PLAIN TALE
THE HI

RUDYARD KIPLING (1865–1936) was born in Bombay in December 1865. He returned to India from England in the autumn of 1882, shortly before his seventeenth birthday, to work as a journalist first on the *Civil and Military Gazette* in Lahore, then on the *Pioneer* at Allahabad. The poems and stories he wrote over the next seven years laid the foundation of his literary reputation, and soon after his return to London in 1889 he found himself world-famous. Throughout his life his works enjoyed great acclaim and popularity, but he came to seem increasingly controversial because of his political opinions, and it has been difficult to reach literary judgements unclouded by partisan feeling. This series, published half a century after Kipling's death, provides the opportunity for reconsidering his remarkable achievement.

ANDREW RUTHERFORD was Vice-Chancellor, University of London, and former Warden of Goldsmith's College. He was the editor of *Kipling's Early Verse 1879–1889*, *Kipling's Mind and Art* and Kipling's *War Stories and Poems* (Oxford World's Classics). He died in 1998.

OXFORD WORLD'S CLASSICS

*For over 100 years Oxford World's Classics have brought
readers closer to the world's great literature. Now with over 700
titles—from the 4,000-year-old myths of Mesopotamia to the
twentieth century's greatest novels—the series makes available
lesser-known as well as celebrated writing.*

*The pocket-sized hardbacks of the early years contained
introductions by Virginia Woolf, T. S. Eliot, Graham Greene,
and other literary figures which enriched the experience of reading.
Today the series is recognized for its fine scholarship and
reliability in texts that span world literature, drama and poetry,
religion, philosophy and politics. Each edition includes perceptive
commentary and essential background information to meet the
changing needs of readers.*

OXFORD WORLD'S CLASSICS

RUDYARD KIPLING

Plain Tales from the Hills

Edited with an Introduction and Notes by
ANDREW RUTHERFORD

OXFORD
UNIVERSITY PRESS

OXFORD

UNIVERSITY PRESS

Great Clarendon Street, Oxford OX2 6DP

Oxford University Press is a department of the University of Oxford.
It furthers the University's objective of excellence in research, scholarship,
and education by publishing worldwide in

Oxford New York

Athens Auckland Bangkok Bogotá Buenos Aires Calcutta
Cape Town Chennai Dar es Salaam Delhi Florence Hong Kong Istanbul
Karachi Kuala Lumpur Madrid Melbourne Mexico City Mumbai
Nairobi Paris São Paulo Shanghai Singapore Taipei Tokyo Toronto Warsaw

with associated companies in Berlin Ibadan

Oxford is a registered trade mark of Oxford University Press
in the UK and in certain other countries

Published in the United States
by Oxford University Press Inc., New York

First published by Oxford University Press as a World's Classics paperback 1987
Reissued as an Oxford World's Classics paperback 2001
Reissued 2009

British Library Cataloguing in Publication Data

Data available

Library of Congress Cataloging in Publication Data

Kipling, Rudyard, 1865–1936.
Plain tales from the hills.
(Oxford world's classics)
Originally published: Calcutta : Thacker, Spink, 1888.
Bibliography: p.
1. India—History—British occupation, 1765–1947—
Fiction. I. Rutherford, Andrew. II. Title. III. Series.
PR4854.P6 1987 823'.8 86–12851

ISBN 978–0–19–953861–4

12

Printed and bound in Great Britain
by Clays Ltd, Elcograf S.p.A.

CONTENTS

GENERAL PREFACE

RUDYARD KIPLING (1865–1936) was for the last decade of the nineteenth century and at least the first two decades of the twentieth the most popular writer in English, in both verse and prose, throughout the English-speaking world. Widely regarded as the greatest living English poet and story-teller, winner of the Nobel Prize for Literature, recipient of honorary degrees from the Universities of Oxford, Cambridge, Edinburgh, Durham, McGill, Strasbourg, and the Sorbonne, he also enjoyed popular acclaim that extended far beyond academic and literary circles.

He stood, it can be argued, in a special relation to the age in which he lived. He was primarily an artist, with his individual vision and techniques, but his was also a profoundly representative consciousness. He seems to give expression to a whole phase of national experience, symbolizing in appropriate forms (as Lascelles Abercrombie said the epic poet must do) the 'sense of the significance of life he [felt] acting as the unconscious metaphysic of the time'.[1] He is in important ways a spokesman for his age, with its sense of imperial destiny, its fascinated contemplation of the unfamiliar world of soldiering, its confidence in engineering and technology, its respect for craftsmanship, and its dedication to Carlyle's gospel of work. That age is one about which many Britons—and to a lesser extent Americans and West Europeans—now feel an exaggerated sense of guilt; and insofar as Kipling was its spokesman, he has become our scapegoat. Hence, in part at least, the tendency in recent decades to dismiss him so contemptuously, so unthinkingly, and so mistakenly. Whereas if we approach him more historically, less hysterically, we shall find in this very relation to his age a cultural phenomenon of absorbing interest.

Here, after all, we have the last English author to appeal to readers of all social classes and all cultural groups, from

[1] Cited in E. M. W. Tillyard, *The Epic Strain in the English Novel*, London, 1958, p. 15.

lowbrow to highbrow; and the last poet to command a mass audience. He was an author who could speak directly to the man in the street, or for that matter in the barrack-room or factory, more effectively than any left-wing writer of the 'thirties or the present day, but who spoke just as directly and effectively to literary men like Edmund Gosse and Andrew Lang; to academics like David Masson, George Saintsbury, and Charles Eliot Norton; to the professional and service classes (officers and other ranks alike) who took him to their hearts; and to creative writers of the stature of Henry James, who had some important reservations to record, but who declared in 1892 that 'Kipling strikes me personally as the most complete man of genius (as distinct from fine intelligence) that I have ever known', and who wrote an enthusiastic introduction to *Mine Own People* in which he stressed Kipling's remarkable appeal to the sophisticated critic as well as to the common reader.[2]

An innovator and a virtuoso in the art of the short story, Kipling does more than any of his predecessors to establish it as a major genre. But within it he moves confidently between the poles of sophisticated simplicity (in his earliest tales) and the complex, closely organized, elliptical and symbolic mode of his later works which reveal him as an unexpected contributor to modernism.

He is a writer who extends the range of English literature in both subject-matter and technique. He plunges readers into new realms of imaginative experience which then become part of our shared inheritance. His anthropological but warmly human interest in mankind in all its varieties produces, for example, sensitive, sympathetic vignettes of Indian life and character which culminate in *Kim*. His sociolinguistic experiments with proletarian speech as an artistic medium in *Barrack-Room Ballads* and his rendering of the life of private soldiers in all their unregenerate humanity gave a new dimension to war literature. His portrayal of Anglo-Indian life

---

[2] See *Kipling: The Critical Heritage*, ed. Roger Lancelyn Green, London, 1971, pp. 159–60. *Mine Own People*, published in New York in 1891, was a collection of stories nearly all of which were to be subsumed in *Life's Handicap* later that year.

ranges from cynical triviality in some of the *Plain Tales from the Hills* to the stoical nobility of the best things in *Life's Handicap* and *The Day's Work*. Indeed Mrs Hauksbee's Simla, Mulvaney's barrack-rooms, Dravot and Carnehan's search for a kingdom in Kafiristan, Holden's illicit, star-crossed love, Stalky's apprenticeship, Kim's Grand Trunk Road, 'William' 's famine relief expedition, and the Maltese Cat's game at Umballa, establish the vanished world of Empire for us (as they established the unknown world of Empire for an earlier generation), in all its pettiness and grandeur, its variety and energy, its miseries, its hardships, and its heroism.

In a completely different vein Kipling's genius for the animal fable as a means of inculcating human truths opens up a whole new world of joyous imagining in the two *Jungle Books*. In another vein again are the stories in which he records his delighted discovery of the English countryside, its people and traditions, after he had settled at Bateman's in Sussex: England, he told Rider Haggard in 1902, 'is the most wonderful foreign land I have ever been in'[3]; and he made it peculiarly his own. Its past gripped his imagination as strongly as its present, and the two books of Puck stories show what Eliot describes as 'the development of the imperial . . . into the historical imagination.'[4] In another vein again he figures as the bard of engineering and technology. From the standpoint of world history, two of Britain's most important areas of activity in the nineteenth century were those of industrialism and imperialism, both of which had been neglected by literature prior to Kipling's advent. There is a substantial body of work on the Condition of England Question and the socio-economic effects of the Industrial Revolution; but there is comparatively little imaginative response in literature (as opposed to painting) to the extraordinary inventive energy, the dynamic creative power, which manifests itself in (say) the work of engineers like Telford, Rennie, Brunel, and the brothers Stephenson—men who revolutionized communications within Britain by their

[3] *Rudyard Kipling to Rider Haggard*, ed. Morton Cohen, London, 1965, p. 51.
[4] T. S. Eliot, *On Poetry and Poets*, London, 1957, p. 247.

road, rail and harbour systems, producing in the process masterpieces of industrial art, and who went on to revolutionize ocean travel as well. Such achievements are acknowledged on a sub-literary level by Samuel Smiles in his best-selling *Lives of the Engineers* (1861-2). They are acknowledged also by Carlyle, who celebrates the positive as well as denouncing the malign aspects of the transition from the feudal to the industrial world, insisting as he does that the true modern epic must be technological, not military: 'For we are to bethink us that the Epic verily is not *Arms and the Man*, but *Tools and the Man*,—an infinitely wider kind of Epic.'[5] That epic has never been written in its entirety, but Kipling came nearest to achieving its aims in verses like 'McAndrew's Hymn' (*The Seven Seas*) and stories like 'The Ship that Found Herself' and 'Bread upon the Waters' (*The Day's Work*) in which he shows imaginative sympathy with the machines themselves as well as sympathy with the men who serve them. He comes nearer, indeed, than any other author to fulfilling Wordsworth's prophecy that

If the labours of men of Science should ever create any material revolution, direct or indirect, in our condition, and in the impressions which we habitually receive, the Poet will sleep then no more than at present, but he will be ready to follow the steps of the Man of Science, not only in those general indirect effects, but he will be at his side, carrying sensation into the midst of the objects of the Science itself.[6]

This is one aspect of Kipling's commitment to the world of work, which, as C. S. Lewis observes, 'imaginative literature in the eighteenth and nineteenth centuries had [with a few exceptions] quietly omitted, or at least thrust into the background', though it occupies most of the waking hours of most men:

And this did not merely mean that certain technical aspects of life were unrepresented. A whole range of strong sentiments and emotions—for many men, the strongest of all—went with them. . . . It was Kipling who first reclaimed for literature this enormous territory.[7]

[5] *Past and Present* (1843), Book iv, ch.1. Cf. ibid., Book iii, ch. 5.

[6] *Lyrical Ballads*, ed. R. L. Brett and A. R. Jones, London, 1963, pp. 253-4.

[7] 'Kipling's World', *Literature and Life: Addresses to the English Association*, London, 1948, pp. 59-60.

He repudiates the unspoken assumption of most novelists that the really interesting part of life takes place outside working hours: men at work or talking about their work are among his favourite subjects. The qualities men show in their work, and the achievements that result from it (bridges built, ships salvaged, pictures painted, famines relieved) are the very stuff of much of Kipling's fiction. Yet there also runs through his *œuvre*, like a figure in the carpet, a darker, more pessimistic vision of the impermanence, the transience—but not the worthlessness—of all achievement. This underlies his delighted engagement with contemporary reality and gives a deeper resonance to his finest work, in which human endeavour is celebrated none the less because it must ultimately yield to death and mutability.

ANDREW RUTHERFORD

INTRODUCTION

Plain Tales from the Hills was Kipling's first volume of prose fiction. Published in Calcutta in January 1888, just after his twenty-second birthday, it is a remarkable manifestation of precocious literary talent and a key document of Anglo-Indian social history.

The tales, most of which were published in the *Civil and Military Gazette* between November 1886 and June 1887,[1] were plain in the sense of being simple, straightforward, unelaborated: but there is also a suppressed pun in the title on the opposition between Plains and Hills. This opposition, geographical, social, and psychological, was a major factor in the life of British India in Kipling's day.

The Plains were where teeming millions of Indians lived out their lives; where troops were stationed in cantonments not for active service, which was to be sought then on the North-West Frontier or in Burma, but as garrisons to maintain internal security; and where British administrators toiled year-in, year-out, in an almost obsessive adherence to the gospel of work and their own Platonic ideals of good government. In the Punjab and North India generally the climate was agreeable enough from October to March, but from April to September the excessive heat made life almost unendurable. (This is why, in Kipling's poem 'Pagett, M.P.' in *Departmental Ditties*, the globe-trotting Member of Parliament who 'came on a four months visit, to "study the East" in November' was persuaded to sign an agreement vowing to stay till September—so that he would be forced to learn by personal experience what living conditions for his countrymen in India were really like.)

The only relief from the heat, discomfort, and diseases of the Plains was a leave spent in the Hills—that is to say, at one of the Hill Stations built at a sufficient altitude to provide cool, pleasant conditions comparable with those at Home.

---

[1] See below, pp. xvi–xviii.

My month's leave at Simla, or whatever Hill Station my people went to, was pure joy [Kipling recalled in his old age]—every golden hour counted. It began in heat and discomfort, by rail and road. It ended in the cool evening, with a wood fire in one's bedroom, and next morn—thirty more of them ahead!—the early cup of tea, the Mother who brought it in, and the long talks of us all together again.[2]

As this implies, it was not uncommon for married men to send their womenfolk to the Hills for more extended periods, for the sake of their health, though the men themselves could join them only for limited periods, unless they secured Government posts which guaranteed a more extended stay. Society in the Hill Stations, therefore, was shifting and kaleidoscopic—a mixture of long-stay residents and transients, of whom the latter might be bachelors or married men, from the Army or the Civil Administration. The Stations developed their own distinctive patterns of social life, with diversions such as riding, walking, picnicing, amateur theatricals, gymkhanas, painting or sketching, dancing, light flirtation, serious courtship, and not infrequently adulterous or quasi-adulterous intrigue. Philandering with unmarried girls was *tabu* in Anglo-India, but standards for married women were more flexible, and while the majority were by all accounts as virtuous as their sisters in Victorian England, grass-widows like Mrs Hauksbee or Mrs Reiver played a dominant role in many Stations. The extreme case (as opposed to the ambiguities so well conveyed in *Plain Tales from the Hills*) is sketched by Kipling in one of his 'Nursery Rhymes for Little Anglo-Indians':

> I had a little husband
> Who gave me all his pay.
> I left him for Mussoorie,
> A hundred miles away.

> I dragged my little husband's name
> Through heaps of social mire,
> And joined him in October,
> As good as you'd desire.[3]

[2] *Something of Myself*, London, 1937, p. 57.
[3] From *Echoes*, Lahore, 1884.

Mussoorie, Murree, Naini Tal, Dalhousie, and Darjeeling were all well-known Hill Stations in the lower Himalayas, but by far the most famous was Simla. Its site, some 7,000 feet above sea level, had been retained in British hands after the Gurkha War of 1814–16. Houses were built there in the course of the 1820s, and by the mid-century it had become the most fashionable of Hill resorts, patronized by Governor-Generals and Commanders-in-Chief. A remarkable development took place in 1864 when Sir John Lawrence, the new Viceroy and one of the Titans of the old Punjab administration, decided that Simla should become the summer residence of the Government of India. He was influenced partly by his own state of health, partly by his view of the strategic importance of North-West India, and partly by his conviction that the climate of Simla would allow a greater volume of work to be carried through than would be conceivable in the heat of Calcutta. The decision was seen as controversial, both then and later. The expatriate commercial community in Calcutta could not see why, if its members stayed there throughout the year, Government officials could not do the same: it deplored the expense of the move and the way it distanced Government from the governed. Attacks on 'the Simla Exodus' or 'the Exodus to the Hills' were still frequent in the 1880s—Kipling makes fun of them in his poem 'A Tale of Two Cities' in *Departmental Ditties*—but by then it was firmly established practice that the Viceroy and his staff, the Members of Council, the Secretariat, and the Commander-in-Chief and *his* staff, all left Calcutta at the start of the hot weather, returning in October. For these six months the Indian sub-continent was ruled from Simla (where the Supreme Government was joined by the Provincial Government of the Punjab); and the effect was to make Simla a centre of power as well as pleasure. 'There the Hierarchy lived,' wrote Kipling afterwards, 'and one saw and heard the machinery of administration stripped bare.'[4] Opportunities for promotion and for patronage abounded, or so it was widely believed; the number, rank and importance of long-stay residents increased; and to the normal routine of a Hill

[4] *Something of Myself*, p. 57.

Station there were added the splendours of Viceregal hospitality, the pomp, panache and glitter of a Court. Simla was
nicknamed 'Olympus', as the abode of remote and self-
indulgent deities who governed the destinies of mankind,
and 'Capua', after the chief city of Campania which had
become in Roman times a byword for wealth, luxury and
decadence.

Kipling first visited Simla for a month's leave in the
summer of 1883, as the guest of one of the proprietors of the
Civil and Military Gazette: 'The month was a round of
picnics, dances, theatricals and so on—and I flirted with the
bottled up energy of a year on my lips,' he told one of his
aunts.[5] In 1884 he joined his family at the less fashionable
station of Dalhousie; but he returned to Simla in 1885 for a
three-and-a-half month sojourn as special correspondent for
the *Civil and Military Gazette*, reporting on the Simla social
scene. In one of his father's letters we get a glimpse of him,
one cheek disfigured by a 'Lahore sore', practising waltzing in
preparation for this assignment—his proprietors having told
him that as he was going to represent the paper, he *must* waltz
well. He soon had the entrée to the very highest circles, since
the new Viceroy, Lord Dufferin, had been quick to appreciate
the intelligence and wit of the Kipling parents—'Dulness and
Mrs Kipling cannot exist in the same room,' he once declared
—and the family came to figure frequently on invitation lists
to viceregal entertainments. Kipling returned to Simla each
year thereafter for his annual leave, increasingly fêted for his
own literary achievements, and in spite of his youth he came
to know all the leading members of government, and to move
confidently through the society which was to provide him
with so much copy.

For the remainder of the year he was based in Lahore, the
capital of the Punjab, where he worked as assistant-editor of
the *Civil and Military Gazette* until his transfer to the *Pioneer*
in Allahabad late in 1887. The editorial staff consisted of only
two Europeans; the paper appeared six days a week
throughout the year apart from one day's break at Christmas

[5] Letter of 14 August 1883, to Edith Macdonald (Rare Book and Special
Collections Division, Library of Congress).

and Easter; the work was unremitting; and an unsympathetic editor, Stephen Wheeler, proved a hard task-master. E. Kay Robinson, who succeeded him as editor in 1886, tells us that besides reporting outside the office Kipling's daily work was, briefly,

(1) To prepare for the press all the telegrams of the day; (2) to provide all the extracts and paragraphs [i.e. from Anglo-Indian, Indian, English, and other newspapers]; (3) to make headed articles out of official reports, etc; (4) to write such editorial notes as he might have time for; (5) to look generally after all sports, out-station and local intelligence; (6) to read all proofs except the editorial matter.[6]

He also had to vet the presentation and content of external contributions to the paper. He reviewed new books and theatrical performances. He reported on race-meetings and official functions like the opening of new bridges or hospitals. He provided regular features on 'The Week in Lahore'; and when taking his one month's holiday a year he often acted as special correspondent from Simla. He was also sent from time to time on special assignments—to cover, for example, the Rawalpindi Durbar of 1885 when the Viceroy received the Amir of Afghanistan on a state visit, or the installation of a new Maharajah of Kashmir in 1886. It was a regimen which at first seemed incompatible with any writing of his own, and Wheeler actively discouraged his creative work; but his urge to write was irrepressible, and when Kay Robinson took over in 1886 with instructions to put some sparkle into the paper, he had the sense to give Kipling his head. *Plain Tales from the Hills* were among the first fruits of that policy.

Of the forty stories in the *Plain Tales* volume of 1888, eight appeared there for the first time. These were 'Thrown Away', 'False Dawn', 'Cupid's Arrows', 'Beyond the Pale', 'The Rout of the White Hussars', 'The Bronkhorst Divorce-Case', 'The Madness of Private Ortheris' and 'To be Filed for Reference'. All the others had already been published in the *Civil and Military Gazette*. Three of these had appeared individually without any 'Plain Tales' heading: 'The Gate of

---

[6] 'Mr Kipling as Journalist', *The Academy*, vol. i (1896). Cited in *Kipling: Interviews and Recollections*, ed. Harold Orel, London, 1983, vol. i, p. 87.

the Hundred Sorrows' on 26 September 1884; 'In the House of Suddhoo' (under the title 'Section 420 I.P.C.') on 30 April 1886; and 'The Story of Muhammad Din' on 8 September 1886. The remaining twenty-nine were from a series of thirty-nine stories, numbered but unsigned, which appeared under the general title 'Plain Tales from the Hills' on the dates indicated below:

Of the ten items in the original series (marked here with asterisks) which were not included in the collected volume, two—'Bitters Neat' and 'Haunted Subalterns'—are unquestionably by Kipling. He included them in the *Plain Tales* volume (1897) of the Outward Bound Edition and the Edition de Luxe of his collected works; and they also figure in the *Plain Tales* volume of the posthumous Sussex Edition which he prepared in the last years of his life. These two stories are printed in the present edition as appendices. It seems unlikely that any of the remaining eight are by his hand. He and his sister Trix had collaborated in 1884 on a book of verses, *Echoes. By Two Writers*. In 1885 they and their parents had collaborated on a collection of poems and stories published as *Quartette. The Christmas Annual of the Civil and Military Gazette. By Four Anglo-Indian Writers*. And it seems clear that in their original conception the 'Plain Tales' were also to have been a collaborative effort. One of the stories, 'A Pinchbeck Goddess', is undoubtedly by Trix, who later expanded it into a novel; and it seems probable that most if not all the other uncollected pieces are also her work. In his marginalia to Admiral Chandler's *Summary of the Work of Rudyard Kipling, Including Items Ascribed to Him* (New York, 1930), Kipling repudiates with the formula 'not mine R.K.' the items 'Love-in-a-Mist', 'Love: a "Miss"', 'A Straight Flush', 'A Pinchbeck Goddess' (which he also attributes explicitly to Trix), 'Our Theatricals', and ' A Little Learning', while 'How it Happened' is marked 'NOT R.K.' This evidence is not wholly conclusive, since these marginalia can be shown to contain occasional inaccuracies at other points, and scholarly opinion is divided, but I find no case for including any of these seven items or 'A Scrap of Paper' in the present edition.

The fact that the Plain Tales appeared originally in the *Civil and Military Gazette* and that, when first collected, they were published in Calcutta, reminds us that they were written for Anglo-Indian readers familiar with the world portrayed. Such readers loved to see their own life reflected accurately, even if satirically, in prose or verse. Hence the popularity amongst them of such works as G. F. Atkinson's *Curry and Rice* (1859), with its sketches of 'Our Station', 'Our Judge's Wife', etc.; G. O. Trevelyan's *The Competition Wallah* (1864), which Kipling won as a school prize for his poem on 'The Battle of Assaye'; Florence Marryat's *'Gup'.*[7] *Sketches of Anglo-Indian Life and Character* (1868); 'Aliph Cheem' (W. Yeldham)'s *Lays of Ind* (1871), described as 'Comical, Satirical and Descriptive Poems illustrative of English Life in India'; I. T. Prichard's *Chronicles of Budgepore, or Sketches of Life in Upper India* (1870–80); H. S. Cunningham's *Chronicles of Dustypore. A Tale of Modern Anglo-Indian Society* (1875); and G. R. Aberigh-Mackay's *Twenty-One Days in India, or the Tour of Sir Ali Baba K.C.B.* (1880), with its delightfully ironic sketches of types ranging from the Viceroy to the Grass Widow ('little Mrs Lollipop') in Nephelococcygia—that is to say, in the Cloud-Cuckoo-Land of Simla.[8] What this literature reflects above all is the sense shared by authors and public alike that Anglo-Indian life was so distinctive, so remarkable a mutation from the norms of English society, as to merit sustained literary attention. As the reviewer of a now-forgotten novel—perhaps Kipling himself—wrote in the *Civil and Military Gazette* for 15 December 1885,

An Anglo-Indian novel will always find Anglo-Indian readers who are sometimes inclined to wonder that all the world does not shew an equal interest in pictures of an existence which must be ranked among the curiosities of modern life. We affect to be *blasé*, and put on an air of dreary resignation when we speak of the dulness of our surroundings; but we are at heart willing enough to follow a capable writer who will thoroughly describe our lives of monotonous work,

[7] *Gup*: gossip.
[8] She is mentioned more than once by Kipling. See for example *From Sea to Sea*, London, 1900, II, 238; and *Kipling's India*, ed. Thomas Pinney, London, 1986, pp. 118, 120, 124.

in which is interwoven, with painful regularity of pattern, a gay chequer work of equally monotonous play. But the book must be well done to satisfy those who really know Indian life . . . we like to see the story of our lives told by 'one who knows'!

Kipling was pre-eminently 'one who knew', and if his knowingness is sometimes overdone, this is partly due to a youthful simulation of maturity and partly to an exuberant sense of how much he really *did* know, from experience and observation, of the multifarious world of India. As he told his cousin Margaret Burne-Jones in February 1889 on the eve of his departure, he had 'tried to get to know folk from the barrack room and the brothel, to the Ballroom and the Viceroy's Council', and he had in a little measure succeeded.[9]

Often the night got into my head [he recalled in his autobiography] . . . and I would wander till dawn in all manner of odd places—liquor-shops, gambling and opium dens, which are not a bit mysterious, wayside entertainments such as puppet-shows, native dances; or in and about the narrow gullies under the Mosque of Wazir Khan for the sheer sake of looking. . . . One would come home, just as the light broke, in some night-hawk of a hired carriage which stank of hookah-fumes, jasmine-flowers, and sandal-wood; and if the driver were moved to talk, he told one a good deal.[10]

Hence the knowledge he required for stories like 'The Gate of the Hundred Sorrows', 'In the House of Suddhoo', and 'Beyond the Pale'; while his meetings with the soldiery at Fort Lahore and Mian Mir Cantonments a few miles away gave the background for Mulvaney, Ortheris and Learoyd. ('Having no position to consider, and my trade enforcing it, I could move at will in the fourth dimension. I came to realise the bare horrors of the private's life. . . .')[11] If Anglo-India dominates *Plain Tales from the Hills*, these excursions into other social worlds add new dimensions to the series.

So too do Kipling's—or the narrator's—changes of view-point. His identification with Anglo-Indian race prejudice

---

[9] Kipling Papers, University of Sussex.
[10] *Something of Myself*, pp. 53–4.
[11] Ibid., p. 56.

in 'Kidnapped' contrasts sharply with the hostility he shows towards it in 'Lispeth', which he selected as the opening story for the volume. Admiration for the Raj alternates with debunking and irreverence. Social shibboleths are both defended and defied. Compassion co-exists strangely with cynicism, sometimes even in the same story, with flippant, hard-boiled comments masking and protecting deeper feelings. We shall look in vain in *Plain Tales* for consistency of attitude or a coherent value system. The stories are notations of experience, brilliant vignettes, jeux d'esprit, which document the life around him but which do not mediate, and are not assimilated to, a unified vision of the kind that informs some of his later volumes. Nor is this to be regretted. 'Unadjusted impressions have their value,' as Hardy wrote of one collection of his poems, 'and the road to a true philosophy of life seems to lie in humbly recording diverse readings of its phenomena as they are forced on us by chance and change.'[12]

Kipling's own philosophy of life was still in process of formation, though the diverse phenomena which he was now recording (not particularly humbly) would contribute to it. But his delight in life's diversity was always crucial to his fiction, as suggested by his later volume title *A Diversity of Creatures. Plain Tales from the Hills* are entertainments—superb entertainments—based on his eager, inexhaustible interest in the human comedy; and perhaps the best introduction to them is his inscription in the copy he presented to Mrs Hill in Allahabad in March 1888:

> Between the gum pot and the shears,
>   The weapons of my grimy trade,
> In divers moods and various years
>   These forty foolish yarns were made.

> And some were writ to fill a page
>   And some—but these are not so many—
> To soothe a finely moral rage
>   And all to turn an honest penny.

[12] Preface to 'Poems of the Past and the Present', *Complete Poetical Works*, ed. Samuel Hynes, vol. i (Oxford, 1982), p. 113.

And some I gathered from my friends
  And some I looted from my foes,
And some—All's fish that Heaven sends—
  Are histories of private woes.

And some are Truth, and some are Lie,
  And some exactly half and half,
I've heard some made a woman cry—
  I *know* some made a woman laugh.

I do not view them with delight
  And, since I know that you may read 'em,
I'd like to thoroughly rewrite,
  Remould, rebuild, retouch, reword 'em.

Would they were worthier. That's too late—
  Cracked pictures stand no further stippling.
Forgive the faults.

March '88

To Mrs Hill

From Rudyard Kipling[13]

[13] Edmonia Hill, 'The Young Kipling', *Atlantic Monthly*, vol. 157 (1936), p. 407.

NOTE ON THE TEXT[1]

THE text of Kipling's works has never been subjected to scholarly analysis, and a full investigation of the textual history of *Plain Tales from the Hills* would go far beyond the bounds of this edition.

The most significant changes were made by Kipling when he revised the versions published in the *Civil and Military Gazette* for the First Edition of 1888. It was at this stage that verse headings were added to the stories; and the stories themselves, originally written at high speed, in astonishingly rapid succession, were subjected to extensive revision.

Sometimes whole sentences are re-written. (I shall cite examples from a single story.) 'Indian racing is skittles, and mean skittles at that' becomes 'Indian racing is immoral, and expensively immoral. Which is much worse' (p. 122). 'But my business is to describe the Broken Link Handicap—not to pretend to be virtuous because the fun of one particular vice does not appeal to me' becomes 'But, if you have no conscience and no sentiments, and good hands, and some knowledge of pace, and ten years' experience of horses, and several thousand rupees a month, I believe that you can occasionally contrive to pay your shoeing-bills' (p. 122). 'He is lost somewhere in this big India of ours' becomes 'To the best of my knowledge and belief he spoke the truth' (p. 126). Sometimes completely new material is introduced, as in the passage 'He was of no brand, being one of an ear-nicked mob taken into the *Bucephalus* at £4-10s. a head to make up freight, and sold raw and out of condition at Calcutta for Rs.275. People who lost money on him called him a "brumby"; but if any horse had "Harpoon's" shoulders and the "Gin's" temper, "Shackles" was that horse' (p. 123). These sentences have no equivalent in the newspaper version. Sometimes statements are expanded, to give added point. '*Every* peculiarity of a course is worth remembering' becomes '*Every* peculiarity of a course is worth remembering in a country where rats play the mischief

with the elephant-litter, and Stewards build jumps to suit
their own stables' (p. 123–4). 'The mare was called *The Lady
Regula Baddun*' becomes 'The mare was, as a delicate tribute
to Mrs. Reiver, called "The Lady Regula Baddun" ' (p. 124).
Sometimes the phrasing is altered in the interests of
terseness or precision. 'He wasn't going to stand dictation'
becomes 'He objected to dictation' (p. 123). 'At your ordinary
pitch' becomes 'at ordinary pitch' (p. 123); 'speak with'
becomes 'speak from with' (p. 123); 'his nerve was a good deal
shaken' becomes 'his nerve had been shaken' (p. 124); 'You
see, he began' becomes 'He began' (p. 124); 'He hadn't
education enough' becomes 'He had no education' (p. 124);
'As Shackles shortened his stride to take the turn and the two
came abreast' becomes 'As "Shackles" went short to take the
turn and came abreast' (p. 125); and 'cantered back to the
Grand Stand thanking Providence' becomes 'cantered back to
the Stand' (p. 126). There are minor verbal alterations:
'clearly, all' becomes 'clearly that all', 'too well' becomes 'far
too well', 'you know his wife' becomes 'you are fond of his
wife' (all p. 122); 'country, say, with' becomes 'country, with'
(p. 122); 'raking' becomes 'racking' and 'want lynching. He
was' becomes 'want lynching, and was' (p. 124); and 'spurs'
becomes 'heels' (p. 126). There are also changes of
punctuation, capitalization etc.; and sometimes of allusion:
'the Currency Commission' is substituted for 'the
Retrenchment Committee' on p. 126.

All these examples are drawn from 'The Broken-Link
Handicap', but examination of the text of other stories shows
that it is not in any way exceptional. The preparation of the
First Edition involved a major revision of the text throughout.
Kipling cuts many passages of superfluous or flabby verbiage.
The original preamble to 'Kidnapped', for example, contained
the following: 'Ask a child of four to order the clothes it would
like to dress in all its life; and the dear little innocent will
point out a sailor's suit, with lots of brass buttons, a lanyard,
and a shiny hat. Very few grown men care for brass buttons
and low, turn-down collars' (cf. p. 97). 'His Wedded Wife' had
the passage 'The "Shikarris" are not to be confused with the
"Inextinguishables", though they hold the same views on

polo and dances and all the serious business of life. Both
Regiments are high caste . . .' (cf. p. 116). And 'Miss
Youghal's Sais' contained the sentence 'The old man was
doing the paternal lover in fine style' (cf. p. 27). All these are
cut, and many like them.

Kipling also cuts out some local and temporary allusions:
the reference to infant-marriage at the beginning of 'Kidnapped' was followed in the newspaper version by the phrase
'and Rukhmabai's case is an atrocity and so on' (cf. p. 97)—an
allusion to a *cause célèbre* in which an educated Hindu lady was
being compelled to grant conjugal rights to a man to whom
she had been married in childhood, but with whom she had
never lived, and never wished to live, as his wife. In the same
story the suggestion that 'an Awful Warning, in the shape of
a love-match that has gone wrong', should be 'chained to the
trees in the courtyard' was followed by the simile 'like the
bears in the Lawrence Hall Gardens'—a reference directed to
his original audience in Lahore and the Punjab. This
comparison, like the reference to Rukhmabai, is cut in the
First Edition, aimed at a wider Indian public the following
year. There is also some reduction of his use of Indian words:
'*nokri*' becomes 'service' (p. 26); '*jharuns* and *degchies* and all
the mean worry of housekeeping' becomes simply 'all the
mean worry of housekeeping' (p. 69); 'a flaming *chit*' becomes
'a flaming "character"' (p. 96); 'a charpoy' becomes 'a
bedstead' (p. 100); 'the *chabutra* outside' becomes 'the
platform outside the Mess House' (p. 117); 'his *shouk*'
becomes 'his strong point' (p. 120); and so on.

Above all, there is a pervasive policy of revision in the
interests of crisper, more precise, more vivid writing, which
involves scores of amendments in individual stories. It is easy
to cite instances. The unappealing description of the newly
arrived subaltern from Home as having 'beefy red splotches
on his cheeks' is changed to the more evocative phrase 'the red
of sappy English beef on [Second Edition: 'in'] his cheeks'
(p. 116). The Senior Subaltern's terrier which at a moment of
tension for his master was hunting for fleas 'full in the open
space' is now more precisely located 'full in the open space in
the centre, by the whist-tables' (p. 119). The rambling

opening of this story read 'Shakespeare or some one else says something about worms turning if you tread on them long enough; or, if it isn't worms, it's beetles and giants, which are practically the same.' It is compressed in the First Edition to 'Shakespeare says something about worms, or it may be giants or beetles, turning if you tread on them too severely' (p. 116). The improvement in such individual examples is self-evident; but it is impossible, without the tabulation of many hundred variant readings, to demonstrate the overall, cumulative effect of Kipling's reworking of the stories.

Subsequent revisions are minor in comparison. The Second Edition of 1889 is almost identical with the First, though there is a significant addition to 'The Conversion of Aurelian McGoggin'—the passage 'For this reason. The Deputy is above the Assistant, the Commissioner above the Deputy, the Lieutenant-Governor above the Commissioner, and the Viceroy above all four, under the orders of the Secretary of State, who is responsible to the Empress. If the Empress be not responsible to her Maker—if there is no Maker for her to be responsible to—the entire system of Our administration must be wrong. Which is manifestly impossible' (cf. p. 182). There is also a limited number of detailed amendments. In 'Kidnapped', for example, the over-emphasis of 'Mrs. Hauksbee went to the wedding, and was *so* astonished when Peythroppe did not appear' is modified by the change of '*so*' to the more dead-pan 'much'; just as the proposition 'Twelve-bores *do* kick rather curiously' is modified by the omission of '*do*' (both p. 100). The 'whole howling, seething smash of the Maribyrnong Plate' is changed by the omission of 'howling' (p. 125); 'she pulled a paper from her breast, like a queen, saying' becomes 'she pulled a paper from her breast, saying imperially' (p. 120); 'spoke' is replaced by the more Scriptural 'spake' on p. 99; *kutcha* (temporary) becomes 'dusty' (p. 20); and there are other examples. But the incidence of change in this edition is much less significant.

The Third Edition of 1890 was in fact the first English edition published by Macmillan and Co. (whereas the First and Second Editions had been published by Thacker, Spink and Co. of Calcutta). The text underwent further revision.

The phrase 'out here' is replaced by 'in India' throughout; and, not surprisingly, there is a further reduction in the use of Indian vocabulary. Thus 'a *memsahib*' becomes 'a white woman' (pp. 7–8); 'the *shroff*' becomes 'the bankers' (p. 18); 'dead on the *charpoy*' becomes 'dead on the bed' (p. 20); '*chamar* or *faquir*' becomes 'hide-dresser or priest' (p. 24); '*mimbar*-board' becomes 'sounding-board' (p. 25); 'a *purdah nashin*' becomes 'a *purdah nashin* or woman who lives behind the veil' (p. 32); 'kul' becomes 'to-morrow' (p. 55); 'the day's bazaar' becomes 'the day's market' (p. 60); 'a good, sound, *pukka* one' becomes 'a good, sound one' (p. 76); 'chaprassi' becomes 'orderly' and '*Hauksbee Sahib ki Mem*' 'Mrs Hauksbee' (p. 77); 'a *jhairun*' becomes 'a towel' and '*dal-bhat* and *kijri*' 'water an' rice' (pp. 86–7); '*bhoosa*' becomes 'hay' (p. 91); '*jats*' becomes 'farmers' (p. 148); *methrani* (First Edition) or '*metrani*' (Second Edition) becomes 'sweeper' (p. 181); 'a *mehter*' becomes 'a sweeper' (p. 182); 'the *Kansamah*' (butler) becomes 'the servants' (p. 199) and there are other examples. '*Bund*' becomes 'Dam', to be changed back to '*Bund*' in the Sussex Edition (p. 48), just as '*Lat Sahib*' becomes '*Lord Sahib*', to be changed back to 'Lat Sahib' in the Sussex Edition (p. 146). There are other minor revisions: 'the wrinkled, unclean creature, very much of the texture and appearance of charred rag' (First Edition), became 'the bleared, wrinkled creature, so like a wisp of charred rag' in the Second Edition, and now assumes its final form, 'the bleared, wrinkled creature, exactly like a wisp of charred rag' (p. 11); 'Hayes' becomes 'Captain Hayes' (p. 44); 'd—d' becomes 'damned' (p. 119); etc. And there are some substantial changes, like the substitution of 'But this has done him no good in the eyes of the Indian Government' (p. 24) for 'But what good has this done him with the Government? None in the world. He has never got Simla for his charge; and his name is almost unknown to Englishmen.'

The text of the Third Edition was used for Macmillan's Uniform Edition, which was first published in 1899, and which was for decades the most widely read edition of Kipling's works. That edition has been used as the copy-text for the present volume. It has, however, been amended in some minor aspects in the light of Kipling's revision of the text of *Plain Tales* for the Sussex Edition. The first proofs of this are stamped '12 September 1931', and Kipling's autograph amendments (which go beyond simple proof-correction) have been preserved in the Macmillan Archive).[2] These I have used selectively. It could be argued that their unique authority outweighs all other considerations, but caution should be observed in dealing with revisions made more than forty years after the work's publication in the form with which we are familiar. When, for example, the Major in 'Thrown Away' asks '*Does* a man shoot *tetur* with a revolver and writing-case' (p. 19), he is using the authentic mixture of English and the vernacular which was typical of British practice in India. To change '*tetur*' to 'partridge', as Kipling does in the Sussex Edition is a concession to contemporary readers which detracts from the original, so I retain the reading '*tetur*'. To substitute 'That was her programme' for 'This was her programme' in 'Lispeth' (p. 9), or 'That hurt his feelings' for 'This hurt his feelings' in 'Thrown Away' (p. 18) is to lose something of the immediacy and to distance us from the protagonists; so I retain the reading 'This'. To change 'T.G.' (Travelling Gentleman) to 'Globe-trotter' or 'G.T.' as Kipling does (p. 195) is to lose a social nuance of the 1880s, and again I retain the original reading. On the other hand, Kipling's revision of his soldiers' speech shows an attempt to improve on his earlier phonetic transcription: he notes, for example, that while Ortheris and Learoyd drop their 'aitches', Mulvaney never does; and I incorporate his amendments.

A great many changes are trivial in nature. There are points of spelling—he now prefers 'veranda' to 'verandah', 'fakir' to 'faquir', 'Peterhof' to 'Peterhoff', 'Narkanda' to 'Narkunda', 'Darjeeling' to 'Darjiling', 'hookah' to 'huqa', etc.—but in general I retain the original spellings for their period flavour, though I accept his standardizing of one form, e.g. 'khitmutgar' in place of variants like 'khitmagar' and 'khitmatgar'. There is a lot of rather arbitrary juggling with

[2] British Library, Add. MS. 55852.

upper and lower case, and I do not accept the capitalization of 'Dreams of Avarice' (p. 49), 'Vessel of Wrath' (p. 66) or 'Little Man' (p. 90) which make for over-emphasis. Nor do I accept the arbitrary change to lower case for 'Station' and 'Sir' throughout, or 'Bagi road' for 'Bagi Road' (p. 8); though the capital at 'Gardens' which he introduces in 'False Dawn' (p. 36) makes the useful point that *public* gardens are what he is referring to.

There is much minor amendment of small points of punctuation, eliminating intrusive commas, adjusting misplaced apostrophes, tidying up little irregularities or blunders: these corrections have mostly been incorporated. I have, however, resisted changes which affect characteristic mannerisms of the earlier text—for example, a statement which ends with a semi-colon, to be followed by a laconic comment. Kipling now tends to substitute a full stop, with a new sentence in apposition; but I have preferred the earlier and more familiar form. I have also retained many dashes where he now substitutes commas or colons; I have not inserted the commas he proposes after 'For God's sake' (p. 22) and 'For Heaven's sake' (p. 28), since these reduce the sense of urgency; just as the proposed change of 'it need not stop you, Tom' to 'it needn't stop you, Tom' (p. 13) would detract from Mrs Cusack-Bremmil's sad dignity. Kipling usefully and unobtrusively tidies up inconsistencies: the Uniform Edition refers both to the Boy's ring and to his rings in 'Thrown Away', but he now settles for the singular; and it was indeed *Mrs* Vezzis, not her daughter, who imposed the hard conditions on Michele D'Cruze (p. 61).

In general I have sought to incorporate his revisions where these seem significant or useful, while rejecting them if they seem merely arbitrary or disruptive of an aesthetic effect already achieved. I have thus employed a measure of subjective editorial judgement, for which I make no apology. I have also corrected a number of misprints which had survived his various revisions.

SELECT BIBLIOGRAPHY

THE standard bibliography is J. McG. Stewart's *Rudyard Kipling: A Bibliographical Catalogue*, ed. A. Yeats (1959). Reference may also be made to two earlier works: Flora V. Livingston's *Bibliography of the Works of Rudyard Kipling* (1927) with its *Supplement* (1938), and Lloyd H. Chandler's *Summary of the Work of Rudyard Kipling, Including Items ascribed to Him* (1930). We still await a bibliography which will take account of the findings of modern scholarship over the last quarter-century.

The official biography, authorized by Kipling's daughter Elsie, is Charles Carrington's *Rudyard Kipling: His Life and Work* (1955; 3rd edn., revised 1978). Other full-scale biographies are Lord Birkenhead's *Rudyard Kipling* (1978) and Angus Wilson's *The Strange Ride of Rudyard Kipling* (1977). Briefer, copiously illustrated surveys are provided by Martin Fido's *Rudyard Kipling* (1974) and Kingsley Amis's *Rudyard Kipling and his World* (1975), which combine biography and criticism, as do the contributions to *Rudyard Kipling: the man, his work and his world* (also illustrated), ed. John Gross (1972). Information on particular periods of his life is also to be found in such works as A. W. Baldwin, *The Macdonald Sisters* (1960); Alice Macdonald Fleming (*née* Kipling), 'Some Childhood Memories of Rudyard Kipling' and 'More Childhood Memories of Rudyard Kipling', *Chambers Journal*, 8th series, vol. 8 (1939); L. C. Dunsterville, *Stalky's Reminiscences* (1928); G. C. Beresford, *Schooldays with Kipling* (1936); E. Kay Robinson, 'Kipling in India', *McClure's Magazine*, vol. 7 (1896); Edmonia Hill, 'The Young Kipling', *Atlantic Monthly*, vol. 157 (1936); *Kipling's Japan*, ed. Hugh Cortazzi and George Webb (1988); H. C. Rice, *Rudyard Kipling in New England* (1936); Frederic Van de Water, *Rudyard Kipling's Vermont Feud* (1937); Julian Ralph, *War's Brighter Side* (1901); Angela Thirkell, *Three Houses* (1931); *Rudyard Kipling to Rider Haggard: The Record of a Friendship*, ed. Morton Cohen (1965); and *'O Beloved Kids': Rudyard Kipling's Letters to his Children*, ed. Elliott L. Gilbert (1983). Useful background on the India he knew is provided by 'Philip Woodruff' (Philip Mason) in *The Men Who Ruled India* (1954), and by Pat Barr and Ray Desmond in their illustrated *Simla: A Hill Station in British India* (1978).

Kipling's own autobiography, *Something of Myself* (1937), is idiosyncratic but indispensable.

The early reception of Kipling's work is usefully documented in *Kipling: The Critical Heritage*, ed. Roger Lancelyn Green (1971). Richard Le Gallienne's *Rudyard Kipling: A Criticism* (1900), Cyril Falls's *Rudyard Kipling: A Critical Study* (1915), André Chevrillon's *Three Studies in English Literature* (1923) and *Rudyard Kipling* (1936), Edward Shanks's *Rudyard Kipling: A Study in Literature and Political Ideas* (1940), and Hilton Brown's *Rudyard Kipling: A New Appreciation* (1945) were all serious attempts at reassessment; while Ann M. Weygandt's study of *Kipling's Reading and Its Influence on His Poetry* (1939), and (in more old-fashioned vein) Ralph Durand's *Handbook to the Poetry of Rudyard Kipling* (1914) remain useful pieces of scholarship.

T. S. Eliot's introduction to *A Choice of Kipling's Verse* (1941; see *On Poetry and Poets*, 1957) began a period of more sophisticated reappraisal. There are influential essays by Edmund Wilson (1941; see *The Wound and the Bow*), George Orwell (1942; see his *Critical Essays*, 1946), Lionel Trilling (1943; see *The Liberal Imagination*, 1951), W. H. Auden (1943; see *New Republic*, vol. 109), and C. S. Lewis (1948; see *They Asked for a Paper*, 1962). These were followed by a series of important book-length studies which include J. M. S. Tompkins, *The Art of Rudyard Kipling* (1959); C. A. Bodelsen, *Aspects of Kipling's Art* (1964); Roger Lancelyn Green, *Kipling and the Children* (1965); Louis L. Cornell, *Kipling in India* (1966); and Bonamy Dobrée, *Rudyard Kipling: Realist and Fabulist* (1967), which follows on from his earlier studies in *The Lamp and the Lute* (1929) and *Rudyard Kipling* (1951). There were also two major collections of critical essays: *Kipling's Mind and Art*, ed. Andrew Rutherford (1964); and *Kipling and the Critics*, ed. Elliot L. Gilbert (1965). Nirad C. Chaudhuri's essay on *Kim* as 'The Finest Story about India—in English' (1957) is reprinted in John Gross's collection (see above). *The Readers' Guide to Rudyard Kipling's Work*, ed. R. E. Harbord (8 vols., privately printed, 1961–72) is an eccentric compilation, packed with useful information but by no means infallible.

Other studies devoted in whole or in part to Kipling include Richard Faber, *The Vision and the Need: Late Victorian Imperialist Aims* (1966); T. R. Henn, *Kipling* (1967); Alan Sandison, *The Wheel of Empire* (1967); Herbert L. Sussman, *Victorians and the Machine: The Literary Response to Technology* (1968); P. J. Keating, *The Working Classes in Victorian Fiction* (1971); Elliot L. Gilbert, *The Good Kipling: Studies in the Short Story* (1972);

Jeffrey Meyers, *Fiction and the Colonial Experience* (1972); Shamsul Islam, *Kipling's 'Law'* (1975); J. S. Bratton, *The Victorian Popular Ballad* (1975); Philip Mason, *Kipling: The Glass, The Shadow and The Fire* (1975); John Bayley, *The Uses of Division* (1976); M. Van Wyk Smith, *Drummer Hodge: The Poetry of the Anglo-Boer War 1899–1902* (1978); Stephen Prickett, *Victorian Fantasy* (1979); Martin Green, *Dreams of Adventure, Deeds of Empire* (1980); J. A. McClure, *Kipling and Conrad* (1981); R. F. Moss, *Rudyard Kipling and the Fiction of Adolescence* (1982); S. S. Azfar Husain, *The Indianness of Rudyard Kipling: A Study in Stylistics* (1983); and Norman Page, *A Kipling Companion* (1984); B. J. Moore-Gilbert, *Kipling and 'Orientalism'* (1986); Sandra Kemp, *Kipling's Hidden Narratives* (1988); Norah Crook, *Kipling's Myths of Love and Death* (1989); and Ann Parry, *The Poetry of Rudyard Kipling* (1992); while further collections of essays include *Rudyard Kipling*, ed. Harold Bloom (1987); *Kipling Considered*, ed. Phillip Mallet (1989); and *Critical Essays on Rudyard Kipling*, ed. Harold Orel (1989). Among the most important recent studies are Edward Said, *Culture and Imperialism* (1991); Sara Suleri, *The Rhetoric of English India* (1992); Zohrah T. Sullivan, *Narratives of Empire: The Fictions of Rudyard Kipling* (1993); and Peter Keating, *Kipling the Poet* (1994).

Two important additions to the available corpus of Kipling's writings are *Kipling's India: Uncollected Sketches*, ed. Thomas Pinney (1986); and *Early Verse by Rudyard Kipling 1879–89: Unpublished, Uncollected and Rarely Collected Poems*, ed. Andrew Rutherford (1986). Indispensable is Pinney's edition of *The Letters of Rudyard Kipling*, in four volumes.

A CHRONOLOGY OF KIPLING'S
LIFE AND WORKS

THE dates given here for Kipling's works are those of first authorized publication in volume form, whether this was in India, America, or England. (The dates of subsequent editions are not listed.) It should be noted that individual poems and stories collected in these volumes had in many cases appeared in newspapers or magazines of earlier dates. For full details see James McG. Stewart, *Rudyard Kipling: A Bibliographical Catalogue*, ed. A. W. Yeats, Toronto, 1959; but see also the editors' notes in this World's Classics series.

1865   Rudyard Kipling born at Bombay on 30 December, son of John Lockwood Kipling and Alice Kipling (*née* Macdonald).

1871   In December Rudyard and his sister Alice Macdonald Kipling ('Trix'), who was born in 1868, are left in the charge of Captain and Mrs Holloway at Lorne Lodge, Southsea ('The House of Desolation'), while their parents return to India.

1877   Alice Kipling returns from India in March/April and removes the children from Lorne Lodge, though Trix returns there subsequently.

1878   Kipling is admitted in January to the United Services College at Westward Ho! in Devon. First visit to France with his father that summer. (Many visits later in his life.)

1880   Meets and falls in love with Florence Garrard, a fellow-boarder of Trix's at Southsea and prototype of Maisie in *The Light that Failed*.

1881   Appointed editor of the *United Services College Chronicle*. *Schoolboy Lyrics* privately printed by his parents in Lahore, for limited circulation.

1882   Leaves school at end of summer term. Sails for India on 20 September; arrives Bombay on 18 October. Takes up post as assistant-editor of the *Civil and Military Gazette* in Lahore in the Punjab, where his father is now Principal of the Mayo College of Art and Curator of the Lahore Museum. Annual leaves from 1883 to 1888 are spent at Simla, except in 1884 when the family goes to Dalhousie.

1884   *Echoes* (by Rudyard and Trix, who has now rejoined the family in Lahore).

1885   *Quartette* (a Christmas Annual by Rudyard, Trix, and their parents).

1886   *Departmental Ditties*.

1887   Transferred in the autumn to the staff of the *Pioneer*, the *Civil and Military Gazette*'s sister-paper, in Allahabad in the North-West Provinces. As special correspondent in Rajputana he writes the articles later collected as 'Letters of Marque' in *From Sea to Sea*. Becomes friendly with Professor and Mrs Hill, and shares their bungalow.

1888   *Plain Tales from the Hills*. Takes on the additional responsibility of writing for the *Week's News*, a new publication sponsored by the *Pioneer*.

1888–9   *Soldiers Three*; *The Story of the Gadsbys*; *In Black and White*; *Under the Deodars*; *The Phantom Rickshaw*; *Wee Willie Winkie*.

1889   Leaves India on 9 March; travels to San Francisco with Professor and Mrs Hill via Rangoon, Singapore, Hong Kong, and Japan. Crosses the United States on his own, writing the articles later collected in *From Sea to Sea*. Falls in love with Mrs Hill's sister Caroline Taylor. Reaches Liverpool in October, and makes his début in the London literary world.

1890   Enjoys literary success, but suffers breakdown. Visits Italy. *The Light that Failed*.

1891   Visits South Africa, Australia, New Zealand, and (for the last time) India. Returns to England on hearing of the death of his American friend Wolcott Balestier. *Life's Handicap*.

1892   Marries Wolcott's sister Caroline Starr Balestier ('Carrie') in January. (The bride is given away by Henry James.) Their world tour is cut short by the loss of his savings in the collapse of the Oriental Banking Company. They establish their home at Brattleboro in Vermont, on the Balestier family estate. Daughter Josephine born in December. *The Naulahka* (written in collaboration with Wolcott Balestier). *Barrack-Room Ballads*.

1893   *Many Inventions*.

1894   *The Jungle Book*.

1923   *The Irish Guards in the Great War; Land and Sea Tales for Scouts and Guides.*

1924   Daughter Elsie marries Captain George Bambridge, MC.

1926   *Debits and Credits.*

1927   Voyage to Brazil.

1928   *A Book of Words.*

1930   *Thy Servant a Dog.* Visit to the West Indies.

1932   *Limits and Renewals.*

1933   *Souvenirs of France.*

1936   Kipling's death, 18 January.

1937   *Something of Myself For My Friends Known and Unknown.*

1937–9 *The Complete Works of Rudyard Kipling,* Sussex Edition. Prepared by Kipling in the last years of his life, this edition contains some previously uncollected items; but in spite of its title it does not include all his works.

1939   Death of Mrs Kipling.

1940   *The Definitive Edition of Rudyard Kipling's Verse.* This is the last of the series of 'Inclusive Editions' of his verse published in 1919, 1921, 1927, and 1933. In spite of its title the edition is far from definitive in terms of its inclusiveness or textual authority.

1948   Death of Kipling's sister Trix (Mrs John Fleming).

1976   Death of Kipling's daughter Elsie (Mrs George Bambridge).

Plain Tales from the Hills

TO

THE WITTIEST WOMAN IN INDIA*

I DEDICATE THIS BOOK

PREFACE

EIGHT-AND-TWENTY of these tales* appeared originally in the *Civil and Military Gazette*. I am indebted to the kindness of the Proprietors of that paper for permission to reprint them. The remaining tales are, more or less, new.

RUDYARD KIPLING.

Lispeth*

Look, you have cast out Love! What Gods are these
   You bid me please?
The Three in One, the One in Three? Not so!
   To my own gods I go.
It may be they shall give me greater ease
Than your cold Christ and tangled Trinities.

                                    The Convert.

SHE was the daughter of Sonoo, a Hill-man of the Himalayas,
and Jadéh his wife. One year their maize failed, and two bears
spent the night in their only opium poppy-field just above the
Sutlej Valley* on the Kotgarh* side; so, next season, they
turned Christian, and brought their baby to the Mission to be
baptized. The Kotgarh Chaplain christened her Elizabeth,
and 'Lispeth' is the Hill or *pahari* pronunciation.

Later, cholera came into the Kotgarh Valley and carried off
Sonoo and Jadéh, and Lispeth became half servant, half
companion, to the wife of the then Chaplain of Kotgarh. This
was after the reign of the Moravian missionaries* in that
place, but before Kotgarh had quite forgotten her title of
'Mistress of the Northern Hills.'

Whether Christianity improved Lispeth, or whether the
gods of her own people would have done as much for her
under any circumstances, I do not know; but she grew very
lovely. When a Hill-girl grows lovely, she is worth travelling
fifty miles over bad ground to look upon. Lispeth had a Greek
face—one of those faces people paint so often, and see so
seldom. She was of a pale, ivory colour, and, for her race,
extremely tall. Also, she possessed eyes that were wonderful;
and, had she not been dressed in the abominable print-cloths
affected by Missions, you would, meeting her on the hillside
unexpectedly, have thought her the original Diana* of the
Romans going out to slay.

Lispeth took to Christianity readily, and did not abandon it
when she reached womanhood, as do some Hill-girls. Her own
people hated her because she had, they said, become a white

woman and washed herself daily; and the Chaplain's wife did
not know what to do with her. One cannot ask a stately
goddess, five feet ten in her shoes, to clean plates and dishes.
She played with the Chaplain's children and took classes in
the Sunday School, and read all the books in the house, and
grew more and more beautiful, like the Princesses in fairy
tales. The Chaplain's wife said that the girl ought to take
service in Simla as a nurse or something 'genteel.' But Lispeth
did not want to take service. She was very happy where she
was.

When travellers—there were not many in those years—came
in to Kotgarh, Lispeth used to lock herself into her own room
for fear they might take her away to Simla, or out into the
unknown world.

One day, a few months after she was seventeen years old,
Lispeth went out for a walk. She did not walk in the manner
of English ladies—a mile and a half out, with a carriage-ride
back again. She covered between twenty and thirty miles in
her little constitutionals, all about and about, between
Kotgarh and Narkunda.* This time she came back at full
dusk, stepping down the breakneck descent into Kotgarh with
something heavy in her arms. The Chaplain's wife was dozing
in the drawing-room when Lispeth came in breathing heavily
and very exhausted with her burden. Lispeth put it down
on the sofa, and said simply, 'This is my husband. I found
him on the Bagi Road. He has hurt himself. We will nurse
him, and when he is well your husband shall marry him to
me.'

This was the first mention Lispeth had ever made of her
matrimonial views, and the Chaplain's wife shrieked with
horror. However, the man on the sofa needed attention first.
He was a young Englishman, and his head had been cut to the
bone by something jagged. Lispeth said she had found him
down the hillside, and had brought him in. He was breathing
queerly and was unconscious.

He was put to bed and tended by the Chaplain, who knew
something of medicine; and Lispeth waited outside the door
in case she could be useful. She explained to the Chaplain that
this was the man she meant to marry; and the Chaplain and

his wife lectured her severely on the impropriety of her conduct. Lispeth listened quietly, and repeated her first proposition. It takes a great deal of Christianity to wipe out uncivilised Eastern instincts, such as falling in love at first sight. Lispeth, having found the man she worshipped, did not see why she should keep silent as to her choice. She had no intention of being sent away, either. She was going to nurse that Englishman until he was well enough to marry her. This was her programme.

After a fortnight of slight fever and inflammation, the Englishman recovered coherence and thanked the Chaplain and his wife, and Lispeth—especially Lispeth—for their kindness. He was a traveller in the East, he said—they never talked about 'globe-trotters' in those days, when the P. & O*. fleet was young and small—and had come from Dehra Dun* to hunt for plants and butterflies among the Simla hills. No one at Simla, therefore, knew anything about him. He fancied that he must have fallen over the cliff while reaching out for a fern on a rotten tree-trunk, and that his coolies must have stolen his baggage and fled. He thought he would go back to Simla when he was a little stronger. He desired no more mountaineering.

He made small haste to go away, and recovered his strength slowly. Lispeth objected to being advised either by the Chaplain or his wife; therefore the latter spoke to the Englishman, and told him how matters stood in Lispeth's heart. He laughed a good deal, and said it was very pretty and romantic, but, as he was engaged to a girl at Home, he fancied that nothing would happen. Certainly he would behave with discretion. He did that. Still he found it very pleasant to talk to Lispeth, and walk with Lispeth, and say nice things to her, and call her pet names while he was getting strong enough to go away. It meant nothing at all to him, and everything in the world to Lispeth. She was very happy while the fortnight lasted, because she had found a man to love.

Being a savage by birth, she took no trouble to hide her feelings and the Englishman was amused. When he went away, Lispeth walked with him up the Hill as far as Narkunda, very troubled and very miserable. The Chaplain's wife, being a good Christian and disliking anything in the shape of fuss or scandal—Lispeth was beyond her management entirely—had told the Englishman to tell Lispeth that he was coming back to marry her. 'She is but a child, you know, and, I fear, at heart a heathen,' said the Chaplain's wife. So all the twelve miles up the Hill the Englishman, with his arm round Lispeth's waist, was assuring the girl that he would come back and marry her; and Lispeth made him promise over and over again. She wept on the Narkunda Ridge till he had passed out of sight along the Muttiani* path.

Then she dried her tears and went in to Kotgarh again, and said to the Chaplain's wife, 'He will come back and marry me. He has gone to his own people to tell them so.' And the Chaplain's wife soothed Lispeth and said, 'He will come back.' At the end of two months Lispeth grew impatient, and was told that the Englishman had gone over the seas to England. She knew where England was, because she had read little geography primers; but, of course, she had no conception of the nature of the sea, being a Hill-girl. There was an old puzzle-map of the World in the house. Lispeth had played with it when she was a child. She unearthed it again, and put it together of evenings, and cried to herself, and tried to imagine where her Englishman was. As she had no ideas of distance or steamboats her notions were somewhat wild. It would not have made the least difference had she been perfectly correct; for the Englishman had no intention of coming back to marry a Hill-girl. He forgot all about her by the time he was butterfly-hunting in Assam. He wrote a book on the East afterwards. Lispeth's name did not appear there.

At the end of three months Lispeth made daily pilgrimage to Narkunda to see if her Englishman was coming along the road. It gave her comfort, and the Chaplain's wife finding her happier thought that she was getting over her 'barbarous and most indelicate folly.' A little later the walks ceased to help Lispeth, and her temper grew very bad. The Chaplain's wife thought this a profitable time to let her know the real state of affairs—that the Englishman had only promised his love to keep her quiet—that he had never meant anything, and that it was wrong and improper of Lispeth to think of marriage with an Englishman, who was of a superior clay, besides being promised in marriage to a girl of his own people. Lispeth said that all this was clearly impossible because he had said he loved her, and the Chaplain's wife had, with her own lips, asserted that the Englishman was coming back.

'How can what he and you said be untrue?' asked Lispeth.

'We said it as an excuse to keep you quiet, child,' said the Chaplain's wife.

'Then you have lied to me,' said Lispeth, 'you and he?'

The Chaplain's wife bowed her head, and said nothing. Lispeth was silent too for a little time; then she went out down the valley, and returned in the dress of a Hill-girl—infamously dirty, but without the nose-stud and ear-rings. She had her hair braided into the long pigtail, helped out with black thread, that Hill-women wear.

'I am going back to my own people,' said she. 'You have killed Lispeth. There is only left old Jadéh's daughter—the daughter of a *pahari** and the servant of Tarka Devi.* You are all liars, you English.'

By the time that the Chaplain's wife had recovered from the shock of the announcement that Lispeth had 'verted to her mother's gods the girl had gone; and she never came back.

She took to her own unclean people savagely, as if to make up the arrears of the life she had stepped out of; and, in a little time, she married a woodcutter who beat her after the manner of *paharis,* and her beauty faded soon.*

'There is no law whereby you can account for the vagaries of the heathen,' said the Chaplain's wife, 'and I believe that Lispeth was always at heart an infidel.' Seeing she had been taken into the Church of England at the mature age of five weeks, this statement does not do credit to the Chaplain's wife.

Lispeth was a very old woman when she died. She had always a perfect command of English, and when she was sufficiently drunk could sometimes be induced to tell the story of her first love-affair.

It was hard then to realise that the bleared, wrinkled creature, exactly like a wisp of charred rag, could ever have been 'Lispeth of the Kotgarh Mission.'

Three and—an Extra

*When halter and heel-ropes are slipped, do not give chase
with sticks but with gram.*   Punjabi Proverb.*

AFTER marriage arrives a reaction, sometimes a big,
sometimes a little one; but it comes sooner or later, and must
be tided over by both parties if they desire the rest of their
lives to go with the current.

In the case of the Cusack-Bremmils this reaction did not set
in till the third year after the wedding. Bremmil was hard to
hold at the best of times; but he was a beautiful husband until
the baby died and Mrs. Bremmil wore black, and grew thin,
and mourned as though the bottom of the Universe had fallen
out. Perhaps Bremmil ought to have comforted her. He tried
to do so, but the more he comforted the more Mrs. Bremmil
grieved, and, consequently, the more uncomfortable grew
Bremmil. The fact was that they both needed a tonic. And
they got it. Mrs. Bremmil can afford to laugh now, but it was
no laughing matter to her at the time.

Mrs. Hauksbee appeared on the horizon; and where she
existed was fair chance of trouble. At Simla her by-name was
the 'Stormy Petrel.' She had won that title five times to my
own certain knowledge. She was a little, brown, thin, almost
skinny, woman, with big, rolling, violet-blue eyes, and the
sweetest manners in the world. You had only to mention her
name at afternoon teas for every woman in the room to rise
up and call her not blessed. She was clever, witty, brilliant,
and sparkling beyond most of her kind; but possessed of many
devils of malice and mischievousness. She could be nice,
though, even to her own sex. But that is another story.

Bremmil went off at score* after the baby's death and the
general discomfort that followed, and Mrs. Hauksbee annexed
him. She took no pleasure in hiding her captives. She annexed
him publicly, and saw that the public saw it. He rode with
her, and walked with her, and talked with her, and picnicked

with her, and tiffined* at Peliti's* with her, till people put up
their eyebrows and said, 'Shocking!' Mrs. Bremmil stayed at
home, turning over the dead baby's frocks and crying into the
empty cradle. She did not care to do anything else. But some
eight dear, affectionate lady-friends explained the situation at
length to her in case she should miss the cream of it. Mrs.
Bremmil listened quietly, and thanked them for their good
offices. She was not as clever as Mrs. Hauksbee, but she was
no fool. She kept her own counsel, and did not speak to
Bremmil of what she had heard. This is worth remembering.
Speaking to or crying over a husband never did any good yet.

When Bremmil was at home, which was not often, he was
more affectionate than usual; and that showed his hand. The
affection was forced, partly to soothe his own conscience and
partly to soothe Mrs. Bremmil. It failed in both regards.

Then 'the A.-D.-C.* in Waiting was commanded by Their
Excellencies, Lord and Lady Lytton,* to invite Mr. and Mrs.
Cusack-Bremmil to Peterhoff* on July 26 at 9-30 P.M.'—
'Dancing' in the bottom left-hand corner.

'I can't go,' said Mrs. Bremmil, 'it is too soon after poor
little Florrie . . . but it need not stop you, Tom.'

She meant what she said then, and Bremmil said that he
would go just to put in an appearance. Here he spoke the
thing which was not; and Mrs. Bremmil knew it. She
guessed—a woman's guess is much more accurate than a
man's certainty—that he had meant to go from the first, and
with Mrs. Hauksbee. She sat down to think, and the outcome
of her thoughts was that the memory of a dead child was
worth considerably less than the affections of a living
husband. She made her plan and staked her all upon it. In that
hour she discovered that she knew Tom Bremmil thoroughly,
and this knowledge she acted on.

'Tom,' said she, 'I shall be dining out at the Longmores' on
the evening of the 26th. You'd better dine at the Club.'

This saved Bremmil from making an excuse to get away and
dine with Mrs. Hauksbee, so he was grateful, and felt small
and mean at the same time—which was wholesome. Bremmil
left the house at five for a ride. About half-past five in the
evening a large leather-covered basket came in from Phelps's*

for Mrs. Bremmil. She was a woman who knew how to dress; and she had not spent a week on designing that dress and having it gored, and hemmed, and herring-boned, and tucked and rucked (or whatever the terms are), for nothing. It was a gorgeous dress—slight mourning.* I can't describe it, but it was what *The Queen* calls 'a creation'—a thing that hit you straight between the eyes and made you gasp. She had not much heart for what she was going to do; but as she glanced at the long mirror she had the satisfaction of knowing that she had never looked so well in her life. She was a large blonde and, when she chose, carried herself superbly.

After the dinner at the Longmores' she went on to the dance—a little late—and encountered Bremmil with Mrs. Hauksbee on his arm. That made her flush, and as the men crowded round her for dances she looked magnificent. She filled up all her dances except three, and those she left blank. Mrs. Hauksbee caught her eye once, and knew it was war— real war—between them. She started handicapped in the struggle, for she had ordered Bremmil about just the least little bit in the world too much, and he was beginning to resent it. Moreover, he had never seen his wife look so lovely. He stared at her from doorways, and glared at her from passages as she went about with her partners; and the more he stared, the more taken was he. He could scarcely believe that this was the woman with the red eyes and the black stuff gown who used to weep over the eggs at breakfast.

Mrs. Hauksbee did her best to hold him in play, but, after two dances, he crossed over to his wife and asked for a dance.

'I'm afraid you've come too late, *Mister* Bremmil,' she said, with her eyes twinkling.

Then he begged her to give him a dance, and, as a great favour, she allowed him the fifth waltz. Luckily Five stood vacant on his programme. They danced it together, and there was a little flutter round the room. Bremmil had a sort of a notion that his wife could dance, but he never knew she danced so divinely. At the end of that waltz he asked for another—as a favour, not as a right; and Mrs. Bremmil said, 'Show me your programme, dear!' He showed it as a naughty little schoolboy hands up contraband sweets to a master.

There was a fair sprinkling of 'H's on it, besides 'H' at supper. Mrs. Bremmil said nothing, but she smiled contemptuously, ran her pencil through Seven and Nine—two 'H's—and returned the card with her own name written above—a pet name that only she and her husband used. Then she shook her finger at him, and said laughing, 'Oh, you silly, *silly* boy!'

Mrs. Hauksbee heard that, and—she owned as much—felt she had the worst of it. Bremmil accepted Seven and Nine gratefully. They danced Seven, and sat out Nine in one of the little tents. What Bremmil said and what Mrs. Bremmil did is no concern of any one.

When the band struck up 'The Roast Beef of Old England,'* the two went out into the verandah, and Bremmil began looking for his wife's dandy (this was before 'rickshaw days)* while she went into the cloak-room. Mrs. Hauksbee came up and said, 'You take me in to supper, I think, Mr. Bremmil?' Bremmil turned red and looked foolish, 'Ah—h'm! I'm going home with my wife, Mrs. Hauksbee. I think there has been a little mistake.' Being a man, he spoke as though Mrs. Hauksbee were entirely responsible.

Mrs. Bremmil came out of the cloak-room in a swan's-down cloak with a white 'cloud'* round her head. She looked radiant; and she had a right to.

The couple went off into the darkness together, Bremmil riding very close to the dandy.

Then said Mrs. Hauksbee to me—she looked a trifle faded and jaded in the lamplight—'Take my word for it, the silliest woman can manage a clever man; but it needs a very clever woman to manage a fool.'

Then we went in to supper.

Thrown Away*

And some are sulky, while some will plunge.
  (*So ho! Steady! Stand still, you!*)
Some you must gentle, and some you must lunge.*
  (*There! There! Who wants to kill you?*)
Some—there are losses in every trade—
Will break their hearts ere bitted and made,
Will fight like fiends as the rope cuts hard,
And die dumb-mad in the breaking-yard.
               Toolungala Stockyard Chorus.

TO rear a boy under what parents call the 'sheltered life system' is, if the boy must go into the world and fend for himself, not wise, Unless he be one in a thousand he has certainly to pass through many unnecessary troubles; and may, possibly, come to extreme grief simply from ignorance of the proper proportions of things.

Let a puppy eat the soap in the bath-room or chew a newly-blacked boot. He chews and chuckles until, by and by, he finds out that blacking and Old Brown Windsor* make him very sick; so he argues that soap and boots are not wholesome. Any old dog about the house will soon show him the unwisdom of biting big dogs' ears. Being young, he remembers and goes abroad, at six months, a well-mannered little beast with a chastened appetite. If he had been kept away from boots, and soap, and big dogs till he came to the trinity full-grown and with developed teeth, consider how fearfully sick and thrashed he would be! Apply that notion to the 'sheltered life,' and see how it works. It does not sound pretty, but it is the better of two evils.

There was a Boy once who had been brought up under the 'sheltered life' theory; and the theory killed him dead. He stayed with his people all his days, from the hour he was born till the hour he went into Sandhurst* nearly at the top of the list. He was beautifully taught in all that wins marks by a private tutor, and carried the exta weight of 'never having given his parents an hour's anxiety in his life.' What he learnt at Sandhurst beyond the regular routine is of no great consequence. He looked about him, and he found soap and blacking, so to speak, very good. He ate a little, and came out of Sandhurst not so high as he went in. Then there was an interval and a scene with his people, who expected much from him. Next a year of living unspotted from the world in a third-rate depôt battalion* where all the juniors were children and all the seniors old women; and lastly, he came out to India, where he was cut off from the support of his parents, and had no one to fall back on in time of trouble except himself.

Now India is a place beyond all others where one must not take things too seriously—the mid-day sun always excepted. Too much work and too much energy kill a man just as effectively as too much assorted vice or too much drink. Flirtation does not matter, because every one is being transferred, and either you or she leave the Station and never return. Good work does not matter, because a man is judged by his worst output, and another man takes all the credit of his best as a rule. Bad work does not matter, because other men do worse, and incompetents hang on longer in India than anywhere else. Amusements do not matter, because you must repeat them as soon as you have accomplished them once, and most amusements only mean trying to win another person's money. Sickness does not matter, because it's all in the day's work, and if you die, another man takes over your place and your office in the eight hours between death and burial. Nothing matters except Home-furlough and acting allowances,* and these only because they are scarce. It is a slack country, where all men work with imperfect instruments; and the wisest thing is to escape as soon as ever you can to some place where amusement is amusement and a reputation worth the having.

But this Boy—the tale is as old as the Hills*—came out, and took all things seriously. He was pretty and was petted. He took the pettings seriously, and fretted over women not worth saddling a pony to call upon. He found his new free life in India very good. It does look attractive in the beginning, from a subaltern's point of view— all ponies, partners, dancing, and so on. He tasted it as the puppy tastes the soap. Only he came late to the eating, with a grown set of teeth. He had no sense of balance—just like the puppy—and could not understand why he was not treated with the consideration he received under his father's roof. This hurt his feelings.

He quarrelled with other boys and, being sensitive to the marrow, remembered these quarrels, and they excited him. He found whist, and gymkhanas, and things of that kind (meant to amuse one after office) good; but he took them seriously too, just as seriously as he took the 'head' that followed after drink. He lost his money over whist and gymkhanas because they were new to him.

He took his losses seriously, and wasted as much energy and interest over a two-goldmohur* race for maiden *ekka*-ponies* with their manes hogged, as if it had been the Derby. One-half of this came from inexperience—much as the puppy squabbles with the corner of the hearthrug—and the other half from the dizziness bred by stumbling out of his quiet life into the glare and excitement of a livelier one. No one told him about the soap and the blacking, because an average man takes it for granted that an average man is ordinarily careful in regard to them. It was pitiful to watch The Boy knocking himself to pieces, as an over-handled colt falls down and cuts himself when he gets away from his groom.

This unbridled license in amusements not worth the trouble of breaking line for, much less rioting over, endured for six months—all through one cold weather—and then we thought that the heat and the knowledge of having lost his money and health and lamed his horses would sober The Boy down, and he would stand steady. In ninety-nine cases out of a hundred this would have happened. You can see the principle working in any Indian Station. But this particular case fell through because The Boy was sensitive and took things seriously—as I may have said some seven times before. Of course, we could not tell how his excesses struck him personally. They were nothing very heartbreaking or above the average. He might be crippled for life financially, and want a little nursing. Still the memory of his performances would wither away in one hot weather, and the bankers would help him to tide over the money-troubles. But he must have taken another view altogether, and have believed himself ruined beyond redemption. His Colonel talked to him severely when the cold weather ended. That made him more wretched than ever; and it was only an ordinary 'Colonel's wigging'!

What follows is a curious instance of the fashion in which we are all linked together and made responsible for one another. *The* thing that kicked the beam in The Boy's mind was a remark that a woman made when he was talking to her. There is no use in repeating it, for it was only a cruel little sentence, rapped out before thinking, that made him flush to the roots of his hair. He kept himself to himself for three days, and then put in for two days' leave to go shooting near a Canal Engineer's Rest House* about thirty miles out. He got his leave, and that night at Mess was noisier and more offensive than ever. He said that he was 'going to shoot big game,' and left at half-past ten o'clock in an *ekka*. Partridge—which was the only thing a man could get near the Rest House—is not big game; so every one laughed.

Next morning one of the Majors came in from short leave, and heard that The Boy had gone out to shoot 'big game.' The Major had taken an interest in the Boy, and had, more than once, tried to check him. The Major put up his eyebrows when he heard of the expedition, and went to The Boy's rooms, where he rummaged.

Presently he came out and found me leaving cards on the Mess. There was no one else in the ante-room.

He said, 'The Boy has gone out shooting. *Does* a man shoot *tetur** with a revolver and writing-case?'

I said, 'Nonsense, Major!' for I saw what was in his mind.

He said, 'Nonsense or no nonsense, I'm going to the Canal now—at once. I don't feel easy.'

Then he thought for a minute, and said, 'Can you lie?'

'You know best,' I answered. 'It's my profession.'

'Very well,' said the Major, 'you must come out with me now—at once—in an *ekka* to the Canal to shoot black-buck. Go and put on *shikar*-kit*—*quick*—and drive here with a gun.'

The Major was a masterful man, and I knew that he would not give orders for nothing. So I obeyed, and on return found the Major packed up in an *ekka*—gun-cases and food slung below—all ready for a shooting-trip.

He dismissed the driver and drove himself. We jogged along quietly while in the station; but, as soon as we got to the dusty road across the plains, he made that pony fly. A country-bred* can do nearly anything at a pinch. We covered the thirty miles in under three hours, but the poor brute was nearly dead.

Once I said, 'What's the blazing hurry, Major?'

He said quietly, 'The Boy has been alone, by himself for—one, two, five,—fourteen hours now! I tell you, I don't feel easy.'

This uneasiness spread itself to me, and I helped to beat the pony.

When we came to the Canal Engineer's Rest House the Major called for The Boy's servant; but there was no answer. Then we went up to the house, calling for The Boy by name; but there was no answer.

'Oh, he's out shooting,' said I.

Just then I saw through one of the windows a little hurricane-lamp burning. This was at four in the afternoon. We both stopped dead in the verandah, holding our breath to catch every sound; and we heard, inside the room, the '*brr—brr—brr* of a multitude of flies. The Major said nothing, but he took off his helmet and we entered very softly.

The Boy was dead on the bed in the centre of the bare, lime-washed room. He had shot his head nearly to pieces with his revolver. The gun-cases were still strapped, so was the bedding, and on the table lay The Boy's writing-case with photographs. He had gone away to die like a poisoned rat!

The Major said to himself softly, 'Poor Boy! Poor, *poor* devil!' Then he turned away from the bed and said, 'I want your help in this business.'

Knowing The Boy was dead by his own hand, I saw exactly what that help would be, so I passed over to the table, took a chair, lit a cheroot, and began to go through the writing-case; the Major looking over my shoulder and repeating to himself, 'We came too late!—Like a rat in a hole!—Poor, *poor* devil!'

The Boy must have spent half the night in writing to his people, to his Colonel, and to a girl at Home; and as soon as he had finished, must have shot himself, for he had been dead a long time when we came in.

I read all that he had written, and passed over each sheet to the Major as I finished it.

We saw from his accounts how very seriously he had taken everything. He wrote about 'disgrace which he was unable to bear'—'indelible shame'—'criminal folly'—'wasted life,' and so on; besides a lot of private things to his father and mother much too sacred to put into print. The letter to the girl at Home was the most pitiful of all, and I choked as I read it. The Major made no attempt to keep dry-eyed. I respected him for that. He read and rocked himself to and fro, and simply cried like a woman without caring to hide it. The letters were so dreary and hopeless and touching. We forgot all about The Boy's follies, and only thought of the poor Thing on the bed and the scrawled sheets in our hands. It was utterly impossible to let the letters go Home. They would have broken his father's heart and killed his mother after killing her belief in her son.

At last the Major dried his eyes openly, and said, 'Nice sort of thing to spring on an English family! What shall we do?'

I said, knowing what the Major had brought me out for,— 'The Boy died of cholera. We were with him at the time. We can't commit ourselves to half-measures. Come along.'

Then began one of the most grimly comic scenes I have ever taken part in—the concoction of a big, written lie, bolstered with evidence, to soothe The Boy's people at Home. I began the rough draft of the letter, the Major throwing in hints here and there while he gathered up all the stuff that The Boy had written and burnt it in the fireplace. It was a hot, still evening when we began, and the lamp burned very badly. In due course I made the draft to my satisfaction, setting forth how The Boy was the pattern of all virtues, beloved by his regiment, with every promise of a great career before him, and so on; how we had helped him through the sickness—it was no time for little lies, you will understand—and how he had died without pain. I choked while I was putting down these things and thinking of the poor people who would read them. Then I laughed at the grotesqueness of the affair, and the laughter mixed itself up with the choke—and the Major said that we both wanted drinks.

I am afraid to say how much whisky we drank before the letter was finished. It had not the least effect on us. Then we took off The Boy's watch, locket, and ring.

Lastly, the Major said, 'We must send a lock of hair too. A woman values that.'

But there were reasons why we could not find a lock fit to send. The Boy was black-haired, and so was the Major, luckily. I cut off a piece of the Major's hair above the temple with a knife, and put it into the packet we were making. The laughing-fit and the chokes got hold of me again, and I had to stop. The Major was nearly as bad; and we both knew that the worst part of the work was to come.

We sealed up the packet, photographs, locket, seals,* ring, letter, and lock of hair with The Boy's sealing-wax and The Boy's seal.

Then the Major said, 'For God's sake let's get outside— away from the room—and think!'

We went outside, and walked on the banks of the Canal for an hour, eating and drinking what we had with us, until the moon rose. I know now exactly how a murderer feels. Finally, we forced ourselves back to the room with the lamp and the Other Thing in it, and began to take up the next piece of work. I am not going to write about this. It was too horrible. We burned the bedstead and dropped the ashes into the Canal; we took up the matting of the room and treated that in the same way. I went off to a village and borrowed two big hoes,*—I did not want the villagers to help,—while the Major arranged—the other matters. It took us four hours' hard work to make the grave. As we worked, we argued out whether it was right to say as much as we remembered of the Burial of the Dead. We compromised things by saying the Lord's Prayer with a private unofficial prayer for the peace of the soul of The Boy. Then we filled in the grave and went into the verandah— not the house—to lie down to sleep. We were dead tired.

When we woke the Major said wearily, 'We can't go back till to-morrow. We must give him a decent time to die in. He died early *this* morning, remember. That seems more natural.'

So the Major must have been lying awake all the time, thinking.

I said, 'Then why didn't we bring the body back to cantonments?'

The Major thought for a minute. 'Because the people bolted when they heard of the cholera. And the *ekka* has gone!'

That was strictly true. We had forgotten all about the *ekka*-pony, and he had gone home.

So we were left there alone, all that stifling day, in the Canal Rest House, testing and re-testing our story of The Boy's death to see if it was weak in any point. A native appeared in the afternoon, but we said that a *Sahib* was dead of cholera, and he ran away. As the dust gathered, the Major told me all his fears about The Boy, and awful stories of suicide or nearly-carried-out suicide—tales that made one's hair crisp. He said that he himself had once gone into the same Valley of the Shadow* as The Boy, when he was young and new to the country; so he understood how things fought together in The Boy's poor jumbled head. He also said that youngsters, in their repentant moments, consider their sins much more serious and ineffaceable than they really are. We talked together all through the evening and rehearsed the story of the death of The Boy. As soon as the moon was up, and The Boy, theoretically, just buried, we struck across country for the Station. We walked from eight till six o'clock in the morning; but though we were dead tired, we did not forget to go to The Boy's rooms and put away his revolver with the proper amount of cartridges in the pouch. Also to set his writing-case on the table. We found the Colonel and reported the death, feeling more like murderers than ever. Then we went to bed and slept the clock round, for there was no more in us.

The tale had credence as long as was necessary; for every one forgot about The Boy before a fortnight was over. Many people, however, found time to say that the Major had behaved scandalously in not bringing in the body for a regimental funeral. The saddest thing of all was the letter from The Boy's mother to the Major and me—with big inky blisters all over the sheet. She wrote the sweetest possible things about our great kindness, and the obligation she would be under to us as long as she lived.

All things considered, she was under an obligation, but not exactly as she meant.

Miss Youghal's Sais*

When Man and Woman are agreed, what can the Kazi* do?
Proverb.

SOME people say that there is no romance in India. Those people are wrong. Our lives hold quite as much romance as is good for us. Sometimes more.

Strickland was in the Police, and people did not understand him; so they said he was a doubtful sort of man and passed by on the other side.* Strickland had himself to thank for this. He held the extraordinary theory that a Policeman in India should try to know as much about the natives as the natives themselves. Now, in the whole of Upper India there is only one man who can pass for Hindu or Mahommedan, hide-dresser* or priest, as he pleases. He is feared and respected by the natives from the Ghor Kathri* to the Jamma Musjid;* and he is supposed to have the gift of invisibility and executive control over many Devils. But this has done him no good in the eyes of the Indian Government.

Strickland was foolish enough to take that man for his model; and, following out his absurd theory, dabbled in unsavoury places which no respectable man would think of exploring—all among the native riff-raff. He educated himself in this peculiar way for seven years, and people could not appreciate it. He was perpetually 'going Fantee'* among natives, which, of course, no man with any sense believes in. He was initiated into the *Sat Bhai* at Allahabad once, when he was on leave; he knew the Lizzard-Song of the Sansis,* and the *Hálli-Hukk* dance,* which is a religious can-can of a startling kind. When a man knows who dance the *Hálli-Hukk*, and how, and when, and where, he knows something to be proud of. He has gone deeper than the skin. But Strickland was not proud, though he had helped once, at Jagadhri,* at the Painting of the Death Bull, which no Englishman must even look upon; had mastered the thieves'-patter of the *chángars;** had taken a Eusufzai* horse-thief alone near Attock; and had stood under the sounding-board of a Border mosque and conducted service in the manner of a Sunni Mollah.*

His crowning achievement was spending eleven days as a *faquir* or priest in the gardens of Baba Atal* at Amritsar, and there picking up the threads of the great Nasiban Murder Case. But people said, justly enough, 'Why on earth can't Strickland sit in his office and write up his diary, and recruit, and keep quiet, instead of showing up the incapacity of his seniors?' So the Nasiban Murder Case did him no good departmentally; but, after his first feeling of wrath, he returned to his outlandish custom of prying into native life. When a man once acquires a taste for this particular amusement, it abides with him all his days. It is the most fascinating thing in the world—Love not excepted. Where other men took ten days to the Hills, Strickland took leave for what he called *shikar*,* put on the disguise that appealed to him at the time, stepped down into the brown crowd, and was swallowed up for a while. He was a quiet, dark young fellow—spare, black-eyed—and, when he was not thinking of something else, a very interesting companion. Strickland on Native Progress as he had seen it was worth hearing. Natives hated Strickland; but they were afraid of him. He knew too much.

When the Youghals came into the station, Strickland—very gravely, as he did everything— fell in love with Miss Youghal; and she, after a while, fell in love with him because she could not understand him. Then Strickland told the parents; but Mrs. Youghal said she was not going to throw her daughter into the worst paid Department in the Empire, and old Youghal said, in so many words, that he mistrusted Strickland's ways and works, and would thank him not to speak or write to his daughter any more. 'Very well,' said Strickland, for he did not wish to make his lady-love's life a burden. After one long talk with Miss Youghal he dropped the business entirely.

The Youghals went up to Simla in April.

In July Strickland secured three months' leave on 'urgent private affairs.' He locked up his house—though not a native in the Province would wittingly have touched 'Estreekin Sahib's' gear for the world—and went down to see a friend of his, an old dyer, at Tarn Taran.*

Here all trace of him was lost, until a *sais* or groom met me on the Simla Mall with this extraordinary note:—

DEAR OLD MAN,—Please give bearer a box of cheroots—Supers, No. 1, for preference. They are freshest at the Club. I'll repay when I reappear; but at present I'm out of society.—Yours,

E. STRICKLAND.

I ordered two boxes, and handed them over to the *sais* with my love. That *sais* was Strickland, and he was in old Youghal's employ, attached to Miss Youghal's Arab.* The poor fellow was suffering for an English smoke, and knew that, whatever happened, I should hold my tongue till the business was over.

Later on, Mrs. Youghal, who was wrapped up in her servants, began talking at houses where she called of her paragon among *saises*—the man who was never too busy to get up in the morning and pick flowers for the breakfast-table, and who blacked—actually *blacked*—the hoofs of his horse like a London coachman! The turn-out of Miss Youghal's Arab was a wonder and a delight. Strickland—Dulloo, I mean—found his reward in the pretty things that Miss Youghal said to him when she went out riding. Her parents were pleased to find she had forgotten all her foolishness for young Strickland, and said she was a good girl.

Strickland vows that the two months of his service were the most rigid mental discipline he has ever gone through. Quite apart from the little fact that the wife of one of his fellow-*saises* fell in love with him and then tried to poison him with arsenic because he would have nothing to do with her, he had to school himself into keeping quiet when Miss Youghal went out riding with some man who tried to flirt with her, and he was forced to trot behind carrying the blanket* and hearing every word! Also, he had to keep his temper when he was slanged in the theatre porch by a policeman—especially once when he was abused by a Naik* he had himself recruited from Isser Jang* village—or, worse still, when a young subaltern called him a pig for not making way quickly enough.

But the life had its compensations. He obtained great insight into the ways and thefts of *saises*—enough, he says, to have summarily convicted half the population of the Punjab if he had been on business. He became one of the leading players at knuckle-bones,* which all *jhampánies** and many *saises* play while they are waiting outside the Government House or the Gaiety Theatre* of nights; he learned to smoke tobacco that was three-fourths cowdung; and he heard the wisdom of the grizzled Jemadar* of the Government House grooms. Whose words are valuable. He saw many things which amused him; and he states, on honour, that no man can appreciate Simla properly till he has seen it from the *sais*'s point of view. He also says that, if he chose to write all he saw his head would be broken in several places.

Strickland's account of the agony he endured on wet nights, hearing the music and seeing the lights in 'Benmore,'* with his toes tingling for a waltz and his head in a horse-blanket, is rather amusing. One of these days Strickland is going to write a little book on his experiences. That book will be worth buying, and even more worth suppressing.

Thus he served faithfully as Jacob served for Rachel;* and his leave was nearly at an end when the explosion came. He had really done his best to keep his temper in the hearing of the flirtations I have mentioned; but he broke down at last. An old and very distinguished General took Miss Youghal for a ride, and began that specially offensive 'you're-only-a-little-girl' sort of flirtation—most difficult for a woman to turn aside deftly, and most maddening to listen to. Miss Youghal was shaking with fear at the things he said in the hearing of her *sais*. Dulloo—Strickland—stood it as long as he could. Then he caught hold of the General's bridle, and, in most fluent English, invited him to step off and be flung over the cliff. Next minute Miss Youghal began to cry, and Strickland saw that he had hopelessly given himself away, and everything was over.

The General nearly had a fit, while Miss Youghal was sobbing out the story of the disguise and the engagement that was not recognised by the parents. Strickland was furiously angry with himself, and more angry with the General for forcing his hand; so he said nothing, but held the horse's head and prepared to thrash the General as some sort of satisfaction. But when the General had thoroughly grasped the story, and knew who Strickland was, he began to puff and blow in the saddle, and nearly rolled off with laughing. He said Strickland deserved a V.C., if it were only for putting on a *sais*'s blanket. Then he called himself names, and vowed that he deserved a thrashing, but he was too old to take it from Strickland. Then he complimented Miss Youghal on her lover. The scandal of the business never struck him; for he was a nice old man, with a weakness for flirtations. Then he laughed again, and said that old Youghal was a fool. Strickland let go of the cob's head, and suggested that the General had better help them if that was his opinion. Strickland knew Youghal's weakness for men with titles and letters after their names and high official position. 'It's rather like a forty-minute farce,' said the General, 'but, begad, I *will* help, if it's only to escape that tremendous thrashing I deserve. Go along to your home, my *sais*-Policeman, and change into decent kit, and I'll attack Mr. Youghal. Miss Youghal, may I ask you to canter home and wait?'

*   *   *

About seven minutes later there was a wild hurroosh at the Club. A *sais*, with blanket and head-rope, was asking all the men he knew: 'For Heaven's sake lend me decent clothes!' As the men did not recognise him, there were some peculiar scenes before Strickland could get a hot bath, with soda in it, in one room, a shirt here, a collar there, a pair of trousers elsewhere, and so on. He galloped off, with half the Club wardrobe on his back, and an utter stranger's pony under him, to the house of old Youghal. The General, arrayed in purple and fine linen,* was before him. What the General had said Strickland never knew, but Youghal received Strickland with moderate civility; and Mrs. Youghal, touched by the devotion of the transformed Dulloo, was almost kind. The General beamed and chuckled, and Miss Youghal came in, and, almost before old Youghal knew where he was, the parental consent had been wrenched out, and Strickland had departed with Miss Youghal to the Telegraph Office to wire for his European kit. The final embarrassment was when a stranger attacked him on the Mall and asked for the stolen pony.

In the end, Strickland and Miss Youghal were married, on the strict understanding that Strickland should drop his old ways, and stick to Departmental routine, which pays best and leads to Simla.* Strickland was far too fond of his wife, just then, to break his word, but it was a sore trial to him; for the streets and the bazars, and the sounds in them, were full of meaning to Strickland, and these called to him to come back and take up his wanderings and his discoveries. Some day I will tell you how he broke his promise to help a friend. That was long since, and he has, by this time, been nearly spoilt for what he would call *shikar*. He is forgetting the slang, and the beggar's cant, and the marks, and the signs, and the drift of the under-currents, which, if a man would master, he must always continue to learn.

But he fills in his Departmental returns beautifully.

'Yoked with an Unbeliever'*

I am dying for you, and you are dying for another.
Punjabi Proverb.

WHEN the Gravesend tender* left the P. & O. steamer for
Bombay and went back to catch the train to Town, there were
many people in it crying. But the one who wept most, and
most openly, was Miss Agnes Laiter. She had reason to cry,
because the only man she ever loved—or ever could love, so
she said—was going out to India; and India, as every one
knows, is divided equally between jungle, tigers, cobras,
cholera, and sepoys.

Phil Garron, leaning over the side of the steamer in the rain,
felt very unhappy too; but he did not cry. He was sent out to
'tea.'* What 'tea' meant he had not the vaguest idea, but
fancied that he would have to ride on a prancing horse over
hills covered with tea-vines, and draw a sumptuous salary for
doing so; and he was very grateful to his uncle for getting him
the berth. He was really going to reform all his slack, shiftless
ways, save a large proportion of his magnificent salary yearly,
and in a very short time return to marry Agnes Laiter. Phil
Garron had been lying loose on his friends' hands for three
years, and, as he had nothing to do, he naturally fell in love.
He was very nice; but he was not strong in his views and
opinions and principles, and though he never came to actual
grief, his friends were thankful when he said good-bye, and
went out to this mysterious 'tea' business near Darjiling.*
They said, 'God bless you, dear boy! Let us never see your
face again,'—or at least that was what Phil was given to
understand.

When he sailed, he was very full of a great plan to prove
himself several hundred times better than any one had given
him credit for—to work like a horse, and triumphantly marry
Agnes Laiter. He had many good points besides his good
looks; his only fault being that he was weak, the least little bit

in the world weak. He had as much notion of economy as the Morning Sun;* and yet you could not lay your hand on any one item, and say, 'Herein Phil Garron is extravagant or reckless.' Nor could you point out any particular vice in his character; but he was 'unsatisfactory' and as workable as putty.

Agnes Laiter went about her duties at home—her family objected to the engagement—with red eyes, while Phil was sailing to Darjiling—a 'port on the Bengal Ocean,'* as his mother used to tell her friends. He was popular enough on board ship, made many acquaintances and a moderately large liquor-bill, and sent off huge letters to Agnes Laiter at each port. Then he fell to work on his plantation, somewhere between Darjiling and Kangra,* and, though the salary and the horse and the work were not quite all he had fancied, he succeeded fairly well, and gave himself much unnecessary credit for his perseverance.

In the course of time, as he settled more into collar, and his work grew fixed before him, the face of Agnes Laiter went out of his mind and only came when he was at leisure, which was not often. He would forget all about her for a fortnight, and remember her with a start, like a schoolboy who has forgotten to learn his lesson. She did not forget Phil, because she was of the kind that never forgets. Only, another man—a really desirable young man—presented himself before Mrs. Laiter; and the chance of a marriage with Phil was as far off as ever; and his letters were so unsatisfactory; and there was a certain amount of domestic pressure brought to bear on the girl; and the young man really was an eligible person as incomes go; and the end of all things was that Agnes married him, and wrote a tempestuous whirlwind of a letter to Phil in the wilds of Darjiling, and said she should never know a happy moment all the rest of her life. Which was a true prophecy.

Phil received that letter, and held himself ill-treated. This was two years after he had come out; but by dint of thinking fixedly of Agnes Laiter, and looking at her photograph, and patting himself on the back for being one of the most constant lovers in history, and warming to the work as he went on, he really fancied that he had been very hardly used. He sat down and wrote one final letter—a really pathetic 'world without end, amen,' epistle; explaining how he would be true to Eternity, and that all women were very much alike, and he would hide his broken heart, etc. etc.; but if, at any future time, etc. etc., he could afford to wait, etc. etc., unchanged affections, etc. etc., return to her old love, etc. etc., for eight closely-written pages. From an artistic point of view it was very neat work, but an ordinary Philistine, who knew the state of Phil's real feelings—not the ones he rose to as he went on writing—would have called it the thoroughly mean and selfish work of a thoroughly mean and selfish weak man. But this verdict would have been incorrect. Phil paid for the postage, and felt every word he had written for at least two days and a half. It was the last flicker before the light went out.

That letter made Agnes Laiter very unhappy, and she cried and put it away in her desk, and became Mrs. Somebody Else for the good of her family. Which is the first duty of every Christian maid.

Phil went his ways, and thought no more of his letter, except as an artist thinks of a neatly touched-in sketch. His ways were not bad, but they were not altogether good until they brought him across Dunmaya, the daughter of a Rajput* ex-Subadar-Major* of our Native Army. The girl had a strain of Hill blood in her and, like the Hill-women, was not a *purdah-nashin* or woman who lives behind the veil. Where Phil met her, or how he heard of her, does not matter. She was a good girl and handsome, and, in her way, very clever and shrewd; though, of course, a little hard. It is to be remembered that Phil was living very comfortably, denying himself no small luxury, never putting by a penny, very satisfied with himself and his good intentions, was dropping all his English correspondents one by one, and beginning more and more to look upon India as his home. Some men fall this way, and they are of no use afterwards. The climate where he was stationed was good, and it really did not seem to him that there was any reason to return to England.

He did what many planters have done before him—that is to say, he made up his mind to marry a Hill-girl and settle down. He was seven-and-twenty then, with a long life before him, but no spirit to go through with it. So he married Dunmaya by the forms of the English Church, and some fellow-planters said he was a fool, and some said he was a wise man. Dunmaya was a thoroughly honest girl, and, in spite of her reverence for an Englishman, had a reasonable estimate of her husband's weaknesses. She managed him tenderly, and became, in less than a year, a very passable imitation of an English lady in dress and carriage. It is curious to think that a Hill-man after a lifetime's education is a Hill-man still; but a Hill-woman can in six months master most of the ways of her English sisters. There was a coolie-woman once . . . But that is another story. Dunmaya dressed by preference in black and yellow, and looked well.

Meantime Phil's letter lay in Agnes Laiter's desk, and now and again she would think of poor, resolute, hard-working Phil among the cobras and tigers of Darjiling, toiling in the vain hope that she might come back to him. Her husband was worth ten Phils, except that he had rheumatism of the heart. Three years after he was married,—and after he had tried Nice and Algeria for his complaint,—he went to Bombay, where he died, and set Agnes free. Being a devout woman, she looked on his death and the place of it as a direct interposition of Providence, and when she had recovered from the shock, she took out and re-read Phil's letter with the 'etc. etc.,' and the big dashes, and the little dashes, and kissed it several times. No one knew her in Bombay; she had her husband's income, which was a large one, and Phil was close at hand. It was wrong and improper, of course, but she decided, as heroines do in novels, to find her old lover, to offer him her hand and her gold, and with him spend the rest of her life in some spot far from unsympathetic souls. She sat for two months, alone in Watson's Hotel,* elaborating this decision, and the picture was a pretty one. Then she set out in search of Phil Garron, asssistant on a tea plantation with a more than usually unpronounceable name.

*   *   *

She found him. She spent a month over it, for his plantation was not in the Darjiling district at all, but nearer Kangra. Phil was very little altered, and Dunmaya was very nice to her.

Now the particular sin and shame of the whole business is that Phil, who really is not worth thinking of twice, was and is loved by Dunmaya, and more than loved by Agnes, the whole of whose life he seems to have spoilt.

Worst of all, Dunmaya is making a decent man of him; and he will ultimately be saved from perdition through her training.

Which is manifestly unfair.

False Dawn*

To-night God knows what thing shall tide,
     The Earth is racked and fain—*
Expectant, sleepless, open-eyed;
     And we, who from the Earth were made,
     Thrill with our Mother's pain.

                                    In Durance.

NO man will ever know the exact truth of this story; though
women may sometimes whisper it to one another after a
dance, when they are putting up their hair for the night and
comparing lists of victims. A man, of course, cannot assist at
these functions. So the tale must be told from the outside—in
the dark—all wrong.

Never praise a sister to a sister, in the hope of your
compliments reaching the proper ears, and so preparing the
way for you later on. Sisters are women first, and sisters
afterwards; and you will find that you do yourself harm.

Saumarez knew this when he made up his mind to propose
to the elder Miss Copleigh. Saumarez was a strange man, with
few merits so far as men could see, though he was popular
with women, and carried enough conceit to stock a Viceroy's
Council and leave a little over for the Commander-in-Chief's
Staff. He was a Civilian*. Very many women took an interest
in Saumarez, perhaps, because his manner to them was
offensive. If you hit a pony over the nose at the outset of your
acquaintance, he may not love you, but he will take a deep
interest in your movements ever afterwards. The elder Miss
Copleigh was nice, plump, winning, and pretty. The younger
was not so pretty, and, from men disregarding the hint set
forth above, her style was repellent and unattractive. Both
girls had, practically, the same figure, and there was a strong
likeness between them in look and voice; though no one could
doubt for an instant which was the nicer of the two.

Saumarez made up his mind, as soon as they came into the

Station from Behar,* to marry the elder one. At least, we all
made sure that he would, which comes to the same thing. She
was two-and-twenty, and he was thirty-three, with pay and
allowances of nearly fourteen hundred rupees a month. So the
match, as we arranged it, was in every way a good one.
Saumarez was his name, and summary was his nature, as a
man once said. Having drafted his Resolution, he formed a
select Committee of One to sit upon it, and resolved to take
his time. In our unpleasant slang, the Copleigh girls 'hunted
in couples'. That is to say, you could do nothing with one
without the other. They were very loving sisters; but their
mutual affection was sometimes inconvenient. Saumarez held
the balance-hair true between them, and none but himself
could have said to which side his heart inclined, though every
one guessed. He rode with them a good deal and danced with
them, but he never succeeded in detaching them from each
other for any length of time.

Women said that the two girls kept together through deep
mistrust, each fearing that the other would steal a march on
her. But that has nothing to do with a man. Saumarez was
silent for good or bad, and as business-likely attentive as he
could be, having due regard to his work and his polo. Beyond
doubt both girls were fond of him.

As the hot weather drew nearer and Saumarez made no sign,
women said that you could see their trouble in the eyes of the
girls—that they were looking strained, anxious, and irritable.
Men are quite blind in these matters unless they have more
of the woman than the man in their composition; in which
case it does not matter what they say or think. I maintain it
was the hot April days that took the colour out of the Copleigh
girls' cheeks. They should have been sent to the Hills early.
No one—man or woman—feels an angel when the hot weather
is approaching. The younger sister grew more cynical, not to
say acid, in her ways; and the winningness of the elder wore
thin. There was effort in it.

The Station wherein all these things happened was, though
not a little one, off the line of rail, and suffered through want
of attention. There were no Gardens or bands or amusements
worth speaking of, and it was nearly a day's journey to come

into Lahore for a dance. People were grateful for small things to interest them.

About the beginning of May, and just before the final exodus of Hill-goers, when the weather was very hot and there were not more than twenty people in the Station, Saumarez gave a moonlight riding-picnic at an old tomb,* six miles away, near the bed of the river. It was a 'Noah's Ark' picnic;* and there was to be the usual arrangement of quarter-mile intervals between each couple on account of the dust. Six couples came altogether, including chaperons. Moonlight picnics are useful just at the very end of the season, before all the girls go away to the Hills. They lead to understandings, and should be encouraged by chaperons, especially those whose girls look sweetest in riding-habits. I knew a case once. . . . But that is another story. That picnic was called the 'Great Pop Picnic,' because every one knew Saumarez would propose then to the eldest Miss Copleigh; and, besides his affair, there was another which might possibly come to happiness. The social atmosphere was heavily charged and wanted clearing.

We met at the parade-ground at ten: the night was fearfully hot. The horses sweated even at walking-pace, but anything was better than sitting still in our own dark houses. When we moved off under the full moon we were four couples, one triplet, and Me. Saumarez rode with the Copleigh girls, and I loitered at the tail of the procession wondering with whom Saumarez would ride home. Every one was happy and contented: but we all felt that things were going to happen. We rode slowly; and it was nearly midnight before we reached the old tomb, facing the ruined tank,* in the decayed gardens where we were going to eat and drink. I was late in coming up; and, before I went in to the garden, I saw that the horizon to the north carried a faint, dun-coloured feather. But no one would have thanked me for spoiling so well-managed an entertainment as this picnic—and a dust-storm, more or less, does no great harm.

We gathered by the tank. Some one had brought out a banjo—which is a most sentimental instrument—and three or four of us sang. You must not laugh at this. Our amusements in out-of-the-way Stations are very few indeed. Then we talked in groups or together, lying under the trees, with the

sun-baked roses dropping their petals on our feet, until supper
was ready. It was a beautiful supper, as cold and as iced as you
could wish; and we stayed long over it.

I had felt that the air was growing hotter and hotter; but
nobody seemed to notice it until the moon went out and a
burning hot wind began lashing the orange-trees with a sound
like the noise of the sea. Before we knew where we were the
dust-storm was on us, and everything was roaring, whirling
darkness. The supper-table was blown bodily into the tank.
We were afraid of staying anywhere near the old tomb for fear
it might be blown down. So we felt our way to the orange-trees
where the horses were picketed* and waited for the storm to
blow over. Then the little light that was left vanished, and you
could not see your hand before your face. The air was heavy
with dust and sand from the bed of the river, that filled boots
and pockets, and drifted down necks, and coated eyebrows and
moustaches. It was one of the worst dust-storms of the year.
We were all huddled together close to the trembling horses,
with the thunder chattering overhead, and the lightning
spurting like water from a sluice, all ways at once. There was
no danger, of course, unless the horses broke loose. I was
standing with my head downwind and my hands over my
mouth, hearing the trees thrashing each other. I could not see
who was next me till the flashes came. Then I found that I was
packed near Saumarez and the eldest Miss Copleigh, with my
own horse just in front of me. I recognised the eldest Miss
Copleigh, because she had a puggree* round her helmet, and
the younger had not. All the electricity in the air had gone into
my body, and I was quivering and tingling from head to
foot—exactly as a corn shoots and tingles before rain. It was
a grand storm. The wind seemed to be picking up the earth
and pitching it to leeward in great heaps; and the heat beat up
from the ground like the Day of Judgment.

The storm lulled slightly after the first half-hour, and I
heard a despairing little voice close to my ear, saying to itself,
quietly and softly, as if some lost soul were flying about with
the wind, 'Oh my God!' Then the younger Miss Copleigh
stumbled into my arms, saying, 'Where is my horse? Get my
horse. I want to go home. I want to go home. Take me home.'

I thought that the lightning and the black darkness had frightened her; so I said there was no danger, but she must wait till the storm blew over. She answered, 'It is not that! I want to go home! Oh, take me away from here!'

I said that she could not go till the light came; but I felt her brush past me and go away. It was too dark to see where. Then the whole sky was split open with one tremendous flash, as if the end of the world were coming, and all the women shrieked.

Almost directly after this I felt a man's hand on my shoulder, and heard Saumarez bellowing in my ear. Through the rattling of the trees and howling of the wind I did not catch his words at once, but at last I heard him say, 'I've proposed to the wrong one! What shall I do?' Saumarez had no occasion to make this confidence to me. I was never a friend of his, nor am I now; but I fancy neither of us were ourselves just then. He was shaking as he stood with excitement, and I was feeling queer all over with the electricity. I could not think of anything to say except, 'More fool you for proposing in a dust-storm.' But I did not see how that would improve the mistake.

Then he shouted, 'Where's Edith—Edith Copleigh?' Edith was the younger sister. I answered out of my astonishment, 'What do you want with *her?*' For the next two minutes he and I were shouting at each other like maniacs,—he vowing that it was the younger sister he had meant to propose to all along, and I telling him, till my throat was hoarse, that he must have made a mistake! I cannot account for this except, again, by the fact that we were neither of us ourselves. Everything seemed to me like a bad dream—from the stamping of the horses in the darkness to Saumarez telling me the story of his loving Edith Copleigh from the first. He was still clawing my shoulder and begging me to tell him where Edith Copleigh was, when another lull came and brought light with it, and we saw the dust-cloud forming on the plain in front of us. So we knew the worst was over. The moon was low down, and there was just the glimmer of the false dawn that comes about an hour before the real one. But the light was very faint, and the dun cloud roared like a bull. I wondered where Edith

Copleigh had gone; and as I was wondering I saw three things together: First, Maud Copleigh's face come smiling out of the darkness and move towards Saumarez who was standing by me. I heard the girl whisper, 'George,' and slide her arm through the arm that was not clawing my shoulder, and I saw that look on her face which only comes once or twice in a lifetime—when a woman is perfectly happy and the air is full of trumpets and gorgeously-coloured fire, and the Earth turns into cloud because she loves and is loved. At the same time, I saw Saumarez's face as he heard Maud Copleigh's voice, and, fifty yards away from the clump of orange-trees, I saw a brown holland habit* getting upon a horse.

It must have been my state of over-excitement that made me so ready to meddle with what did not concern me. Saumarez was moving off to the habit; but I pushed him back and said, 'Stop here and explain. I'll fetch her back!' And I ran out to get at my own horse. I had a perfectly unnecessary notion that everything must be done decently and in order, and that Saumarez's first care was to wipe the happy look out of Maud Copleigh's face. All the time I was linking up the curb-chain I wondered how he would do it.

I cantered after Edith Copleigh, thinking to bring her back slowly on some pretence or another. But she galloped away as soon as she saw me, and I was forced to ride after her in earnest. She called back over her shoulder—'Go away! I'm going home. Oh, go away!' two or three times; but my business was to catch her first, and argue later. The ride fitted in with the rest of the evil dream. The ground was very rough, and now and again we rushed through the whirling, choking 'dust-devils'* in the skirts of the flying storm. There was a burning hot wind blowing that brought up a stench of stale brick-kilns with it; and through the half-light and through the dust-devils, across that desolate plain, flickered the brown holland habit on the gray horse. She headed for the Station at first. Then she wheeled round and set off for the river through beds of burnt-down jungle-grass, bad even to ride pig over.* In cold blood I should never have dreamed of going over such a country at night, but it seemed quite right and natural with the lightning crackling overhead, and a reek like the smell of the Pit in my nostrils. I rode and shouted, and she bent forward and lashed her horse, and the aftermath of the dust-storm came up, and caught us both, and drove us down wind like pieces of paper.

I don't know how far we rode; but the drumming of the horse-hoofs and the roar of the wind and the race of the faint blood-red moon through the yellow mist seemed to have gone on for years and years, and I was literally drenched with sweat from my helmet to my gaiters when the gray stumbled, recovered himself, and pulled up dead lame. My brute was used up altogether. Edith Copleigh was bare headed, plastered with dust, and crying bitterly. 'Why can't you let me alone?' she said. 'I only wanted to get away and go home. Oh, *please* let me go!'

'You have got to come back with me, Miss Copleigh. Saumarez has something to say to you.'

It was a foolish way of putting it; but I hardly knew Miss Copleigh, and, though I was playing Providence at the cost of my horse, I could not tell her in as many words what Saumarez had told me. I thought he could do that better himself. All her pretence about being tired and wanting to go home broke down, and she rocked herself to and fro in the saddle as she sobbed, and the hot wind blew her black hair to leeward. I am not going to repeat what she said, because she was utterly unstrung.

This was the cynical Miss Copleigh, and I, almost an utter stranger to her, was trying to tell her that Saumarez loved her, and she was to come back to hear him say so. I believe I made myself understood, for she gathered the gray together and made him hobble somehow, and we set off for the tomb, while the storm went thundering down to Umballa* and a few big drops of warm rain fell. I found out that she had been standing close to Saumarez when he proposed to her sister, and had wanted to go home to cry in peace, as an English girl should. She dabbed her eyes with her pocket-handkerchief as we went along, and babbled to me out of sheer lightness of heart and hysteria. That was perfectly unnatural; and yet, it seemed all right at the time and in the place. All the world was only the two Copleigh girls, Saumarez and I, ringed in with the lightning and the dark; and the guidance of this misguided world seemed to lie in my hands.

When we returned to the tomb in the deep, dead stillness that followed the storm, the dawn was just breaking and nobody had gone away. They were waiting for our return. Saumarez most of all. His face was white and drawn. As Miss Copleigh and I limped up, he came forward to meet us, and, when he helped her down from her saddle, he kissed her before all the picnic. It was like a scene in a theatre, and the likeness was heightened by all the dust-white, ghostly-looking men and women under the orange-trees clapping their hands—as if they were watching a play—at Saumarez's choice. I never knew anything so un-English in my life.

Lastly, Saumarez said we must all go home or the Station would come out to look for us, and would I be good enough to ride home with Maud Copleigh? Nothing would give me greater pleasure, I said.

So we formed up, six couples in all, and went back two by two; Saumarez walking at the side of Edith Copleigh, who was riding his horse. Maud Copleigh did not talk to me at any length.

The air was cleared; and, little by little, as the sun rose, I felt we were all dropping back again into ordinary men and women, and that the 'Great Pop Picnic' was a thing altogether apart and out of the world—never to happen again. It had gone with the dust-storm and the tingle in the hot air.

I felt tired and limp, and a good deal ashamed of myself as I went in for a bath and some sleep.

There is a woman's version of this story, but it will never be written . . . unless Maud Copleigh cares to try.

The Rescue of Pluffles*

> Thus, for a season, they fought it fair—
> She and his cousin May—
> Tactful, talented, debonnaire,
> Decorous foes were they;
> But never can battle of man compare
> With merciless feminine fray.
>
> *Two and One.* ¹

MRS. HAUKSBEE was sometimes nice to her own sex. Here is a story to prove this; and you can believe just as much as ever you please.

Pluffles was a subaltern in the 'Unmentionables.'* He was callow, even for a subaltern. He was callow all over—like a canary that had not finished fledging itself. The worst of it was that he had three times as much money as was good for him; Pluffles' Papa being a rich man, and Pluffles being the only son. Pluffles' Mamma adored him. She was only a little less callow than Pluffles, and she believed everything he said.

Pluffles' weakness was not believing what people said. He preferred what he called trusting to his own judgment. He had as much judgment as he had seat or hands;* and this preference tumbled him into trouble once or twice. But the biggest trouble Pluffles ever manufactured came about at Simla—some years ago, when he was four-and-twenty.

He began by trusting to his own judgment as usual, and the result was that, after a time, he was bound hand and foot to Mrs. Reiver's 'rickshaw wheels.

There was nothing good about Mrs. Reiver, unless it was her dress. She was bad from her hair—which started life on a Brittany girl's head— to her boot-heels, which were two and three-eighth inches high. She was not honestly mischievous like Mrs. Hauksbee; she was wicked in a businesslike way.

There was never any scandal—she had not generous impulses enough for that. She was the exception which proved the rule that Anglo-Indian ladies are in every way as nice as their sisters at Home. She spent her life in proving that rule.

Mrs. Hauksbee and she hated each other fervently. They hated far too much to clash; but the things they said of each other were startling—not to say original. Mrs. Hauksbee was honest—honest as her own front-teeth—and, but for her love of mischief, would have been a woman's woman. There was no honesty about Mrs. Reiver; nothing but selfishness. And at the beginning of the season poor little Pluffles fell a prey to her. She laid herself out to that end, and who was Pluffles to resist? He trusted to his judgment, and he got judged.

I have seen Captain Hayes* argue with a tough horse—I have seen a tonga-driver* coerce a stubborn pony—I have seen a riotous setter broken to gun by a hard keeper—but the breaking-in of Pluffles of the 'Unmentionables' was beyond all these. He learned to fetch and carry like a dog, and to wait like one, too, for a word from Mrs. Reiver. He learned to keep appointments which Mrs. Reiver had no intention of keeping. He learned to take thankfully dances which Mrs. Reiver had no intention of giving him. He learned to shiver for an hour and a quarter on the windward side of Elysium* while Mrs. Reiver was making up her mind to come for a ride. He learned to hunt for a 'rickshaw, in a light dress-suit under pelting rain, and to walk by the side of that 'rickshaw when he had found it. He learned what it was to be spoken to like a coolie and ordered about like a cook. He learned all this and many other things besides. And he paid for his schooling.

Perhaps, in some hazy way, he fancied that it was fine and impressive, that it gave him a status among men, and was altogether the thing to do. It was nobody's business to warn Pluffles that he was unwise. The pace that season was too good to inquire; and meddling with another man's folly is always thankless work. Pluffles' Colonel should have ordered him back to his regiment when he heard how things were going. But Pluffles had got himself engaged to a girl in England the last time he went Home; and, if there was one thing more than another that the Colonel detested, it was a married subaltern.* He chuckled when he heard of the education of Pluffles, and said it was good training for the

boy. But it was not good training in the least. It led him
into spending money beyond his means, which were good·
above that, the education spoilt an average boy and made it a
tenth-rate man of an objectionable kind. He wandered into a
bad set, and his little bill at the jewellers' was a thing to
wonder at.

Then Mrs. Hauksbee rose to the occasion. She played her
game alone, knowing what people would say of her; and she
played it for the sake of a girl she had never seen. Pluffles'
fiancée was to come out, under chaperonage of an aunt, in
October, to be married to Pluffles.

At the beginning of August Mrs. Hauksbee discovered that
it was time to interfere. A man who rides much knows exactly
what a horse is going to do next before he does it. In the
same way, a woman of Mrs. Hauksbee's experience knows
accurately how a boy will behave under certain circumstances—notably when he is infatuated with one of Mrs.
Reiver's stamp. She said that, sooner or later, little Pluffles
would break off that engagement for nothing at all—simply to
gratify Mrs. Reiver, who, in return, would keep him at her
feet and in her service just so long as she found it worth her
while. She said she knew the signs of these things. If she did
not no one else could.

Then she went forth to capture Pluffles under the guns of
the enemy; just as Mrs. Cusack-Bremmil* carried away
Bremmil under Mrs. Hauksbee's eyes.

This particular engagement lasted seven weeks—we called it
the Seven Weeks' War*—and was fought out inch by inch on
both sides. A detailed account would fill a book, and would
be incomplete then. Any one who knows about these things
can fit in the details for himself. It was a superb fight—there
will never be another like it as long as Jakko Hill* stands—and
Pluffles was the prize of victory. People said shameful things
about Mrs. Hauksbee. They did not know what she was
playing for. Mrs. Reiver fought partly because Pluffles was
useful to her, but mainly because she hated Mrs. Hauksbee,
and the matter was a trial of strength between them. No one
knows what Pluffles thought. He had not many ideas at the
best of times, and the few he possessed made him conceited.

Mrs. Hauksbee said, 'The boy must be caught; and the only way of catching him is by treating him well.'

So she treated him as a man of the world and of experience so long as the issue was doubtful. Little by little Pluffles fell away from his old allegiance and came over to the enemy, by whom he was made much of. He was never sent on out-post duty after 'rickshaws any more, nor was he given dances which never came off, nor were the drains on his purse continued. Mrs. Hauksbee held him on the snaffle;* and, after his treatment at Mrs. Reiver's hands, he appreciated the change.

Mrs. Reiver had broken him of talking about himself, and made him talk about her own merits. Mrs. Hauksbee acted otherwise, and won his confidence, till he mentioned his engagement to the girl at Home, speaking of it in a high and mighty way as a piece of boyish folly. This was when he was taking tea with her one afternoon, and discoursing in what he considered a gay and fascinating style. Mrs. Hauksbee had seen an earlier generation of his stamp bud and blossom, and decay into fat Captains and tubby Majors.

At a moderate estimate there were about three-and-twenty sides to that lady's character. Some men say more. She began to talk to Pluffles after the manner of a mother, and as if there had been three hundred years, instead of fifteen,* between them. She spoke with a sort of throaty quaver in her voice which had a soothing effect, though what she said was anything but soothing. She pointed out the exceeding folly, not to say meanness, of Pluffles' conduct, and the smallness of his views. Then he stammered something about 'trusting to his own judgment as a man of the world;' and this paved the way for what she wanted to say next. It would have withered up Pluffles had it come from any other woman; but, in the soft cooing style in which Mrs. Hauksbee put it, it only made him feel limp and repentant—as if he had been in some superior kind of church. Little by little, very softly and pleasantly, she began taking the conceit out of Pluffles, as they take the ribs out of an umbrella before re-covering it. She told him what she thought of him and his judgment and his knowledge of the world; and how his performances had made him ridiculous to other people; and how it was his intention to make love to herself if she gave him the chance. Then she said that marriage would be the making of him; and drew a pretty little picture—all rose and opal—of the Mrs. Pluffles of the future going through life relying on the judgment and knowledge of the world of a husband who had nothing to reproach himself with. How she reconciled these two statements she alone knew. But they did not strike Pluffles as conflicting.

Hers was a perfect little homily—much better than any clergyman could have given—and it ended with touching allusions to Pluffles' Mamma and Papa, and the wisdom of taking his bride Home.

Then she sent Pluffles out for a walk, to think over what she had said. Pluffles left, blowing his nose very hard and holding himself very straight. Mrs. Hauksbee laughed.

What Pluffles had intended to do in the matter of the engagement only Mrs. Reiver knew, and she kept her own counsel to her death. She would have liked it spoiled as a compliment, I fancy.

Pluffles enjoyed many talks with Mrs. Hauksbee during the next few days. They were all to the same end, and they helped Pluffles in the path of Virtue.

Mrs. Hauksbee wanted to keep him under her wing to the last. Therefore she discountenanced his going down to Bombay to get married. 'Goodness only knows what might happen by the way!' she said. 'Pluffles is cursed with the curse of Reuben,* and India is no fit place for him!'

In the end the *fiancée* arrived with her aunt; and Pluffles, having reduced his affairs to some sort of order—here again Mrs. Hauksbee helped him—was married.

Mrs. Hauksbee gave a sigh of relief when both the 'I wills' had been said, and went her way.

Pluffles took her advice about going Home. He left the Service and is now raising speckled cattle inside green-painted fences somewhere in England. I believe he does this very judiciously. He would have come to extreme grief in India.

For these reasons, if any one says anything more than usually nasty about Mrs. Hauksbee, tell him the story of the Rescue of Pluffles.

Cupid's Arrows*

Pit where the buffalo cooled his hide,
By the hot sun emptied, and blistered and dried;
Log in the plume-grass, hidden and lone;
Bund* where the earth-rat's mounds are strown;
Cave in the bank where the sly stream steals;
Aloe that stabs at the belly and heels,
Jump if you dare on a steed untried—
Safer it is to go wide—go wide!
Hark, from in front where the best men ride:—
'Pull to the off, boys! Wide! Go wide!'
                                        The Peora Hunt.

ONCE upon a time there lived at Simla a very pretty girl, the
daughter of a poor but honest District and Sessions Judge. She
was a good girl, but could not help knowing her power and
using it. Her Mamma was very anxious about her daughter's
future, as all good Mammas should be.

When a man is a Commissioner* and a bachelor, and has the
right of wearing open-work jam-tart jewels in gold and
enamel* on his clothes, and of going through a door before
every one except a Member of Council,* a Lieutenant-
Governor,* or a Viceroy, he is worth marrying. At least, that
is what ladies say. There was a Commissioner in Simla, in
those days, who was, and wore and did all I have said. He was
a plain man—an ugly man—the ugliest man in Asia, with two
exceptions. His was a face to dream about and try to carve on
a pipe-head afterwards. His name was Saggott—Barr-
Saggott—Anthony Barr-Saggott and six letters* to follow.
Departmentally, he was one of the best men the Government
of India owned. Socially, he was like unto a blandishing
gorilla.

When he turned his attentions to Miss Beighton, I believe
that Mrs. Beighton wept with delight at the reward
Providence had sent her in her old age.

Mr. Beighton held his tongue. He was an easy-going man.

A Commissioner is very rich. His pay is beyond the dreams of avarice—is so enormous that he can afford to save and scrape in a way that would almost discredit a Member of Council. Most Commissioners are mean; but Barr-Saggott was an exception. He entertained royally; he horsed himself well; he gave dances; he was a power in the land; and he behaved as such.

Consider that everything I am writing of took place in an almost pre-historic era in the history of British India. Some folk may remember the years before lawn-tennis was born when we all played croquet. There were seasons before that, if you will believe me, when even croquet had not been invented, and archery—which was revived in England in 1844—was as great a pest as lawn-tennis is now. People talked learnedly about 'holding' and 'loosing,' 'steles,'* 'reflexed bows,' '56-pound bows,' 'backed' or 'self-yew bows,' as we talk about 'rallies,' 'volleys,' 'smashes,' 'returns,' and '16-ounce rackets.'

Miss Beighton shot divinely over ladies' distance—60 yards that is—and was acknowledged the best lady archer in Simla. Men called her 'Diana of Tara-Devi.'*

Barr-Saggott paid her great attention; and, as I have said, the heart of her mother was uplifted in consequence. Kitty Beighton took matters more calmly. It was pleasant to be singled out by a Commissioner with letters after his name, and to fill the hearts of other girls with bad feelings. But there was no denying the fact that Barr-Saggott was phenomenally ugly; and all his attempts to adorn himself only made him more grotesque. He was not christened 'The *Langur*'—which means gray ape—for nothing. It was pleasant, Kitty thought, to have him at her feet, but it was better to escape from him and ride with the graceless Cubbon—the man in a Dragoon Regiment at Umballa—the boy with a handsome face and no prospects. Kitty liked Cubbon more than a little. He never pretended for a moment that he was anything less than head over heels in love with her; for he was an honest boy. So Kitty fled, now and again, from the stately wooings of Barr-Saggott to the company of young Cubbon, and was scolded by her Mamma in consequence. 'But, Mother,' she said, 'Mr. Saggott is such—such a—is so *fearfully* ugly, you know!'

'My dear,' said Mrs. Beighton piously, 'we cannot be other than an all-ruling Providence has made us. Besides, you will take precedence of your own Mother, you know? Think of that and be reasonable.'

Then Kitty put up her little chin and said irreverent things about precedence, and Commissioners, and matrimony. Mr. Beighton rubbed the top of his head; for he was an easy-going man.

Late in the season, when he judged that the time was ripe, Barr-Saggott developed a plan which did great credit to his administrative powers. He arranged an archery-tournament for ladies, with a most sumptuous diamond-studded bracelet as prize. He drew up his terms skilfully, and every one saw that the bracelet was a gift to Miss Beighton; the acceptance carrying with it the hand and the heart of Commissioner Barr-Saggott. The terms were a St. Leonard's Round—thirty-six shots at sixty yards—under the rules of the Simla Toxophilite Society.

All Simla was invited. There were beautifully arranged tea-tables under the deodars* at Annandale,* where the Grand Stand is now; and, alone in its glory, winking in the sun, sat the diamond bracelet in a blue velvet case. Miss Beighton was anxious—almost too anxious—to compete. On the appointed afternoon all Simla rode down to Annandale to witness the Judgment of Paris* turned upside down. Kitty rode with young Cubbon, and it was easy to see that the boy was troubled in his mind. He must be held innocent of everything that followed. Kitty was pale and nervous, and looked long at the bracelet. Barr-Saggott was gorgeously dressed, even more nervous than Kitty, and more hideous than ever.

Mrs. Beighton smiled condescendingly, as befitted the mother of a potential Commissioneress, and the shooting began; all the world standing in a semicircle as the ladies came out one after the other.

Nothing is so tedious as an archery competition. They shot, and they shot, and they kept on shooting, till the sun left the valley, and little breezes got up in the deodars, and people waited for Miss Beighton to shoot and win. Cubbon was at one horn of the semicircle round the shooters, and Barr-

Saggott at the other. Miss Beighton was last on the list. The
scoring had been weak, and the bracelet, with Commissioner
Barr-Saggott, was hers to a certainty.

The Commissioner strung her bow with his own sacred
hands. She stepped forward, looked at the bracelet, and her
first arrow went true to a hair—full into the heart of the
'gold'—counting nine points.

Young Cubbon on the left turned white, and his Devil
prompted Barr-Saggott to smile. Now horses used to shy when
Barr-Saggott smiled. Kitty saw that smile. She looked to her
left-front, gave an almost imperceptible nod to Cubbon, and
went on shooting.

I wish I could describe the scene that followed. It was out
of the ordinary and most improper. Miss Kitty fitted her arrows
with immense deliberation, so that every one might see what
she was doing. She was a perfect shot; and her 46-pound bow
suited her to a nicety. She pinned the wooden legs of the target
with great care four successive times. She pinned the wooden
top of the target once, and all the ladies looked at each other.
Then she began some fancy shooting at the white, which if you
hit it, counts exactly one point. She put five arrows into the
white. It was wonderful archery; but, seeing that her business
was to make 'golds' and win the bracelet, Barr-Saggott turned
a delicate green like young water-grass. Next, she shot over the
target twice, then wide to the left twice—always with the same
deliberation—while a chilly hush fell over the company, and
Mrs. Beighton took out her handkerchief. Then Kitty shot at
the ground in front of the target, and split several arrows. Then
she made a red—or seven points—just to show what she could
do if she liked, and she finished up her amazing performance
with some more fancy shooting at the target supports. Here
is her score as it was pricked off:—

	Gold.	Red.	Blue	Black	White.	Total Hits	Total Score
Miss Beighton	1	1	0	0	5	7	21

Barr-Saggott looked as if the last few arrow-heads had been
driven into his legs instead of the target's, and the deep

stillness was broken by a little snubby, mottled, half-grown girl saying in a shrill voice of triumph, 'Then *I've* won!'

Mrs. Beighton did her best to bear up; but she wept in the presence of the people. No training could help her through such a disappointment. Kitty unstrung her bow with a vicious jerk, and went back to her place, while Barr-Saggott was trying to pretend that he enjoyed snapping the bracelet on the snubby girl's raw, red wrist. It was an awkward scene—most awkward. Every one tried to depart in a body and leave Kitty to the mercy of her Mamma.

But Cubbon took her away instead, and—the rest isn't worth printing.

The Three Musketeers*

An' when the war began,* we chased the bold Afghan,
An' we made the bloomin' Ghazi* for to flee, boys O!
An' we marched into Kabul, an' we tuk the Balar 'Issar,
An' we taught 'em to respec' the British Soldier.

Barrack-Room Ballad.

MULVANEY, Ortheris, and Learoyd are Privates in B Company of a Line Regiment,* and personal friends of mine. Collectively, I think, but am not certain, they are the worst men in the regiment so far as genial blackguardism goes.

They told me this story in the Umballa* Refreshment Room while we were waiting for an up-train. I supplied the beer. The tale was cheap at a gallon and a half.

All men know Lord Benira Trig. He is a Duke, or an Earl, or something unofficial; also a Peer; also a Globe-trotter. On all three counts, as Ortheris says, ''e didn't deserve no consideration.' He was out in India for three months collecting materials for a book on 'Our Eastern Impedimenta,'* and quartering himself upon everybody, like a Cossack* in evening-dress.

His particular vice—because he was a Radical,* men said— was having garrisons turned out for his inspection. He would then dine with the Officer Commanding, and insult him, across the Mess table, about the appearance of the troops. That was Benira's way.

He turned out troops once too often. He came to Helanthami Cantonment on a Tuesday. He wished to go shopping in the bazar on Wednesday, and he 'desired' the troops to be turned out on a Thursday.* *On—a—Thursday.* The Officer Commanding could not well refuse; for Benira was a Lord. There was an indignation meeting of subalterns in the ante-room, to call the Colonel pet names.

'But the rale dimonstrashin,' said Mulvaney, 'was in B Comp'ny barrick; we three headin' ut.'

Mulvaney climbed on to the refreshment-bar, settled

himself comfortably by the beer, and went on, 'When the row was at uts foinest an' B Comp'ny was fur goin' out to murther this man Thrigg on the p'rade-groun', Learoyd here takes up his helmut an' sez—fwhat was ut ye said?'

'Ah said,' said Learoyd, 'gie us t' brass. Tak oop a sub-scripshun, lads, for to put off t' p'rade, an' if t' p'rade's not put off, ah'll gie t' brass back agean. That's wot ah said. All B Coomp'ny knawed me. Ah took oop a big subscripshun—fower rupees eight annas* 'twere—an' ah went oot to turn t' job over. Mulvaney an' Orth'ris coom with me.'

'We three raises the Divil in couples gin'rally,' explained Mulvaney.

Here Ortheris interrupted. "Ave you read the papers?' said he.

'Sometimes,' I said.

'We 'ad read the papers, an' we put hup a faked decoity,* a—a sedukshun.'

'*Ab*dukshin, ye cockney,' said Mulvaney.

'*Ab*dukshun or *se*dukshun—no great odds. Any'ow, we arranged to take an' put Mister Benhira out o' the way till Thursday was hover, or 'e too busy to rux 'isself about p'raids. *Hi* was the man wot said, "We'll make a few rupees off o' the business."'

'We hild a Council av War,' continued Mulvaney, 'walkin' roun' by the Artill'ry Lines. I was Prisidint, Learoyd was Minister av Finance, an' little Orth'ris here was——'

'A bloomin' Bismarck! *Hi* made the 'ole show pay.'

'This interferin' bit av a Benira man,' said Mulvaney, 'did the thrick for us himself; for, on me sowl, we hadn't a notion av what was to come afther the next minut'. He was shoppin' in the bazar on fut. 'Twas dhrawin' dusk thin, an' we stud watchin' the little man hoppin' in an' out av the shops, thryin' to injuce the naygurs to *mallum* his bat.* Prisintly, he sthrols up, his arrums full av thruck, an' he sez in a consiquinsha¹ way, shticking out his little belly, "Me good men," sez he "have ye seen the Kernel's b'roosh*!"—"B'roosh?" says Learoyd. "There's no b'roosh here—nobbut a *ekka* *' – "Fwhat's that?" sez Thrigg. Learoyd shows him wan down the sthreet, an' he sez, "How thruly Orientil! I will ride on a *ekka*." I saw thin that our Rigimintal Saint was for givin' Thrigg over to us neck an' brisket. I purshued a *ekka*, an' I sez to the dhriver-divil, I sez, "Ye black limb, there's a *Sahib* comin' for this *ekka*. He wants to go *jildi** to the Padsahi Jhil*"—'twas about tu moiles away—"to shoot snipe—*chirria*. You dhrive *Jehannum ke marfik*, *mallum**—like Hell? 'Tis no manner av use *bukkin'** to the *Sahib*, bekaze he doesn't *samjao** your talk. Av he *bolos** anything, just you *choop* and *chel*.* *Dekker?** Go *arsty** for the first *arder** mile from cantonmints. Thin *chel*, *Shaitan ke marfik*,* an' the *chooper* you *choops* an' the *jildier* you *chels* the better *kooshy** will that *Sahib* be; an' here's a rupee for ye!"

The *ekka*-man knew there was somethin' out av the common in the air. He grinned an' sez, "*Bote achee!** I goin' damn fast." I prayed the Kernel's b'roosh wudn't arrive till me darlin' Benira by the grace av God was undher weigh. The little man puts his thruck into the *ekka* an' scuttles in like a fat guinea-pig; niver offerin' us the price av a dhrink for our services in helpin' him home. "He's off to the Padsahi *jhil*," sez I to the others.'

Ortheris took up the tale—

'Jist then, little Buldoo kim up, 'oo was the son of one of the Artillery grooms—'e would 'av made a 'evinly newspaper-boy in London, bein' sharp an' fly to all manner o' games. 'E 'ad bin watchin' us puttin' Mister Benhira into 'is temp'ry baroosh, an' 'e sez, "What *'ave* you been a doin' of, *Sahibs?*" sez 'e. Learoyd 'e caught 'im by the ear an 'e sez—'

'Ah says,' went on Learoyd, '"Young mon, that mon's gooin' to have t' goons out o' Thursday—to-morrow—an' thot's more work for you, young mon. Now, sitha, tak' a *tat* an' a *lookri*,* an' ride tha domdest to t' Padsahi Jhil. Cotch thot there *hekka*, and tell t' driver in your lingo thot you've coom to tak' his place. T' *Sahib* doesn't speak t' *bat*, an' he's a little mon. Drive t' *hekka* into t' Padsahi Jhil into t' watter. Leave t' *Sahib* theer an' roon hoam; an' here's a rupee for tha." '

Then Mulvaney and Ortheris spoke together in alternate fragments: Mulvaney leading (You must pick out the two speakers as best you can):—'He was a knowin' little divil was Bhuldoo,— 'e sez *bote achee* an' cuts—wid a wink in his oi—

but *Hi* sez there's money to be made—an' I wanted to see the ind av the campaign—so *Hi* sez we'll double hout to the Padsahi Jhil—an' save the little man from bein' dacoited by the murtherin' Bhuldoo—an' turn hup like reskooers in a Victoria* Melodramma—so we doubled for the *jhil*, an' prisintly there was the divil av a hurroosh behind us an' three bhoys on grasscuts' ponies come by, poundin' along for the dear life—s'elp me Bob, if Buldoo 'adn't raised a rig'lar *harmy* of decoits—to do the job in shtile. An' we ran, an' they ran, shplittin' with laughin', till we gets near the *jhil*— and 'ears sounds of distress floatin' molloncolly on the hevenin' hair.' (Ortheris was growing poetical under the influence of the beer. The duet recommenced: Mulvaney leading again.)

'Thin we heard Bhuldoo, the decoit, shoutin' to the *ekka* man, an' wan of the young divils brought his stick down on the top av the *ekka*-cover, an' Benira Thrigg inside howled "Murther an' Death." Buldoo takes the reins and dhrives like mad for the *jhil*, havin' dishpersed the *ekka*-dhriver—'oo cum up to us an' 'e sez, sez 'e, "That *Sahib's* nigh mad with funk! Wot devil's work 'ave you led me into?"—"Hall right," sez we, "you catch that there pony an' come along. This *Sahib's* been decoited, an' we're going to resky 'im!" Sez the driver, "Decoits! Wot decoits? That's Buldoo the *budmash**"— "Bhuldoo be shot!" sez we. "'Tis a woild dissolute Paythan frum the hills. There's about eight av thim coercin' the *Sahib*. You remimber that an you'll get another rupee!" Thin we heard the *whop-whop-whop* av the *ekka* turnin' over, an' a splash av water an' the voice av Benira Thrigg callin' upon God to forgive his sins—an' Buldoo an' 'is friends squatterin' in the water like boys in the Serpentine.'

Here the Three Musketeers retired simultaneously into the beer.

'Well? What came next?' said I.

'Fwhat nex'?' answered Mulvaney, wiping his mouth. 'Wud ye let three bould sodger-bhoys lave the ornamint av the House av Lords to be dhrowned an' dacoited in a *jhil*? We formed line av quarther-column an' we discinded upon the inimy. For the better part av tin minut's you could not hear

yersilf spake. The *tattoo** was screamin' in chune wid Benira
Thrigg an' Bhuldoo's army, an' the shticks was whistlin'
roun' the *ekka*, an' Orth'ris was beatin' the *ekka*-cover wid his
fistes, an' Learoyd yellin', "Look out for their knives!" an' me
cuttin' into the dark, right an' lef', dishpersin' arrmy corps av
Paythans. Holy Mother av Moses! 'Twas more disp'rit than
Ahmid Kheyl wid Maiwand* thrown in. Afther a while
Bhuldoo an' his bhoys flees. Have ye iver seen a rale live Lord
thryin' to hide his nobility undher a fut an' a half av brown
swamp-wather? 'Tis the livin' image av a water-carrier's
goatskin wid the shivers. It tuk toime to pershuade me frind
Benira he was not disimbowilled: an' more toime to get out
the *ekka*. The dhriver come up afther the battle, swearin' he
tuk a hand in repulsin' the inimy. Benira was sick wid the fear.
We escorted him back, very slow, to cantonmints, for that an'
the chill to soak into him. It suk! Glory be to the Rig'mintil
Saint, but it suk to the marrow av Lord Benira Thrigg!'

Here Ortheris, slowly, with immense pride—"E sez, "You
har my noble preservers," sez 'e. "You har a *h*onour to the
British Harmy," sez 'e. With that 'e describes the hawful band
of decoits wot set on 'im. There was about forty of 'em an' 'e
was hoverpowered by numbers, so 'e was; but 'e never lorst
'is presence of mind, so 'e didn't. 'E guv the *h*ekka-driver five
rupees for 'is noble assistance, an' 'e said 'e would see to us
after 'e 'ad spoken to the Col'nel. For we was a *h*onour to the
Regiment, we was.'

'An' we three,' said Mulvaney, with a seraphic smile, 'have
dhrawn the par-ti-cu-lar attinshin av Bobs Bahadur* more
than wanst. But he's a rale good little man is Bobs. Go on,
Orth'ris, my son.'

'Then we leaves 'im at the Col'nel's 'ouse, werry sick, an'
we cuts hover to B Comp'ny barrick an' we sez we 'ave saved
Benira from a bloody doom, an' the chances was agin there
bein' p'raid on Thursday. About ten minutes later come three
envelicks, one for each of us. S'elp me Bob, if the old bloke
'adn't guv us a fiver apiece—sixty-four rupees in the bazar! On
Thursday 'e was in 'orspital recoverin' from 'is sanguinary
encounter with a gang of Paythans, an' B Comp'ny was
drinkin' 'emselves into Clink* by squads. So there never was

no Thursday p'raid. But the Col'nel, when 'e 'eard of our galliant conduck, 'e sez, "Hi know there's been some devilry somewheres," sez 'e, "but I can't bring it 'ome to you three." '

'An' my privit imprisshin is,' said Mulvaney, getting off the bar and turning his glass upside down, 'that, av they had known they wudn't have brought ut home. 'Tis flyin' in the face, firstly av Natur', secon' av the Rig'lations, an' third the will av Terence Mulvaney, to hould p'rades av Thursdays.'

'Good, ma son!' said Learoyd; 'but, young mon, what's t' notebook for?'

'Let be,' said Mulvaney; 'this time next month we're in the *Sherapis.** 'Tis immortal fame the gentleman's goin' to give us. But kape it dhark till we're out av the range av me little frind Bobs Bahadur.'

And I have obeyed Mulvaney's order!

His Chance in Life*

Then a pile of heads he laid—
Thirty thousands heaped on high—
All to please the Kafir* maid,
Where the Oxus ripples by.
Grimly spake Atulla Khan:—
'Love hath made this thing a Man.'
Oatta's Story.

IF you go straight away from Levées and Government House
Lists, past Trades' Balls—far beyond everything and
everybody you ever knew in your respectable life—you cross,
in time, the Borderline where the last drop of White blood
ends and the full tide of Black sets in. It would be easier to
talk to a new-made Duchess on the spur of the moment than
to the Borderline folk without violating some of their
conventions or hurting their feelings. The Black and the
White mix very quaintly in their ways. Sometimes the White
shows in spurts of fierce, childish pride—which is Pride of
Race run crooked—and sometimes the Black in still fiercer
abasement and humility, half-heathenish customs and strange,
unaccountable impulses to crime. One of these days, this
people—understand they are far lower than the class whence
Derozio,* the man who imitated Byron, sprung—will turn out
a writer or a poet; and then we shall know how they live and
what they feel. In the meantime, any stories about them
cannot be absolutely correct in fact or inference.

Miss Vezzis came from across the Borderline to look after
some children who belonged to a lady until a regularly
ordained nurse could come out. The lady said Miss Vezzis was
a bad, dirty nurse and inattentive. It never struck her that
Miss Vezzis had her own life to lead and her own affairs to
worry over, or that these affairs were the most important
things in the world to Miss Vezzis. Very few mistresses admit
this sort of reasoning. Miss Vezzis was as black as a boot, and,
to our standard of taste, hideously ugly. She wore cotton-print

gowns and bulgy shoes; and when she lost her temper with the children, she abused them in the language of the Borderline—which is part English, part Portuguese, and part Native. She was not attractive; but she had her pride, and she preferred being called 'Miss Vezzis.'

Every Sunday she dressed herself wonderfully and went to see her Mamma, who lived, for the most part, on an old cane chair in a greasy *tussur*-silk* dressing-gown and a big rabbit-warren of a house full of Vezzises, Pereiras, Ribieras, Lisboas, and Gonsalveses, and a floating population of loafers; besides fragments of the day's market, garlic, stale incense, clothes thrown on the floor, petticoats hung on strings for screens, old bottles, pewter crucifixes, dried *immortelles*,* pariah puppies, plaster images of the Virgin, and hats without crowns. Miss Vezzis drew twenty rupees a month for acting as nurse, and she squabbled weekly with her Mamma as to the percentage to be given towards housekeeping. When the quarrel was over, Michele D'Cruze used to shamble across the low mud wall of the compound and make love to Miss Vezzis after the fashion of the Borderline, which is hedged about with much ceremony. Michele was a poor, sickly weed and very black; but he had his pride. He would not be seen smoking a *huqa** for anything; and he looked down on natives as only a man with seven-eighths native blood in his veins can. The Vezzis Family had their pride too. They traced their descent from a mythical platelayer who had worked on the Sone Bridge when railways were new in India, and they valued their English origin. Michele was a Telegraph Signaller on Rs.35 a month. The fact that he was in Government employ made Mrs. Vezzis lenient to the shortcomings of his ancestors.

There was a compromising legend—Dom* Anna the tailor brought it from Poonani*—that a black Jew of Cochin* had once married into the D'Cruze family; while it was an open secret that an uncle of Mrs. D'Cruze was, at that very time, doing menial work, connected with cooking, for a Club in Southern India! He sent Mrs. D'Cruze seven rupees eight annas a month; but she felt the disgrace to the family very keenly all the same.

However, in the course of a few Sundays, Mrs. Vezzis

brought herself to overlook these blemishes, and gave her
consent to the marriage of her daughter with Michele, on
condition that Michele should have at least fifty rupees a
month to start married life upon. This wonderful prudence
must have been a lingering touch of the mythical platelayer's
Yorkshire blood; for across the Borderline people take a pride
in marrying when they please—not when they can.

Having regard to his departmental prospects, Mrs. Vezzis
might as well have asked Michele to go away and come back
with the Moon in his pocket. But Michele was deeply in love
with Miss Vezzis, and that helped him to endure. He
accompanied Miss Vezzis to Mass one Sunday, and after
Mass, walking home through the hot stale dust with her hand
in his, he swore by several Saints, whose names would not
interest you, never to forget Miss Vezzis; and she swore by her
Honour and the Saints—the oath runs rather curiously; '*In
nomine Sanctissimae**—*' (whatever the name of the she-Saint
is) and so forth, ending with a kiss on the forehead, a kiss on
the left cheek, and a kiss on the mouth—never to forget
Michele.

Next week Michele was transferred, and Miss Vezzis
dropped tears upon the window-sash of the 'Intermediate'*
compartment as he left the Station.

If you look at the telegraph-map of India you will see a long
line skirting the coast from Backergunge to Madras. Michele
was ordered to Tibasu, a little Sub-office one-third down this
line, to send messages on from Berhampur to Chicacola, and
to think of Miss Vezzis and his chances of getting fifty rupees
a month out of office-hours. He had the noise of the Bay of
Bengal and a Bengali Babu* for company; nothing more. He
sent foolish letters, with crosses tucked inside the flaps of the
envelopes, to Miss Vezzis.

When he had been at Tibasu for nearly three weeks his
chance came.

Never forget that unless the outward and visible signs of
Our Authority are always before a native he is as incapable as
a child of understanding what authority means, or where is the
danger of disobeying it. Tibasu was a forgotten little place
with a few Orissa* Mahommedans in it. These, hearing

nothing of the Collector-*Sahib** for some time, and heartily despising the Hindu Sub-Judge, arranged to start a little Mohurrum* riot of their own. But the Hindus turned out and broke their heads; when, finding lawlessness pleasant, Hindus and Mahommedans together raised an aimless sort of Donnybrook* just to see how far they could go. They looted each other's shops, and paid off private grudges in the regular way. It was a nasty little riot, but not worth putting in the newspapers.

Michele was working in his office when he heard the sound that a man never forgets all his life—the '*ah-yah*' of an angry crowd. (When that sound drops about three tones, and changes to a thick, droning *ut*, the man who hears it had better go away if he is alone.) The Native Police Inspector ran in and told Michele that the town was in an uproar and coming to wreck the Telegraph Office. The Babu put on his cap and quietly dropped out of the window; while the Police Inspector, afraid, but obeying the old race-instinct which recognises a drop of White blood as far as it can be diluted, said, 'What orders does the *Sahib* give?'

The '*Sahib*' decided Michele. Though horribly frightened, he felt that, for the hour, he, the man with the Cochin Jew and the menial uncle in his pedigree, was the only representative of English authority in the place. Then he thought of Miss Vezzis and the fifty rupees, and took the situation on himself. There were seven native policemen in Tibasu, and four crazy smooth-bore muskets among them. All the men were gray with fear, but not beyond leading. Michele dropped the key of the telegraph instrument, and went out, at the head of his army, to meet the mob. As the shouting crew came round a corner of the road, he dropped and fired; the men behind him loosing off instinctively at the same time.

The whole crowd—curs to the back-bone—yelled and ran, leaving one man dead and another dying in the road. Michele was sweating with fear; but he kept his weakness under, and went down into the town, past the house where the Sub-Judge had barricaded himself. The streets were empty. Tibasu was more frightened than Michele, for the mob had been taken at the right time.

Michele returned to the Telegraph-Office, and sent a message to Chicacola asking for help. Before an answer came, he received a deputation of the elders of Tibasu, telling him that the Sub-Judge said his actions generally were 'unconstitutional,' and trying to bully him. But the heart of Michele D'Cruze was big and white in his breast, because of his love for Miss Vezzis, the nurse-girl, and because he had tasted for the first time Responsibility and Success. Those two make an intoxicating drink, and have ruined more men than ever has Whisky. Michele answered that the Sub-Judge might say what he pleased, but, until the Assistant Collector came, he, the Telegraph Signaller, was the Government of India in Tibasu, and the elders of the town would be held accountable for further rioting. Then they bowed their heads and said, 'Show mercy!' or words to that effect, and went back in great fear; each accusing the other of having begun the rioting.

Early in the dawn, after a night's patrol with his seven policemen, Michele went down the road, musket in hand, to meet the Assistant Collector who had ridden in to quell Tibasu. But, in the presence of this young Englishman, Michele felt himself slipping back more and more into the native; and the tale of the Tibasu Riots ended, with the strain on the teller, in an hysterical outburst of tears, bred by sorrow that he had killed a man, shame that he could not feel as uplifted as he had felt through the night, and childish anger that his tongue could not do justice to his great deeds. It was the White drop in Michele's veins dying out, though he did not know it.

But the Englishman understood; and, after he had schooled those men of Tibasu, and had conferred with the Sub-Judge till that excellent official turned green, he found time to draft an official letter describing the conduct of Michele. Which letter filtered through the Proper Channels, and ended in the transfer of Michele up-country once more, on the Imperial salary of sixty-six rupees a month.

So he and Miss Vezzis were married with great state and ancientry;* and now there are several little D'Cruzes sprawling about the verandahs of the Central Telegraph Office.

But, if the whole revenue of the Department he serves were to be his reward, Michele could never, never repeat what he did at Tibasu for the sake of Miss Vezzis the nurse-girl.

Which proves that, when a man does good work out of all proportion to his pay, in seven cases out of nine there is a woman at the back of the virtue.

The two exceptions must have suffered from sunstroke.

Watches of the Night*

> What is in Brahmin's* books, that is in the Brahmin's
> heart. Neither you nor I knew there was so much evil in the
> world.   *Hindu Proverb.*

THIS began in a practical joke; but it has gone far enough
now, and is getting serious.

Platte, the Subaltern, being poor, had a Waterbury* watch
and a plain leather guard.*

The Colonel had a Waterbury watch also, and, for guard, the
lip-strap of a curb-chain. Lip-straps make the best watch-
guards. They are strong and short. Between a lip-strap and an
ordinary leather-guard there is no great difference; between one
Waterbury watch and another none at all. Every one in the
Station knew the Colonel's lip-strap. He was not a horsey man,
but he liked people to believe he had been one once; and he wove
fantastic stories of the hunting-bridle to which this particular
lip-strap had belonged. Otherwise he was painfully religious.

Platte and the Colonel were dressing at the Club—both late
for their engagements, and both in a hurry. That was *Kismet.*＊
The two watches were on a shelf below the looking-glass—
guards hanging down. That was carelessness. Platte changed
first, snatched a watch, looked in the glass, settled his tie, and
ran. Forty seconds later the Colonel did exactly the same
thing, each man taking the other's watch.

You may have noticed that many religious people are deeply
suspicious. They seem—for purely religious purposes, of
course—to know more about iniquity than the Unregenerate.
Perhaps they were specially bad before they became
converted! At any rate, in the imputation of things evil, and
in putting the worst construction on things innocent, a certain
type of good people may be trusted to surpass all others. The
Colonel and his Wife were of that type. But the Colonel's
Wife was the worst. She manufactured the Station scandal,

and—talked to her ayah.* Nothing more need be said. The
Colonel's Wife broke up the Laplaces' home. The Colonel's
Wife stopped the Ferris-Haughtrey engagement. The
Colonel's Wife induced young Buxton to keep his wife down
in the Plains through the first year of the marriage. Wherefore
little Mrs. Buxton died, and the baby with her. These things
will be remembered against the Colonel's Wife so long as
there is a regiment in the country.

But to come back to the Colonel and Platte. They went
several ways from the dressing-room. The Colonel dined with
two Chaplains, while Platte went to a bachelor party, and
whist to follow.

Mark how things happen! If Platte's groom had put the new
saddle-pad on the mare, the butts of the territs* would not
have worked through the worn leather and the old pad into the
mare's withers, when she was coming home at two o'clock in
the morning. She would not have reared, bolted, fallen into a
ditch, upset the cart, and sent Platte flying over an aloe-hedge
on to Mrs. Larkyn's well-kept lawn; and this tale would never
have been written. But the mare did all these things, and while
Platte was rolling over and over on the turf, like a shot rabbit,
the watch and guard flew from his waistcoat—as an Infantry
Major's sword hops out of the scabbard when they are firing
a *feu-de-joie**—and rolled and rolled in the moonlight, till it
stopped under a window.

Platte stuffed his handkerchief under the pad, put the cart
straight, and went home.

Mark again how *Kismet* works! This would not arrive once
in a hundred years. Towards the end of his dinner with the
two ChaplainsQthe Colonel let out his waistcoat and leaned
over the table to look at some Mission Reports. The bar of the
watch-guard worked through the button-hole, and the
watch—Platte's watch—slid quietly on to the carpet; where
the bearer found it next morning and kept it.

Then the Colonel went home to the wife of his bosom; but
the driver of the carriage was drunk and lost his way. So the
Colonel returned at an unseemly hour and his excuses were
not accepted. If the Colonel's Wife had been an ordinary
vessel of wrath* appointed for destruction, she would have

known that when a man stays away on purpose, his excuse is always sound and original. The very baldness of the Colonel's explanation proved its truth.

See once more the workings of *Kismet*. The Colonel's watch which came with Platte hurriedly on to Mrs. Larkyn's lawn, chose to stop just under Mrs. Larkyn's window, where she saw it early in the morning, recognised it, and picked it up. She had heard the crash of Platte's cart at two o'clock that morning, and his voice calling the mare names. She knew Platte and liked him. That day she showed him the watch and heard his story. He put his head on one side, winked and said, 'How disgusting! Shocking old man! With his religious training, too! I should send the watch to the Colonel's Wife and ask for explanations.'

Mrs. Larkyn thought for a minute of the Laplaces—whom she had known when Laplace and his wife believed in each other—and answered, 'I will send it. I think it will do her good. But, remember, we must *never* tell her the truth.'

Platte guessed that his own watch was in the Colonel's possession, and thought that the return of the lip-strapped Waterbury with a soothing note from Mrs. Larkyn would merely create a small trouble for a few minutes. Mrs. Larkyn knew better. She knew that any poison dropped would find good holding-ground in the heart of the Colonel's Wife.

The packet, and a note containing a few remarks on the Colonel's calling hours, were sent over to the Colonel's Wife, who wept in her own room and took counsel with herself.

If there was one woman under Heaven whom the Colonel's Wife hated with holy fervour, it was Mrs. Larkyn. Mrs. Larkyn was a frivolous lady, and called the Colonel's Wife 'old cat.' The Colonel's Wife said that somebody in Revelation* was remarkably like Mrs. Larkyn. She mentioned other Scripture people* as well: from the Old Testament. But the Colonel's Wife was the only person who cared or dared to say anything against Mrs. Larkyn. Every one else accepted her as an amusing, honest little body. Wherefore, to believe that her husband had been shedding watches under that 'Thing's' window at ungodly hours, coupled with the fact of his late arrival on the previous night, was . . .

At this point she rose up and sought her husband. He denied everything except the ownership of the watch. She besought him, for his Soul's sake to speak the truth. He denied afresh, with two bad words. Then a stony silence held the Colonel's Wife, while a man could draw his breath five times.

The speech that followed is no affair of mine or yours. It was made up of wifely and womanly jealousy; knowledge of old age and sunk cheeks; deep mistrust born of the text that says even little babies' hearts are as bad as they make them; rancorous hatred of Mrs. Larkyn, and the tenets of the creed of the Colonel's Wife's upbringing.

Over and above all was the damning lip-strapped Waterbury, ticking away in the palm of her shaking, withered hand. At that hour, I think, the Colonel's Wife realised a little of the restless suspicion she had injected into old Laplace's mind; a little of poor Miss Haughtrey's misery; and some of the canker that ate into Buxton's heart as he watched his wife dying before his eyes. The Colonel stammered and tried to explain. Then he remembered that his watch had disappeared; and the mystery grew greater. The Colonel's Wife talked and prayed by turns till she was tired, and went away to devise means for chastening the stubborn heart of her husband. Which, translated, means, in our slang, 'tail-twisting'.*

Being deeply impressed with the doctrine of Original Sin, she could not believe in the face of appearances. She knew too much, and jumped to the wildest conclusions.

But it was good for her. It spoilt her life, as she had spoilt the life of the Laplaces. She had lost her faith in the Colonel, and—here the creed-suspicion came in—he might, she argued, have erred many times, before a merciful Providence, at the hands of so unworthy an instrument as Mrs. Larkyn, had established his guilt. He was a bad, wicked, gray-haired profligate. This may sound too sudden a revulsion for a long-wedded wife; but it is a venerable fact that, if a man or woman makes a practice of, and takes a delight in, believing and spreading evil of people indifferent to him or her, he or she will end in believing evil of folk very near and dear. You may think, also, that the mere incident of the watch was too small

and trivial to raise this misunderstanding. It is another aged
fact that, in life as well as racing, all the worst accidents
happen at little ditches and cut-down fences. In the same way,
you sometimes see a woman who would have made a Joan of
Arc in another century and climate, threshing herself to pieces
over all the mean worry of housekeeping. . . . But that is
another story.

Her belief only made the Colonel's Wife more wretched,
because it insisted so strongly on the villainy of men.
Remembering what she had done, it was pleasant to watch her
unhappiness, and the penny-farthing attempts she made to
hide it from the Station. But the Station knew and laughed
heartlessly; for they had heard the story of the watch, with
much dramatic gesture, from Mrs. Larkyn's lips.

Once or twice Platte said to Mrs. Larkyn, seeing that the
Colonel had not cleared himself, 'This thing has gone far
enough. I move we tell the Colonel's Wife how it happened.'
Mrs. Larkyn shut her lips and shook her head, and vowed the
the Colonel's Wife must bear her punishment as best she
could. Now Mrs. Larkyn was a frivolous woman, in whom
none would have suspected deep hate. So Platte took no
action, and came to believe gradually, from the Colonel's
silence, that the Colonel must have run off the line somewhere
that night, and, therefore, preferred to stand sentence on the
lesser count of rambling into other people's compounds* out
of calling-hours. Platte forgot about the watch business after
a while, and moved down-country with his regiment. Mrs.
Larkyn went home when her husband's tour of Indian service
expired. She never forgot.

But Platte was quite right when he said that the joke
had gone too far. The mistrust and the tragedy of it—which
we outsiders cannot see and do not believe in—are killing
the Colonel's Wife, and are making the Colonel wretched.
If either of them read this story, they can depend upon
its being a fairly true account of the case, and can kiss and
make friends.

Shakespeare alludes to the pleasure of watching an Engineer
being shelled by his own Battery.* Now this shows that poets
should not write about what they do not understand. Any one

could have told him that Sappers and Gunners are perfectly different branches of the Service. But, if you correct the sentence, and substitute Gunner for Sapper, the moral comes just the same.

The Other Man*

When the earth was sick and the skies were gray
    And the woods were rotted with rain,
The Dead Man rode through the autumn day
    To visit his love again.

Old Ballad

FAR back in the 'seventies,' before they had built any Public-Offices* at Simla, and the broad road round Jakko* lived in a pigeon-hole in the P. W. D.* hovels, her parents made Miss Gaurey marry Colonel Schreiderling. He could not have been much more than thirty-five years her senior; and, as he lived on two hundred rupees a month* and had money of his own, he was well off. He belonged to good people , and suffered in the cold weather from lung-complaints. In the hot weather he dangled on the brink of heat-apoplexy; but it never quite killed him.

Understand, I do not blame Schreiderling. He was a good husband according to his lights, and his temper only failed him when he was being nursed: which was some seventeen days in each month. He was almost generous to his wife about money matters, and that, for him, was a concession. Still Mrs. Schreiderling was not happy. They married her when she was this side of twenty and had given all her poor little heart to another man. I have forgotten his name, but we will call him the Other Man. He had no money and no prospects. He was not even good-looking; and I think he was in the Commissariat or Transport.* But, in spite of all these things, she loved him very badly; and there was some sort of an engagement between the two when Schreiderling appeared and told Mrs. Gaurey that he wished to marry her daughter. Then the other engagement was broken off—washed away by Mrs. Gaurey's tears, for that lady governed her house by weeping over disobedience to her authority and the lack of reverence she received in her old age. The daughter did not take after her mother. She never cried; not even at the wedding.

The Other Man bore his loss quietly, and was transferred to as bad a station as he could find. Perhaps the climate consoled him. He suffered from intermittent fever, and that may have distracted him from his other trouble. He was weak about the heart also. Both ways. One of the valves was affected, and the fever made it worse. This showed itself later on.

Then many months passed, and Mrs. Schreiderling took to being ill. She did not pine away like people in story-books, but she seemed to pick up every form of illness that went about a Station, from simple fever upwards. She was never more than ordinarily pretty at the best of times; and the illnesses made her ugly. Schreiderling said so. He prided himself on speaking his mind.

When she ceased being pretty, he left her to her own devices, and went back to the lairs of his bachelordom. She used to trot up and down Simla Mall* in a forlorn sort of way, with a gray Terai hat* well on the back of her head, and a shocking bad saddle under her. Schreiderling's generosity stopped at the horse. He said that any saddle would do for a woman as nervous as Mrs. Schreiderling. She never was asked to dance, because she did not dance well; and she was so dull and uninteresting, that her box very seldom had any cards in it. Schreiderling said that if he had known she was going to be such a scarecrow after her marriage he would never have married her. He always prided himself on speaking his mind, did Schreiderling.

He left her at Simla one August, and went down to his regiment. Then she revived a little, but she never recovered her looks. I found out at the Club that the Other Man was coming up sick—very sick—on an off chance of recovery. The fever and the heart-valve had nearly killed him. She knew that too, and she knew—what I had no interest in knowing—when he was coming up. I suppose he wrote to tell her. They had not seen each other since a month before the wedding. And here comes the unpleasant part of the story.

A late call kept me down at the Dovedell Hotel till dusk one evening. Mrs. Schreiderling had been flitting up and down the Mall all the afternoon in the rain. Coming up along the

Cart-Road a tonga* passed me, and my pony, tired with standing so long, set off at a canter. Just by the road down to the Tonga Office Mrs. Schreiderling, dripping from head to foot, was waiting for the tonga. I turned uphill as the tonga was no affair of mine, and just then she began to shriek. I went back at once and saw, under the Tonga Office lamps, Mrs. Schreiderling kneeling in the wet road by the back seat of the newly-arrived tonga, screaming hideously. Then she fell face down in the dirt as I came up.

Sitting in the back seat, very square and firm, with one hand on the awning-stanchion and the wet pouring off his hat and moustache, was the Other Man—dead. The sixty-mile uphill jolt* had been too much for his valves, I suppose. The tonga-driver said, 'This Sahib died two stages out of Solon.* Therefore, I tied him with a rope, lest he should fall out by the way, and so came to Simla. Will the Sahib give me *bukshish?* *It*,' pointing to the Other Man, 'should have given me one rupee.'

The Other Man sat with a grin on his face, as if he enjoyed the joke of his arrival; and Mrs. Schreiderling, in the mud, began to groan. There was no one except us four in the office, and it was raining heavily. The first thing was to take Mrs. Schreiderling home, and the second was to prevent her name from being mixed up with the affair. The tonga-driver received five rupees to find a bazar 'rickshaw for Mrs. Schreiderling. He was to tell the Tonga Babu* afterwards of the Other Man, and the Babu was to make such arrangements as seemed best.

Mrs. Schreiderling was carried into the shed out of the rain, and for three-quarters of an hour we two waited for the 'rickshaw. The Other Man was left exactly as he had arrived. Mrs. Schreiderling would do everything but cry, which might have helped her. She tried to scream as soon as her senses came back, and then she began praying for the Other Man's soul. Had she not been as honest as the day, she would have prayed for her own soul too. I waited to hear her do this, but she did not. Then I tried to get some of the mud off her habit. Lastly, the 'rickshaw came, and I got her away—partly by force. It was a terrible business from beginning to end; but most of all when the 'rickshaw had to squeeze between the wall and the tonga, and she saw by the lamplight that thin, yellow hand grasping the awning-stanchion.

She was taken home just as every one was going to a dance at Viceregal Lodge—'Peterhoff'* it was then—and the doctor found out that she had fallen from her horse, that I had picked her up at the back of Jakko, and really deserved great credit for the prompt manner in which I had secured medical aid. She did not die—men of Schreiderling's stamp marry women who don't die easily. They live and grow ugly.

She never told of her one meeting, since her marriage, with the Other Man; and, when the chill and cough following the exposure of that evening allowed her abroad, she never by word or sign alluded to having met me by the Tonga Office. Perhaps she never knew.

She used to trot up and down the Mall, on that shocking bad saddle, looking as if she expected to meet some one round the corner every minute. Two years afterwards she went Home, and died—at Bournemouth, I think.

Schreiderling, when he grew maudlin at Mess, used to talk about 'my poor dear wife.' He always set great store on speaking his mind, did Schreiderling.

Consequences*

Rosicrucian* subtleties
In the Orient had rise;
Ye may find their teachers still
Under Jacatālā's Hill.*
Seek ye Bombast Paracelsus,
Read what Flood the Seeker* tells us
Of the Dominant that runs
Through the Cycles of the Suns—
Read my story last, and see
Luna at her apogee.*

THERE are yearly appointments, and two-yearly appointments, and five-yearly appointments at Simla, and there are, or used to be, permanent appointments, whereon you stayed up for the term of your natural life, and secured red cheeks and a nice income. Of course, you could descend in the cold weather; for Simla is rather dull then.

Tarrion came from goodness knows where—all away and away in some forsaken part of Central India, where they call Pachmari a Sanitarium,* and drive behind trotting-bullocks,* I believe. He belonged to a regiment; but what he really wanted to do was to escape from his regiment and live in Simla for ever and ever. He had no preference for anything in particular, beyond a good horse and a nice partner. He thought he could do everything well; which is a beautiful belief when you hold it with all your heart. He was clever in many ways, and good to look at, and always made people round him comfortable—even in Central India.

So he went up to Simla, and, because he was clever and amusing, he gravitated naturally to Mrs. Hauksbee, who could forgive everything but stupidity. Once he did her great service by changing the date on an invitation-card for a big dance which Mrs. Hauksbee wished to attend, but couldn't, because she had quarrelled with the A.-D.-C.*, who took care, being a mean man, to invite her to a small dance on the 6th instead of the big Ball of the 26th. It was a very clever piece of forgery; and when Mrs. Hauksbee showed the A.-D.-C. her invitation-card, and chaffed him mildly for not better managing his vendettas, he really thought that he had made a mistake; and—which was wise—realised that it was no use to fight with Mrs. Hauksbee. She was grateful to Tarrion, and asked what she could do for him. He said simply, 'I'm a Freelance up here on leave, on the lookout for what I can loot. I haven't a square inch of interest* in all Simla. My name isn't known to any man with an appointment in his gift, and I want an appointment—a good, sound one. I believe you can do anything you turn yourself to. Will you help me?' Mrs. Hauksbee thought for a minute, and passed the lash of her riding-whip through her lips, as was her custom when thinking. Then her eyes sparkled and she said, 'I will'; and she shook hands on it. Tarrion, having perfect confidence in this great woman, took no further thought of the business at all, except to wonder what sort of an appointment he would win.

Mrs. Hauksbee began calculating the prices of all the Heads of Departments and Members of Council she knew, and the more she thought the more she laughed, because her heart was in the game and it amused her. Then she took a Civil List and ran over a few of the appointments. (There are some beautiful appointments in the Civil List.) Eventually, she decided that, though Tarrion was too good for the Political Department, she had better begin by trying to place him there. Her own plans to this end do not matter in the least, for Luck or Fate played into her hands, and she had nothing to do but to watch the course of events and take the credit of them.

All Viceroys, when they first come out, pass through the Diplomatic Secrecy craze. It wears off in time; but they all catch it in the beginning, because they are new to the country. The particular Viceroy* who was suffering from the complaint just then—this was a long time ago, before Lord Dufferin* ever came from Canada, or Lord Ripon* from the bosom of the English Church—had it very badly; and the result was that men who were new to keeping official secrets went about looking unhappy; and the Viceroy plumed himself on the way in which he had instilled notions of reticence into his Staff.

Now, the Supreme Government have a careless custom of committing what they do to printed papers. These papers deal with all sorts of things—from the payment of Rs. 200 to a 'secret service' native, up to rebukes administered to Vakils and Motamids* of Native States,* and rather brusque letters to Native Princes, telling them to put their houses in order, to refrain from kidnapping women, or filling offenders with pounded red pepper, and eccentricities of that kind. Of course, these things could never be made public, because Native Princes never err officially, and their States are officially as well administered as Our territories. Also, the private allowances to various queer people are not exactly matters to put into newspapers, though they give quaint reading sometimes. When the Supreme Government is at Simla these papers are prepared there, and go round to the people who ought to see them in office-boxes or by post. The principle of secrecy was to that Viceroy quite as important as the practice, and he held that a benevolent despotism liqc Ours should never allow even little things, such as appointments of subordinate clerks, to leak out till the proper time. He was always remarkable for his principles.

There was a very important batch of papers in preparation at that time. It had to travel from one end of Simla to the other by hand. It was not put into an official envelope, but a large, square, pale pink one; the matter being in MS. on soft crinkly paper.* It was addressed to 'The Head Clerk, etc. etc.' Now, between 'The Head Clerk, etc. etc.' and 'Mrs. Hauksbee' and a flourish, is no very great difference, if the address be written in a very bad hand, as this was. The orderly who took the envelope was not more of an idiot than most orderlies. He merely forgot where this most unofficial cover was to be delivered, and so asked the first Englishman he met, who happened to be a man riding down to Annandale* in a great hurry. The Englishman hardly looked at it, said, 'Mrs. Hauksbee,' and went on. So did the orderly, because that letter was the last in stock and he wanted to get his work over. There was no book to sign;* he thrust the letter into Mrs. Hauksbee's bearer's hands and went off to smoke with a friend. Mrs. Hauksbee was expecting some cut-out pattern things in flimsy paper from a friend. As soon as she got the big square packet, therefore, she said, 'Oh, the dear creature!' and tore it open with a paper-knife, and all the MS. enclosures tumbled out on the floor.

Mrs Hauksbee began reading. I have said the batch was rather important. That is quite enough for you to know. It referred to some correspondence, two measures, a peremptory order to a native chief, and two dozen other things. Mrs. Hauksbee gasped as she read, for the first glimpse of the naked machinery of the Great Indian Government, stripped of its casings, and lacquer, and paint, and guard-rails, impresses even the most stupid man. And Mrs. Hauksbee was a clever woman. She was a little afraid at first, and felt as if she had taken hold of a lightning-flash by the tail, and did not quite know what to do with it. There were remarks and initials at the side of the papers; and some of the remarks were rather more severe than the papers. The initials belonged to men who are all dead or gone now; but they were great in their day. Mrs. Hauksbee read on and thought calmly as she read. Then the value of her trove struck her, and she cast about for the best method of using it. Then Tarrion dropped in, and they read through all the papers together, and Tarrion, not knowing how she had come by them, vowed that Mrs. Hauksbee was the greatest woman on earth. Which I believe was true or nearly so.

'The honest course is always the best,' said Tarrion, after an hour and a half of study and conversation. 'All things considered, the Intelligence Branch is about my form. Either that or the Foreign Office. I go to lay siege to the High Gods in their Temples.'

He did not seek a little man, or a little big man, or a weak Head of a strong Department, but he called on the biggest and strongest man that the Government owned, and explained that he wanted an appointment at Simla on a good salary. The compound insolence of this amused the Strong Man, and, as he had nothing to do for the moment, he listened to the proposals of the audacious Tarrion. 'You have, I presume, some special qualifications, besides the gift of self-assertion, for the claims you put forward?' said the Strong Man. 'That,

Sir,' said Tarrion, 'is for you to judge.' Then he began, for he had a good memory, quoting a few of the more important notes in the papers—slowly and one by one as a man drops chlorodyne* into a glass. When he had reached the peremptory order—and it was a very peremptory order—the Strong Man was troubled. Tarrion wound up—'And I fancy that special knowledge of this kind is at least as valuable for, let us say, a berth in the Foreign Office, as the fact of being the nephew of a distinguished officer's wife.' That hit the Strong Man hard, for the last appointment to the Foreign Office had been by black favour, and he knew it.

'I'll see what I can do for you,' said the Strong Man.

'Many thanks,' said Tarrion. Then he left, and the Strong Man departed to see how the appointment was to be blocked.

*   *   *

Followed a pause of eleven days; with thunders and lightnings and much telegraphing. The appointment was not a very important one, carrying only between Rs.500 and Rs.700 a month; but, as the Viceroy said, it was the principle of diplomatic secrecy that had to be maintained, and it was more than likely that a boy so well supplied with special information would be worth translating. So they translated Tarrion. They must have suspected him, though he protested that his information was due to singular talents of his own. Now, much of this story, including the after-history of the missing envelope, you must fill in for yourself, because there are reasons why it cannot be written. If you do not know about things Up Above, you won't understand how to fill in, and you will say it is impossible.

What the Viceroy said* when Tarrion was introduced to him was—'This is the boy who "rushed" the Government of India, is it? Recollect, Sir, that is not done twice.' So he must have known something.

What Tarrion said when he saw his appointment gazetted was—'If Mrs. Hauksbee were twenty years younger, and I her husband, I should be Viceroy of India in fifteen years.'

What Mrs. Hauksbee said, when Tarrion thanked her, almost with tears in his eyes, was first—'I told you so!' and next, to herself—'What fools men are!'

The Conversion of Aurelian McGoggin*

Ride with an idle whip, ride with an unused heel,
But, once in a way, there will come a day
When the colt must be taught to feel
The lash that falls, and the curb that galls, and the sting of
the rowelled steel.

*Life's Handicap.**

THIS is not a tale exactly. This is a Tract; and I am immensely proud of it. Making a Tract is a Feat.

Every man is entitled to his own religious opinions; but no man—least of all a junior—has a right to thrust these down other men's throats. The Government sends out weird Civilians now and again; but McGoggin was the queerest exported for a long time. He was clever—brilliantly clever—but his cleverness worked the wrong way. Instead of keeping to the study of the vernaculars, he had read some books written by a man called Comte,* I think, and a man called Spencer.* (You will find these books in the Library.) They deal with people's insides from the point of view of men who have no stomachs. There was no order against his reading them; but his Mamma should have smacked him. They fermented in his head, and he came out to India with a rarefied religion over and above his work. It was not much of a creed. It only proved that men had no souls, and there was no God and no hereafter, and that you must worry along somehow for the good of Humanity.

One of its minor tenets seemed to be that the one thing more sinful than giving an order was obeying it. At least, that was what McGoggin said; but I suspect he had misread his primers.

I do not say a word against this creed. It was made up in Town* where there is nothing but machinery and asphalte and building—all shut in by the fog. Naturally, a man grows to think that there is no one higher than himself, and that the Metropolitan Board of Works made everything. But in India,

where you really see humanity—raw, brown, naked humanity
—with nothing between it and the blazing sky, and only the
used-up, overhandled earth underfoot, the notion somehow
dies away, and most folk come back to simpler theories. Life,
in India, is not long enough to waste in proving that there is
no one in particular at the head of affairs. For this reason. The
Deputy* is above the Assistant, the Commissioner above the
Deputy, the Lieutenant-Governor above the Commissioner,
and the Viceroy above all four, under the orders of the
Secretary of State,* who is responsible to the Empress. If the
Empress be not responsible to her Maker—if there is no
Maker for her to be responsible to—the entire system of Our
administration must be wrong; which is manifestly
impossible. At Home men are to be excused. They are stalled
up a good deal and get intellectually 'beany.'* When you take
a gross, 'beany' horse to exercise, he slavers and slobbers over
the bit till you can't see the horns. But the bit is there just the
same. Men do not get 'beany' in India. The climate and the
work are against playing bricks with words.

If McGoggin had kept his creed, with the capital letters and
the endings in 'ism,' to himself, no one would have cared; but
his grandfathers on both sides had been Wesleyan preachers,*
and the preaching strain came out in his mind. He wanted
every one at the Club to see that they had no souls too, and
to help him to eliminate his Creator. As a good many men told
him, *he* undoubtedly had no soul, because he was so young,
but it did not follow that his seniors were equally
undeveloped; and, whether there was another world or not, a
man still wanted to read his papers in this. 'But that is not the
point—that is not the point!' Aurelian used to say. Then men
threw sofa-cushions at him and told him to go to any
particular place he might believe in. They christened him
'The Blastoderm,'*—he said he came from a family of that
name somewhere, in the prehistoric ages,—and by insult and
laughter strove to choke him dumb, for he was an unmitigated
nuisance at the Club, besides being an offence to the older
men. His Deputy Commissioner, who was working on the
Frontier when Aurelian was rolling on a bed-quilt, told him
that, for a clever boy, Aurelian was a very big idiot. And, if he

had gone on with his work, he would have been caught up to
the Secretariat in a few years. He was of the type that goes
there—all head, no physique and a hundred theories. Not a
soul was interested in McGoggin's soul. He might have had
two, or none, or somebody else's. His business was to obey
orders and keep abreast of his files, instead of devastating the
Club with 'isms'.

He worked brilliantly; but he could not accept any order
without trying to better it. That was the fault of his creed. It
made men too responsible and left too much to their honour.
You can sometimes ride an old horse in a halter, but never a
colt. McGoggin took more trouble over his cases than any of
the men of his year. He may have fancied that thirty-page
judgments on fifty-rupee cases—both sides perjured to the
gullet—advanced the cause of Humanity. At any rate, he
worked too much, and worried and fretted over the rebukes
he received, and lectured away on his ridiculous creed out of
office, till the Doctor had to warn him that he was overdoing
it. No man can toil eighteen annas in the rupee* in June
without suffering. But McGoggin was still intellectually
'beany' and proud of himself and his powers, and he would
take no hint. He worked nine hours a day steadily.

'Very well,' said the Doctor, 'you'll break down, because
you are over-engined for your beam.' McGoggin was a little
man.

One day the collapse came—as dramatically as if it had been
meant to embellish a Tract.

It was just before the Rains. We were sitting in the verandah
in the dead, hot, close air, gasping and praying that the black-
blue clouds would let down and bring the cool. Very, very far
away, there was a faint whisper, which was the roar of the
Rains breaking over the river. One of the men heard it, got out
of his chair, listened and said, naturally enough, 'Thank God!'

Then The Blastoderm turned in his place and said, 'Why?
I assure you it's only the result of perfectly natural causes—
atmospheric phenomena of the simplest kind. Why you
should, therefore, return thanks to a Being who never did
exist—who is only a figment——'

'Blastoderm,' grunted the man in the next chair, 'dry up and throw me over the *Pioneer*.*. We know all about your figments.' The Blastoderm reached out to the table, took up one paper, and jumped as if something had stung him. Then he handed the paper.

'As I was saying,' he went on slowly and with an effort—'due to perfectly natural causes—perfectly natural causes. I mean——'

'Hi! Blastoderm, you've given me the *Calcutta Mercantile Advertiser*.'

The dust got up in little whorls, while the tree-tops rocked and the kites whistled. But no one was looking at the coming of the Rains. We were all staring at The Blastoderm, who had risen from his chair and was fighting with his speech. Then he said, still more slowly—

'Perfectly conceivable——dictionary——red oak——amenable——cause——retaining——shuttle-cock——alone.'

'Blastoderm's drunk,' said one man. But The Blastoderm was not drunk. He looked at us in a dazed sort of way, and began motioning with his hands in the half light as the clouds closed overhead. Then—with a sceam—

'What is it?——Can't——reserve——attainable——market——obscure——'

But the speech seemed to freeze in him, and—just as the lightning shot two tongues that cut the whole sky into three pieces and the rain fell in quivering sheets—The Blastoderm was struck dumb. He stood pawing and champing like a hard-held horse, and his eyes were full of terror.

The Doctor came over in three minutes, and heard the story. 'It's aphasia,*' he said. 'Take him to his room. I knew the smash would come.' We carried The Blastoderm across in the pouring rain to his quarters, and the Doctor gave him bromide of potassium to make him sleep.

Then the Doctor came back to us and told us that aphasia was like all the arrears of 'Punjab Head'* falling in a lump; and that only once before—in the case of a sepoy—had he met with so complete a case. I have seen mild aphasia in an overworked man, but this sudden dumbness was uncanny—though, as The Blastoderm himself might have said, due to 'perfectly natural causes.'

'He'll have to take leave after this,' said the Doctor. 'He won't be fit for work for another three months. No; it isn't insanity or anything like it. It's only complete loss of control over the speech and memory. I fancy it will keep The Blastoderm quiet, though.'

Two days later The Blastoderm found his tongue again. The first question he asked was—'What was it?' The Doctor enlightened him. 'But I can't understand it!' said The Blastoderm. 'I'm quite sane; but I can't be sure of my mind, it seems—my *own* memory—can I?'

'Go up into the Hills for three months, and don't think about it,' said the Doctor.

'But I can't understand it,' repeated The Blastoderm. 'It was my *own* mind and memory.'

'I can't help it,' said the Doctor; 'there are a good many things you can't understand; and, by the time you have put in my length of service, you'll know exactly how much a man dare call his own in this world.'

The stroke cowed The Blastoderm. He could not understand it. He went into the Hills in fear and trembling, wondering whether he would be permitted to reach the end of any sentence he began.

This gave him a wholesome feeling of mistrust. The legitimate explanation, that he had been over-working himself, failed to satisfy him. Something had wiped his lips of speech, as a mother wipes the milky lips of her child, and he was afraid—horribly afraid.

So the Club had rest when he returned; and if ever you come across Aurelian McGoggin laying down the law on things Human—he doesn't seem to know as much as he used to about things Divine—put your forefinger to your lip for a moment, and see what happens.

Don't blame me if he throws a glass at your head.

The Taking of Lungtungpen*

So we loosed a bloomin' volley,
   An' we made the beggars cut,
An' when our pouch was emptied out,
   We used the bloomin' butt.
      Ho! My!
      Don't yer come anigh
When Tommy is a-playin' with the baynit an' the butt.
                                    *Barrack-Room Ballad.**

MY friend Private Mulvaney told me this, sitting on the
parapet of the road to Dagshai,* when we were hunting
butterflies together. He had theories about the Army, and
coloured clay pipes perfectly. He said that the young soldier
is the best to work with, 'on account av the surpassin'
innocince av the choild.'

'Now, listen!' said Mulvaney, throwing himself full length
on the wall in the sun. 'I'm a born scutt* av the barrick-room!
The Army's mate an' dhrink to me, bekaze I'm wan av the few
that can't quit ut. I've put in sivinteen years, an' the
pipeclay's* in the marrow av me. Av I cud have kept out av
wan big dhrink a month, I wud have been a Hon'ry Lift'nint
by this time—a nuisince to my betthers, a laughin'-shtock to
my aquils, an' a curse to meself. Bein' fwhat I am, I'm Privit
Mulvaney, wid no good-conduc' pay an' a devourin' thirst.
Always barrin' me little frind Bobs Bahadur,* I know as much
about the Army as most men.'

I said something here.

'Wolseley* be shot! Betune you an' me an' that butterfly
net, he's a ramblin', incoherint sort av a divil, wid wan eye on
the Quane an' the Coort, an' the other on his blessed silf—
everlastin'ly playin' Saysar and Alexandrier* rowled into a
lump. Now Bobs is a sinsible little man. Wid Bobs an' a few
three-year-olds,* I'd swape any army av the earth into a towel,
an' throw ut away aftherwards. Faith, I'm not jokin'! 'Tis the
bhoys—the raw bhoys—that don't know fwhat a bullut

manes, an' wudn't care av they did—that do the work. They're crammed wid bull-mate till they fairly *ramps* wid good livin'; and thin, av they don't fight, they blow each other's hids off. 'Tis the trut' I'm tellin' you. They shud be kept on water an' rice in the hot weather; but there'd be a mut'ny av 'twas done.

Did ye iver hear how Privit Mulvaney tuk the town av Lungtungpen? I thought not! 'Twas the Lift'nint got the credit; but 'twas me planned the schame. A little before I was invilided from Burma, me an' four-an'-twenty young wans undher a Lift'nint Brazenose, was ruinin' our dijeshins thryin' to catch dacoits.* An' such double-inded divils I niver knew! 'Tis only a *dah** an' a Snider* that makes a dacoit. Widout thim, he's a paceful cultivator, an' felony for to shoot. We hunted, an' we hunted, an' tuk fever an' elephints now an' again; but no dacoits. Evenshually, we *puckarowed** wan man. "Trate him tinderly," sez the Lift'nint. So I tuk him away into the jungle, wid the Burmese Interprut'r an' my clanin'-rod. Sez I to the man, "My paceful squireen," sez I, "you shquot on your hunkers an' dimonstrate to *my* frind here, where *your* frinds are whin they're at home?" Wid that I introjuced him to the clanin'-rod, an' he comminst to jabber; the Interprut'r interprutin' in betweens, an' me helpin' the Intilligince Departmint wid my clanin'-rod whin the man misremimbered.

Prisintly, I learn that, acrost the river, about nine miles away, was a town just dhrippin' wid dahs, an' bohs* an' arrows, an' dacoits, an' elephints, an' *jingles.** "Good!" sez I; "this office will now close!"

That night I went to the Lift'nint an' communicates my informashin. I never thought much av Lift'nint Brazenose till that night. He was shtiff wid books an' the-ouries, an' all manner av thrimmin's no manner av use. "Town, did ye say?" sez he. "Acordin' to the the-ouries av War, we shud wait for reinforcements."—"Faith!" thinks I, "we'd betther dig our graves thin"; for the nearest throops was up to their shtocks in the marshes out Mimbu way. "But," sez the Lift'nint, "since 'tis a speshil case, I'll make an excepshin. We'll visit this Lungtungpen tonight."

The bhoys was fairly woild wid deloight whin I tould 'em;

an', by this an' that, they wint through the jungle like buck-rabbits. About midnight we come to the shtrame which I had clane forgot to minshin to my orf'cer. I was on, ahead, wid four bhoys, an' I thought that the Lift'nint might want to the-ourise. 'Shtrip bhoys!" sez I. "Shtrip to the buff, an' shwim in where glory waits!"—"But I *can't* shwim!" sez two av thim. "To think I should live to hear that from a bhoy wid a board-school edukashin!" sez I. "Take a lump av timbher, an' me an' Conolly here will ferry ye over, ye young ladies!"

We got an ould tree-trunk, an' pushed off wid the kits an' the rifles on ut. The night was chokin' dhark, an' just as we was fairly embarked, I heard the Lift'nint behind av me callin' out. "There's a bit av a *nullah** here, Sorr," sez I, "but I can feel the bottom already." So I cud, for I was not a yard from the bank.

"Bit av a *nullah*! Bit av an eshtury!" sez the Lift'nint. "Go on, ye mad Irishman! Shtrip bhoys!" I heard him laugh; an' the bhoys begun shtrippin' an' rollin' a log into the wather to put their kits on. So me an' Conolly shtruck out through the warm wather wid our log, an' the rest come on behind.

That shtrame was miles woide! Orth'ris, on the rear-rank log, whispers we had got into the Thames below Sheerness by mistake. "Kape on shwimmin', ye little blayguard," sez I, "an' don't go pokin' your dirty jokes at the Irriwaddy."—"Silince, men!" sings out the Lift'nint. So we shwum on into the black dhark, wid our chests on the logs, trustin' in the Saints an' the luck av the British Army.

Evenshually we hit ground—a bit av sand—an' a man. I put my heel on the back av him. He skreeched an' ran.

"*Now* we've done ut!" sez Lift'nint Brazenose. "Where the Divil *is* Lungtungpen?" There was about a minute and a half to wait. The bhoys laid a hoult av their rifles an' some thried to put their belts on; we was marchin' wid fixed baynits av coorse. Thin we knew where Lungtungpen was; for we had hit the river-wall av ut in the dhark, an' the whole town blazed wid thim messin' *jingles* an' Sniders like a cat's back on a frosty night. They was firin' all ways at wanst; but over our hids into the shtrame.

"Have you got your rifles?" sez Brazenose, "Got 'em!" sez

Orth'ris. "I've got that thief Mulvaney's for all my back-pay,
an' she'll kick my heart sick wid that blunderin' long shtock
av hers."—"Go on!" yells Brazenose, whippin' his sword out.
"Go on an' take the town! An' the Lord have mercy on our
sowls!"

Thin the bhoys gave wan devastatin' howl, an' pranced into
the dhark, feelin' for the town, an' blindin' an' stiffin'* like
Cavalry Ridin' Masters whin the grass pricked their bare legs.
I hammered wid the butt at some bamboo-thing that felt wake,
an' the rest come an' hammered contagious, while the *jingles*
was jinglin', an' feroshus yells from inside was shplittin' our
ears. We was too close undher the wall for thim to hurt us.

Evenshually, the thing, whatever ut was, bruk; an' the six-
and-twinty av us tumbled, wan afther the other, nakid as we
was borrun, into the town of Lungtungpen. There was a
*melly** av a sumpshus kind for a whoile; but whether they tuk
us, all white an' wet, for a new breed av' divil, or a new kind
av dacoit, I don't know. They ran as though we was both, an'
we wint into thim, baynit an' butt, shriekin' wid laughin'.
There was torches in the shtreets, an' I saw little Orth'ris
rubbin' his shoulther ivry time he loosed my long-shtock
Martini; an' Brazenose walkin' into the gang wid his sword,
like Diarmid* av the Gowlden Collar—barrin' he hadn't a
stitch av clothin' on him. We diskivered elephints wid dacoits
undher their bellies, an', fwhat wid wan thing an' another, we
was busy till mornin' takin' possession av the town av
Lungtungpen.

Thin we halted an' formed up, the wimmen howlin' in the
houses an' Lift'nint Brazenose blushin' pink in the light av
the mornin' sun. 'Twas the most ondasint p'rade I iver tuk a
hand in. Foive-and-twenty privits an' an orf'cer av the Line
in review ordher, an' not as much as wud dust a fife betune
'em all in the way av clothin'! Eight av us had their belts an'
pouches on; but the rest had gone in wid a handful av
cartridges an' the skin God gave thim. *They* was as nakid as
Vanus!

"Number off from the right!" sez the Lift'nint. "Odd
numbers fall out to dress; even numbers pathrol the town till
relieved by the dressing party." Let me tell you, pathrollin'

a town wid nothing on is an ex*pay*rience. I pathrolled for tin minutes, an' begad, before 'twas over, I blushed. The wimmen laughed so. I niver blushed before or since; but I blushed all over my carkiss thin. Orth'ris didn't pathrol. He sez only, "Portsmith Barricks, an' the 'Ard* av a Sunday!" Thin he lay down an' rowled any ways wid laughin'.

Whin we was all dhressed we counted the dead—sivinty-foive dacoits besides wounded. We tuk five elephints, a hunder' an' sivinty Sniders, two hunder' dahs, and a lot av other burglarious thruck. Not a man av us was hurt—excep' maybe the Lift'nint, an' him from the shock to his dasincy.

The Headman av Lungtungpen, who surrindered himsilf, asked the Interprut'r—"Av the English fight like that wid their clo'es off, what in the wurruld do they do wid their clo'es on?" Orth'ris began rowlin' his eyes an' crackin' his fingers an' dancin' a step-dance for to impress the Headman. He ran to his house; an' we spint the rest av the day carryin' the Lift'nint on our shoulthers round the town, an' playin' wid the Burmese babies—fat, little, brown little divils, as pretty as picturs.

Whin I was inviladed for the dysent'ry to India, I sez to the Lift'nint, "Sorr," sez I, "you've the makin's in you av a great man; but, av you'll let an ould sodger spake, you're too fond av the-ourisin'." He shuk hands wid me and sez, "Hit high, hit low, there's no plasin' you, Mulvaney. You've seen me waltzin' through Lungtungpen like a Red Injin widout the war-paint, an' you say I'm too fond av the-ourisin'?"—"Sorr," sez I, for I loved the bhoy, "I wud waltz wid you in that condishin through *Hell*, an' so wud the rest av the men!" Thin I wint down-shtrame in the flat* an' left him my blessin'. May the Saints carry ut where ut shud go, for he was a fine upstandin' young orf'cer.

To reshume. Fwhat I've said jist shows the use av three-year-olds. Wud fifty seasoned sodgers have taken Lung-tungpen in the dhark that way? No! They'd know the risk av fever and chill; let alone the shootin'. Two hundher' might have done ut. But the three-year-olds know little an' care less; an' where there's no fear there's no danger. Catch thim young, feed thim high, an' by the honour av that great little man

Bobs, behind a good orf'cer, 'tisn't only dacoits they'd smash wid their clo'es off—'tis Con-ti-nental Ar-r-r-mies! They tuk Lungtungpen nakid; an' they'd take St. Pethersburg in their dhrawers? Begad, they would that!

Here's your pipe, Sorr. Shmoke her tinderly wid honey-dew,* afther letting the reek av the Canteen plug die away. But 'tis no good, thanks to you all the same, fillin' my pouch wid your chopped hay. Canteen baccy's like the Army; ut shpoils a man's taste for moilder things.'

So saying, Mulvaney took up his butterfly-net, and returned to barracks.

A Germ-Destroyer*

Pleasant it is for the Little Tin Gods
When great Jove nods;
But Little Tin Gods make their little mistakes
In missing the hour when great Jove wakes.

AS a general rule, it is inexpedient to meddle with questions
of State in a land where men are highly paid to work them out
for you. This tale is a justifiable exception.

Once in every five years, as you know, we indent for a new
Viceroy; and each Viceroy imports, with the rest of his
baggage, a Private Secretary, who may or may not be the real
Viceroy, just as Fate ordains. Fate looks after the Indian
Empire because it is so big and so helpless.

There was a Viceroy once who brought out with him a
turbulent Private Secretary—a hard man with a soft manner
and a morbid passion for work. This Secretary was called
Wonder—John Fennil Wonder. The Viceroy possessed no
name—nothing but a string of counties and two-thirds of the
alphabet after them. He said, in confidence, that he was the
electro-plated figurehead of a golden administration, and he
watched in a dreamy, amused way Wonder's attempts to draw
matters which were entirely outside his province into his own
hands. 'When we are all cherubim together,' said His
Excellency once, 'my dear, good friend Wonder will head the
conspiracy for plucking out Gabriel's tail-feathers or stealing
Peter's keys. *Then* I shall report him.'

But, though the Viceroy did nothing to check Wonder's
officiousness, other people said unpleasant things. May be the
Members of Council began it; but, finally, all Simla agreed
that there was 'too much Wonder and too little Viceroy' in
that rule. Wonder was always quoting 'His Excellency.' It was
'His Excellency this,' 'His Excellency that,' 'In the opinion of
His Excellency,' and so on. The Viceroy smiled; but he did
ιot heed. He said that, so long as his old men squabbled with

his 'dear, good Wonder,' they might be induced to leave the
Immemorial East in peace.

'No wise man has a Policy,' said the Viceroy. 'A Policy is
the blackmail levied on the Fool by the Unforeseen. I am not
the former, and I do not believe in the latter.'

I do not quite see what this means, unless it refers to an
Insurance Policy. Perhaps it was the Viceroy's way of saying,
'Lie low.'

That season came up to Simla one of those crazy people
with only a single idea. These are the men who make things
move; but they are not nice to talk to. This man's name was
Mellish, and he had lived for fifteen years on land of his own,
in Lower Bengal, studying cholera. He held that cholera was
a germ that propagated itself as it flew through a muggy
atmosphere; and stuck in the branches of trees like a wool-
flake. The germ could be rendered sterile, he said, by
'Mellish's Own Invincible Fumigatory'—a heavy violet-black
powder—'the result of fifteen years' scientific investigation,
Sir!'

Inventors seem very much alike as a caste. They talk loudly,
especially about 'conspiracies of monopolists;' they beat upon
the table with their fists; and they secrete fragments of their
inventions about their persons.

Mellish said that there was a Medical 'Ring' at Simla,
headed by the Surgeon-General, who was in league,
apparently, with all the Hospital Assistants in the Empire. I
forget exactly how he proved it, but it had something to do
with 'skulking up to the Hills'; and what Mellish wanted was
the independent evidence of the Viceroy—'Steward of our
Most Gracious Majesty the Queen, Sir.' So Mellish went up
to Simla, with eighty-four pounds of Fumigatory in his trunk,
to speak to the Viceroy and to show him the merits of the
invention.

But it is easier to see a Viceroy than to talk to him, unless
you chance to be as important as Mellishe of Madras. He was
a six-thousand-rupee man, so great that his daughters never
'married.' They 'contracted alliances'. He himself was not
paid. He 'received emoluments,' and his journeys about the
country were 'tours of observation.' His business was to stir
up the people in Madras with a long pole—as you stir up tench

in a pond—and the people had to come up out of their comfortable old ways and gasp—'This is Enlightenment and Progress. Isn't it fine!' Then they gave Mellishe statues and jasmine garlands, in the hope of getting rid of him.

Mellishe came up to Simla 'to confer with the Viceroy.' That was one of his perquisites. The Viceroy knew nothing of Mellishe except that he was 'one of those middle-class deities who seem necessary to the spiritual comfort of this paradise of the Middle-classes,' and that, in all probability, he had 'suggested, designed, founded, and endowed all the public institutions in Madras.' Which proves that His Excellency, though dreamy, had experience of the ways of six-thousand-rupee men.

Mellishe's name was E. Mellishe, and Mellish's was E. S. Mellish, and they were both staying at the same hotel, and the Fate that looks after the Indian Empire ordained that Wonder should blunder and drop the final '*e*'; that the Chaprassi should help him, and that the note which ran—

DEAR MR. MELLISH,—Can you set aside your other engagements, and lunch with us at two to-morrow? His Excellency has an hour at your disposal then,

should be given to Mellish with the Fumigatory. He nearly wept with pride and delight, and at the appointed hour cantered to Peterhoff,* a big paper-bag full of the Fumigatory in his coat-tail pockets. He had his chance, and he meant to make the most of it. Mellishe of Madras had been so portentously solemn about his 'conference' that Wonder had arranged for a private tiffin,—no A.-D.-C.s, no Wonder, no one but the Viceroy, who said plaintively that he feared being left alone with unmuzzled autocrats like the great Mellishe of Madras.

But his guest did not bore the Viceroy. On the contrary, he amused him. Mellish was nervously anxious to go straight to his Fumigatory, and talked at random until tiffin was over and His Excellency asked him to smoke. The Viceroy was pleased with Mellish because he did not talk 'shop.'

As soon as the cheroots were lit, Mellish spoke like a man; beginning with his cholera-theory, reviewing his fifteen years'

'scientific labours,' the machinations of the 'Simla Ring,' and
the excellence of his Fumigatory, while the Viceroy watched
him between half-shut eyes and thought—'Evidently this is
the wrong tiger; but it is an original animal.' Mellish's hair
was standing on end with excitement, and he stammered. He
began groping in his coat-tails and, before the Viceroy knew
what was about to happen, he had tipped a bagful of his
powder into the big silver ash-tray.

'J-j-judge for yourself, Sir,' said Mellish. 'Y' Excellency
shall judge for yourself! Absolutely infallible, on my honour.'

He plunged the lighted end of his cigar into the powder,
which began to smoke like a volcano, and send up fat, greasy
wreaths of copper-coloured smoke. In five seconds the room
was filled with a most pungent and sickening stench—a reek
that took fierce hold of the trap of your windpipe and shut it.
The powder hissed and fizzed, and sent out blue and green
sparks, and the smoke rose till you could neither see, nor
breathe, nor gasp. Mellish, however, was used to it.

'Nitrate of strontia,' he shouted; 'baryta, bone-meal,
etcetera! Thousand cubic feet smoke per cubic inch. Not a
germ could live—not a germ, Y' Excellency!'

But His Excellency had fled, and was coughing at the foot
of the stairs, while all Peterhoff hummed like a hive. Red
Lancers* came in, and the head Chaprassi* who speaks
English came in, and macebearers came in, and ladies ran
downstairs screaming, 'Fire'; for the smoke was drifting
through the house and oozing out of the windows, and
bellying along the verandahs, and wreathing and writhing
across the gardens. No one could enter the room where
Mellish was lecturing on his Fumigatory till that unspeakable
powder had burned itself out.

Then an Aide-de-Camp, who desired the V.C., rushed
through the rolling clouds and hauled Mellish into the hall.
The Viceroy was prostrate with laughter, and could only
waggle his hands feebly at Mellish, who was shaking a fresh
bagful of powder at him.

'Glorious! Glorious!' sobbed His Excellency. 'Not a germ,
as you justly observe, could exist! I can swear it. A
magnificent success!'

Then he laughed till the tears came, and Wonder, who had caught the real Mellishe snorting on the Mall, entered and was deeply shocked at the scene. But the Viceroy was delighted, because he saw that Wonder would presently depart. Mellish with the Fumigatory was also pleased, for he felt that he had smashed the Simla Medical 'Ring.'

*   *   *

Few men could tell a story like his Excellency when he took the trouble, and his account of 'my dear, good Wonder's friend with the powder' went the round of Simla, and flippant folk made Wonder unhappy by their remarks.

But His Excellency told the tale once too often—for Wonder. As he meant to do. It was at a Seepee Picnic.* Wonder was sitting just behind the Viceroy.

'And I really thought for a moment,' wound up His Excellency, 'that my dear, good Wonder had hired an assassin to clear his way to the throne!'

Every one laughed; but there was a delicate sub-tinkle in the Viceroy's tone which Wonder understood. He found that his health was giving way; and the Viceroy allowed him to go, and presented him with a flaming 'character' for use at Home among big people.

'My fault entirely,' said His Excellency, in after seasons, with a twinkle in his eye. 'My inconsistency must always have been distasteful to such a masterly man.'

Kidnapped*

There is a tide in the affairs of men
Which, taken any way you please, is bad,
And strands them in forsaken guts and creeks
No decent soul would think of visiting.
You cannot stop the tide; but, now and then,
You may arrest some rash adventurer,
Who—h'm—will hardly thank you for your pains.
Vibart's Moralities.

WE are a high-caste and enlightened race, and infant-marriage is very shocking, and the consequences are sometimes peculiar; but, nevertheless, the Hindu notion—which is the Continental notion, which is the aboriginal notion—of arranging marriages irrespective of the personal inclinations of the married, is sound. Think for a minute, and you will see that it must be so; unless, of course, you believe in 'affinities.' In which case you had better not read this tale. How can a man who has never married, who cannot be trusted to pick up at sight a moderately sound horse, whose head is hot and upset with visions of domestic felicity, go about the choosing of a wife? He cannot see straight or think straight if he tries; and the same disadvantages exist in the case of a girl's fancies. But when mature, married, and discreet people arrange a match between a boy and a girl, they do it sensibly, with a view to the future, and the young couple live happily ever afterwards. As everybody knows.

Properly speaking, Government should establish a Matrimonial Department, efficiently officered, with a Jury of Matrons, a Judge of the Chief Court, a Senior Chaplain, and an Awful Warning, in the shape of a love-match that has gone wrong, chained to the trees in the courtyard. All marriages should be made through the Department, which might be subordinate to the Educational Department, under the same penalty as that attaching to the transfer of land without a stamped document. But Government won't take suggestions.

It pretends that it is too busy. However, I will put my notion on record, and explain the example that illustrates the theory.

Once upon a time there was a good young man—a first-class officer in his own Department—a man with a career before him and, possibly, a K.C.I.E.* at the.end of it. All his superiors spoke well of him, because he knew how to hold his tongue and his pen at the proper times. There are, to-day, only eleven men in India who possess this secret; and they have all, with one exception, attained great honour and enormous incomes.

This good young man was quiet and self-contained—too old for his years by far. Which always carries its own punishment. Had a Subaltern, or a Tea-Planter's Assistant, or anybody who enjoys life and has no thought for to-morrow, done what he tried to do, not a soul would have cared. But when Peythroppe—the estimable, virtuous, economical, quiet, hard-working, young Peythroppe—fell, there was a flutter through five Departments.

The manner of his fall was in this way. He met a Miss Castries—d'Castries it was originally, but the family dropped the d' for administrative reasons—and he fell in love with her even more energetically than he worked. Understand clearly that there was not a breath of a word to be said against Miss Castries—not a shadow of a breath. She was good and very lovely—possessed what innocent people at Home call a 'Spanish' complexion, with thick blue-black hair growing low down on the forehead, into a 'widow's peak,' and big violet eyes under eyebrows as black and as straight as the borders of a *Gazette Extraordinary** when a big man dies. But——but—— but——Well, she was a *very* sweet girl and very pious, but for many reasons she was 'impossible.' Quite so. All good Mammas know what 'impossible' means. It was obviously absurd that Peythroppe should marry her. The little opal-tinted onyx at the base of her finger-nails said this as plainly as print. Further, marriage with Miss Castries meant marriage with several other Castries—Honorary Lieutenant* Castries her Papa, Mrs. Eulalie Castries her Mamma, and all the ramifications of the Castries family, on incomes ranging from Rs. 175 to Rs. 470 a month, and *their* wives and connections again.

It would have been cheaper for Peythroppe to have assaulted a Commissioner with a dog-whip, or to have burned the records of a Deputy-Commissioner's office, than to have contracted an alliance with the Castries. It would have weighted his after-career less—even under a Government which never forgets and *never* forgives. Everybody saw this but Peythroppe. He was going to marry Miss Castries, he was—being of age and drawing a good income—and woe betide the house that would not afterwards receive Mrs. Virginie Saulez Peythroppe with the deference due to her husband's rank. That was Peythroppe's ultimatum, and any remonstrance drove him frantic.

These sudden madnesses most afflict the sanest men. There was a case once—but I will tell you of that later on. You cannot account for the mania except under a theory directly contradicting the one about the Place wherein marriages are made. Peythroppe was burningly anxious to put a millstone round his neck at the outset of his career; and argument had not the least effect on him. He was going to marry Miss Castries, and the business was his own business. He would thank you to keep your advice to yourself. With a man in this condition mere words only fix him in his purpose. Of course he cannot see that marriage in India does not concern the individual but the Government he serves.

Do you remember Mrs. Hauksbee—the most wonderful woman in India? She saved Pluffles from Mrs. Reiver, won Tarrion his appointment in the Foreign Office, and was defeated in open field by Mrs. Cusack-Bremmil. She heard of the lamentable condition of Peythroppe, and her brain struck out the plan that saved him. She had the wisdom of the Serpent, the logical coherence of the Man, the fearlessness of the Child, and the triple intuition of the Woman. Never—no, never—as long as a tonga buckets down the Solon dip,* or the couples go a-riding at the back of Summer Hill,* will there be such a genius as Mrs. Hauksbee. She attended the consultation of Three Men on Peythroppe's case; and she stood up with the lash of her riding-whip between her lips and spake.

*   *   *

Three weeks later Peythroppe dined with the Three Men, and the *Gazette of India* came in. Peythroppe found to his surprise that

he had been gazetted a month's leave. Don't ask me how this
was managed. I believe firmly that, if Mrs. Hauksbee gave the
order, the whole Great Indian Administration would stand on
its head. The Three Men had also a month's leave each.
Peythroppe put the *Gazette* down and said bad words. Then
there came from the compound the soft 'pad-pad' of camels—
'thieves' camels,' the Bikaneer* breed that don't bubble and
howl when they sit down and get up.

After that, I don't know what happened. This much is
certain. Peythroppe disappeared—vanished like smoke—and
the long foot-rest chair in the house of the Three Men was
broken to splinters. Also a bedstead departed from one of the
bedrooms.

Mrs. Hauksbee said that Mr. Peythroppe was shooting in
Rajputana with the Three Men; so we were compelled to
believe her.

At the end of the month Peythroppe was gazetted twenty
days' extension of leave; but there was wrath and lamentation
in the house of Castries. The marriage-day had been fixed, but
the bridegroom never came; and the D'Silvas, Pereiras, and
Ducketts lifted their voices and mocked Honorary Lieutenant
Castries as one who had been basely imposed on. Mrs.
Hauksbee went to the wedding, and was much astonished
when Peythroppe did not appear. After seven weeks
Peythroppe and the Three Men returned from Rajputana.
Peythroppe was in hard, tough condition, rather white, and
more self-contained than ever.

One of the Three Men had a cut on his nose, caused by the
kick of a gun. Twelve-bores kick rather curiously.

Then came Honorary Lieutenant Castries, seeking for the
blood of his perfidious son-in-law to be. He said things—
vulgar and 'impossible' things which showed the raw, rough
'ranker' below the 'Honorary,' and I fancy Peythroppe's eyes
were opened. Anyhow, he held his peace till the end, when he
spoke briefly. Honorary Lieutenant Castries asked for a 'peg'*
before he went away to die or bring a suit for breach of
promise.

Miss Castries was a *very* good girl. She said that she would
have no breach of promise suits. She said that, if she was not

a lady, she was refined enough to know that ladies kept their broken hearts to themselves; and, as she ruled her parents, nothing happened. Later on, she married a most respectable and gentlemanly person. He travelled for an enterprising firm in Calcutta, and was all that a good husband should be.

So Peythroppe came to his right mind again, and did much good work, and was honoured by all who knew him. One of these days he will marry; but he will marry a sweet pink-and-white maiden, on the Government House List, with a little money and some influential connections, as every wise man should. And he will never, all his life, tell her what happened during the seven weeks of his shooting-tour in Rajputana.

But just think how much trouble and expense—for camel-hire is not cheap, and those Bikaneer brutes had to be fed like humans—might have been saved by a properly conducted Matrimonial Department, under the control of the Director-General of Education, but corresponding direct with the Viceroy!

The Arrest of Lieutenant Golightly*

'I've forgotten the countersign,' sez 'e.
'Oh! You 'ave, 'ave you?' sez I.
'But I'm the Colonel,' sez 'e.
'Oh! You are, are you?' sez I. 'Colonel nor no Colonel,
you waits 'ere till I'm relieved, an' the Sarjint reports on
your ugly old mug. *Choop!** sez I.

*   *   *

An' s'welp me soul, 'twas the Colonel after all! But I was
a recruity then.
The Unedited Autobiography of Private Ortheris.

IF there was one thing on which Golightly prided himself
more than another, it was looking like 'an Officer and a
Gentleman.' He said it was for the honour of the Service that
he attired himself so elaborately; but those who knew him best
said that it was just personal vanity. There was no harm about
Golightly—not an ounce. He recognised a horse when he saw
one, and could do more than fill a cantle.* He played a very
fair game at billiards, and was a sound man at the whist-table.
Every one liked him; and nobody ever dreamed of seeing him
handcuffed on a station platform as a deserter. But this sad
thing happened.

He was going down from Dalhousie, at the end of his
leave—riding down. He had run his leave as fine as he dared,
and wanted to come down in a hurry.

It was fairly warm at Dalhousie, and, knowing what to
expect below, he descended in a new *khaki* suit—tight-
fitting—of a delicate olive-green; a peacock-blue tie, white
collar, and a snowy white *solah** helmet. He prided himself on
looking neat even when he was riding post.* He did look neat,
and he was so deeply concerned about his appearance before
he started that he quite forgot to take anything but some small
change with him. He left all his notes at the hotel. His
servants had gone down the road before him, to be ready in

waiting at Pathankote* with a change of gear. That was what
he called travelling in 'light marching-order.' He was proud
of his faculty of organisation—what we call *bundobust*.

Twenty-two miles out of Dalhousie it began to rain—not a
mere Hill-shower, but a good, tepid, monsoonish downpour.
Golightly bustled on, wishing that he had brought an
umbrella. The dust on the roads turned into mud, and the
pony mired a good deal. So did Golightly's *khaki* gaiters. But
he kept on steadily and tried to think how pleasant the coolth
was.

His next pony was rather a brute at starting, and,
Golightly's hands being slippery with the rain, contrived to
get rid of Golightly at a corner. He chased the animal, caught
it, and went ahead briskly. The spill had not improved his
clothes or his temper, and he had lost one spur. He kept the
other one employed. By the time that stage was ended the
pony had had as much exercise as he wanted, and, in spite
of the rain, Golightly was sweating freely. At the end of
another miserable half hour Golightly found the world
disappear before his eyes in clammy pulp. The rain had
turned the pith of his huge and snowy *solah-topee** into an evil-
smelling dough, and it had closed on his head like a half-
opened mushroom. Also the green lining was beginning to
run.

Golightly did not say anything worth recording here. He
tore off and squeezed up as much of the brim as was in his
eyes and ploughed on. The back of the helmet was flapping
on his neck, and the sides stuck to his ears, but the leather
band and green lining kept things roughly together, so that
the hat did not actually melt away where it flapped.

Presently, the pulp and the green stuff made a sort of slimy
mildew which ran over Golightly in several directions—down
his back and bosom for choice. The *khaki* colour ran too—it
was really shocking bad dye—and sections of Golightly were
brown, and patches were violet, and contours were ochre, and
streaks were brick-red, and blotches were nearly white,
according to the nature and peculiarities of the dye. When he
took out his handkerchief to wipe his face, and the green of
the hat-lining and the purple stuff that had soaked through on

to his neck from the tie became thoroughly mixed, the effect was amazing.

Near Dhar the rain stopped and the evening sun came out and dried him up slightly. It fixed the colours, too. Three miles from Pathankote the last pony fell dead lame, and Golightly was forced to walk. He pushed on into Pathankote to find his servants. He did not know then that his *khitmutgar** had stopped by the roadside to get drunk, and would come on the next day saying that he had sprained his ankle. When he got into Pathankote he couldn't find his servants, his boots were stiff and ropy with mud, and there were large quantities of dust about his body. The blue tie had run as much as the *khaki*. So he took it off with the collar and threw it away. Then he said something about servants generally and tried to get a peg. He paid eight annas for the drink, and this revealed to him that he had only six annas more in his pocket—or in the world as he stood at that hour.

He went to the Station-Master to negotiate for a first-class ticket to Khasa,* where he was stationed. The booking-clerk said something to the Station-Master, the Station-Master said something to the Telegraph Clerk, and the three looked at him with curiosity. They asked him to wait for half an hour, while they telegraphed to Umritsar for authority. So he waited and four constables came and grouped themselves picturesquely round him. Just as he was preparing to ask them to go away, the Station-Master said that he would give the *Sahib* a ticket to Umritsar, if the *Sahib* would kindly come inside the booking-office. Golightly stepped inside, and the next thing he knew was that a constable was attached to each of his legs and arms, while the Station-Master was trying to cram a mail-bag over his head.

There was a very fair scuffle all round the booking-office, and Golightly took a nasty cut over his eye through falling against a table. But the constables were too much for him, and they and the Station-Master handcuffed him securely. As soon as the mail-bag was slipped, he began expressing his opinions, and the head constable said, 'Without doubt this is the soldier-Englishman we required. Listen to the abuse!' Then Golightly asked the Station-Master what the this and the that the proceedings meant. The Station-Master told him he was 'Private John Binkle of the——Regiment, 5 ft. 9 in., fair hair, gray eyes, and a dissipated appearance, no marks on the body,' who had deserted a fortnight ago. Golightly began explaining at great length; and the more he explained the less the Station-Master believed him. He said that no Lieutenant could look such a ruffian as did Golightly, and that his instructions were to send his capture under proper escort to Umritsar. Golightly was feeling very damp and uncomfortable, and the language he used was not fit for publication, even in an expurgated form. The four constables saw him safe to Umritsar in an 'intermediate' compartment,* and he spent the four-hour journey in abusing them as fluently as his knowledge of the vernaculars allowed.

At Umritsar he was bundled out on the platform into the arms of a Corporal and two men of the——Regiment. Golightly drew himself up and tried to carry off matters jauntily. He did not feel too jaunty in handcuffs, with four constables behind him, and the blood from the cut on his forehead stiffening on his left cheek. The Corporal was not jocular either. Golightly got as far as—'This is a very absurd mistake, my men,' when the Corporal told him to 'stow his lip' and come along. Golightly did not want to come along. He explained very well indeed, until the Corporal cut in with— 'You a orficer! It's the like o' you as brings disgrace on the likes of us. Bloomin' fine orficer you are! I know your regiment. The Rogue's March* is the quickstep where you come from. You're a black shame to the Service.'

Golightly kept his temper, and began explaining all over again from the beginning. Then he was marched out of the rain into the refreshment-room, and told not to make a qualified fool of himself. The men were going to run him up to Fort Govindghar. And 'running up' is a performance almost as undignified as the Frog March.

Golightly was nearly hysterical with rage and the chill and the mistake and the handcuffs and headache that the cut on his forehead had given him. He really laid himself out to express what was in his mind. When he had quite finished and his throat was feeling dry, one of the men said, 'I've 'eard a

few beggars in the clink* blind, stiff and crack on a bit;* but
I've never 'eard any one to touch this 'ere "orficer." ' They
were not angry with him. They rather admired him. They had
some beer at the refreshment-room, and offered Golightly
some too, because he had 'swore won'erful'. They asked him
to tell them all about the adventures of Private John Binkle
while he was loose on the country-side; and that made
Golightly wilder than ever. If he had kept his wits about him
he would have been quiet until an officer came; but he
attempted to run.

Now the butt of a Martini* in the small of your back hurts
a great deal, and rotten, rain-soaked *khaki* tears easily when
two men are yerking at your collar.

Golightly rose from the floor feeling very sick and giddy,
with his shirt ripped open all down his breast and nearly all
down his back. He yielded to his luck, and at that point the
down-train from Lahore came in, carrying one of Golightly's
Majors.

This is the Major's evidence in full—

'There was the sound of a scuffle in the second-class
refreshment-room, so I went in and saw the most villainous
loafer that I ever set eyes on. His boots and breeches were
plastered with mud and beer-stains. He wore a muddy-white
dunghill sort of thing on his head, and it hung down in slips
on his shoulders which were a good deal scratched. He was
half in and half out of a shirt as nearly in two pieces as it could
be, and he was begging the guard to look at the name on the
tail of it. As he had rucked the shirt all over his head I couldn't
at first see who he was, but I fancied that he was a man in the
first stage of D.T. from the way he swore while he wrestled
with his rags. When he turned round, and I had made
allowances for a lump as big as a pork-pie over one eye, and
some green war-paint on the face, and some violet stripes
round the neck, I saw that it was Golightly. He was very glad
to see me,' said the Major, 'and he hoped I would not tell the
Mess about it. *I* didn't, but you can, if you like, now that
Golightly has gone Home.'

Golightly spent the greater part of that summer in trying to
get the Corporal and the two soldiers tried by Court-Martial

for arresting an 'officer and a gentleman.' They were, of course, very sorry for their error. But the tale leaked into the regimental canteen, and thence ran about the Province.

In the House of Suddhoo*

A stone's throw out on either hand
From that well-ordered road we tread,
  And all the world is wild and strange:
Churel* and ghoul and Djinn* and sprite
Shall bear us company to-night,
For we have reached the Oldest Land
  Wherein the Powers of Darkness range.
                From the Dusk to the Dawn.

THE house of Suddhoo, near the Taksali Gate,* is two
storeyed, with four carved windows of old brown wood, and
a flat roof. You may recognise it by five red hand-prints
arranged like the Five of Diamonds on the whitewash between
the upper windows. Bhagwan Dass the grocer and a man who
says he gets his living by seal-cutting live in the lower storey
with a troop of wives, servants, friends, and retainers. The
two upper rooms used to be occupied by Janoo and Azizun,
and a little black-and-tan terrier that was stolen from an
Englishman's house and given to Janoo by a soldier. To-day,
only Janoo lives in the upper rooms. Suddhoo sleeps on the
roof generally, except when he sleeps in the street. He used
to go to Peshawar in the cold weather to visit his son who sells
curiosities near the Edwardes' Gate,* and then he slept under
a real mud roof. Suddhoo is a great friend of mine, because
his cousin had a son who secured, thanks to my
recommendation, the post of head-messenger to a big firm in
the Station. Suddhoo says that God will make me a
Lieutenant-Governor one of these days. I daresay his
prophecy will come true. He is very, very old, with white hair
and no teeth worth showing, and he has outlived his wits—
outlived nearly everything except his fondness for his son
at Peshawar. Janoo and Azizun are Kashmiris, Ladies of the
City, and theirs was an ancient and more or less honourable
profession; but Azizun has since married a medical student
from the North-West and has settled down to a most

respectable life somewhere near Bareilly. Bhagwan Dass is an extortioner and an adulterator. He is very rich. The man who is supposed to get his living by seal-cutting pretends to be very poor. This lets you know as much as is necessary of the four principal tenants in the house of Suddhoo. Then there is Me of course; but I am only the chorus that comes in at the end to explain things. So I do not count.

Suddhoo was not clever. The man who pretended to cut seals was the cleverest of them all—Bhagwan Dass only knew how to lie—except Janoo. She was also beautiful, but that was her own affair.

Suddhoo's son at Peshawar was attacked by pleurisy, and old Suddhoo was troubled. The seal-cutter man heard of Suddhoo's anxiety and made capital out of it. He was abreast of the times. He got a friend in Peshawar to telegraph daily accounts of the son's health. And here the story begins.

Suddhoo's cousin's son told me, one evening, that Suddhoo wanted to see me; that he was too old and feeble to come personally, and that I should be conferring an everlasting honour on the House of Suddhoo if I went to him. I went; but I think, seeing how well off Suddhoo was then, that he might have sent something better than an *ekka*,* which jolted fearfully, to haul out a future Lieutenant-Governor to the City on a muggy April evening. The *ekka* did not run quickly. It was full dark when we pulled up opposite the door of Ranjit Singh's* Tomb near the main gate of the Fort. Here was Suddhoo, and he said that by reason of my condescension, it was absolutely certain that I should become a Lieutenant-Governor while my hair was yet black. Then we talked about the weather and the state of my health, and the wheat crops, for fifteen minutes, in the Huzuri Bagh,* under the stars.

Suddhoo came to the point at last. He said that Janoo had told him that there was an order of the *Sirkar** against magic, because it was feared that magic might one day kill the Empress of India. I didn't know anything about the state of the law; but I fancied that something interesting was going to happen. I said that so far from magic being discouraged by the Government it was highly commended. The greatest officials of the State practised it themselves. (If the Financial

Statement* isn't magic, I don't know what is.) Then, to encourage him further, I said that, if there was any *jadoo*** afoot, I had not the least objection to giving it my countenance and sanction, and to seeing that it was clean *jadoo*—white magic, as distinguished from the unclean *jadoo* which kills folk. It took a long time before Suddhoo admitted that this was just what he had asked me to come for. Then he told me, in jerks and quavers, that the man who said he cut seals was a sorcerer of the cleanest kind; that every day he gave Suddhoo news of the sick son in Peshawar more quickly than the lightning could fly, and that this news was always corroborated by the letters. Further, that he had told Suddhoo how a great danger was threatening his son, which could be removed by clean *jadoo*; and, of course, heavy payment. I began to see exactly how the land lay, and told Suddhoo that I also understood a little *jadou* in the Western line, and would go to his house to see that everything was done decently and in order. We set off together; and on the way Suddhoo told me that he had paid the seal-cutter between one hundred and two hundred rupees already; and the *jadoo* of that night would cost two hundred more. Which was cheap, he said, considering the greatness of his son's danger; but I do not think he meant it.

The lights were all cloaked in the front of the house when we arrived. I could hear awful noises from behind the seal-cutter's shop-front, as if some one were groaning his soul out. Suddhoo shook all over, and while we groped our way upstairs told me that the *jadoo* had begun. Janoo and Azizun met us at the stair-head, and told us that the *jadoo*-work was coming off in their rooms, because there was more space there. Janoo is a lady of a free-thinking turn of mind. She whispered that the *jadoo* was an invention to get money out of Suddhoo, and that the seal-cutter would go to a hot place when he died. Suddhoo was nearly crying with fear and old age. He kept walking up and down the room in the half-light, repeating his son's name over and over again, and asking Azizun if the seal-cutter ought not to make a reduction in the case of his own landlord. Janoo pulled me over to the shadow in the recess of the carved bow-windows. The boards were up, and the rooms were only lit by one tiny oil-lamp. There was no chance of my being seen if I stayed still.

Presently, the groans below ceased, and we heard steps on the staircase. That was the seal-cutter. He stopped outside the door as the terrier barked and Azizun fumbled at the chain, and he told Suddhoo to blow out the lamp. This left the place in jet darkness, except for the red glow from the two *huqas* that belonged to Janoo and Azizun. The seal-cutter came in, and I heard Suddhoo throw himself down on the floor and groan. Azizun caught her breath, and Janoo backed on to one of the beds with a shudder. There was a clink of something metallic, and then shot up a pale blue-green flame near the ground. The light was just enough to show Azizun, pressed against one corner of the room with the terrier between her knees; Janoo, with her hands clasped, leaning forward as she sat on the bed; Suddhoo, face-down, quivering, and the seal-cutter.

I hope I may never see another man like that seal-cutter. He was stripped to the waist, with a wreath of white jasmine as thick as my wrist round his forehead, a salmon coloured loin-cloth round his middle, and a steel bangle on each ankle. This was not awe-inspiring. It was the face of the man that turned me cold. It was blue-gray in the first place. In the second, the eyes were rolled back till you could only see the whites of them; and, in the third, the face was the face of a demon—a ghoul—anything you please except of the sleek, oily old ruffian who sat in the daytime over his turning-lathe downstairs. He was lying on his stomach with his arms turned and crossed behind him, as if he had been thrown down pinioned. His head and neck were the only parts of him off the floor. They were nearly at right angles to the body, like the head of a cobra at spring. It was ghastly. In the centre of the room, on the bare earth floor, stood a big, deep, brass basin, with a pale blue-green light floating in the centre like a night-light. Round that basin the man on the floor wriggled himself three times. How he did it I do not know. I could see the muscles ripple along his spine and fall smooth again; but I could not see any other motion. The head seemed the only thing alive about him, except that slow curl and uncurl of the labouring back-muscles. Janoo from the bed was breathing seventy to the minute; Azizun held her hands before her eyes; and old Suddhoo, fingering at the dirt that had got into his white beard, was crying to himself. The horror of it was that the creeping, crawly thing made no sound—only crawled! And, remember, this lasted for ten minutes, while the terrier whined, and Azizun shuddered, and Janoo gasped, and Suddhoo cried!

I felt the hair lift at the back of my head, and my heart thump like a thermantidote* paddle. Luckily, the seal-cutter betrayed himself by his most impressive trick and made me calm again. After he had finished that unspeakable triple crawl, he stretched his head away from the floor as high as he could, and sent out a jet of fire from his nostrils. Now, I knew how fire-spouting is done—I can do it myself—so I felt at ease. The business was a fraud. If he had only kept to that crawl without trying to raise the effect, goodness knows what I might not have thought. Both the girls shrieked at the jet of fire and the head dropped, chin-down on the floor, with a thud; the whole body lying then like a corpse with its arms trussed. There was a pause of five full minutes after this, and the blue-green flame died down. Janoo stooped to settle one of her anklets, while Azizun turned her face to the wall and took the terrier in her arms. Suddhoo put out an arm mechanically to Janoo's *huqa*, and she slid it across the floor with her foot. Directly above the body and on the wall were a couple of flaming portraits, in stamped-paper frames, of the Queen and the Prince of Wales. They looked down on the performance, and to my thinking, seemed to heighten the grotesqueness of it all.

Just when the silence was getting unendurable, the body turned over and rolled away from the basin to the side of the room, where it lay stomach-up. There was a faint 'plop' from the basin—exactly like the noise a fish makes when it takes a fly—and the green light in the centre revived.

I looked at the basin, and saw, bobbing in the water, the dried, shrivelled, black head of a native baby—open eyes, open mouth, and shaved scalp. It was worse, being so very sudden, than the crawling exhibition. We had no time to say anything before it began to speak.

Read Poe's account* of the voice that came from the mesmerised dying man, and you will realise less than one-half of the horror of that head's voice.

There was an interval of a second or two between each word, and a sort of 'ring, ring, ring,' in the note of the voice, like the timbre of a bell. It pealed slowly, as if talking to itself, for several minutes before I got rid of my cold sweat. Then the blessed solution struck me. I looked at the body lying near the doorway, and saw, just where the hollow of the throat joins on the shoulders, a muscle that had nothing to do with any man's regular breathing twitching away steadily. The whole thing was a careful reproduction of the Egyptian teraphim* that one reads about sometimes; and the voice was as clever and as appalling a piece of ventriloquism as one could wish to hear. All this time the head was 'lip-lip-lapping' against the side of the basin, and speaking. It told Suddhoo, on his face again whining, of his son's illness and of the state of the illness up to the evening of that very night. I always shall respect the seal-cutter for keeping so faithfully to the time of the Peshawar telegrams. It went on to say that skilled doctors were night and day watching over the man's life; and that he would eventually recover if the fee to the potent sorcerer, whose servant was the head in the basin, were doubled.

Here the mistake from the artistic point of view came in. To ask for twice your stipulated fee in a voice that Lazarus* might have used when he rose from the dead, is absurd. Janoo, who is really a woman of masculine intellect, saw this as quickly as I did, I heard her say '*Asli nahin! Fareib!*'* scornfully under her breath; and just as she said so the light in the basin died out, the head stopped talking, and we heard the room door creak on its hinges. Then Janoo struck a match, lit the lamp, and we saw that head, basin, and seal-cutter were gone. Suddhoo was wringing his hands, and explaining to any one who cared to listen, that, if his chances of eternal salvation depended on it, he could not raise another two hundred rupees. Azizun was nearly in hysterics in the corner; while Janoo sat down composedly on one of the beds to discuss the probabilities of the whole thing being a *bunao*, or 'make-up.'

I explained as much as I knew of the seal-cutter's way of *jadoo*; but her argument was much more simple—'The magic that is always demanding gifts is no true magic,' said she. 'My mother told me that the only potent love-spells are those which are told you for love. This seal-cutter man is a liar and a devil. I dare not tell, do anything, or get anything done, because I am in debt to Bhagwan Dass the *bunnia** for two gold rings and a heavy anklet. I must get my food from his shop. The seal-cutter is the friend of Bhagwan Dass, and he would poison my food. A fool's *jadoo* has been going on for ten days, and has cost Suddhoo many rupees each night. The seal-cutter used black hens and lemons and *mantras** before. He never showed us anything like this till to-night. Azizun is a fool, and will be a *purdahnashin** soon. Suddhoo has lost his strength and his wits. See now! I had hoped to get from Suddhoo many rupees while he lived, and many more after his death; and behold, he is spending everything on that offspring of a devil and a she-ass, the seal-cutter!'

Here I said, 'But what induced Suddhoo to drag me into the business? Of course I can speak to the seal-cutter, and he shall refund. The whole thing is child's talk—shame—and senseless.'

'Suddhoo *is* an old child,' said Janoo. 'He has lived on the roofs these seventy years and is as senseless as a milch-goat. He brought you here to assure himself that he was not breaking any law of the *Sirkar*, whose salt he ate many years ago. He worships the dust off the feet of the seal-cutter, and that cow-devourer* has forbidden him to go and see his son. What does Suddhoo know of your laws or the lightning-post? I have to watch his money going day by day to that lying beast below.'

Janoo stamped her foot on the floor and nearly cried with vexation; while Suddhoo was whimpering under a blanket in the corner, and Azizun was trying to guide the pipe-stem to his foolish old mouth.

*   *   *

Now, the case stands thus. Unthinkingly, I have laid myself open to the charge of aiding and abetting the seal-cutter in

obtaining money under false pretences, which is forbidden by
Section 420 of the Indian Penal Code. I am helpless in the
matter for these reasons. I cannot inform the Police. What
witnesses would support my statements? Janoo refuses flatly,
and Azizun is a veiled woman somewhere near Bareilly—lost
in this big India of ours. I dare not again take the law into my
own hands, and speak to the seal-cutter; for certain am I that,
not only would Suddhoo disbelieve me, but this step would
end in the poisoning of Janoo, who is bound hand and foot by
her debt to the *bunnia*. Suddhoo is an old dotard; and
whenever we meet mumbles my idiotic joke that the *Sirkar*
rather patronises the Black Art than otherwise. His son is well
now; but Suddhoo is completely under the influence of the
seal-cutter, by whose advice he regulates the affairs of his life.
Janoo watches daily the money that she hoped to wheedle out
of Suddhoo taken by the seal-cutter, and becomes daily more
furious and sullen.

She will never tell, because she dare not; but, unless
something happens to prevent her, I am afraid that the seal-
cutter will die of cholera—the white arsenic kind—about the
middle of May. And thus I shall be privy to a murder in the
House of Suddhoo.

His Wedded Wife*

Cry 'Murder!' in the market-place, and each
Will turn upon his neighbour anxious eyes
That ask—'Art thou the man?' We hunted Cain,
Some centuries ago, across the world.
That bred the fear our own misdeeds maintain
To-day.

Vibart's Moralities.

SHAKESPEARE says something about worms, or it may be
giants or beetles,* turning if you tread on them too severely.
The safest plan is never to tread on a worm—not even on the
last new subaltern from Home, with his buttons hardly out of
their tissue-paper, and the red of sappy English beef in his
cheeks. This is a story of the worm that turned. For the sake
of brevity, we will call Henry Augustus Ramsay Faizanne
'The Worm,' though he really was an exceedingly pretty boy,
without a hair on his face, and with a waist like a girl's, when
he came out to the Second 'Shikarris'* and was made unhappy
in several ways. The 'Shikarris' are a high-caste regiment, and
you must be able to do things well—play a banjo, or ride more
than a little, or sing, or act,—to get on with them.

The Worm did nothing except fall off his pony, and knock
chips out of gate-posts with his trap. Even that became
monotonous after a time. He objected to whist, cut the cloth
at billiards, sang out of tune, kept very much to himself, and
wrote to his Mamma and sisters at Home. Four of these five
things were vices which the 'Shikarris' objected to and set
themselves to eradicate. Every one knows how subalterns are,
by brother subalterns, softened and not permitted to be
ferocious. It is good and wholesome, and does no one any
harm, unless tempers are lost; and then there is trouble. There
was a man once—

The 'Shikarris' *shikarred* The Worm very much, and he
bore everything without winking. He was so good and so
anxious to learn, and flushed so pink, that his education was

cut short, and he was left to his own devices by every one
except the Senior Subaltern, who continued to make life a
burden to The Worm. The Senior Subaltern meant no harm;
but his chaff was coarse and he didn't quite understand where
to stop. He had been waiting too long for his Company; and
that always sours a man. Also he was in love, which made him
worse.

One day, after he had borrowed The Worm's trap for a lady
who never existed, had used it himself all the afternoon, had
sent a note to The Worm, purporting to come from the lady,
and was telling the Mess all about it, The Worm rose in his
place and said, in his quiet, lady-like voice—'That was a very
pretty sell; but I'll lay you a month's pay to a month's pay
when you get your step, that I work a sell on you that you'll
remember for the rest of your days, and the Regiment after
you when you're dead or broke.'* The Worm wasn't angry in
the least, and the rest of the Mess shouted. Then the Senior
Subaltern looked at The Worm from the boots upwards, and
down again, and said—'Done, Baby.' The Worm held the rest
of the Mess to witness that the bet had been taken, and retired
into a book with a sweet smile.

Two months passed, and the Senior Subaltern still educated
The Worm, who began to move about a little more as the hot
weather came on. I have said that the Senior Subaltern was in
love. The curious thing is that a girl was in love with the
Senior Subaltern. Though the Colonel said awful things, and
the Majors snorted, and the married Captains looked
unutterable wisdom, and the juniors scoffed, those two were
engaged.

The Senior Subaltern was so pleased with getting his
Company and his acceptance at the same time that he forgot
to bother The Worm. The girl was a pretty girl, and had
money of her own. She does not come into this story at all.

One night, at the beginning of the hot weather, all the Mess,
except The Worm, who had gone to his own room to write
Home letters, were sitting on the platform outside the Mess
House. The Band had finished playing, but no one wanted to
go in. And the Captains' wives were there also. The folly of
a man in love is unlimited. The Senior Subaltern had been

holding forth on the merits of the girl he was engaged to, and the ladies were purring approval while the men yawned, when there was a rustle of skirts in the dark, and a tired, faint voice lifted itself.

'Where's my husband?'

I do not wish in the least to reflect on the morality of the 'Shikarris'; but it is on record that four men jumped up as if they had been shot. Three of them were married men. Perhaps they were afraid that their wives had come from Home unbeknownst. The fourth said that he had acted on the impulse of the moment. He explained this afterwards.

Then the voice cried, 'Oh, Lionel!' Lionel was the Senior Subaltern's name. A woman came into the little circle of light by the candles on the peg-tables, stretching out her hands to the dark where the Senior Subaltern was, and sobbing. We rose to our feet, feeling that things were going to happen and ready to believe the worst. In this bad, small world of ours, one knows so little of the life of the next man—which, after all, is entirely his own concern—that one is not surprised when a crash comes. Anything might turn up any day for any one. Perhaps the Senior Subaltern had been trapped in his youth. Men are crippled that way occasionally. We didn't know; we wanted to hear; and the Captains' wives were as anxious as we. If he had been trapped he was to be excused; for the woman from nowhere, in the dusty shoes and gray travelling-dress, was very lovely, with black hair and great eyes full of tears. She was tall, with a fine figure, and her voice had a running sob in it pitiful to hear. As soon as the Senior Subaltern stood up, she threw her arms round his neck, and called him 'my darling,' and said she could not bear waiting alone in England, and his letters were so short and cold, and she was his to the end of the world, and would he forgive her? This did not sound quite like a lady's way of speaking. It was too demonstrative.

Things seemed black indeed, and the Captains' wives peered under their eyebrows at the Senior Subaltern, and the Colonel's face set like the Day of Judgment framed in gray bristles, and no one spoke for a while.

Next the Colonel said, very shortly, 'Well, Sir?' and the

woman sobbed afresh. The Senior Subaltern was half choked
with the arms round his neck, but he gasped out—'It's a
damned lie! I never had a wife in my life!'—'Don't swear,' said
the Colonel. 'Come into the Mess. We must sift this clear
somehow,' and he sighed to himself, for he believed in his
'Shikarris,' did the Colonel.

We trooped into the ante-room, under the full lights and
there we saw how beautiful the woman was. She stood up in
the middle of us all, sometimes choking with crying, then hard
and proud, and then holding out her arms to the Senior
Subaltern. It was like the fourth act of a tragedy. She told us
how the Senior Subaltern had married her when he was Home
on leave eighteen months before; and she seemed to know all
that we knew, and more too, of his people and his past life.
He was white and ashy-gray, trying now and again to break
into the torrent of her words; and we, noting how lovely she
was and what a criminal he looked, esteemed him a beast of
the worst kind. We felt sorry for him, though.

I shall never forget the indictment of the Senior Subaltern
by his wife. Nor will he. It was so sudden, rushing out of the
dark, unannounced, into our dull lives. The Captains' wives
stood back; but their eyes were alight, and you could see that
they had already convicted and sentenced the Senior
Subaltern. The Colonel seemed five years older. One Major
was shading his eyes with his hand and watching the woman
from underneath it. Another was chewing his moustache and
smiling quietly as if he were witnessing a play. Full in the
open space in the centre, by the whist-tables, the Senior
Subaltern's terrier was hunting for fleas. I remember all this
as clearly as though a photograph were in my hand. I
remember the look of horror on the Senior Subaltern's face.
It was rather like seeing a man hanged, but much more
interesting. Finally, the woman wound up by saying that the
Senior Subaltern carried a double F. M. in tattoo on his left
shoulder. We all knew that, and to our innocent minds it
seemed to clinch the matter. But one of the bachelor Majors
said very politely, 'I presume that your marriage-certificate
would be more to the purpose?'

That roused the woman. She stood up and sneered at the

Senior Subaltern for a cur, and abused the Major and the
Colonel and all the rest. Then she wept, and then she pulled
a paper from her breast, saying imperially, 'Take that! And let
my husband—my lawfully wedded husband—read it aloud—if
he dare!'

There was a hush, and the men looked into each other's eyes
as the Senior Subaltern came forward in a dazed and dizzy
way, and took the paper. We were wondering, as we stared,
whether there was anything against any one of us that might
turn up later on. The Senior Subaltern's throat was dry; but,
as he ran his eye over the paper, he broke out into a hoarse
cackle of relief, and said to the woman, 'You young
blackguard!' But the woman had fled through a door, and on
the paper was written, 'This is to certify that I, The Worm,
have paid in full my debts to the Senior Subaltern, and,
further, that the Senior Subaltern is my debtor, by agreement
on the 23rd of February, as by the Mess attested, to the extent
of one month's Captain's pay, in the lawful currency of the
Indian Empire.'

Then a deputation set off for The Worm's quarters, and
found him, betwixt and between, unlacing his stays, with the
hat, wig, and serge dress, on the bed. He came over as he was,
and the 'Shikarris' shouted till the Gunners' Mess sent over
to know if they might have a share of the fun. I think we were
all, except the Colonel and the Senior Subaltern, a little
disappointed that the scandal had come to nothing. But that
is human nature. There could be no two words about The
Worm's acting. It leaned as near to a nasty tragedy as anything
this side of a joke can. When most of the Subalterns sat upon
him with sofa-cushions to find out why he had not said that
acting was his strong point, he answered very quietly, 'I don't
think you ever asked me. I used to act at Home with my
sisters.' But no acting with girls could account for The
Worm's display that night. Personally, I think it was in bad
taste; besides being dangerous. There is no sort of use in
playing with fire, even for fun.

The 'Shikarris' made him President of the Regimental
Dramatic Club; and, when the Senior Subaltern paid up his
debt, which he did at once, The Worm sank the money in

scenery and dresses. He was a good Worm; and the 'Shikarris' are proud of him. The only drawback is that he has been christened 'Mrs. Senior Subaltern'; and, as there are now two Mrs. Senior Subalterns in the Station, this is sometimes confusing to strangers.

Later on, I will tell you of a case something like this,* but with all the jest left out and nothing in it but real trouble.

The Broken-Link Handicap*

While the snaffle holds, or the long-neck* stings,
While the big beam tilts,* or the last bell rings,
While horses are horses to train and to race,
Then women and wine take second place
        For me—for me—
        While a short 'ten-three'*
Has a field to squander or fence to face!
        *Song of the G. R.**

THÉRE are more ways of running a horse* to suit your book than pulling his head off in the straight. Some men forget this. Understand clearly that all racing is rotten—as everything connected with losing money must be. In India, in addition to its inherent rottenness, it has the merit of being two-thirds sham; looking pretty on paper only. Every one knows every one else far too well for business purposes. How on earth can you rack and harry and post a man for his losings, when you are fond of his wife, and live in the same Station with him? He says, 'On the Monday following,' 'I can't settle just yet.' You say, 'All right, old man,' and think yourself lucky if you pull off nine hundred out of a two-thousand-rupee debt. Any way you look at it, Indian racing is immoral, and expensively immoral; which is much worse. If a man wants your money he ought to ask for it, or send round a subscription-list, instead of juggling about the country with an Australian larrikin;* a 'brumby,'* with as much breed as the boy; a brace of *chumars** in gold-laced caps; three or four *ekka*-ponies* with hogged manes, and a switch-tailed demirep* of a mare called Arab because she has a kink in her flag.* Racing leads to the *shroff** quicker than anything else. But if you have no conscience and no sentiments, and good hands, and some knowledge of pace, and ten years' experience of horses, and several thousand rupees a month, I believe that you can occasionally contrive to pay your shoeing-bills.

Did you ever know Shackles—b. w. g., 15.1⅜*—coarse,

loose, mule-like ears—barrel as long as a gate-post—tough as a telegraph-wire—and the queerest brute that ever looked through a bridle? He was of no brand, being one of an ear-nicked mob taken into the *Bucephalus* at £4:10s. a head to make up freight, and sold raw and out of condition at Calcutta for Rs.275. People who lost money on him called him a 'brumby'; but if ever any horse had Harpoon's shoulders and The Gin's* temper, Shackles was that horse. Two miles was his own particular distance. He trained himself, ran himself, and rode himself; and, if his jockey insulted him by giving him hints, he shut up at once and bucked the boy off. He objected to dictation. Two or three of his owners did not understand this, and lost money in consequence. At last he was bought by a man who discovered that, if a race was to be won, Shackles, and Shackles only, would win it in his own way, so long as his jockey sat still. This man had a riding-boy called Brunt—a lad from Perth, West Australia—and he taught Brunt, with a trainer's whip, the hardest thing a jock can learn—to sit still, to sit still, and to keep on sitting still. When Brunt fairly grasped this truth, Shackles devastated the country. No weight could stop him at his own distance; and the fame of Shackles spread from Ajmir* in the South, to Chedputter* in the North. There was no horse like Shackles, so long as he was allowed to do his work in his own way. But he was beaten in the end; and the story of his fall is enough to make angels weep.

At the lower end of the Chedputter race-course, just before the turn into the straight, the track passes close to a couple of old brick-mounds enclosing a funnel-shaped hollow. The big end of the funnel is not six feet from the railings on the off-side. The astounding peculiarity of the course is that, if you stand at one particular place, about half a mile away, inside the course, and speak at ordinary pitch, your voice just hits the funnel of the brick-mounds and makes a curious whining echo there. A man discovered this one morning by accident while out training with a friend. He marked the place to stand and speak from with a couple of bricks, and he kept his knowledge to himself. *Every* peculiarity of a course is worth remembering in a country where rats play the mischief with

the elephant-litter, and Stewards* build jumps to suit their
own stables. This man ran a very fairish country-bred,* a
long, racking high mare with the temper of a fiend, and the
paces of an airy wandering seraph—a drifty, glidy stretch. The
mare was, as a delicate tribute to Mrs. Reiver, called 'The
Lady Regula Baddun'—or for short, Regula Baddun.

Shackles' jockey, Brunt, was a quite well-behaved boy, but
his nerve had been shaken. He began his career by riding
jump-races in Melbourne, where a few Stewards want
lynching, and was one of the jockeys who came through the
awful butchery—perhaps you will recollect it—of the
Maribyrnong Plate. The walls were colonial ramparts—logs of
*jarrah** spiked into masonry—with wings as strong as Church
buttresses. Once in his stride, a horse had to jump or fall. He
couldn't run out. In the Maribyrnong Plate twelve horses
were jammed at the second wall. Red Hat, leading, fell this
side, and threw out The Gled, and the ruck came up behind
and the space between wing and wing was one struggling,
screaming, kicking shambles. Four jockeys were taken out
dead; three were very badly hurt, and Brunt was among the
three. He told the story of the Maribyrnong Plate sometimes;
and when he described how Whalley on Red Hat said, as the
mare fell under him—'God ha' mercy, I'm done for!' and how,
next instant, Sithee There and White Otter had crushed the
life out of poor Whalley, and the dust hid a small hell of men
and horses, no one marvelled that Brunt had dropped jump-
races and Australia together. Regula Baddun's owner knew
that story by heart. Brunt never varied it in the telling. He had
no education.

Shackles came to the Chedputter Autumn races one year,
and his owner walked about insulting the sportsmen of
Chedputter generally, till they went to the Honorary Secretary
in a body and said, 'Appoint handicappers, and arrange a race
which shall break Shackles and humble the pride of his owner.'
The Districts rose against Shackles and sent up of their best:
Ousel, who was supposed to be able to do his mile in 1-53;*
Petard, the stud-bred, trained by a cavalry regiment who knew
how to train; Gringalet, the ewe-lamb of the 75th; Bobolink,
the pride of Peshawar; and many others.

They called that race The Broken-Link Handicap, because it was to smash Shackles; and the Handicappers piled on the weights, and the Fund gave eight hundred rupees, and the distance was 'round the course for all horses.' Shackles' owner said, 'You can arrange the race with regard to Shackles only. So long as you don't bury him under weight-cloths, I don't mind.' Regula Baddun's owner said, 'I throw in my mare to fret Ousel. Six furlongs is Regula's distance, and she will then lie down and die. So also will Ousel, for his jockey doesn't understand a waiting race.' Now, this was a lie, for Regula had been in work for two months at Dehra, and her chances were good, always supposing that Shackles broke a blood-vessel—or Brunt moved on him.

The plunging in the lotteries* was fine. They filled eight thousand-rupee lotteries on the Broken-Link Handicap, and the account in the *Pioneer* said that 'favouritism was divided.' In plain English, the various contingents were wild on their respective horses; for the Handicappers had done their work well. The Honorary Secretary shouted himself hoarse through the din; and the smoke of the cheroots was like the smoke, and the rattling of the dice-boxes like the rattle of small-arm fire.

Ten horses started—very level—and Regula Baddun's owner cantered out on his hack to a place inside the circle of the course, where two bricks had been thrown. He faced towards the brick-mounds at the lower end of the course and waited.

The story of the running is in the *Pioneer*. At the end of the first mile, Shackles crept out of the ruck, well on the outside, ready to get round the turn, lay hold of the bit and spin up the straight before the others knew he had got away. Brunt was sitting still, perfectly happy, listening to the 'drum-drum-drum' of the hoofs behind, and knowing that, in about twenty strides, Shackles would draw one deep breath and go up the last half-mile like the Flying Dutchman. As Shackles went short to take the turn and came abreast of the brick-mound, Brunt heard, above the noise of the wind in his ears, a whining, wailing voice on the offside, saying—'God ha' mercy, I'm done for!' In one stride, Brunt saw the whole seething smash of the Maribyrnong Plate before him, started in his saddle, and gave a yell of terror. The start brought the heels into Shackles' side, and the scream hurt Shackles' feelings. He couldn't stop dead; but he put out his feet and slid along for fifty yards, and then, very gravely and judicially, bucked off Brunt—a shaking, terror-stricken lump—while Regula Baddun made a neck-and-neck race with Bobolink up the straight, and won by a short head—Petard a bad third. Shackles' owner, in the Stand, tried to think that his field-glasses had gone wrong. Regula Baddun's owner, waiting by the two bricks, gave one deep sigh of relief, and cantered back to the Stand. He had won, in lotteries and bets, about fifteen thousand.

It was a Broken-link Handicap with a vengeance. It broke nearly all the men concerned, and nearly broke the heart of Shackles' owner. He went down to interview Brunt. The boy lay, livid and gasping with fright, where he had tumbled off. The sin of losing the race never seemed to strike him. All he knew was that Whalley had 'called' him, that the 'call' was a warning; and, were he cut in two for it, he would never get up again. His nerve had gone altogether, and he only asked his master to give him a good thrashing, and let him go. He was fit for nothing, he said. He got his dismissal, and crept up to the paddock, white as chalk, with blue lips, his knees giving way under him. People said nasty things in the paddock; but Brunt never heeded. He changed into tweeds, took his stick and went down the road, still shaking with fright, and muttering over and over again—'God ha' mercy, I'm done for!' To the best of my knowledge and belief he spoke the truth.

So now you know how the Broken-link Handicap was run and won. Of course you don't believe it. You would credit anything about Russia's designs on India, or the recommendations of the Currency Commission;* but a little bit of sober fact is more than you can stand.

Beyond the Pale*

Love heeds not caste nor sleep a broken bed. I went in
search of love and lost myself.   *Hindu Proverb.*

A MAN should, whatever happens, keep to his own caste,
race, and breed. Let the White go to the White and the Black
to the Black. Then, whatever trouble falls is in the ordinary
course of things—neither sudden, alien, nor unexpected.

This is the story of a man who wilfully stepped beyond the
safe limits of decent everyday society, and paid for it heavily.

He knew too much in the first instance; and he saw too
much in the second. He took too deep an interest in native life;
but he will never do so again.

Deep away in the heart of the City, behind Jitha Megji's
*bustee,** lies Amir Nath's Gully,* which ends in a dead-wall
pierced by one grated window. At the head of the Gully is a
big cowbyre, and the walls on either side of the Gully are
without windows. Neither Suchet Singh nor Gaur Chand
approve of their women-folk looking into the world. If Durga
Charan had been of their opinion he would have been a happier
man to-day, and little Bisesa would have been able to knead
her own bread. Her room looked out through the grated window
into the narrow dark Gully where the sun never came and where
the buffaloes wallowed in the blue slime. She was a widow,
about fifteen years old, and she prayed the Gods, day and night,
to send her a lover; for she did not approve of living alone.

One day, the man—Trejago his name was—came into Amir
Nath's Gully on an aimless wandering; and, after he had passed
the buffaloes, stumbled over a big heap of cattle-food.

Then he saw that the Gully ended in a trap, and heard a little
laugh from behind the grated window. It was a pretty little
laugh, and Trejago, knowing that, for all practical purposes,
the old *Arabian Nights* are good guides, went forward to the
window, and whispered that verse of 'The Love Song of Har
Dyal' which begins:—

Can a man stand upright in the face of the naked Sun; or a Lover in the Presence of his Beloved?

If my feet fail me, O Heart of my Heart, am I to blame, being blinded by the glimpse of your beauty?

There came the faint *tchink* of a woman's bracelets from behind the grating, and a little voice went on with the song at the fifth verse:—

Alas! alas! Can the Moon tell the Lotus of her love when the Gate of Heaven is shut and the clouds gather for the rains?

They have taken my Beloved, and driven her with the pack-horses to the North.

There are iron chains on the feet that were set on my heart.

Call to the bowmen to make ready——

The voice stopped suddenly, and Trejago walked out of Amir Nath's Gully, wondering who in the world could have capped 'The Love Song of Har Dyal' so neatly.

Next morning, as he was driving to office, an old woman threw a packet into his dogcart. In the packet was the half of a broken glass-bangle, one flower of the blood-red *dhak*,* a pinch of *bhusa*,* or cattle-food, and eleven cardamoms. That packet was a letter—not a clumsy compromising letter, but an innocent unintelligible lover's epistle.

Trejago knew far too much about these things, as I have said. No Englishman should be able to translate object-letters. But Trejago spread all the trifles on the lid of his office-box and began to puzzle them out.

A broken glass-bangle stands for a Hindu widow all India over; because, when her husband dies, a woman's bracelets are broken on her wrists. Trejago saw the meaning of the little bit of glass. The flower of the *dhak* means diversely 'desire,' 'come,' 'write,' or 'danger,' according to the other things with it. One cardamom means 'jealousy'; but when any article is duplicated in an object-letter, it loses its symbolic meaning and stands merely for one of a number indicating time, or, if incense, curds, or saffron be sent also, place. The message ran then—'A widow—*dhak* flower and *bhusa*,—at eleven o'clock.' The pinch of *bhusa* enlightened Trejago. He saw—this kind of letter leaves much to instinctive knowledge—that the *bhusa*

referred to the big heap of cattle-food over which he had fallen
in Amir Nath's Gully, and that the message must come from
the person behind the grating; she being a widow. So the
mesage ran then—'A widow, in the Gully in which is the heap
of *bhusa*, desires you to come at eleven o'clock.'

Trejago threw all the rubbish into the fireplace and laughed.
He knew that men in the East do not make love under
windows at eleven in the forenoon, nor do women fix
appointments a week in advance. So he went, that very night
at eleven, into Amir Nath's Gully, clad in a *boorka*,* which
cloaks a man as well as a woman. Directly the gongs of the
City made the hour, the little voice behind the grating took
up 'The Love Song of Har Dyal' at the verse where the
Patha. irl calls upon Har Dyal to return. The song is really
pretty in the Vernacular. In English you miss the wail of it
It runs something like this—

Alone upon the housetops, to the North
　I turn and watch the lightning in the sky,—
The glamour of thy footsteps in the North,
　Come back to me, Beloved, or I die!

Below my feet the still bazar is laid
　Far, far, below the weary camels lie,—
The camels and the captives of thy raid.
　Come back to me, Beloved, or I die!

My father's wife is old and harsh with years,
　And drudge of all my father's house am I.—
My bread is sorrow and my drink is tears,
　Come back to me, Beloved, or I die!

As the song stopped, Trejago stepped up under the grating
and whispered—'I am here.'

Bisesa was good to look upon.

That night was the beginning of many strange things, and
of a double life so wild that Trejago to-day sometimes wonders
if it were not all a dream. Bisesa, or her old handmaiden who
had thrown the object-letter, had detached the heavy grating
from the brick-work of the wall; so that the window slid
inside, leaving only a square of raw masonry into which an
active man might climb.

In the day-time, Trejago drove through his routine of office-work, or put on his calling-clothes and called on the ladies of the Station, wondering how long they would know him if they knew of poor little Bisesa. At night, when all the City was still, came the walk under the evil-smelling *boorka*, the patrol through Jitha Megji's *bustee*, the quick turn into Amir Nath's Gully between the sleeping cattle and the dead walls, and then, last of all, Bisesa, and the deep, even breathing of the old woman who slept outside the door of the bare little room that Durga Charan allotted to his sister's daughter. Who or what Durga Charan was, Trejago never inquired; and why in the world he was not discovered and knifed never occurred to him till his madness was over, and Bisesa. . . . But this comes later.

Bisesa was an endless delight to Trejago. She was as ignorant as a bird; and her distorted versions of the rumours from the outside world, that had reached her in her room, amused Trejago almost as much as her lisping attempts to pronounce his name—'Christopher.' The first syllable was always more than she could manage, and she made funny little gestures with her roseleaf hands, as one throwing the name away, and then, kneeling before Trejago, asked him, exactly as an Englishwoman would do, if he were sure he loved her. Trejago swore that he loved her more than any one else in the world. Which was true.

After a month of this folly, the exigencies of his other life compelled Trejago to be especially attentive to a lady of his acquaintance. You may take it for a fact that anything of this kind is not only noticed and discussed by a man's own race, but by some hundred and fifty natives as well. Trejago had to walk with this lady and talk to her at the Band-stand, and once or twice to drive with her; never for an instant dreaming that this would affect his dearer, out-of-the-way life. But the news flew, in the usual mysterious fashion, from mouth to mouth, till Bisesa's duenna heard of it and told Bisesa. The child was so troubled that she did the household work evilly, and was beaten by Durga Charan's wife in consequence.

A week later Bisesa taxed Trejago with the flirtation. She understood no gradations and spoke openly. Trejago laughed,

and Bisesa stamped her little feet—little feet, light as marigold flowers, that could lie in the palm of a man's one
hand.

Much that is written about Oriental passion and
impulsiveness is exaggerated and compiled at second-hand,
but a little of it is true; and when an Englishman finds that
little, it is quite as startling as any passion in his own proper
life. Bisesa raged and stormed, and finally threatened to kill
herself if Trejago did not at once drop the alien *Memsahib* who
had come between them. Trejago tried to explain, and to show
her that she did not understand these things from a Western
standpoint. Bisesa drew herself up, and said simply—

'I do not. I know only this—it is not good that I should have
made you dearer than my own heart to me, *Sahib*. You are an
Englishman. I am only a black girl'—she was fairer than bar-
gold in the Mint,—'and the widow of a black man.'

Then she sobbed and said—'But on my soul and my
Mother's soul, I love you. There shall no harm come to you,
whatever happens to me.'

Trejago argued with the child, and tried to soothe her, but
she seemed quite unreasonably disturbed. Nothing would
satisfy her save that all relations between them should end. He
was to go away at once. And he went. As he dropped out of
the window she kissed his forehead twice, and he walked home
wondering.

A week, and then three weeks, passed without a sign from
Bisesa. Trejago, thinking that the rupture had lasted quite
long enough, went down to Amir Nath's Gully for the fifth
time in the three weeks, hoping that his rap at the sill of the
shifting grating would be answered. He was not disappointed.

There was a young moon, and one stream of light fell down
into Amir Nath's Gully, and struck the grating which was
drawn away as he knocked. From the black dark Bisesa held
out her arms into the moonlight. Both hands had been cut off
at the wrists, and the stumps were nearly healed.

Then, as Bisesa bowed her head between her arms and
sobbed, some one in the room grunted like a wild beast, and
something sharp—knife, sword, or spear,—thrust at Trejago
in his *boorka*. The stroke missed his body, but cut into one

of the muscles of the groin, and he limped slightly from the wound for the rest of his days.

The grating went into its place. There was no sign whatever from inside the house,—nothing but the moonlight strip on the high wall, and the blackness of Amir Nath's Gully behind.

The next thing Trejago remembers, after raging and shouting like a madman between those pitiless walls, is that he found himself near the river as the dawn was breaking, threw away his *boorka* and went home bareheaded.

*   *   *

What was the tragedy—whether Bisesa had, in a fit of causeless despair, told everything, or the intrigue had been discovered and she tortured to tell; whether Durga Charan knew his name and what became of Bisesa—Trejago does not know to this day. Something horrible had happened, and the thought of what it must have been comes upon Trejago in the night now and again, and keeps him company till the morning. One special feature of the case is that he does not know where lies the front of Durga Charan's house. It may open on to a courtyard common to two or more houses, or it may lie behind any one of the gates of Jitha Megji's *bustee*. Trejago cannot tell. He cannot get Bisesa—poor little Bisesa—back again. He has lost her in the City where each man's house is as guarded and as unknowable as the grave; and the grating that opens into Amir Nath's Gully has been walled up.

But Trejago pays his calls regularly, and is reckoned a very decent sort of man.

There is nothing peculiar about him, except a slight stiffness, caused by a riding-strain, in the right leg.

In Error*

They burnt a corpse upon the sand—
The light shone out afar;
It guided home the plunging boats
That beat from Zanzibar.
Spirit of Fire, where'er Thy altars rise,
Thou art Light of Guidance to our eyes!

Salsette Boat-Song.

THERE is hope for a man who gets publicly and riotously
drunk more often than he ought to do; but there is no hope
for the man who drinks secretly and alone in his own house—
the man who is never seen to drink.

This is a rule; so there must be an exception to prove it.
Moriarty's case was that exception.

He was a Civil Engineer, and the Government, very kindly,
put him quite by himself in an out-district, with nobody but
natives to talk to and a great deal of work to do. He did his
work well in the four years he was utterly alone; but he picked
up the vice of secret and solitary drinking, and came up out
of the wilderness more old and worn and haggard than the
dead-alive life had any right to make him. You know the
saying, that a man who has been alone in the jungle for more
than a year is never quite sane all his life after. People credited
Moriarty's queerness of manner and moody ways to the
solitude, and said that it showed how Government spoilt the
futures of its best men. Moriarty had built himself the plinth
of a very good reputation in the bridge-dam-girder line. But
he knew, every night of the week, that he was taking steps to
undermine that reputation with L.L.L. and Christopher* and
little nips of liqueurs, and filth of that kind. He had a sound
constitution and a great brain, or else he would have broken
down and died like a sick camel in the District; as better men
have done before him.

Government ordered him to Simla after he had come out of the desert; and he went up meaning to try for a post then vacant. That season, Mrs. Reiver—perhaps you will remember her—was in the height of her power, and many men lay under her yoke. Everything bad that could be said has already been said about Mrs. Reiver, in another tale. Moriarty was heavily-built and handsome, very quiet, and nervously anxious to please his neighbours when he wasn't sunk in a brown study. He started a good deal at sudden noises or if spoken to without warning; and, when you watched him drinking his glass of water at dinner, you could see the hand shake a little. But all this was put down to nervousness, and the quiet, steady, sip-sip-sip, fill and sip-sip-sip again that went on in his own room when he was by himself, was never known. Which was miraculous, seeing how everything in a man's private life is public property in India.

Moriarty was drawn, not into Mrs. Reiver's set, because they were not his sort, but into the power of Mrs. Reiver, and he fell down in front of her and made a goddess of her. This was due to his coming fresh out of the jungle to a big town. He could not scale things properly or see who was what.

Because Mrs. Reiver was cold and hard he said she was stately and dignified. Because she had no brains, and could not talk cleverly, he said she was reserved and shy. Mrs. Reiver shy! Because she was unworthy of honour or reverence from any one, he reverenced her from a distance and dowered her with all the virtues in the Bible and most of those in Shakespeare.

This big, dark, abstracted man who was so nervous when a pony cantered behind him, used to moon in the train of Mrs. Reiver, blushing with pleasure when she threw a word or two his way. His admiration was strictly platonic; even other women saw and admitted this. He did not move out in Simla, so he heard nothing against his idol: which was satisfactory. Mrs. Reiver took no special notice of him, beyond seeing that he was added to her list of admirers, and going for a walk with him now and then, just to show that he was her property, claimable as such. Moriarty must have done most of the talking, for Mrs. Reiver couldn't talk much to a man of his stamp; and the little she said could not have been profitable. What Moriarty believed in, as he had good reason to, was Mrs. Reiver's influence over him, and, in that belief, he set himself seriously to try to do away with the vice that only he himself knew of.

His experiences while he was fighting with it must have been peculiar, but he never described them. Sometimes he would hold off from everything except water for a week. Then, on a rainy night, when no one had asked him out to dinner, and there was a big fire in his room, and everything comfortable, he would sit down and make a big night of it by adding little nip to little nip, planning big schemes of reformation meanwhile, until he threw himself on his bed hopelessly drunk. He suffered next morning.

One night the big crash came. He was troubled in his own mind over his attempts to make himself 'worthy of the friendship' of Mrs. Reiver. The past ten days had been very bad ones, and the end of it all was that he received the arrears of two and three-quarter years of sipping in one attack of *delirium tremens* of the subdued kind; beginning with suicidal depression, going on to fits and starts and hysteria, and ending with downright raving. As he sat in a chair in front of the fire, or walked up and down the room picking a handkerchief to pieces, you heard what poor Moriarty really thought of Mrs. Reiver, for he raved about her and his own fall for the most part; though he ravelled some P. W. D.* accounts into the same skein of thought. He talked and talked, and talked in a low dry whisper to himself, and there was no stopping him. He seemed to know that there was something wrong, and twice tried to pull himself together and confer rationally with the Doctor; but his mind ran out of control at once, and he fell back to a whisper and the story of his troubles. It is terrible to hear a big man babbling like a child of all that a man usually locks up, and puts away in the deep of his heart. Moriarty read out his very soul for the benefit of any one who was in the room between ten-thirty that night and two-forty-five next morning.

From what he said, one gathered how immense an influence Mrs. Reiver held over him, and how thoroughly he felt for his own lapse. His whisperings cannot, of course, be put down here; but they were very instructive—as showing the errors of his estimates.

* * *

When the trouble was over, and his few acquaintances were pitying him for the bad attack of jungle-fever that had so pulled him down, Moriarty swore a big oath to himself and went abroad again with Mrs. Reiver till the end of the season, adoring her in a quiet and deferential way as an angel from heaven. Later on, he took to riding—not hacking, but honest riding—which was good proof that he was improving, and you could slam doors behind him without his jumping to his feet with a gasp. That, again, was hopeful.

How he kept his oath, and what it cost him in the beginning nobody knows. He certainly managed to compass the hardest thing that a man who has drunk heavily can do. He took his peg* and wine at dinner; but he never drank alone, and never let what he drank have the least hold on him.

Once he told a bosom-friend the story of his great trouble, and how the 'influence of a pure honest woman, and an angel as well,' had saved him. When the man—startled at anything good being laid to Mrs. Reiver's door—laughed, it cost him Moriarty's friendship. Moriarty, who is married now to a woman ten thousand times better than Mrs. Reiver—a woman who believes that there is no man on earth as good and clever as her husband—will go down to his grave vowing and protesting that Mrs. Reiver saved him from ruin in both worlds.

That she knew anything of Moriarty's weakness nobody believed for a moment. That she would have cut him dead, thrown him over, and acquainted all her friends with her discovery, if she had known of it, nobody who knew her doubted for an instant.

Moriarty thought her something she never was, and in that belief saved himself; which was just as good as though she had been everything that he had imagined.

But the question is, What claim will Mrs. Reiver have to the credit of Moriarty's salvation, when her day of reckoning comes?

A Bank Fraud*

He drank strong waters and his speech was coarse;
    He purchased raiment and forbore to pay;
He stuck a trusting junior with a horse,
    And won Gymkhanas in a doubtful way.
Then, 'twixt a vice and folly, turned aside
To do good deeds and straight to cloak them, lied.
The Mess-Room.

I F Reggie Burke were in India now he would resent this tale being told; but as he is in Hong-Kong and won't see it, the telling is safe. He was the man who worked the big fraud on the Sind and Sialkote Bank. He was manager of an upcountry Branch, and a sound practical man with a large experience of native loan and insurance work. He could combine the frivolities of ordinary life with his work, and yet do well. Reggie Burke rode anything that would let him get up, danced as neatly as he rode, and was wanted for every sort of amusement in the Station.

As he said himself, and as many men found out rather to their surprise, there were two Burkes, both very much at your service. 'Reggie Burke,' between four and ten,* ready for anything from a hot-weather gymkhana to a riding-picnic, and, between ten and four,* 'Mr. Reginald Burke, Manager of the Sind and Sialkote Branch Bank.' You might play polo with him one afternoon and hear him express his opinions when a man crossed;* and you might call on him next morning to raise a two-thousand-rupee loan* on a five-hundred-pound insurance policy, eighty pounds paid in premiums. He would recognise you, but you might have some trouble in recognising him.

The Directors of the Bank—it had its head-quarters in Calcutta, and its General Manager's word carried weight with the Government—picked their men well. They had tested Reggie up to a fairly severe breaking-strain. They trusted him just as much as Directors ever trust Managers. You must see for yourself whether their trust was misplaced.

Reggie's Branch was in a big Station, and worked with the usual staff—one Manager, one Accountant, both English, a Cashier, and a horde of native clerks; besides the Police patrol at nights outside. The bulk of its work, for it was in a thriving District, was *hoondi** and accommodation* of all kinds. A fool has no grip of this sort of business; and a clever man who does not go about among his clients, and know more than a little of their affairs, is worse than a fool. Reggie was young-looking, clean-shaved, with a twinkle in his eye, and a head that nothing short of a gallon of the Gunners' Madeira could make any impression on.

One day, at a big dinner, he announced casually that the Directors had shifted on to him a Natural Curiosity, from England, in the Accountant line. He was perfectly correct. Mr. Silas Riley, Accountant, was a most curious animal—a long, gawky, rawboned Yorkshireman, full of the savage self-conceit that blossoms only in the best county in England. Arrogance was a mild word for the mental attitude of Mr. S. Riley. He had worked himself up, after seven years, to a Cashier's position in a Huddersfield Bank; and all his experience lay among the factories of the North. Perhaps he would have done better on the Bombay side, where they are happy with one-half per cent profits, and money is cheap. He was useless for Upper India and a wheat Province, where a man wants a large head and a touch of imagination if he is to turn out a satisfactory balance-sheet.

He was wonderfully narrow-minded in business, and, being new to the country, had no notion that Indian banking is totally distinct from Home work. Like most clever self-made men, he had much simplicity in his nature; and, somehow or other, had construed the ordinarily polite terms of his letter of engagement into a belief that the Directors had chosen him on account of his special and brilliant talents, and that they set great store by him. This notion grew and crystallised; thus adding to his natural North-country conceit. Further, he was delicate, suffered from some trouble in his chest, and was short in his temper.

You will admit that Reggie had reason to call his new Accountant a Natural Curiosity. The two men failed to hit it off at all. Riley considered Reggie a wild, feather-headed idiot, given to Heaven only knew what dissipation in low places called 'Messes,' and totally unfit for the serious and solemn vocation of banking. He could never get over Reggie's look of youth and 'you-be-damned' air; and he couldn't understand Reggie's friends—clean-built, careless men in the Army—who rode over to big Sunday breakfasts at the Bank, and told sultry stories till Riley got up and left the room. Riley was always showing Reggie how the business ought to be conducted, and Reggie had more than once to remind him that seven years' limited experience between Huddersfield and Beverley did not qualify a man to steer a big up-country business. Then Riley sulked, and referred to himself as a pillar of the Bank and a cherished friend of the Directors, and Reggie tore his hair. If a man's English subordinates fail him in India, he comes to a hard time indeed, for native help has strict limitations. In the winter Riley went sick for weeks at a time with his lung complaint, and this threw more work on Reggie. But he preferred it to the everlasting friction when Riley was well.

One of the Travelling Inspectors of the Bank discovered these collapses and reported them to the Directors. Now, Riley had been foisted on the Bank by an M.P., who wanted the support of Riley's father who, again, was anxious to get his son out to a warmer climate because of those lungs. The M.P. had an interest in the Bank; but one of the Directors wanted to advance a nominee of his own; and, after Riley's father had died, he made the rest of the Board see that an Accountant who was sick for half the year had better give place to a healthy man. If Riley had known the real story of his appointment he might have behaved better; but, knowing nothing, his stretches of sickness alternated with restless, persistent, meddling irritation of Reggie, and all the hundred ways in which conceit in a subordinate situation can find play. Reggie used to call him striking and hair-curling names behind his back as a relief to his own feelings; but he never abused him to his face, because he said, 'Riley is such a frail beast that half of his loathsome conceit is due to pains in the chest.'

Late one April, Riley went very sick indeed. The Doctor punched him and thumped him, and told him he would be better before long. Then the Doctor went to Reggie and said—'Do you know how sick your Accountant is?'—'No!' said Reggie; 'the worse the better, confound him! He's a clacking nuisance when he's well. I'll let you take away the Bank Safe if you can drug him silent for this hot weather.'

But the Doctor did not laugh—'Man, I'm not joking,' he said. 'I'll give him another three months in his bed and a week or so more to die in. On my honour and reputation that's all the grace he has in this world. Consumption has hold of him to the marrow.'

Reggie's face changed at once into the face of 'Mr. Reginald Burke,' and he answered, 'What can I do?'—'Nothing,' said the Doctor; 'for all practical purposes the man is dead already. Keep him quiet and cheerful, and tell him he's going to recover. That's all. I'll look after him to the end, of course.'

The Doctor went away, and Reggie sat down to open the evening mail. His first letter was one from the Directors, intimating for his information that Mr. Riley was to resign, under a month's notice, by the terms of his agreement, telling Reggie that their letter to Riley would follow, and advising Reggie of the coming of a new Accountant, a man whom Reggie knew and liked.

Reggie lit a cheroot, and, before he had finished smoking, he had sketched the outline of a fraud. He put away—burked*—the Directors' letter, and went in to talk to Riley, who was as ungracious as usual, and fretting himself over the way the Bank would run during his illness. He never thought of the extra work on Reggie's shoulders, but solely of the damage to his own prospects of advancement. Then Reggie assured him that everything would be well, and that he, Reggie, would confer with Riley daily on the management of the Bank. Riley was a little soothed, but he hinted in as many words that he did not think much of Reggie's business capacity. Reggie was humble. And he had letters in his desk from the Directors that a Gilbarte or a Hardie* might have been proud of!

The days passed in the big darkened house, and the Directors' letter of dismissal to Riley came and was put away by Reggie, who, every evening, brought the books to Riley's room, and showed him what had been going forward, while Riley snarled. Reggie did his best to make statements pleasing to Riley, but the Accountant was sure that the Bank was going to rack and ruin without him. In June, as the lying in bed told on his spirit, he asked whether his absence had been noted by the Directors, and Reggie said that they had written most sympathetic letters, hoping that he would be able to resume his valuable services before long. He showed Riley the letters; and Riley said that the Directors ought to have written to him direct. A few days later, Reggie opened Riley's mail in the half-light of the room, and gave him the sheet—not the envelope—of a letter to Riley from the Directors. Riley said he would thank Reggie not to interfere with his private papers, especially as Reggie knew he was too weak to open his own letters. Reggie apologised.

Then Riley's mood changed, and he lectured Reggie on his evil ways: his horses and his bad friends. 'Of course lying here, on my back, Mr. Burke, I can't keep you straight; but when I'm well, I *do* hope you'll pay some heed to my words.' Reggie, who had dropped polo, and dinners. and tennis and all, to attend to Riley, said that he was penitent, and settled Riley's head on the pillow, and heard him fret and contradict in hard, dry, hacking whispers, without a sign of impatience. This, at the end of a heavy day's office work, doing double duty, in the latter half of June.

When the new Accountant came, Reggie told him the facts of the case, and announced to Riley that he had a guest staying with him. Riley said that he might have had more consideration than to entertain his 'doubtful friends' at such a time. Reggie made Carron, the new Accountant, sleep at the Club in consequence. Carron's arrival took some of the heavy work off his shoulders, and he had time to attend to Riley's exactions—to explain, soothe, invent, and settle and re-settle the poor wretch in bed, and to forge complimentary letters from Calcutta. At the end of the first month Riley wished to send some money home to his mother. Reggie sent the draft. At the end of the second month Riley's salary came in just the same. Reggie paid it out of his own pocket, and, with it, wrote Riley a beautiful letter from the Directors.

Riley was very ill indeed, but the flame of his life burnt unsteadily. Now and then he would be cheerful and confident about the future, sketching plans for going Home and seeing his mother. Reggie listened patiently when the office-work was over, and encouraged him.

At other times Riley insisted on Reggie reading the Bible and grim 'Methody' tracts to him. Out of these tracts he pointed morals directed at his Manager. But he always found time to worry Reggie about the working of the Bank, and to show him where the weak points lay.

This indoor, sickroom life and constant strain wore Reggie down a good deal, and shook his nerves, and lowered his billiard play by forty points. But the business of the Bank, and the business of the sickroom, had to go on, though the glass was 116° in the shade.

At the end of the third month Riley was sinking fast, and had begun to realise that he was very sick. But the conceit that made him worry Reggie kept him from believing the worst. 'He wants some sort of mental stimulant if he is to drag on,' said the Doctor. 'Keep him interested in life if you care about his living.' So Riley, contrary to all the laws of business and finance, received a 25-per-cent rise of salary from the Directors. The 'mental stimulant' succeeded beautifully. Riley was happy and cheerful, and, as is often the case in consumption, healthiest in mind when the body was weakest. He lingered for a full month, snarling and fretting about the Bank, talking of the future, hearing the Bible read, lecturing Reggie on sin, and wondering when he would be able to move abroad.

But at the end of September, one mercilessly hot evening, he rose up in his bed with a little gasp, and said quickly to Reggie—'Mr. Burke, I am going to die. I know it in myself. My chest is all hollow inside, and there's nothing to breathe with. To the best of my knowledge I have done nowt'—he was returning to the talk of his boyhood—'to lie heavy on my conscience. God be thanked, I have been preserved from the grosser forms of sin; and I counsel *you*, Mr. Burke . . .'

Here his voice died down, and Reggie stooped over him.

'Send my salary for September to my Mother . . . done great things with the Bank if I had been spared . . . mistaken policy . . . no fault of mine. . . .'

Then he turned his face to the wall and died.

Reggie drew the sheet over Its face, and went out into the verandah, with his last 'mental stimulant'—a letter of condolence and sympathy from the Dirctors—unused in his pocket.

'If I'd been only ten minutes earlier,' thought Reggie, 'I might have heartened him up to pull through another day.'

Tods' Amendment*

> The World hath set its heavy yoke
> Upon the old white-bearded folk
> Who strive to please the King.
> God's mercy is upon the young,
> God's wisdom in the baby tongue
> That fears not anything.
> *The Parable of Chajju Bhagat.*

NOW Tods' Mamma was a singularly charming woman, and every one in Simla knew Tods. Most men had saved him from death on occasions. He was beyond his *ayah's** control altogether, and perilled his life daily to find out what would happen if you pulled a Mountain Battery mule's tail. He was an utterly fearless young Pagan, about six years old, and the only baby who ever broke the holy calm of the Supreme Legislative Council.

It happened this way: Tods' pet kid got loose, and fled up the hill, off the Boileaugunge* Road, Tods after it, until it burst in to the Viceregal Lodge lawn, then attached to 'Peterhoff.'* The Council were sitting at the time, and the windows were open because it was warm. The Red Lancer* in the porch told Tods to go away; but Tods knew the Red Lancer and most of the Members of Council personally. Moreover, he had firm hold of the kid's collar, and was being dragged all across the flower-bed. 'Give my *salaam** to the long Councillor *Sahib*, and ask him to help me take *Moti** back!' gasped Tods. The Council heard the noise through the open windows; and, after an interval, was seen the shocking spectacle of a Legal Member and a Lieutenant-Governor helping, under the direct patronage of a Commander-in-Chief and a Viceroy, one small and very dirty boy, in a sailor's suit and a tangle of brown hair, to coerce a lively and rebellious kid. They headed it off down the path to the Mall, and Tods went home in triumph and told his Mamma that *all* the Councillor *Sahibs* had been helping him to catch *Moti*

Whereat his Mamma smacked Tods for interfering with the administration of the Empire; but Tods met the Legal Member the next day, and told him in confidence that if the Legal Member ever wanted to catch a goat, he, Tods, would give him all the help in his power. 'Thank you, Tods,' said the Legal Member.

Tods was the idol of some eighty *jhampanis*, and half as many *saises*.* He saluted them all as 'O Brother.' It never entered his head that any living human being could disobey his orders; and he was the buffer between the servants and his Mamma's wrath. The working of that household turned on Tods, who was adored by every one from the *dhobi** to the dog-boy. Even Futteh Khan, the villainous loafer *khit** from Mussoorie, shirked risking Tods' displeasure for fear his co-mates should look down on him.

So Tods had honour in the land from Boileaugunge to Chota Simla,* and ruled justly according to his lights. Of course, he spoke Urdu, but he had also mastered many queer side-speeches like the *chotee bolee** of the women, and held grave converse with shopkeepers and Hill-coolies alike. He was precocious for his age, and his mixing with natives had taught him some of the more bitter truths of life: the meanness and the sordidness of it. He used, over his bread and milk, to deliver solemn and serious aphorisms, translated from the vernacular into the English, that made his Mamma jump and vow that Tods *must* go Home next hot weather.

Just when Tods was in the bloom of his power, the Supreme Legislature were hacking out a Bill for the Sub-Montane Tracts, a revision of the then Act, smaller than the Punjab Land Bill, but affecting a few hundred thousand people none the less. The Legal Member had built, and bolstered, and embroidered, and amended that Bill till it looked beautiful on paper. Then the Council began to settle what they called the 'minor details.' As if any Englishman legislating for natives knows enough to know which are the minor and which are the major points, from the native point of view, of any measure! That Bill was a triumph of 'safe-guarding the interests of the tenant.' One clause provided that land should not be leased on longer terms than five years at a stretch; because, if the landlord had a tenant bound down for, say, twenty years, he would squeeze the very life out of him. The notion was to keep up a stream of independent cultivators in the Sub-Montane Tracts; and ethnologically and politically the notion was correct. The only drawback was that it was altogether wrong. A native's life in India implies the life of his son. Wherefore, you cannot legislate for one generation at a time. You must consider the next from the native point of view. Curiously enough, the native now and then, and in Northern India more particularly, hates being over-protected against himself. There was a Naga village once, where they lived on dead *and* buried Commissariat mules. . . . But that is another story.

For many reasons, to be explained later, the people concerned objected to the Bill. The Native Member of Council knew as much about Punjabis as he knew about Charing Cross. He had said in Calcutta that 'the Bill was entirely in accord with the desires of that large and important class, the cultivators;' and so on, and so on. The Legal Member's knowledge of natives was limited to English-speaking Durbaris,* and his own red *Chaprassis*;* the Sub-Montane Tracts concerned no one in particular; the Deputy Commissioners were a good deal too driven to make representations, and the measure was one which dealt with small land-holders only. Nevertheless, the Legal Member prayed that it might be correct, for he was a nervously conscientious man. He did not know that no man can tell what natives think unless he mixes with them with the varnish off. And not always then. But he did the best he knew. So the measure came up to the Supreme Council for the final touches, while Tods patrolled the Burra* Simla Bazar in his morning rides, and played with the monkey belonging to Ditta Mull, the *bunnia*,* and listened, as a child listens, to all the stray talk about this new freak of the Lat Sahib's.*

One day there was a dinner-party at the house of Tods' Mamma, and the Legal Member came. Tods was in bed, but he kept awake till he heard the bursts of laughter from the men over the coffee. Then he paddled out in his little red flannel dressing-gown and his night-suit, and took refuge by the side of his father, knowing that he would not be sent back. 'See the miseries of having a family!' said Tods' father, giving Tods three prunes, some water in a glass that had been used for claret, and telling him to sit still. Tods sucked the prunes slowly, knowing that he would have to go when they were finished, and sipped the pink water like a man of the world, as he listened to the conversation. Presently, the Legal Member, talking 'shop' to the Head of a Department, mentioned his Bill by its full name—'The Sub-Montane Tracts *Ryotwary** Revised Enactment.' Tods caught the one native word, and lifting up his small voice said—

'Oh, I know *all* about that! Has it been *murramutted** yet, Councillor *Sahib*?'

'How much?' said the Legal Member.

'*Murramutted*—mended.—Put *theek*,* you know—made nice to please Ditta Mull!'

The Legal Member left his place and moved up next to Tods.

'What do you know about *ryotwary*, little man?' he said.

'I'm not a little man, I'm Tods, and I know *all* about it. Ditta Mull, and Choga Lall, and Amir Nath, and—oh, *lakhs** of my friends tell me about it in the bazars when I talk to them.'

'Oh, they do—do they? What do they say, Tods?'

Tods tucked his feet under his red flannel dressing-gown and said—'I must *fink*.'

The Legal Member waited patiently. Then Tods, with infinite compassion—

'You don't speak my talk, do you, Councillor *Sahib*?'

'No; I am sorry to say I do not,' said the Legal Member.

'Very well,' said Tods, 'I must *fink* in English.'

He spent a minute putting his ideas in order, and began very slowly, translating in his mind from the vernacular to English, as many Anglo-Indian children do. You must remember that the Legal Member helped him on by questions when he halted, for Tods was not equal to the sustained flight of oratory that follows.

'Ditta Mull says, "This thing is the talk of a child, and was made up by fools." But *I* don't think you are a fool,

Councillor *Sahib*,' said Tods hastily. 'You caught my goat. This is what Ditta Mull says—"I am not a fool, and why should the Sirkar* say I am a child? *I* can see if the land is good and if the landlord is good. If I am a fool, the sin is upon my own head. For five years I take my ground for which I have saved money, and a wife I take too, and a little son is born." Ditta Mull has one daughter now, but he *says* he will have a son, soon. And he says, "At the end of five years, by this new *bundobust*,* I must go. If I do not go, I must get fresh seals and *takkus*-stamps on the papers, perhaps in the middle of the harvest, and to go to the law-courts once is wisdom, but to go twice is *Jehannum*.*" That is *quite* true,' explained Tods gravely. 'All my friends say so. And Ditta Mull says, "Always fresh *takkus* and paying money to *vakils** and *chaprassis* and law-courts every five years, or else the landlord makes me go. Why do I want to go? Am I a fool ? If I am a fool and do not know, after forty years, good land when I see it, let me die! But if the new *bundobust* says for *fifteen* years, that is good and wise. My little son is a man, and I am burnt,* and he takes the ground or another ground, paying only once for the *takkus*-stamps on the papers, and his little son is born, and at the end of fifteen years is a man too. But what profit is there in five years and fresh papers? Nothing but *dikh*,* trouble, *dikh*. We are not young men who take these lands, but old ones—not farmers, but tradesmen with a little money—and for fifteen years we shall have peace. Nor are we children that the Sirkar should treat us so." '

Here Tods stopped short, for the whole table were listening. The Legal Member said to Tods, 'Is that all?'

'All I can remember,' said Tods. 'But you should see Ditta Mull's big monkey. It's just like a Councillor *Sahib*.'

'Tods! Go to bed,' said his father.

Tods gathered up his dressing-gown tail and departed.

The Legal Member brought his hand down on the table with a crash—'By Jove!' said the Legal Member, 'I believe the boy is right. The short tenure *is* the weak point.'

He left early, thinking over what Tods had said. Now, it was obviously impossible for the Legal Member to play with a *bunnia's* monkey, by way of getting understanding; but he did better. He made inquiries, always bearing in mind the fact that the real native—not the hybrid, University-trained mule—is as timid as a colt, and, little by little, he coaxed some of the men whom the measure concerned most intimately to give in their views, which squared very closely with Tods' evidence.

So the Bill was amended in that clause; and the Legal Member was filled with an uneasy suspicion that Native Members represent very little except the Orders they carry on their bosoms. But he put the thought from him as illiberal. He was a most Liberal man.

After a time the news spread through the bazars that Tods had got the Bill recast in the tenure-clause, and if Tods' Mamma had not interfered, Tods would have made himself sick on the baskets of fruit and pistachio nuts and Cabuli grapes and almonds that crowded the verandah. Till he went Home, Tods ranked some few degrees before the Viceroy in popular estimation. But for the little life of him Tods could not understand why.

In the Legal Member's private-paper-box still lies the rough draft of the Sub-Montane Tracts *Ryotwary* Revised Enactment; and, opposite the twenty-second clause, pencilled in blue chalk, and signed by the Legal Member, are the words '*Tods' Amendment.*'

The Daughter of the Regiment*

Jain 'Ardin' was a Sargint's wife,
  A Sargint's wife wus she.
She married of 'im in Orldershort
  An' comed acrost the sea.
(*Chorus*) 'Ave you never 'eard tell o' Jain 'Ardin'?
                    Jain 'Ardin'?
                    Jain 'Ardin'?
  'Ave you never 'eard tell o' Jain 'Ardin'?
The pride o' the Compan*ee*?
                    Old Barrack-Room Ballad.

'A GENTLEMAN who doesn't know the Circassian Circle*
ought not to stand up for it—puttin' everybody out.' That was
what Miss McKenna said, and the Sergeant who was my *vis-à-
vis** looked the same thing. I was afraid of Miss McKenna.
She was six feet high, all yellow freckles and red hair, and was
simply clad in white satin shoes, a pink muslin dress, an apple-
green stuff sash, and black silk gloves, with yellow roses in her
hair. Wherefore I fled from Miss McKenna and sought my
friend Private Mulvaney, who was at the cant*—refreshment-
table.

'So you've been dancin' wid little Jhansi* McKenna,
Sorr—she that's goin' to marry Corp'ril Slane? Whin you next
conversh wid your lorruds an' your ladies, tell thim you've
danced wid little Jhansi. 'Tis a thing to be proud av.'

But I wasn't proud. I was humble. I saw a story in Private
Mulvaney's eye; and besides, if he stayed too long at the bar,
he would, I knew, qualify for more pack-drill. Now to meet
an esteemed friend doing pack-drill outside the guard-room is
embarrassing, especially if you happen to be walking with his
Commanding Officer.

'Come on to the parade-ground, Mulvaney, it's cooler there,
and tell me about Miss McKenna. What is she, and who is
she, and why is she called "Jhansi"?'

'D'ye mane to say you've niver heard av Ould Pummeloe's*
daughter? An' you thinkin' you know things! I'm wid ye in a
minut' whin me poipe's lit.'

We came out under the stars. Mulvaney sat down on one of
the artillery bridges, and began in the usual way: his pipe
between his teeth, his big hands clasped and dropped between
his knees, and his cap well on the back of his head—

'Whin Mrs. Mulvaney that is, was Miss Shad that was, you
were a dale younger than you are now, an' the Army was
dif'rint in sev'ril e-sen-shuls. Bhoys have no call for to marry
nowadays, an' that's why the Army has so few rale, good,
honust, swearin', strapagin',* tinder-hearted, heavy-futted
wives as ut used to have whin I was a Corp'ril. I was rejuced
aftherwards—but no matther—I was a Corp'ril wanst. In thim
times a man lived an' died wid his rig'mint; an' by natur', he
married whin he was a *man*. Whin I was Corp'ril—Mother av
Hivin, how the rig'mint has died an' been borrun since that
day!—my Colour-Sargint was Ould McKenna, an' a married
man tu. An' his woife—his first woife, for he married three
times did McKenna—was Bridget McKenna, from Portarl-
ington, like mesilf. I've misremembered fwhat her first name
was; but in B Comp'ny we called her "Ould Pummeloe," by
reason av her figure, which was entirely cir-cum-fe-renshill.
Like the big dhrum! Now that woman—God rock her sowl
to rest in glory!—was for everlastin' havin' childher; an'
McKenna, whin the fifth or sixth come squallin' on to the
musther-roll, swore he wud number thim off in future. But
Ould Pummeloe she prayed av him to christen them after the
names av the stations they was borrun in. So there was Colaba
McKenna, an' Muttra McKenna, an' a whole Presidincy* av
other McKennas, an' little Jhansi, dancin' over yonder. Whin
the childher wasn't bornin', they was dying; for, av our
childher die like sheep in these days, they died like flies thin.
I lost me own little Shad—but no matther. 'Tis long ago, and
Mrs. Mulvaney niver had another.

I'm digresshin. Wan divil's hot summer there come an order
from some mad ijjit, whose name I misremember, for the
rig'mint to go upcountry. Maybe they wanted to know how
the new rail carried throops. They knew! On me sowl,

they knew before they was done! Old Pummeloe had just buried Muttra McKenna; an', the season bein' onwholesim, only little Jhansi McKenna, who was four year ould thin, was left on hand.

Foive childher gone in fourteen months. 'Twas harrd, wasn't ut?

So we wint up to our new station in that blazin' heat—may the curse av Saint Lawrence* conshume the man who gave the ordher! Will I iver forget that move? They gave us two wake thrains to the rig'mint; an' we was eight hundher' and sivinty strong. There was A, B, C, an' D Comp'nies in the secon' thrain, wid twelve wimmen, no orficers' ladies, an' thirteen childher. We was to go six hundher' miles, an' railways was new in thim days. Whin we had been a night in the belly av the thrain—the men ragin' in their shirts an' dhrinkin' anything they cud find, an' eatin' bad fruit-stuff whin they cud, for we cudn't stop 'em—I was a Corp'ril thin—the cholera bruk out wid the dawnin' av the day.

Pray to the Saints you may niver see cholera in a throop-thrain! 'Tis like the judgmint av God hittin' down from the nakid sky! We run into a rest-camp—as ut might have been Ludianny,* but not by any manes so comfortable. The Orficer Commandin' sent a telegrapt up the line, three hundher' mile up, askin' for help. Faith, we wanted ut, for ivry sowl av the followers ran for the dear life as soon as the thrain stopped; an' by the time that telegrapt was writ, there wasn't a naygur in the station exceptin' the telegrapt-clerk—an' he only bekaze he was held down to his chair by the scruff av his sneakin' black neck. Thin the day began wid the noise in the carr'ges, an' the rattle av the men on the platform fallin' over, arms an' all, as they stud for to answer the Comp'ny muster-roll before goin' over to the camp. 'Tisn't for me to say what like the cholera was like. May be the Doctor cud ha' tould, av he hadn't dropped on to the platform from the door av a carriage where we was takin' out the dead. He died wid the rest. Some bhoys had died in the night. We tuk out siven, and twenty more was sickenin' as we tuk thim. The wimmen was huddled up anyways, screamin' wid fear.

Sez the Commandin' Orficer, whose name I misremember,

"Take the wimmen over to that tope* av trees yonder. Get thim out av the camp. 'Tis no place for thim."

Ould Pummeloe was sittin' on her beddin'-rowl, thryin' to kape little Jhansi quiet. "Go off to that tope!" sez the Orficer. "Go out av the men's way!"

"Be damned av I do!" sez Ould Pummeloe, an' little Jhansi, squattin' by her mother's side, squeaks out, "Be damned av I do," tu. Thin Ould Pummeloe turns to the wimmen an' she sez, "Are ye goin' to let the bhoys die while you're picnickin', ye sluts?" sez she. "'Tis wather they want. Come on an' help."

Wid that, she turns up her sleeves an' steps out for a well behind the rest-camp—little Jhansi trottin' behind wid a *lotah** an' string, an' the other wimmen followin' like lambs, wid horse-buckets and cookin' pots. Whin all the things was full, Ould Pummeloe marches back into camp—'twas like a battlefield wid all the glory missin'—at the hid av the rig'mint av wimmen.

"McKenna, me man!" she sez, wid a voice on her like grand-roun's* challenge, "tell the bhoys to be quiet. Ould Pummeloe's comin' to look afther thim—wid free dhrinks."

'Thin we cheered, an' the cheerin' in the lines was louder than the noise av the poor divils wid the sickness on thim. But not much.

You see, we was a new an' raw rig'mint in those days, an' we cud make neither head nor tail av the sickness; an' so we was useless. The men was goin' roun' an' about like dumb sheep, waitin' for the nex' man to fall over, an' sayin' undher their spache, "Fwhat is ut? In the name av God, *fwhat* is ut?" 'Twas horrible. But through ut all, up an' down, an' down an' up, wint Ould Pummeloe an' little Jhansi—all we cud see av the baby, undher a dead man's helmut wid the chin-strap swingin' about her little stummick—up an' down wid the wather an' fwhat brandy there was.

Now an' thin Ould Pummeloe, the tears runnin' down her fat, red face, sez, "Me bhoys, me poor, dead, darlin' bhoys!" But, for the most, she was thryin' to put heart into the men an' kape thim stiddy; and little Jhansi was tellin' thim all they wud be "betther in the mornin'." 'Twas a thrick she'd picked

up from hearin' Ould Pummeloe whin Muttra was burnin'
out wid fever. In the mornin'! 'Twas the iverlastin' mornin'
at St. Pether's Gate was the mornin' for seven-an'-twenty
good men; an' twenty more was sick to the death in that bitter,
burnin' sun. But the wimmen worked like angils as I've said,
an' the men like divils, till two doctors come down from
above, and we was rescued.

But, just before that, Ould Pummeloe, on her knees over a
bhoy in my squad—right-cot man to me he was in the
barrick—tellin' him the worrud av the Church that niver
failed a man yet, sez, "Hould me up, bhoys! I'm feelin' bloody
sick!" 'Twas the sun, not the cholera, did ut. She
misremembered she was only wearin' her ould black bonnet,
an' she died wid "McKenna, me man," houldin' her up, an'
the bhoys howled whin they buried her.

That night a big wind blew, an' blew, an' blew, an' blew the
tents flat. But it blew the cholera away, an' niver another case
there was all the while we was waitin'—ten days in quarintin'.
Av you will belave me, the thrack av the sickness in the camp
was for all the wurruld the thrack av a man walkin' four times
in a figur-av-eight through the tents. They say 'tis the
Wandherin' Jew takes the cholera wid him. I believe ut.

An' *that*,' said Mulvaney illogically, 'is the cause why little
Jhansi McKenna is fwhat she is. She was brought up by the
Quartermaster Sargint's wife whin McKenna died, but she
b'longs to B Comp'ny; and this tale I'm tellin' you—*wid* a
proper appreciashin av Jhansi McKenna—I've belted into ivry
recruity av the Comp'ny as he was drafted. 'Faith, 'twas me
belted Corp'ril Slane into askin' the girl!'

'Not really?'

'Man, I did! She's no beauty to look at, but she's Ould
Pummeloe's daughter, an' 'tis my juty to provide for her. Just
before Slane got his promotion I sez to him, "Slane," sez I,
"to-morrow 'twill be insubordinashin av me to chastise you;
but, by the sowl av Ould Pummeloe, who is now in glory, av
you don't give me your wurrud to ask Jhansi McKenna at
wanst, I'll peel the flesh off yer bones wid a brass huk to-night.
'Tis a dishgrace to B Comp'ny she's been single so long!" sez

I. Was I goin' to let a three-year-ould* preshume to discoorse wid me—my will bein' set? No! Slane wint an' asked her. He's a good bhoy is Slane. Wan av these days he'll get into the Com'ssariat an' dhrive a buggy wid his—savin's.* So I provided for Ould Pummeloe's daughter; an' now you go along an' dance agin wid her.'

And I did.

I felt a respect for Miss Jhansi McKenna; and I went to her wedding later on.

Perhaps I will tell you about that* one of these days.

In the Pride of His Youth*

'Stopped in the straight when the race was his own!
Look at him cutting it—cur to the bone!'
'Ask, ere the youngster be rated and chidden,
What did he carry and how was he ridden?
Maybe they used him too much at the start;
Maybe Fate's weight-cloths* are breaking his heart.'

Life's Handicap.

WHEN I was telling you of the joke that The Worm* played off on the Senior Subaltern, I promised a somewhat similar tale, but with all the jest left out. This is that tale.

Dicky Hatt was kidnapped in his early, early youth—neither by landlady's daughter, housemaid, barmaid, nor cook, but by a girl so nearly of his own caste that only a woman could have seen she was just the least little bit in the world below it. This happened a month before he came out to India, and five days after his one-and-twentieth birthday. The girl was nineteen—six years older than Dicky in the things of this world, that is to say—and, for the time, twice as foolish as he.

Excepting, always, falling off a horse there is nothing more fatally easy than marriage before the Registrar. The ceremony cost less than fifty shillings, and is remarkably like walking into a pawn-shop. After the declarations of residence have been put in, four minutes will cover the rest of the proceedings—fees, attestation, and all. Then the Registrar slides the blotting-pad over the names, and says grimly with his pen between his teeth, 'Now you're man and wife;' and the couple walk out into the street feeling as if something were horribly illegal somewhere.

But that ceremony holds and can drag a man to his undoing just as thoroughly as the 'long as ye both shall live' curse from the altar-rails, with the bridesmaids giggling behind, and 'The Voice that breathed o'er Eden'* lifting the roof off. In this manner was Dicky Hatt kidnapped, and he considered it vastly fine, for he had received an appointment in India which carried a magnificent salary from the Home point of view. The marriage was to be kept secret for a year. Then Mrs. Dicky Hatt was to come out, and the rest of life was to be a glorious golden mist. That was how they sketched it under the Addison Road Station* lamps; and, after one short month, came Gravesend* and Dicky steaming out to his new life, and the girl crying in a thirty-shillings-a-week bed-and-living-room, in a back-street off Montpelier Square near the Knightsbridge Barracks.

But the country that Dicky came to was a hard land where men of twenty-one were reckoned very small boys indeed, and life was expensive. The salary that loomed so large six thousand miles away did not go far. Particularly when Dicky divided it by two, and remitted more than the fair half, at 1-6⅞*, to Montpelier Square. One hundred and thirty-five rupees out of three hundred and thirty is not much to live on; but it was absurd to suppose that Mrs. Hatt could exist for ever on the £20 held back by Dicky from his outfit allowance. Dicky saw this and remitted at once; always remembering that Rs.700 were to be paid, twelve months later, for a first-class passage out for a lady. When you add to these trifling details the natural instincts of a boy beginning a new life in a new country and longing to go about and enjoy himself, and the necessity for grappling with strange work—which, properly speaking, should take up a boy's undivided attention—you will see that Dicky started handicapped. He saw it himself for a breath or two; but he did not guess the full beauty of his future.

As the hot weather began, the shackles settled on him and ate into his flesh. First would come letters—big, crossed, seven-sheet letters—from his wife, telling him how she longed to see him, and what a Heaven upon earth would be their property when they met. Then some boy of the chummery* wherein Dicky lodged would pound on the door of his bare little room, and tell him to come out to look at a pony—the very thing to suit him. Dicky could not afford ponies. He had to explain this. Dicky could not afford living in the chummery, modest as it was. He had to explain this before he moved to a single room next the office where he worked all day. He kept house on a green oil-cloth table-cover, one chair, one bedstead, one photograph, one tooth-glass, very strong and thick, a seven-rupee eight-anna filter,* and messing by contract at thirty-seven rupees a month. Which last item was extortion. He had no punkah, for a punkah costs fifteen rupees a month; but he slept on the roof of the office with all his wife's letters under his pillow. Now and again he was asked out to dinner, where he got both a punkah and an iced drink. But this was seldom, for people objected to recognising a boy who had evidently the instincts of a Scotch tallow-chandler, and who lived in such a nasty fashion. Dicky could not subscribe to any amusement, so he found no amusement except the pleasure of turning over his Bank-book and reading what it said about 'loans on approved security.' That cost nothing. He remitted through a Bombay Bank, by the way, and the Station knew nothing of his private affairs.

Every month he sent Home all he could possibly spare for his wife and for another reason which was expected to explain itself shortly, and would require more money.

About this time Dicky was overtaken with the nervous, haunting fear that besets married men when they are out of sorts. He had no pension to look to. What if he should die suddenly, and leave his wife unprovided for? The thought used to lay hold of him in the still, hot nights on the roof, till the shaking of his heart made him think that he was going to die then and there of heart-disease. Now this is a frame of mind which no boy has a right to know. It is a strong man's trouble; but, coming when it did, it nearly drove poor punkah-less, perspiring Dicky Hatt mad. He could tell no one about it.

A certain amount of 'screw'* is as necessary for a man as for a billiard-ball. It makes them both do wonderful things. Dicky needed money badly, and he worked for it like a horse. But, naturally, the men who owned him knew that a boy can live very comfortably on a certain income—pay in India is a matter of age, not merit, you see, and, if their particular boy wished to work like two boys, Business forbid that they should stop him. But Business forbid that they should give him an increase of pay at his present ridiculously immature age. So Dicky won certain rises of salary—ample for a boy—not enough for a wife and a child—certainly too little for the seven-hundred-rupee passage that he and Mrs. Hatt had discussed so lightly once upon a time. And with this he was forced to be content.

Somehow, all his money seemed to fade away in Home drafts and the crushing Exchange,* and the tone of the Home letters changed and grew querulous. 'Why wouldn't Dicky have his wife and the baby out? Surely he had a salary—a fine salary—and it was too bad of him to enjoy himself in India. But would he—could he—make the next draft a little more elastic?' Here followed a list of baby's kit, as long as a Parsee's* bill. Then Dicky, whose heart yearned to his wife and the little son he had never seen—which, again, is a feeling no boy is entitled to—enlarged the draft, and wrote queer half-boy, half-man letters, saying that life was not so enjoyable after all, and would the little wife wait yet a little longer? But the little wife, however much she approved of money, objected to waiting, and there was a strange, hard sort of ring in her letters that Dicky didn't understand. How could he, poor boy?

Later on still—just as Dicky had been told—apropos of another youngster who had 'made a fool of himself' as the saying is—that matrimony would not only ruin his further chances of advancement, but would lose him his present appointment—came the news that the baby, his own little, little son, had died and, behind this, forty lines of an angry woman's scrawl, saying the death might have been averted if certain things, all costing money, had been done, or if the mother and the baby had been with Dicky. The letter struck at Dicky's naked heart; but, not being officially entitled to a baby, he could show no sign of trouble.

How Dicky won through the next four months, and what hope he kept alight to force him into his work, no one dare say. He pounded on, the seven-hundred-rupee passage as far away as ever, and his style of living unchanged, except when he launched into a new filter. There was the strain of his office-work, and the strain of his remittances, and the knowledge of his son's death, which touched the boy more, perhaps, than it would have touched a man; and, beyond all, the enduring strain of his daily life. Gray-headed seniors who approved of his thrift and his fashion of denying himself everything pleasant reminded him of the old saw that says—

> 'If a youth would be distinguished in his art, art, art,
> He must keep the girls away from his heart, heart, heart.'*

And Dicky, who fancied he had been through every trouble that a man is permitted to know, had to laugh and agree; with the last line of his balanced Bank-book jingling in his head day and night.

But he had one more sorrow to digest before the end. There arrived a letter from the little wife—the natural sequence of the others if Dicky had only known it—and the burden of that letter was 'gone with a handsomer man than you.' It was a rather curious production, without stops, something like this—'She was not going to wait for ever and the baby was dead and Dicky was only a boy and he would never set eyes on her again and why hadn't he waved his handkerchief to her when he left Gravesend and God was her judge she was a wicked woman but Dicky was worse enjoying himself in India and this other man loved the ground she trod on and would Dicky ever forgive her for she would never forgive Dicky; and there was no address to write to.'

Instead of thanking his stars that he was free, Dicky discovered exactly how an injured husband feels—again, not at all the knowledge to which a boy is entitled—for his mind went back to his wife as he remembered her in the thirty-shilling 'suite' in Montpelier Square, when the dawn of his last morning in England was breaking, and she was crying in the bed. Whereat he rolled about on his bed and bit his fingers. He never stopped to think whether, if he had met Mrs. Hatt after those two years, he would have discovered that he and she had grown quite different and new persons. This, theoretically, he ought to have done. He spent the night after the English Mail came in rather severe pain.

Next morning Dicky Hatt felt disinclined to work. He argued that he had missed the pleasure of youth. He was tired, and he had tasted all the sorrow in life before three-and-twenty. His Honour was gone—that was the man; and now he, too, would go to the Devil—that was the boy in him. So he put his head down on the green oil-cloth tablecover, and wept before resigning his post, and all it offered.

But the reward of his services came. He was given three days to reconsider himself, and the Head of the establishment, after some telegraphings, said that it was a most unusual step, but, in view of the ability that Mr. Hatt had displayed at such and such a time, at such and such junctures, he was in a position to offer him an infinitely superior post—first on probation and later, in the natural course of things, on confirmation. 'And how much does the post carry?' said Dicky. 'Six hundred and fifty rupees,' said the Head slowly, expecting to see the young man sink with gratitude and joy.

And it came then! The seven-hundred-rupee-passage, and enough to have saved the wife, and the little son, and to have allowed of assured and open marriage, came then. Dicky burst into a roar of laughter—laughter he could not check—nasty, jangling merriment that seemed as if it would go on for ever. When he had recovered himself he said, quite seriously, 'I'm tired of work. I'm an old man now. It's about time I retired. And I will.'

'The boy's mad!' said the Head

I think he was right; but Dicky Hatt never reappeared to settle the question.

Pig*

Go, stalk the red deer o'er the heather,
  Ride, follow the fox if you can!
But, for pleasure and profit together,
  Allow me the hunting of Man—
The chase of the Human, the search for the Soul
  To its ruin,—the hunting of Man.

*The Old Shikarri.**

I BELIEVE the difference began in the matter of a horse,
with a twist in his temper, whom Pinecoffin sold to Nafferton,
and by whom Nafferton was nearly slain. There may have
been other causes of offence; the horse was the official
stalking-horse. Nafferton was very angry; but Pinecoffin
laughed, and said that he had never guaranteed the beast's
manners. Nafferton laughed too, though he vowed that he
would write off his fall against Pinecoffin if he waited five
years. Now, a Dalesman from beyond Skipton will forgive an
injury when the Strid* lets a man live; but a South Devon man
is as soft as a Dartmoor bog. You can see from their names
that Nafferton had the race-advantage of Pinecoffin. He was
a peculiar man, and his notions of humour were cruel. He
taught me a new and fascinating form of *shikar*. He hounded
Pinecoffin from Mithankot to Jagadri, and from Gurgaon to
Abbottabad—up and across the Punjab, a large Province, and
in places remarkably dry. He said that he had no intention of
allowing Assistant Commissioners* to 'sell him pups,' in the
shape of ramping, screaming countrybreds,* without making
their lives a burden to them.

Most Assistant Commisioners develop a bent for some
special work after their first hot weather in the country. The
boys with digestions hope to write their names large on the
Frontier, and struggle for dreary places like Bannu and
Kohat.* The bilious ones climb into the Secretariat; which is
very bad for the liver. Others are bitten with a mania for
District work, Ghaznevid* coins or Persian poetry; while

some, who come of farmers' stock, find that the smell of the Earth after the Rains gets into their blood, and calls them to 'develop the resources of the Province.' These men are enthusiasts. Pinecoffin belonged to their class. He knew a great many facts bearing on the cost of bullocks and temporary wells, and opium-scrapers, and what happens if you burn too much rubbish on a field in the hope of enriching used-up soil. All the Pinecoffins come of a landholding breed, and so the land only took back her own again. Unfortunately—most unfortunately for Pinecoffin—he was a Civilian as well as a farmer. Nafferton watched him, and thought about the horse. Nafferton said, 'See me chase that boy till he drops!' I said, 'You can't get your knife into an Assistant Commissioner.' Nafferton told me that I did not understand the administration of the Province.

Our Government is rather peculiar. It gushes on the agricultural and general information side, and will supply a moderately respectable man with all sorts of 'economic statistics,' if he speaks to it prettily. For instance, you are interested in gold-washing in the sands of the Sutlej.* You pull the string, and find that it wakes up half-a-dozen Departments, and finally communicates, say, with a friend of yours in the Telegraph, who once wrote some notes on the customs of the gold-washers when he was on construction-work in their part of the Empire. He may or may not be pleased at being ordered to write out everything he knows for your benefit. This depends on his temperament. The bigger man you are, the more information and the greater trouble can you raise.

Nafferton was not a big man; but he had the reputation of being very 'earnest.' An 'earnest' man can do much with a Government. There was an earnest man once who nearly wrecked . . . but all India knows *that* story. I am not sure what real 'earnestness' is. A very fair imitation can be manufactured by neglecting to dress decently, by mooning about in a dreamy, misty sort of way, by taking office-work home, after staying in the office till seven, and by receiving crowds of native gentlemen on Sundays. That is one sort of 'earnestness.'

Nafferton cast about for a peg whereon to hang his earnestness, and for a string that would communicate with Pinecoffin. He found both. They were Pig. Nafferton became an earnest inquirer after Pig. He informed the Government that he had a scheme whereby a very large percentage of the British Army in India could be fed, at a very large saving, on Pig. Then he hinted that Pinecoffin might supply him with the 'varied information necessary to the proper inception of the scheme.' So the Government wrote on the back of the letter, 'Instruct Mr. Pinecoffin to furnish Mr. Nafferton with any information in his power.' Government is very prone to writing things on the backs of letters which, later, lead to trouble and confusion.

Nafferton had not the faintest interest in Pig, but he knew that Pinecoffin would flounce into the trap. Pinecoffin was delighted at being consulted about Pig. The Indian Pig is not exactly an important factor in agricultural life; but Nafferton explained to Pinecoffin that there was room for improvement, and corresponded direct with that young man.

You may think that there is not much to be evolved from Pig. It all depends how you set to work. Pinecoffin being a Civilian and wishing to do things thoroughly, began with an essay on the Primitive Pig, the Mythology of the Pig, and the Dravidian* Pig. Nafferton filed that information—twenty-seven foolscap sheets—and wanted to know about the distribution of the Pig in the Punjab, and how it stood the Plains in the hot weather. From this point onwards remember that I am giving you only the barest outlines of the affair—the guy-ropes, as it were, of the web that Nafferton spun round Pinecoffin.

Pinecoffin made a coloured Pig-population map, and collected observations on the comparative longevity of Pig (a) in the sub-montane tracts of the Himalayas, and (b) in the Rechna Doab.* Nafferton filed that, and asked what sort of people looked after Pig. This started an ethnological excursus on swineherds, and drew from Pinecoffin long tables showing the proportion per thousand of the caste in the Derajat.* Nafferton filed that bundle, and explained that the figures which he wanted referred to the Cis-Sutlej states, where he

understood that Pigs were very fine and large, and where he
proposed to start a Piggery. By this time Government had
quite forgotten their instructions to Mr. Pinecoffin. They
were like the gentlemen in Keats' poem*, who turned well-
oiled wheels to skin other people. But Pinecoffin was just
entering into the spirit of the Pig-hunt, as Nafferton well
knew he would do. He had a fair amount of work of his own
to clear away; but he sat up of nights reducing Pig to five
places of decimals for the honour of his Service. He was not
going to appear ignorant of so easy a subject as Pig.

Then Government sent him on special duty to Kohat, to
'inquire into' the big, seven-foot, iron-shod spades of that
District. People had been killing each other with those
peaceful tools; and Government wished to know 'whether a
modified form of agricultural implement could not,
tentatively and as a temporary measure, be introduced among
the agricultural population without needlessly or unduly
exacerbating the existing religious sentiments of the
peasantry.'

Between those spades and Nafferton's Pig, Pinecoffin was
rather heavily burdened.

Nafferton now began to take up '(a) The food-supply of the
indigenous Pig, with a view to the improvement of its
capacities as a flesh-former. (b) The acclimatisation of the
exotic Pig, maintaining its distinctive peculiarities.'
Pinecoffin replied exhaustively that the exotic Pig would
become merged in the indigenous type; and quoted horse-
breeding statistics to prove this. The side-issue was debated at
great length on Pinecoffin's side, till Nafferton owned that he
had been in the wrong, and moved the previous question.
When Pinecoffin had quite written himself out about flesh-
formers, and fibrins, and glucose, and the nitrogenous
constituents of maize and lucerne, Nafferton raised the
question of expense. By this time Pinecoffin, who had been
transferred from Kohat, had developed a Pig theory of his
own, which he stated in thirty-three folio pages—all carefully
filed by Nafferton; who asked for more.

These things took ten months, and Pinecoffin's interest in
the potential Piggery seemed to die down after he had stated

his own views. But Nafferton bombarded him with letters on 'the Imperial aspect of the scheme, as tending to officialise the sale of pork, and thereby calculated to give offence to the Mahommedan population* of Upper India.' He guessed that Pinecoffin would want some broad, free-hand work after his niggling, stippling, decimal details. Pinecoffin handled the latest development of the case in masterly style, and proved that no 'popular ebullition of excitement was to be apprehended.' Nafferton said that there was nothing like Civilian insight in matters of this kind, and lured him up a by-path—'the possible profits to accrue to the Government from the sale of hog-bristles.' There is an extensive literature of hog-bristles, and the shoe, brush, and colourman's trades recognise more varieties of bristles than you would think possible. After Pinecoffin had wondered a little at Nafferton's rage for information, he sent back a monograph, fifty-one pages, on 'Products of the Pig.' This led him, under Nafferton's tender handling, straight to the Cawnpore factories, the trade in hog-skin for saddles—and thence to the tanners. Pinecoffin wrote that pomegranate-seed was the best cure for hog-skin, and suggested—for the past fourteen months had wearied him—that Nafferton should 'raise his pigs before he tanned them.'

Nafferton went back to the second section of his fifth question. How could the exotic Pig be brought to give as much pork as it did in the West and yet 'assume the essentially hirsute characteristics of its Oriental congener'? Pinecoffin felt dazed, for he had forgotten what he had written sixteen months before, and fancied that he was about to reopen the entire question. He was too far involved in the hideous tangle to retreat, and, in a weak moment, he wrote, 'Consult my first letter'; which related to the Dravidian Pig. As a matter of fact, Pinecoffin had still to reach the acclimatisation stage; having gone off on a side-issue on the merging of types.

Then Nafferton really unmasked his batteries! He complained to the Government, in stately language, of 'the paucity of help accorded to me in my earnest attempts to start a potentially remunerative industry, and the flippancy with which my requests for information are treated by a gentleman whose pseudo-scholarly attainments should at least have taught him the primary differences between the Dravidian and the Berkshire variety of the genus *Sus*.* If I am to understand that the letter to which he refers me contains his serious views on the acclimatisation of a valuable, though possible uncleanly, animal, I am reluctantly compelled to believe,' etc. etc.

There was a new man at the head of the Department of Castigation. The wretched Pinecoffin was told that the Service was made for the Country, and not the Country for the Service, and that he had better begin to supply information about Pigs.

Pinecoffin answered insanely that he had written everything that could be written about Pig, and that some furlough was due to him.

Nafferton got a copy of that letter, and sent it, with the essay on the Dravidian Pig, to a down-country paper which printed both in full. The essay was rather high-flown; but if the Editor had seen the stacks of paper, in Pinecoffin's handwriting, on Nafferton's table, he would not have been so sarcastic about the 'nebulous discursiveness and blatant self-sufficiency of the modern Competition-*wallah*,* and his utter inability to grasp the practical issues of a practical question.' Many friends cut out these remarks and sent them to Pinecoffin.

I have already stated that Pinecoffin came of a soft stock. This last stroke frightened and shook him. He could not understand it; but he felt that he had been, somehow, shamelessly betrayed by Nafferton. He realised that he had wrapped himself up in the Pigskin without need, and that he could not well set himself right with his Government. All his acquaintances asked after his 'nebulous discursiveness' or his 'blatant self-sufficiency,' and this made him miserable.

He took a train and went to Nafferton, whom he had not seen since the Pig business began. He also took the cutting from the paper, and blustered feebly and called Nafferton names, and then died down to a watery, weak protest of the 'I-say-it's-too-bad-you-know' order.

Nafferton was very sympathetic.

'I'm afraid I've given you a good deal of trouble, haven't I?' said he.

'Trouble!' whimpered Pinecoffin; 'I don't mind the trouble so much, though that was bad enough; but what I resent is this showing up in print. It will stick to me like a burr all through my service. And I *did* do my best for your interminable swine. It's too bad of you—on my soul it is!'

'I don't know,' said Nafferton. 'Have you ever been stuck with a horse? It isn't the money I mind, though that is bad enough; but what I resent is the chaff that follows, especially from the boy who stuck me. But I think we'll cry quits now.'

Pinecoffin found nothing to say save bad words; and Nafferton smiled ever so sweetly, and asked him to dinner.

The Rout of the White Hussars*

It was not in the open fight
We threw away the sword,
But in the lonely watching
In the darkness by the ford.
The waters lapped, the night-wind blew,
Full-armed the Fear was born and grew,
And we were flying ere we knew
From panic in the night.

Beoni Bar. 1

SOME people hold that an English Cavalry regiment cannot
run. This is a mistake. I have seen four hundred and thirty-
seven sabres flying over the face of the country in abject
terror—have seen the best Regiment that ever drew bridle
wiped off the Army List for the space of two hours. If you
repeat this tale to the White Hussars they will, in all
probability, treat you severely. They are not proud of the
incident.

You may know the White Hussars by their 'side,' which is
greater than that of all the Cavalry Regiments on the roster.
If this is not a sufficient mark, you may know them by their
old brandy. It has been sixty years in the Mess and is worth
going far to taste. Ask for the 'McGaire' old brandy, and see
that you get it. If the Mess Sergeant thinks that you are
uneducated, and that the genuine article will be lost on you,
he will treat you accordingly. He is a good man. But, when
you are at Mess, you must never talk to your hosts about
forced marches or long-distance rides. The Mess are very
sensitive; and, if they think that you are laughing at them, will
tell you so.

As the White Hussars say, it was all the Colonel's fault. He
was a new man, and he ought never to have taken the
Command. He said that the Regiment was not smart enough.
This to the White Hussars, who knew that they could walk
round any Horse, and through any Guns, and over any Foot

on the face of the earth! That insult was the first cause of offence.

Then the Colonel cast* the Drum-Horse—the Drum-Horse of the White Hussars! Perhaps you do not see what an unspeakable crime he had committed. I will try to make it clear. The soul of the Regiment lives in the Drum-Horse who carries the silver kettle-drums. He is nearly always a big piebald Waler.* That is a point of honour; and a Regiment will spend anything you please on a piebald. He is beyond the ordinary laws of casting. His work is very light, and he only manoeuvres at a footpace. Wherefore, so long as he can step out and look handsome, his well-being is assured. He knows more about the Regiment than the Adjutant, and could not make a mistake if he tried.

The Drum-Horse of the White Hussars was only eighteen years old, and perfectly equal to his duties. He had at least six years' more work in him, and carried himself with all the pomp and dignity of a Drum-Major of the Guards. The Regiment had paid Rs.1200 for him.

But the Colonel said that he must go, and he was cast in due form and replaced by a washy, bay beast, as ugly as a mule, with a ewe-neck, rat-tail, and cow-hocks.* The Drummer detested that animal, and the rest of the Band-horses put back their ears and showed the whites of their eyes at the very sight of him. They knew him for an upstart and no gentleman. I fancy that the Colonel's ideas of smartness extended to the Band, and that he wanted to make it take part in the regular parade movements. A Cavalry Band is a sacred thing. It only turns out for Commanding Officers' parades, and the Band Master is one degree more important than the Colonel. He is a High Priest and the 'Keel Row'* is his holy song. The 'Keel Row' is the Cavalry Trot; and the man who has never heard that tune rising, high and shrill, above the rattle of the Regiment going past the saluting-base, has something yet to hear and understand.

When the Colonel cast the Drum-Horse of the White Hussars there was nearly a mutiny.

The officers were angry, the Regiment were furious, and the Bandsmen swore—like troopers. The Drum-Horse was going to be put up to auction—public auction—to be bought, perhaps, by a Parsee* and put into a cart! It was worse than exposing the inner life of the Regiment to the whole world, or selling the Mess Plate to a Jew—a Black Jew.*

The Colonel was a mean man and a bully. He knew what the Regiment thought about his action; and, when the troopers offered to buy the Drum-Horse, he said that their offer was mutinous and forbidden by the Regulations.

But one of the Subalterns—Hogan-Yale, an Irishman— bought the Drum-Horse for Rs.160 at the sale; and the Colonel was wroth. Yale professed repentance—he was unnaturally submissive—and said that, as he had only made the purchase to save the horse from possible ill treatment and starvation, he would now shoot him and end the business. This appeared to soothe the Colonel, for he wanted the Drum-Horse disposed of. He felt that he had made a mistake, and could not of course acknowledge it. Meantime, the presence of the Drum-Horse was an annoyance to him.

Yale took to himself a glass of the old brandy, three cheroots, and his friend Martyn; and they all left the Mess together. Yale and Martyn conferred for two hours in Yale's quarters; but only the bull-terrier who keeps watch over Yale's boot-trees knows what they said. A horse, hooded and sheeted to his ears, left Yale's stables and was taken, very unwillingly, into the Civil Lines. Yale's groom went with him. Two men broke into the Regimental Theatre and took several paint-pots and some large scenery-brushes. Then night fell over the cantonments, and there was a noise as of a horse kicking his loose-box to pieces in Yale's stables. Yale had a big, old, white Waler trap-horse.

The next day was a Thursday, and the men, hearing that Yale was going to shoot the Drum-Horse in the evening, determined to give the beast a regular regimental funeral—a finer one than they would have given the Colonel had he died just then. They got a bullock-cart and some sacking, and mounds and mounds of roses, and the body, under sacking, was carried out to the place where the anthrax cases were cremated; two-thirds of the Regiment following. There was no Band, but they all sang 'The Place where the old Horse died'* as something respectful and appropriate to the occasion. When the corpse was dumped into the grave and the men began throwing down armfuls of roses to cover it, the Farrier-Sergeant ripped out an oath and said aloud, 'Why, it ain't the Drum-Horse any more than it's me!' The Troop-Sergeant-Majors asked him whether he had left his head in the Canteen. The Farrier-Sergeant said that he knew the Drum-Horse's feet as well as he knew his own; but he was silenced when he saw the regimental number burnt in* on the poor stiff, upturned near-fore.

Thus was the Drum-Horse of the White Hussars buried; the Farrier-Sergeant grumbling. The sacking that covered the corpse was smeared in places with black paint; and the Farrier-Sergeant drew attention to this fact. But the Troop-Sergeant-Major of E Troop kicked him severely on the shin, and told him that he was undoubtedly drunk.

On the Monday following the burial, the Colonel sought revenge on the White Hussars. Unfortunately, being at that time temporarily in Command of the Station, he ordered a Brigade field-day. He said that he wished to make the Regiment 'sweat for their damned insolence,' and he carried out his notion thoroughly. That Monday was one of the hardest days in the memory of the White Hussars. They were thrown against a skeleton-enemy, and pushed forward, and withdrawn, and dismounted, and 'scientifically handled' in every possible fashion over dusty country, till they sweated profusely. Their only amusement came late in the day when they fell upon the battery of Horse Artillery and chased it for two miles. This was a personal question, and most of the troopers had money on the event; the Gunners saying openly that they had the legs of the White Hussars. They were wrong. A march-past concluded the campaign, and when the Regiment got back to their Lines the men were coated with dirt from spur to chin-strap.

The White Hussars have one great and peculiar privilege. They won it at Fontenoy,* I think.

Many Regiments possess special rights, such as wearing collars with undress uniform, or a bow of riband between the shoulders, or red and white roses in their helmets on certain days of the year. Some rights are connected with regimental saints, and some with regimental successes. All are valued highly; but none so highly as the right of the White Hussars to have the Band playing when their horses are being watered in the Lines. Only one tune is played, and that tune never varies. I don't know its real name, but the White Hussars call it 'Take me to London again.' It sounds very pretty. The Regiment would sooner be struck off the roster than forego their distinction.

After the 'dismiss' was sounded, the officers rode off home to prepare for stables; and the men filed into the lines riding easy. That is to say, they opened their tight buttons, shifted their helmets, and began to joke or to swear as the humour took them; the more careful slipping off and easing girths and curbs. A good trooper values his mount exactly as much as he values himself, and believes, or should believe, that the two together are irresistible where women or men, girls or guns, are concerned.

Then the Orderly-Officer gave the order, 'Water horses,' and the Regiment loafed off to the squadron-troughs which were in rear of the stables, and between these and the barracks. There were four huge troughs, one for each squadron, arranged en échelon,* so that the whole Regiment could water in ten minutes if it liked. But it lingered for seventeen, as a rule, while the Band played.

The Band struck up as the squadrons filed off to the troughs, and the men slipped their feet out of the stirrups and chaffed each other. The sun was just setting in a big, hot bed of red cloud, and the road to the Civil Lines seemed to run straight into the sun's eye. There was a little dot on the road. It grew and grew till it showed as a horse, with a sort of gridiron-thing on his back. The red cloud glared through the bars of the gridiron. Some of the troopers shaded their eyes with their hands and said—'What the mischief 'as that there 'orse got on 'im?'

In another minute they heard a neigh that every soul—horse and man—in the Regiment knew, and saw, heading straight towards the Band, the dead Drum-Horse of the White Hussars!

On his withers banged and bumped the kettle-drums draped in crape, and on his back, very stiff and soldierly, sat a bareheaded skeleton.

The Band stopped playing, and, for a moment, there was a hush.

Then some one in E Troop—men said it was the Troop-Sergeant-Major—swung his horse round and yelled. No one can account exactly for what happened afterwards; but it seems that at least one man in each troop set an example of panic, and the rest followed like sheep. The horses that had barely put their muzzles into the troughs reared and capered; but as soon as the Band broke, which it did when the ghost of the Drum-Horse was about a furlong distant, all hooves followed suit, and the clatter of the stampede—quite different from the orderly throb and roar of a movement on parade, or the rough horse-play of watering in camp—made them only more terrified. They felt that the men on their backs were afraid of something. When horses once know that, all is over except the butchery.

Troop after troop turned from the troughs and ran—anywhere and everywhere—like spilt quick-silver. It was a most extraordinary spectacle, for men and horses were in all stages of easiness, and the carbine-buckets flopping against their sides urged the horses on. Men were shouting and cursing, and trying to pull clear of the Band which was being chased by the Drum-Horse whose rider had fallen forward and seemed to be spurring for a wager.

The Colonel had gone over to the Mess for a drink. Most of the officers were with him, and the Subaltern of the Day was preparing to go down to the lines, and receive the watering reports from the Troop-Sergeant-Majors. When 'Take me to London again' stopped, after twenty bars, every one in the Mess said, 'What on earth has happened?' A minute later, they heard unmilitary noises, and saw, far across the plain, the White Hussars scattered and broken, and flying.

The Colonel was speechless with rage, for he thought that the Regiment had risen against him or was unanimously drunk. The Band, a disorganised mob, tore past, and at its heels laboured the Drum-Horse—the dead and buried Drum-

Horse—with the jolting, clattering skeleton. Hogan-Yale whispered softly to Martyn—'No wire will stand that treatment,' and the Band, which had doubled like a hare, came back again. But the rest of the Regiment was gone, was rioting all over the Province, for the dusk had shut in, and each man was howling to his neighbour that the Drum-Horse was on his flank. Troop-horses are far too tenderly treated as a rule. They can, in emergencies, do a great deal, even with seventeen stone on their backs; as the troopers found out.

How long this panic lasted I cannot say. I believe that when the moon rose the men saw they had nothing to fear, and, by twos and threes and half-troops, crept back into Cantonments very much ashamed of themselves. Meantime, the Drum-Horse, disgusted at his treatment by old friends, pulled up, wheeled round, and trotted up to the Mess verandah-steps for bread. No one liked to run; but no one cared to go forward till the Colonel made a movement and laid hold of the skeleton's foot. The Band had halted some distance away, and now came back slowly. The Colonel called it, individually and collectively, every evil name that occurred to him at the time; for he had set his hand on the bosom of the Drum-Horse and found flesh and blood. Then he beat the kettle-drums with his clenched fist, and discovered that they were but made of silvered paper and bamboo. Next, still swearing, he tried to drag the skeleton out of the saddle, but found that it had been wired into the cantle.* The sight of the Colonel, with his arms round the skeleton's pelvis and his knee in the old Drum-Horse's stomach, was striking; not to say amusing. He worried the thing off in a minute or two, and threw it down on the ground, saying to the Band—'Here, you curs, that's what you're afraid of.' The skeleton did not look pretty in the twilight. The Band-Sergeant seemed to recognise it, for he began to chuckle and choke. 'Shall I take it away, sir?' said the Band-Sergeant. 'Yes,' said the Colonel, 'take it to Hell, and ride there yourselves!'

The Band-Sergeant saluted, hoisted the skeleton across his saddle-bow, and led off to the stables. Then the Colonel began to make inquiries for the rest of the Regiment, and the language he used was wonderful. He would disband the

Regiment—he would court-martial every soul in it—he would not command such a set of rabble, and so on, and so on. As the men dropped in, his language grew wilder, until at last it exceeded the utmost limits of free speech allowed even to a Colonel of Horse.

Martyn took Hogan-Yale aside and suggested compulsory retirement from the Service as a necessity when all was discovered. Martyn was the weaker man of the two. Hogan-Yale put up his eyebrows and remarked, firstly, that he was the son of a Lord, and, secondly, that he was as innocent as the babe unborn of the theatrical resurrection of the Drum-Horse.

'My instructions,' said Hogan-Yale, with a singularly sweet smile, 'were that the Drum-Horse should be sent back as impressively as possible. I ask you, *am* I responsible if a mule-headed friend sends him back in such a manner as to disturb the peace of mind of a regiment of Her Majesty's Cavalry?'

Martyn said, 'You are a great man, and will in time become a General; but I'd give my chance of a troop* to be safe out of this affair.'

Providence saved Martyn and Hogan-Yale. The Second-in-Command led the Colonel away to the little curtained alcove wherein the Subalterns of the White Hussars were accustomed to play poker of nights; and there, after many oaths on the Colonel's part, they talked together in low tones. I fancy that the Second-in-Command must have represented the scare as the work of some trooper whom it would be hopeless to detect; and I know that he dwelt upon the sin and the shame of making a public laughing-stock of the scare.

'They will call us,' said the Second-in-Command, who had really a fine imagination—'they will call us the "Fly-by-Nights"; they will call us the "Ghost-Hunters"; they will nickname us from one end of the Army List to the other. All the explanation in the world won't make outsiders understand that the officers were away when the panic began. For the honour of the Regiment and for your own sake keep this thing quiet.'

The Colonel was so exhausted with anger that soothing him down was not so difficult as might be imagined. He was made to see, gently and by degrees, that it was obviously impossible to court-martial the whole Regiment, and equally impossible to proceed against any subaltern who, in his belief, had any concern in the hoax.

'But the beast's alive! He's never been shot at all!' shouted the Colonel. 'It's flat flagrant disobedience! I've known a man broke for less— dam' sight less. They're mocking me, I tell you, Mutman! They're mocking me!'

Once more the Second-in-Command set himself to soothe the Colonel, and wrestled with him for half an hour. At the end of that time the Regimental Sergeant-Major reported himself. The situation was rather novel to him; but he was not a man to be put out by circumstances. He saluted and said, 'Regiment all come back, Sir.' Then, to propitiate the Colonel—'An' none of the 'orses any the worse, Sir.'

The Colonel only snorted and answered—'You'd better tuck the men into their cots, then, and see that they don't wake up and cry in the night.' The Sergeant withdrew.

His little stroke of humour pleased the Colonel, and, further, he felt slightly ashamed of the language he had been using. The Second-in-Command worried him again, and the two sat talking far into the night.

Next day but one there was a Commanding Officer's parade, and the Colonel harangued the White Hussars vigorously. The pith of his speech was that, since the Drum-Horse in his old age had proved himself capable of cutting up the whole Regiment, he should return to his post of pride at the head of the Band, *but* the Regiment were a set of ruffians with bad consciences.

The White Hussars shouted, and threw everything movable about them into the air, and when the parade was over they cheered the Colonel till they couldn't speak. No cheers were put up for Lieutenant Hogan-Yale, who smiled very sweetly in the background.

Said the Second-in-Command to the colonel, unofficially—

'These little things ensure popularity, and do not the least affect discipline.'

'But I went back on my word,' said the Colonel.

'Never mind,' said the Second-in-Command. 'The White

Hussars will follow you anywhere from to-day. Regiments are just like women. They will do anything for trinketry.'

A week later, Hogan-Yale received an extraordinary letter from some one who signed himself 'Secretary, *Charity and Zeal*, 3709, E. C.,'* and asked for 'the return of our skeleton which we have reason to believe is in your possession.'

'Who the deuce is this lunatic who trades in bones?' said Hogan-Yale.

'Beg your pardon, Sir,' said the Band-Sergeant, 'but the skeleton is with me, an' I'll return it if you'll pay the carriage into the Civil Lines. There's a coffin with it, Sir.'

Hogan-Yale smiled and handed two rupees to the Band-Sergeant, saying, 'Write the date on the skull, will you?'

If you doubt this story, and know where to go, you can see the date on the skeleton. But don't mention the matter to the White Hussars.

I happen to know something about it, because I helped to prepare the Drum-Horse for his resurrection. He did not take kindly to the skeleton at all.

The Bronckhorst Divorce-Case*

In the daytime, when she moved about me,
  In the night, when she was sleeping at my side,—
I was wearied, I was wearied of her presence,
Day by day and night by night I grew to hate her—
  Would God that she or I had died!

Confessions.

THERE was a man called Bronckhorst—a three-cornered,*
middle-aged man in the Army—gray as a badger, and, some
people said, with a touch of country-blood* in him. That,
however, cannot be proved. Mrs. Bronckhorst was not exactly
young, though fifteen years younger than her husband. She
was a large, pale, quiet woman, with heavy eyelids over weak
eyes, and hair that turned red or yellow as the lights fell on it.

Bronckhorst was not nice in any way. He had no respect for
the pretty public and private lies that make life a little less
nasty than it is. His manner towards his wife was coarse.
There are many things—including actual assault with the
clenched fist—that a wife will endure; but seldom a wife can
bear—as Mrs. Bronckhorst bore—with a long course of brutal,
hard chaff, making light of her weaknesses, her headaches, her
small fits of gaiety, her dresses, her queer little attempts to
make herself attractive to her husband when she knows that
she is not what she has been, and—worst of all—the love that
she spends on her children. That particular sort of heavy-
handed jest was specially dear to Bronckhorst. I suppose that
he had first slipped into it, meaning no harm, in the
honeymoon, when folk find their ordinary stock of
endearments run short, and so go to the other extreme to
express their feelings. A similar impulse makes a man say,
'Hutt,* you old beast!' when a favourite horse nuzzles his
coat-front. Unluckily, when the reaction of marriage sets in,
the form of speech remains, and, the tenderness having died
out, hurts the wife more than she cares to say. But Mrs.
Bronckhorst was devoted to her 'Teddy' as she called him

Perhaps that was why he objected to her. Perhaps—this is only a theory to account for his infamous behaviour later on—he gave way to the queer, savage feeling that sometimes takes by the throat a husband twenty years married, when he sees, across the table, the same, same face of his wedded wife, and knows that, as he has sat facing it, so must he continue to sit until the day of its death or his own. Most men and all women know the spasm. It only lasts for three breaths as a rule, must be a 'throw-back' to times when men and women were rather worse than they are now, and is too unpleasant to be discussed.

Dinner at the Bronckhorsts' was an infliction few men cared to undergo. Bronckhorst took a pleasure in saying things that made his wife wince. When their little boy came in at dessert, Bronckhorst used to give him half a glass of wine, and, naturally enough, the poor little mite got first, riotous, next miserable, and was removed screaming. Bronckhorst asked if that was the way Teddy usually behaved, and whether Mrs. Bronckhorst could not spare some of her time 'to teach the little beggar decency.' Mrs. Bronckhorst, who loved the boy more than her own life, tried not to cry—her spirit seemed to have been broken by her marriage. Lastly, Bronckhorst used to say, 'There! That'll do, that'll do. For God's sake try to behave like a rational woman. Go into the drawing-room.' Mrs. Bronckhorst would go, trying to carry it all off with a smile; and the guest of the evening would feel angry and uncomfortable.

After three years of this cheerful life—for Mrs. Bronckhorst had no women-friends to talk to—the Station was startled by the news that Bronckhorst had instituted proceedings *on the criminal count*,* against a man called Biel, who certainly had been rather attentive to Mrs. Bronckhorst whenever she had appeared in public. The utter want of reserve with which Bronckhorst treated his own dishonour helped us to know that the evidence against Biel would be entirely circumstantial and native. There were no letters; but Bronckhorst said openly that he would rack Heaven and Earth until he saw Biel superintending the manufacture of carpets in the Central Jail. Mrs. Bronckhorst kept entirely to her house, and let charitable folks say what they pleased. Opinions were divided. Some two-thirds of the Station jumped at once to the conclusion that Biel was guilty; but a dozen men who knew and liked him held by him. Biel was furious and surprised. He denied the whole thing, and vowed that he would thrash Bronckhorst within an inch of his life. No jury, we knew, would convict a man on the criminal count on native evidence in a land where you can buy a murder-charge, including the corpse, all complete for fifty-four rupees; but Biel did not care to scrape through by the benefit of a doubt. He wanted the whole thing cleared; but, as he said one night—'He can prove anything with servants' evidence, and I've only my bare word.' This was almost a month before the case came on; and beyond agreeing with Biel, we could do little. All that we could be sure of was that the native evidence would be bad enough to blast Biel's character for the rest of his service; for when a native begins perjury he perjures himself thoroughly. He does not boggle over details.

Some genius at the end of the table whereat the affair was being talked over, said, 'Look here! I don't believe lawyers are any good. Get a man to wire to Strickland, and beg him to come down and pull us through.'

Strickland was about a hundred and eighty miles up the line. He had not long been married to Miss Youghal, but he scented in the telegram a chance of return to the old detective work that his soul lusted after, and next night he came in and heard our story. He finished his pipe and said oracularly, 'We must get at the evidence. *Oorya* bearer, Mussulman *khit* and sweeper *ayah*,* I suppose, are the pillars of the charge. I am on in this piece; but I'm afraid I'm getting rusty in my talk.'

He rose and went into Biel's bedroom, where his trunk had been put, and shut the door. An hour later, we heard him say, 'I hadn't the heart to part with my old make-ups when I married. Will this do?' There was a loathly *faquir* salaaming in the doorway.

'Now lend me fifty rupees,' said Strickland, 'and give me your Words of Honour that you won't tell my wife.'

He got all that he asked for, and left the house while the table drank his health. What he did only he himself knows. A *faquir* hung about Bronckhorst's compound for twelve days. Then a sweeper appeared, and when Biel heard of *him*, he said that Strickland was an angel full-fledged. Whether the sweeper made love to Janki, Mrs. Bronckhorst's *ayah*, is a question which concerns Strickland exclusively.

He came back at the end of three weeks, and said quietly, 'You spoke the truth, Biel. The whole business is put up from beginning to end. 'Jove! It almost astonishes *me!* That Bronckhorst beast isn't fit to live.'

There was uproar and shouting, and Biel said, 'How are you going to prove it? You can't say that you've been trespassing on Bronckhorst's compound in disguise!'

'No,' said Strickland. 'Tell your lawyer-fool, whoever he is, to get up something strong about "inherent improbabilities" and "discrepancies of evidence." He won't have to speak, but it will make him happy. *I'm* going to run this business.'

Biel held his tongue, and the other men waited to see what would happen. They trusted Strickland as men trust quiet men. When the case came off the Court was crowded. Strickland hung about in the verandah of the Court, till he met the Mahommedan *khitmutgar*.* Then he murmured a *faquir's* blessing in his ear, and asked him how his second wife did. The man spun round, and, as he looked into the eyes of 'Estreeken *Sahib*,' his jaw dropped. You must remember that before Strickland was married, he was, as I have told you already, a power among natives. Strickland whispered a rather coarse vernacular proverb to the effect that he was abreast of all that was going on, and went into the Court armed with a gut trainer's-whip.

The Mahommedan was the first witness, and Strickland beamed upon him from the back of the Court. The man moistened his lips with his tongue and, in his abject fear of 'Estreeken *Sahib*,' the *faquir*, went back on every detail of his evidence—said he was a poor man, and God was his witness that he had forgotten everything that Bronckhorst *Sahib* had told him to say. Between his terror of Strickland, the Judge, and Bronckhorst he collapsed weeping.

Then began the panic among the witnesses. Janki, the *ayah*, leering chastely behind her veil, turned gray, and the bearer left the Court. He said that his Mamma was dying, and that it was not wholesome for any man to lie unthriftily in the presence of 'Estreeken *Sahib.*'

Biel said politely to Bronckhorst, 'Your witnesses don't seem to work. Haven't you any forged letters to produce?' But Bronckhorst was swaying to and fro in his chair, and there was a dead pause after Biel had been called to order.

Bronckhorst's Counsel saw the look on his client's face, and without more ado, pitched his papers on the little green baize table, mumbled something about having been misinformed. The whole court applauded wildly, like soldiers at a theatre, and the Judge began to say what he thought.

*   *   *

Biel came out of the Court, and Strickland dropped a gut trainer's-whip in the verandah. Ten minutes later, Biel was cutting Bronckhorst into ribbons behind the old Court cells, quietly and without scandal. What was left of Bronckhorst was sent home in a carriage; and his wife wept over it and nursed it into a man again.

Later on, after Biel had managed to hush up the counter-charge against Bronckhorst of fabricating false evidence, Mrs. Bronckhorst, with her faint, watery smile, said that there had been a mistake, but it wasn't her Teddy's fault altogether. She would wait till her Teddy came back to her. Perhaps he had grown tired of her, or she had tried his patience, and perhaps we wouldn't cut her any more, and perhaps the mothers would let their children play with 'little Teddy' again. He was so lonely. Then the Station invited Mrs. Bronckhorst everywhere, until Bronckhorst was fit to appear in public, when he went Home and took his wife with him. According to latest advices, her Teddy did come back to her, and they are moderately happy. Though, of course, he can never forgive her the thrashing that she was the indirect means of getting for him.

*   *   *

What Biel wants to know is, 'Why didn't I press home the charge against the Bronckhorst orute, and have him run in?'

What Mrs. Strickland wants to know is, 'How *did* my husband bring such a lovely, lovely Waler* from your Station? I know *all* his money affairs; and I'm *certain* he didn't *buy* it.'

What I want to know is, 'How do women like Mrs. Bronckhorst come to marry men like Bronckhorst?'

And my conundrum is the most unanswerable of the three.

Venus Annodomini*

And the years went on,* as the years must do;
But our great Diana was always new—
Fresh, and blooming, and blonde, and fair,
With azure eyes, and with aureate hair;
And all the folk, as they came or went,
Offered her praise to her heart's content.

Diana of Ephesus.

SHE had nothing to do with Number Eighteen in the Braccio
Nuovo* of the Vatican, between Visconti's Ceres and the God
of the Nile. She was purely an Indian deity—an Anglo-Indian
deity, that is to say—and we called her *the* Venus Annodomini,
to distinguish her from other Annodominis of the same
everlasting order. There was a legend among the Hills that she
had once been young; but no living man was prepared to come
forward and say boldly that the legend was true. Men rode up
to Simla, and stayed, and went away and made their name and
did their life's work, and returned again to find the Venus
Annodomini exactly as they had left her. She was as
immutable as the Hills. But not quite so green. All that a girl
of eighteen could do in the way of riding, walking, dancing, picnicking, and over-exertion generally, the Venus
Annodomini did, and showed no sign of fatigue or trace of
weariness. Besides perpetual youth, she had discovered, men
said, the secret of perpetual health; and her fame spread about
the land. From a mere woman, she grew to be an Institution,
insomuch that no young man could be said to be properly
formed, who had not, at some time or another, worshipped at
the shrine of the Venus Annodomini. There was no one like
her, though there were many imitations. Six years in her eyes
were no more than six months to ordinary women; and ten
made less visible impression on her than does a week's fever
on an ordinary woman. Every one adored her, and in return
she was pleasant and courteous to nearly every one. Youth had
been a habit of hers for so long, that she could not part with

it—never realised, in fact, the necessity of parting with it—and took for her more chosen associates young people.

Among the worshippers of the Venus Annodomini was young Gayerson. 'Very Young Gayerson' he was called to distinguish him from his father 'Young' Gayerson, a Bengal Civilian,* who affected the customs—as he had the heart—of youth. 'Very Young' Gayerson was not content to worship placidly and for form's sake, as the other young men did, or to accept a ride or a dance, or a talk from the Venus Annodomini in a properly humble and thankful spirit. He was exacting, and, therefore, the Venus Annodomini repressed him. He worried himself nearly sick in a futile sort of way over her; and his devotion and earnestness made him appear either shy or boisterous or rude, as his mood might vary, by the side of the older men who, with him, bowed before the Venus Annodomini. She was sorry for him. He reminded her of a lad who, three-and-twenty years ago, had professed a boundless devotion for her, and for whom in return she had felt something more than a week's weakness. But that lad had fallen away and married another woman less than a year after he had worshipped her; and the Venus Annodomini had almost—not quite—forgotten his name. 'Very Young' Gayerson had the same big blue eyes and the same way of pouting his underlip when he was excited or troubled. But the Venus Annodomini checked him sternly none the less. Too much zeal was a thing that she did not approve of; preferring instead a tempered and sober tenderness.

'Very Young' Gayerson was miserable, and took no trouble to conceal his wretchedness. He was in the Army—a Line regiment I think, but am not certain—and, since his face was a looking-glass and his forehead an open book, by reason of his innocence, his brothers-in-arms made his life a burden to him and embittered his naturally sweet disposition. No one except 'Very Young' Gayerson, and he never told his views, knew how old 'Very Young' Gayerson believed the Venus Annodomini to be. Perhaps he thought her five-and-twenty, or perhaps she told him that she was this age. 'Very Young' Gayerson would have forded the Indus in flood to carry her lightest word, and had implicit faith in her. Every one liked

him, and every one was sorry when they saw him so bound
a slave of the Venus Annodomini. Every one, too, admitted
that it was not her fault; for the Venus Annodomini differed
from Mrs. Hauksbee and Mrs. Reiver in this particular—she
never moved a finger to attract any one; but, like Ninon de
L'Enclos,* all men were attracted to her. One could admire
and respect Mrs. Hauksbee, despise and avoid Mrs. Reiver,
but one was forced to adore the Venus Annodomini.

'Very Young' Gayerson's papa held a Division, or a
Collectorate, or something administrative, in a particularly
unpleasant part of Bengal—full of Babus* who edited
newspapers proving that 'Young' Gayerson was a 'Nero' and
a 'Scylla' and a 'Charybdis';* and, in additon to the Babus, there
was a good deal of dysentery and cholera abroad for nine months
of the year. 'Young' Gayerson—he was about five-and-forty—
rather liked Babus, they amused him, but he objected to
dysentery, and when he could get away, went to Darjiling* for
the most part. This particular season he fancied that he would
come up to Simla and see his boy. The boy was not altogether
pleased. He told the Venus Annodomini that his father was
coming up, and she flushed a little and said that she should
be delighted to make his acquaintance. Then she looked long
and thoughtfully at 'Very Young' Gayerson, because she was
very, very sorry for him, and he was a very, very big idiot.

'My daughter is coming out in a fortnight, Mr. Gayerson,'
she said.

'Your *what*?' said he.

'Daughter,' said the Venus Annodomini. 'She's been out for
a year at Home already, and I want her to see a little of India.
She is nineteen and a very sensible nice girl I believe.'

'Very Young' Gayerson, who was a short twenty-two years
old, nearly fell out of his chair with astonishment; for he had
persisted in believing, against all belief, in the youth of the
Venus Annodomini. She, with her back to the curtained
window, watched the effect of her sentences and smiled.

'Very Young' Gayerson's papa came up twelve days later,
and had not been in Simla four-and-twenty hours before two
men, old acquaintances of his, had told him how 'Very Young'
Gayerson had been conducting himself.

'Young' Gayerson laughed a good deal, and inquired who the Venus Annodomini might be. Which proves that he had been living in Bengal where nobody knows anything except the rate of Exchange. Then he said boys would be boys, and spoke to his son about the matter. 'Very Young' Gayerson said that he felt wretched and unhappy; and 'Young' Gayerson said that he repented of having helped to bring a fool into the world. He suggested that his son had better cut his leave short and go down to his duties. This led to an unfilial answer, and relations were strained, until 'Young' Gayerson demanded that they should call on the Venus Annodomini. 'Very Young' Gayerson went with his papa, feeling, somehow, uncomfortable and small.

The Venus Annodomini received them graciously, and 'Young' Gayerson said, 'By Jove! It's Kitty!' 'Very Young' Gayerson would have listened for an explanation, if his time had not been taken up with trying to talk to a large, handsome, quiet, well-dressed girl—introduced to him by the Venus Annodomini as her daughter. She was far older in manner, style, and repose than 'Very Young' Gayerson; and, as he realised this thing, he felt sick.

Presently he heard the Venus Annodomini saying, 'Do you know that your son is one of my most devoted admirers?'

'I don't wonder,' said 'Young' Gayerson. Here he raised his voice, 'He follows his father's footsteps. Didn't I worship the ground you trod on, ever so long ago, Kitty—and you haven't changed since then. How strange it all seems!'

'Very Young' Gayerson said nothing. His conversation with the daughter of the Venus Annodomini was, through the rest of the call, fragmentary and disjointed.

* * *

'At five to-morrow, then,' said the Venus Annodomini. 'And mind you are punctual.'

'At five punctually,' said 'Young' Gayerson. 'You can lend your old father a horse, I daresay, youngster, can't you? I'm going for a ride to-morrow afternoon.'

'Certainly,' said 'Very Young' Gayerson. 'I am going down to-morrow morning. My ponies are at your service, Sir.'

The Venus Annodomini looked at him across the half-light of the room, and her big gray eyes filled with moisture. She rose and shook hands with him.

'Good-bye, Tom,' whispered the Venus Annodomini.

The Bisara of Pooree*

Little Blind Fish, thou art marvellous wise,
Little Blind Fish, who put out thy eyes?
Open thy ears while I whisper my wish—
Bring me a lover, thou little Blind Fish.
The Charm of the Bisara.

SOME natives say that it came from the other side of Kulu,*
where the eleven-inch Temple Sapphire is. Others that it was
made at the Devil-Shrine of Ao-Chung in Thibet, was stolen
by a Kafir,* from him by a Gurkha, from him again by a
Lahouli,* from him by a *khitmutgar,** and by this latter sold
to an Englishman, so all its virtue was lost; because, to work
properly, the Bisara of Pooree must be stolen—with bloodshed
if possible, but, at any rate, stolen.

These stories of the coming into India are all false. It was
made at Pooree ages since—the manner of its making would
fill a small book—was stolen by one of the Temple dancing-
girls there, for her own purposes, and then passed on from
hand to hand, steadily northward, till it reached Hanlé:*
always bearing the same name—the Bisara of Pooree. In shape
it is a tiny square box of silver, studded outside with eight
small balas-rubies.* Inside the box, which opens with a
spring, is a little eyeless fish, carved from some sort of dark,
shiny nut and wrapped in a shred of faded gold cloth. That
is the Bisara of Pooree, and it were better for a man to take
a king-cobra in his hand than to touch the Bisara of Pooree.

All kinds of magic are out of date and done away with,
except in India, where nothing changes in spite of the shiny,
top-scum stuff that people call 'civilisation.' Any man who
knows about the Bisara of Pooree will tell you what its powers
are—always supposing that it has been honestly stolen. It is
the only regularly working, trustworthy love-charm in the
country, with one exception. (The other charm is in the hands
of a trooper of the Nizam's* Horse, at a place called Tuprani,

due north of Hyderabad.) This can be depended upon for a fact. Some one else may explain it.

If the Bisara be not stolen, but given or bought or found, it turns against its owner in three years, and leads to ruin or death. This is another fact which you may explain when you have time. Meanwhile, you can laugh at it. At present the Bisara is safe on a hack-pony's neck, inside the blue bead-necklace that keeps off the Evil Eye. If the pony-driver ever finds it, and wears it, or gives it to his wife, I am sorry for him.

A very dirty Hill-coolie woman, with goitre, owned it at Theog* in 1884. It came into Simla from the North before Churton's *khitmutgar* bought it, and sold it, for three times its silver-value, to Churton, who collected curiosities. The servant knew no more what he had bought than the master; but a man looking over Churton's collection of curiosities—Churton was an Assistant Commissioner by the way—saw and held his tongue. He was an Englishman, but knew how to believe. Which shows that he was different from most Englishmen. He knew that it was dangerous to have any share in the little box when working or dormant; for Love unsought is a terrible gift.

Pack—'Grubby' Pack, as we used to call him—was, in every way, a nasty little man who must have crawled into the Army by mistake. He was three inches taller than his sword, but not half so strong. And the sword was a fifty-shilling, tailor-made one. Nobody liked him, and, I suppose, it was his wizenedness and worthlessness that made him fall so hopelessly in love with Miss Hollis, who was good and sweet, and five-feet-seven in her tennis-shoes. He was not content with falling in love quietly, but brought all the strength of his miserable little nature into the business. If he had not been so objectionable, one might have pitied him. He vapoured, and fretted, and fumed, and trotted up and down, and tried to make himself pleasing in Miss Hollis's big, quiet, gray eyes, and failed. It was one of the cases that you sometimes meet, even in our country, where we marry by Code, of a really blind attachment all on one side, without the faintest possibility of return. Miss Hollis looked on Pack as some sort of vermin running about the road. He had no prospects beyond Captain's pay, and no wits to help that out by one penny. In a large-sized man love like his would have been touching. In a good man it would have been grand. He being what he was, it was only a nuisance.

You will believe this much. What you will not believe is what follows: Churton, and The Man who Knew what the Bisara was, were lunching at the Simla Club together. Churton was complaining of life in general. His best mare had rolled out of stable down the cliff and had broken her back; his decisions were being reversed by the upper Courts more than an Assistant Commissioner of eight years' standing has a right to expect; he knew liver and fever, and for weeks past had felt out of sorts. Altogether, he was disgusted and disheartened.

Simla Club dining-room is built, as all the world knows, in two sections, with an arch-arrangement dividing them. Come in, turn to your own left, take the table under the window, and you cannot see any one who has come in, turned to the right, and taken a table on the right side of the arch. Curiously enough, every word that you say can be heard, not only by the other diner, but by the servants beyond the screen through which they bring dinner. This is worth knowing; an echoing-room is a trap to be forewarned against.

Half in fun, and half hoping to be believed, The Man who Knew told Churton the story of the Bisara of Pooree at rather greater length than I have told it to you in this place; winding up with a suggestion that Churton might as well throw the little box down the hill and see whether all his troubles would go with it. In ordinary ears, English ears, the tale was only an interesting bit of folklore. Churton laughed, said that he felt better for his tiffin, and went out. Pack had been tiffining by himself to the right of the arch, and had heard everything. He was nearly mad with his absurd infatuation for Miss Hollis, that all Simla had been laughing about.

It is a curious thing that, when a man hates or loves beyond reason, he is ready to go beyond reason to gratify his feelings; which he would not do for money or power merely. Depend upon it, Solomon would never have built altars to Ashtaroth*

and all those ladies with queer names, if there had not been
trouble of some kind in his *zenana*,* and nowhere else. But
this is beside the story. The facts of the case are these: Pack
called on Churton next day when Churton was out, left his
card, and stole the Bisara of Pooree from its place under the
clock on the mantelpiece. Stole it like the thief he was by
nature! Three days later all Simla was electrified by the news
that Miss Hollis had accepted Pack—the shrivelled rat, Pack!
Do you desire clearer evidence than this? The Bisara of Pooree
had been stolen, and it worked as it had always done when
won by foul means.

There are three or four times in a man's life when he is justified in meddling with other people's affairs to play Providence.

The Man who Knew felt that he was justified; but believing
and acting on a belief are quite different things. The insolent
satisfaction of Pack as he ambled by the side of Miss Hollis,
and Churton's striking release from liver, as soon as the Bisara
of Pooree had gone, decided The Man. He explained to
Churton, and Churton laughed, because he was not brought
up to believe that men on the Government House List steal—
at least little things. But the miraculous acceptance by Miss
Hollis of that tailor, Pack, decided him to take steps on
suspicion. He vowed that he only wanted to find out where
his ruby-studded silver box had vanished to. You cannot
accuse a man on the Government House List of stealing; and
if you rifle his room, you are a thief yourself. Churton,
prompted by The Man who Knew, decided on burglary. If he
found nothing in Pack's room . . . but it is not nice to think
of what would have happened in that case.

Pack went to a dance at Benmore—Benmore was Benmore
in those days, and not an office*—and danced fifteen waltzes
out of twenty-two with Miss Hollis. Churton and The Man
took all the keys that they could lay hands on, and went to Pack's
room in the hotel, certain that his servants would be away. Pack
was a cheap soul. He had not purchased a decent cash-box to
keep his papers in, but one of those native imitations that you
buy for ten rupees. It opened to any sort of key, and there at
the bottom, under Pack's Insurance Policy, lay the Bisara of
Pooree!

Churton called Pack names, put the Bisara of Pooree in his pocket, and went to the dance with The Man. At least, he came in time for supper, and saw the beginning of the end in Miss Hollis's eyes. She was hysterical after supper, and was taken away by her Mamma.

At the dance, with the abominable Bisara in his pocket, Churton twisted his foot on one of the steps leading down to the old Rink, and had to be sent home in a 'rickshaw, grumbling. He did not believe in the Bisara of Pooree any the more for this manifestation, but he sought out Pack and called him some ugly names; and 'thief' was the mildest of them. Pack took the names with the nervous smile of a little man who wants both soul and body to resent an insult, and went his way. There was no public scandal.

A week later Pack got his definite dismissal from Miss Hollis. There had been a mistake in the placing of her affections, she said. So he went away to Madras, where he can do no great harm even if he lives to be a Colonel.

Churton insisted upon The Man who Knew taking the Bisara of Pooree as a gift. The Man took it, went down to the Cart-Road at once, found a cart-pony with a blue bead-necklace, fastened the Bisara of Pooree inside the necklace with a piece of shoe-string and thanked Heaven that he was rid of a danger. Remember, in case you ever find it, that you must not destroy the Bisara of Pooree. I have not time to explain why just now, but the power lies in the little wooden fish. Mr. Gubernatis or Max Müller* could tell you more about it than I.

You will say that all this story is made up. Very well. If ever you come across a little, silver, ruby-studded box, seven-eighths of an inch long by three-quarters wide, with a dark brown wooden fish, wrapped in gold cloth, inside it, keep it. Keep it for three years, and then you will discover for yourself whether my story is true or false.

Better still, steal it as Pack did, and you will be sorry that you had not killed yourself in the beginning.

A Friend's Friend*

Wherefore slew I the stranger? He brought me dishonour.
I saddled my mare Bijli. I set him upon her.
I gave him rice and goat's flesh. He bared me to laughter;
When he was gone from my tent, swift I followed after,
Taking a sword in my hand. The hot wine had filled him:
Under the stars he mocked me. Therefore I killed him.

Hadramauti.

THIS tale must be told in the first person for many reasons. The man whom I want to expose is Tranter of the Bombay side.* I want Tranter black-balled at his Club, divorced from his wife, turned out of the Service, and cast into prison, until I get an apology from him in writing. I wish to warn the world against Tranter of the Bombay side.

You know the casual way in which men pass on acquaintances in India? It is a great convenience, because you can get rid of a man you don't like by writing a letter of introduction and putting him, with it, into the train. T. G.'s* are best treated thus. If you keep them moving, they have no time to say insulting and offensive things about 'Anglo-Indian Society.'

One day, late in the cold weather, I got a letter of preparation from Tranter of the Bombay side, advising me of the advent of a T. G., a man called Jevon; and saying, as usual, that any kindness shown to Jevon would be a kindness to Tranter. Every one knows the regular form of these communications.

Two days afterwards Jevon turned up with his letter of introduction, and I did what I could for him. He was lint-haired, fresh-coloured, and very English. But he held no views about the Government of India. Nor did he insist on shooting tigers on the Station Mall, as some T. G.'s do. Nor did he call us 'colonists,' and dine in a flannel-shirt and tweeds, under that delusion as other T. G.'s do. He was well behaved and very grateful for the little I won for him—most grateful of all when I secured him an invitation for the Afghan Ball, and introduced him to a Mrs. Deemes, a lady for whom I had a great respect and admiration, who danced like the shadow of a leaf in a light wind. I set great store by the friendship of Mrs. Deemes; but, had I known what was coming, I would have broken Jevon's neck with a curtain-pole before getting him that invitation.

But I did not know, and he dined at the Club, I think, on the night of the ball. I dined at home. When I went to the dance, the first man I met asked me whether I had seen Jevon. 'No,' said I. 'He's at the Club. Hasn't he come?'—'Come!' said the man. 'Yes, he's very much come. You'd better look at him.'

I sought for Jevon. I found him sitting on a bench and smiling to himself and a programme. Half a look was enough for me. On that one night, of all others, he had begun a long and thirsty evening by taking too much! He was breathing heavily through his nose, his eyes were rather red, and he appeared very satisfied with all the earth. I put up a little prayer that the waltzing would work off the wine, and went about programme-filling, feeling uncomfortable. But I saw Jevon walk up to Mrs. Deemes for the first dance, and I knew that all the waltzing on the card was not enough to keep Jevon's rebellious legs steady. That couple went round six times. I counted. Mrs. Deemes dropped Jevon's arm and came across to me.

I am not going to repeat what Mrs. Deemes said to me, because she was very angry indeed. I am not going to write what I said to Mrs. Deemes, because I didn't say anything. I only wished that I had killed Jevon first and been hanged for it. Mrs. Deemes drew her pencil through all the dances that I had booked with her, and went away, leaving me to remember that what I ought to have said was that Mrs. Deemes had asked to be introduced to Jevon because he danced well; and that I really had not carefully worked out a plot to get her insulted. But I felt that argument was no good, and that I had better try to stop Jevon from waltzing me into more trouble. He, however, was gone, and about every third dance I set off to hunt for him. This ruined what little pleasure I expected from the entertainment.

Just before supper I caught Jevon at the buffet with his legs wide apart, talking to a very fat and indignant chaperon. 'If this person is a friend of yours, as I understand he is, I would recommend you to take him home,' said she. 'He is unfit for decent society.' Then I knew that goodness only knew what Jevon had been doing, and I tried to get him away.

But Jevon wasn't going; not he. He knew what was good for him, he did; and he wasn't going to be dictated to by any loconial nigger-driver, he wasn't; and I was the friend who had formed his infant mind, and brought him up to buy Benares brassware and fear God, so I was; and we would have many more blazing good drunks together, so we would; and all the she-camels in black silk in the world shouldn't make him withdraw his opinion that there was nothing better than Benedictine to give one an appetite. And then . . . but he was my guest.

I set him in a quiet corner of the supper-room, and went to find a wall-prop that I could trust. There was a good and kindly Subaltern—may Heaven bless that Subaltern, and make him a Commander-in-Chief!—who heard of my trouble. He was not dancing himself, and he owned a head like five-year-old teak-baulks. He said that he would look after Jevon till the end of the ball.

"Don't suppose you much mind what I do with him?' said he.

'Mind!' said I. 'No! You can murder the beast if you like.'

But the Subaltern did not murder him. He trotted off to the supper-room, and sat down by Jevon, drinking peg for peg with him. I saw the two fairly established, and went away, feeling more easy.

When 'The Roast Beef of Old England'* sounded, I heard of Jevon's performances between the first dance and my meeting with him at the buffet. After Mrs. Deemes had cast him off, it seems that he had found his way into the gallery, and offered to conduct the Band or to play any instrument in it just as the Bandmaster pleased.

When the Bandmaster refused, Jevon said that he wasn't appreciated, and he yearned for sympathy. So he trundled downstairs and sat out four dances with four girls, and

proposed to three of them. One of the girls was a married
woman by the way. Then he went into the whist-room, and
fell face-down and wept on the hearth-rug in front of the fire,
because he had fallen into a den of card-sharpers, and his
Mamma had always warned him against bad company. He had
done a lot of other things, too, and had taken about three
quarts of mixed liquors. Besides speaking of me in the most
scandalous fashion!

All the women wanted him turned out, and all the men
wanted him kicked. The worst of it was, that every one said
it was my fault. Now, I put it to you, how on earth could I
have known that this innocent, fluffy T. G. would break out
in this disgusting manner? You see he had gone round the
world nearly, and his vocabulary of abuse was cosmopolitan,
though mainly Japanese, which he had picked up in a low tea-
house at Hakodate.* It sounded like whistling.

While I was listening to first one man and then another
telling me of Jevon's shameless behaviour and asking me for
his blood, I wondered where he was. I was prepared to
sacrifice him to Society on the spot.

But Jevon was gone, and, far away in the corner of the
supper-room, sat my dear, good Subaltern, a little flushed,
eating salad. I went over and said, 'Where's Jevon?'—'In the
cloakroom,' said the Subaltern. 'He'll keep till the women
have gone. Don't you interfere with my prisoner.' I didn't
want to interfere, but I peeped into the cloakroom, and found
my guest put to bed on some rolled-up carpets, all comfy, his
collar free, and a wet swab on his head.

The rest of the evening I spent in making timid attempts to
explain things to Mrs. Deemes and three or four other ladies,
and trying to clear my character—for I am a respectable man—
from the shameful slurs that my guest had cast upon it. Libel
was no word for what he had said.

When I wasn't trying to explain, I was running off to the
cloakroom to see that Jevon wasn't dead of apoplexy. I didn't
want him to die on my hands. He had eaten my salt.

At last that ghastly ball ended, though I was not in the least
restored to Mrs. Deemes' favour. When the ladies had gone,
and some one was calling for songs at the second supper, that

angelic Subaltern told the servants to bring in the *Sahib* who was in the cloakroom, and clear away one end of the supper-table. While this was being done we formed ourselves into a Board of Punishment with the Doctor for President.

Jevon came in on four men's shoulders, and was put down on the table like a corpse in a dissecting-room, while the Doctor lectured on the evils of intemperance, and Jevon snored. Then we set to work.

We corked the whole of his face. We filled his hair with meringue-cream till it looked like a white wig. To protect everything till it dried, a man in the Ordnance Department, who understood the work, luted* a big blue paper cap from a cracker, with meringue-cream, low down on Jevon's forehead. This was punishment, not play, remember. We took gelatine off crackers, and stuck blue gelatine on his nose, and yellow gelatine on his chin, and green and red gelatine on his cheeks, pressing each dab down till it held as firm as gold-beaters' skin.*

We put a ham-frill round his neck, and tied it in a bow in front. He nodded like a mandarin.

We fixed gelatine on the back of his hands, and burnt-corked them inside, and put small cutlet-frills round his wrists, and tied both wrists together with string. We waxed up the ends of his moustache with isinglass.* He looked very martial.

We turned him over, pinned up his coat-tails between his shoulders, and put a rosette of cutlet-frills there. We took up the red cloth from the ball-room to the supper-room, and wound him up in it. There were sixty feet of red cloth, six feet broad; and he rolled up into a big fat bundle, with only that amazing head sticking out.

Lastly, we tied up the surplus of cloth beyond his feet with coconut-fibre string as tightly as we knew how. We were so angry that we hardly laughed at all.

Just as we finished, we heard the rumble of bullock-carts taking away some chairs and things that the General's wife had lent for the ball. So we hoisted Jevon, like a roll of carpets, into one of the carts, and the carts went away.

Now the most extraordinary part of this tale is that never

again did I see or hear anything of Jevon, T. G. He vanished
utterly. He was not delivered at the General's house with the
carpets. He just went into the black darkness of the end of the
night, and was swallowed up. Perhaps he died and was thrown
into the river.

But, alive or dead, I have often wondered how he got rid of
the red cloth and the meringue-cream. I wonder still whether
Mrs. Deemes will ever take any notice of me again, and
whether I shall live down the infamous stories that Jevon set
afloat about my manners and customs between the first and
the ninth waltz of the Afghan Ball. They stick closer than
cream.

Wherefore, I want Tranter of the Bombay side, dead or
alive. But dead for preference.

The Gate of the Hundred Sorrows*

If I can attain Heaven for a pice,* why should you be envious?
                                    Opium Smoker's Proverb.

THIS is no work of mine. My friend, Gabral Misquitta, the
half-caste, spoke it all, between moonset and morning, six
weeks before he died; and I took it down from his mouth as
he answered my questions. So:—

It lies between the Coppersmith's Gully* and the pipe-stem
sellers' quarter, within a hundred yards, too, as the crow flies,
of the Mosque of Wazir Khan.* I don't mind telling any one
this much, but I defy him to find the Gate, however well he
may think he knows the City. You might even go through the
very gully it stands in a hundred times, and be none the wiser.
We used to call the gully 'The Gully of the Black Smoke,'*
but its native name is altogether different of course. A loaded
donkey couldn't pass between the walls; and, at one point, just
before you reach the Gate, a bulged house-front makes people
go along all sideways.

It isn't really a gate though. It's a house. Old Fung-Tching
had it first five years ago. He was a boot-maker in Calcutta.
They say that he murdered his wife there when he was drunk.
That was why he dropped bazar-rum and took to the Black
Smoke instead. Later on, he came up north and opened the
Gate as a house where you could get your smoke in peace and
quiet. Mind you, it was a *pukka,** respectable opium-house,
and not one of those stifling, sweltering *chandoo-khanas** that
you can find all over the City. No; the old man knew his
business thoroughly, and he was most clean for a Chinaman.
He was a one-eyed little chap, not much more than five feet
high, and both his middle fingers were gone. All the same, he
was the handiest man at rolling black pills I have ever seen.
Never seemed to be touched by the Smoke, either; and what
he took day and night, night and day, was a caution. I've been
at it five years, and I can do my fair share of the Smoke with

any one; but I was a child to Fung-Tching that way. All the same, the old man was keen on his money: very keen; and that's what I can't understand. I heard he saved a good deal before he died, but his nephew has got all that now; and the old man's gone back to China to be buried.

He kept the big upper room, where his best customers gathered, as neat as a new pin. In one corner used to stand Fung-Tching's Joss—almost as ugly as Fung-Tching—and there were always sticks burning under his nose; but you never smelt 'em when the pipes were going thick. Opposite the Joss was Fung-Tching's coffin. He had spent a good deal of his savings on that, and whenever a new man came to the Gate he was always introduced to it. It was lacquered black, with red-and-gold writings on it, and I've heard that Fung-Tching brought it out all the way from China. I don't know whether that's true or not, but I know that, if I came first in the evening, I used to spread my mat just at the foot of it. It was a quiet corner, you see, and a sort of breeze from the gully came in at the window now and then. Besides the mats, there was no other furniture in the room—only the coffin, and the old Joss all green and blue and purple with age and polish.

Fung-Tching never told us why he called the place 'The Gate of the Hundred Sorrows.' (He was the only Chinaman I know who used bad-sounding fancy names. Most of them are flowery. As you'll see in Calcutta.) We used to find that out for ourselves. Nothing grows on you so much, if you're white, as the Black Smoke. A yellow man is made different. Opium doesn't tell on him scarcely at all; but white and black suffer a good deal. Of course, there are some people that the Smoke doesn't touch any more than tobacco would at first. They just doze a bit, as one would fall asleep naturally, and next morning they are almost fit for work. Now, I was one of that sort when I began, but I've been at it for five years pretty steadily, and it's different now. There was an old aunt of mine, down Agra way, and she left me a little at her death. About sixty rupees a month secured. Sixty isn't much. I can recollect a time, seems hundreds and hundreds of years ago, that I was getting my three hundred a month, and pickings, when I was working on a big timber-contract in Calcutta.

I didn't stick to that work for long. The Black Smoke does not allow of much other business; and even though I am very little affected by it, as men go, I couldn't do a day's work now to save my life. After all, sixty rupees is what I want. When old Fung-Tching was alive he used to draw the money for me, give me about half of it to live on (I eat very little), and the rest he kept himself. I was free of the Gate at any time of the day and night, and could smoke and sleep there when I liked, so I didn't care. I know the old man made a good thing out of it; but that's no matter. Nothing matters much to me; and besides, the money always came fresh and fresh each month.

There was ten of us met at the Gate when the place was first opened. Me, and two Babus* from a Government Office somewhere in Anarkulli,* but they got the sack and couldn't pay (no man who has to work in the daylight can do the Black Smoke for any length of time straight on); a Chinaman that was Fung-Tching's nephew; a bazar-woman that had got a lot of money somehow; an English loafer—MacSomebody,* I think, but I have forgotten,—that smoked heaps, but never seemed to pay anything (they said he had saved Fung-Tching's life at some trial in Calcutta when he was a barrister); another Eurasian, like myself, from Madras; a half-caste woman, and a couple of men who said they had come from the North. I think they must have been Persians or Afghans or something. There are not more than five of us living now, but we come regular. I don't know what happened to the Babus; but the bazar-woman she died after six months of the Gate, and I think Fung-Tching took her bangles and nose-ring for himself. But I'm not certain. The Englishman, he drank as well as smoked, and he dropped off. One of the Persians got killed in a row at night by the big well near the mosque a long time ago, and the Police shut up the well, because they said it was full of foul air. They found him dead at the bottom of it. So, you see, there is only me, the Chinaman, the half-caste woman that we call the *Memsahib* (she used to live with Fung-Tching), the other Eurasian, and one of the Persians. The *Memsahib* looks very old now. I think she was a young woman when the Gate was opened; but we are all old for the matter of that. Hundreds and hundreds of years old. It's very hard to keep count of time in the Gate, and, besides, time doesn't matter to me. I draw my sixty rupees fresh and fresh every month. A very, very long while ago, when I used to be getting three hundred and fifty rupees a month, and pickings, on a big timber-contract at Calcutta, I had a wife of sorts. But she's dead now. People said that I killed her by taking to the Black Smoke. Perhaps I did, but it's so long since that it doesn't matter. Sometimes when I first came to the Gate, I used to feel sorry for it; but that's all over and done with long ago, and I draw my sixty rupees fresh and fresh every month, and am quite happy. Not *drunk* happy, you know, but always quiet and soothed and contented.

How did I take to it? It began at Calcutta. I used to try it in my own house, just to see what it was like. I never went very far, but I think my wife must have died then. Anyhow, I found myself here, and got to know Fung-Tching. I don't remember rightly how that came about; but he told me of the Gate and I used to go there, and, somehow, I have never got away from it since. Mind you, though, the Gate was a respectable place in Fung-Tching's time, where you could be comfortable and not at all like the *chandoo-khanas* where the niggers go. No; it was clean, and quiet, and not crowded. Of course, there were others besides us ten and the man; but we always had a mat apiece, with a wadded woollen headpiece, all covered with black and red dragons and things, just like the coffin in the corner.

At the end of one's third pipe the dragons used to move about and fight. I've watched 'em many and many a night through. I used to regulate my Smoke that way, and now it takes a dozen pipes to make 'em stir. Besides, they are all torn and dirty, like the mats, and Fung-Tching is dead. He died a couple of years ago, and gave me the pipe I always use now—a silver one, with queer beasts crawling up and down the receiver-bottle below the cup. Before that, I think, I used a big bamboo stem with a copper cup, a very small one, and a green jade mouthpiece. It was a little thicker than a walking-stick stem, and smoked sweet, very sweet. The bamboo seemed to suck up the smoke. Silver doesn't, and I've got to clean it out now and then, that's a great deal of trouble, but I smoke it for

the old man's sake. He must have made a good thing out of
me, but he always gave me clean mats and pillows, and the
best stuff you could get anywhere.

When he died, his nephew Tsin-ling took up the Gate, and
he called it the 'Temple of the Three Possessions;' but we old
ones speak of it as the 'Hundred Sorrows,' all the same. The
nephew does things very shabbily, and I think the *Memsahib*
must help him. She lives with him; same as she used to do
with the old man. The two let in all sorts of low people,
niggers and all, and the Black Smoke isn't as good as it used
to be. I've found burnt bran in my pipe over and over again.
The old man would have died if that had happened in his
time. Besides, the room is never cleaned, and all the mats are
torn and cut at the edges. The coffin is gone—gone to China
again—with the old man and two ounces of Smoke inside it,
in case he should want 'em on the way.

The Joss doesn't get so many sticks burnt under his nose as
he used to; that's a sign of ill-luck, as sure as Death. He's all
brown, too, and no one ever attends to him. That's the
Memsahib's work, I know; because, when Tsin-ling tried to
burn gilt paper before him, she said it was a waste of money,
and, if he kept a stick burning very slowly, the Joss wouldn't
know the difference. So now we've got the sticks mixed with
a lot of glue, and they take half an hour longer to burn, and
smell stinky; let alone the smell of the room by itself. No
business can get on if they try that sort of thing. The Joss
doesn't like it. I can see that. Late at night, sometimes, he
turns all sorts of queer colours—blue and green and red—just
as he used to do when old Fung-Tching was alive; and he rolls
his eyes and stamps his feet like a devil.

I don't know why I don't leave the place and smoke quietly
in a little room of my own in the bazar. Most like, Tsin-ling
would kill me if I went away—he draws my sixty rupees
now—and besides, it's too much trouble, and I've grown to be
very fond of the Gate. It's not much to look at. Not what it
was in the old man's time, but I couldn't leave it. I've seen
so many come in and out. And I've seen so many die here on
the mats that I should be afraid of dying in the open now. I've
seen some things that people would call strange enough; but

nothing is strange when you're on the Black Smoke, except the Black Smoke. And if it was, it wouldn't matter.

Fung-Tching used to be very particular about his people, and never got in any one who'd give trouble by dying messy and such. But the nephew isn't half so careful. He tells everywhere that he keeps a 'first-chop'* house. Never tries to get men in quietly, and make them comfortable like Fung-Tching did. That's why the Gate is getting a little bit more known than it used to be. Among the niggers of course. The nephew daren't get a white, or, for matter of that, a mixed skin into the place. He has to keep us three, of course—me and the *Memsahib* and the other Eurasian. We're fixtures. But he wouldn't give us credit for a pipeful—not for anything.

One of these days, I hope, I shall die in the Gate. The Persian and the Madras man are terribly shaky now. They've got a boy to light their pipes for them. I always do that myself. Most like, I shall see them carried out before me. I don't think I shall ever outlive the *Memsahib* or Tsin-ling. Women last longer than men at the Black Smoke, and Tsin-ling has a deal of the old man's blood in him, though he does smoke cheap stuff. The bazar-woman knew when she was going two days before her time; and she died on a clean mat with a nicely wadded pillow, and the old man hung up her pipe just above the Joss. He was always fond of her, I fancy. But he took her bangles just the same.

I should like to die like the bazar-woman—on a clean, cool mat with a pipe of good stuff between my lips. When I feel I'm going, I shall ask Tsin-ling for them, and he can draw my sixty rupees a month, fresh and fresh, as long as he pleases. Then I shall lie back, quiet and comfortable, and watch the black and red dragons have their last big fight together; and then . . .

Well, it doesn't matter. Nothing matters much to me—only I wish Tsin-ling wouldn't put bran into the Black Smoke.

The Madness of Private Ortheris*

> Oh! Where would I be when my froat was dry?
> Oh! Where would I be when the bullets fly?
> Oh! Where would I be when I come to die?
> > Why,
> Somewheres anigh my chum.
> > If 'e's liquor 'e'll give me some,
> > If I'm dyin' 'e'll 'old my 'ead,
> > An' 'e'll write 'em 'Ome when I'm dead.—
> Gawd send us a trusty chum!
> > > > *Barrack-Room Ballad.*

MY friends Mulvaney and Ortheris had gone on a shooting-expedition for one day. Learoyd was still in hospital, recovering from fever picked up in Burma. They sent me an invitation to join them, and were genuinely pained when I brought beer—almost enough beer to satisfy two Privates of the Line . . . and Me.

"Twasn't for that we bid you welkim, Sorr,' said Mulvaney sulkily. "Twas for the pleasure av your comp'ny.'

Ortheris came to the rescue with—'Well, 'e won't be none the worse for bringin' liquor with 'im. We ain't a file o' Dooks.* We're bloomin' Tommies, ye cantankris Hirishman; an' 'ere's your very good 'ealth!'

We shot all the forenoon, and killed two pariah-dogs, four green parrots, sitting, one kite by the burning-ghaut,* one snake flying, one mud-turtle, and eight crows. Game was plentiful. Then we sat down to tiffin—'bull-mate an' bran-bread,' Mulvaney called it—by the side of the river, and took pot-shots at the crocodiles in the intervals of cutting up the food with our only pocket-knife. Then we drank up all the beer, and threw the bottles into the water and fired at them. After that, we eased belts and stretched ourselves on the warm sand and smoked. We were too lazy to continue shooting.

Ortheris heaved a big sigh, as he lay on his stomach with his head between his fists. Then he swore quietly into the blue sky.

'Fwhat's that for?' said Mulvaney. 'have ye not dhrunk enough?'

'Tott'nim Court Road, an' a gal I fancied there. Wot's the good of sodgerin'?'

'Orth'ris, me son,' said Mulvaney hastily, "tis more than likely you've got throuble in your inside wid the beer. I feel that way mesilf whin my liver gets rusty.'

Ortheris went on slowly, not heeding the interruption—

'I'm a Tommy—a bloomin', eight-anna, dog-stealin' Tommy, with a number instead of a decent name. Wot's the good o' me? If I 'ad a stayed at 'Ome, I might a married that gal and kep' a little shorp in the 'Ammersmith 'Igh.—"S. Orth'ris, Prac-ti-cal Taxi-der-mist." With a stuff' fox, like they 'as in the Haylesbury Dairies, in the winder, an' a little case of blue and yaller glass-heyes, an' a little wife to call "shorp!" "shorp!" when the door-bell rung. As it his, I'm on'y a Tommy—a Bloomin', Gawd-forsaken, Beer-swillin' Tommy. "Rest on your harms—'versed; Stan' at—hease; 'Shun. 'Verse—harms. Right an' lef'—tarrn. Slow—march. 'Alt— front. Rest on your harms—'versed. With blank-cartridge— load." An' that's the end o' me.' He was quoting fragments from Funeral Parties' Orders.

'Stop ut!' shouted Mulvaney. 'Whin ye've fired into nothin' as often as me, over a better man than yoursilf, ye will not make a mock av thim ordhers. 'Tis worse than whistlin' the Dead March in barricks. An' you full as a tick, an' the sun cool, an' all an' all! I take shame for you. Ye're no better than a Pagin—you an' your firin'-parties an' your glass-eyes. Won't you stop ut, Sorr?'

What could I do? Could I tell Ortheris anything that he did not know of the pleasures of his life? I was not a Chaplain nor a Subaltern, and Ortheris had a right to speak as he thought fit.

'Let him run, Mulvaney,' I said. 'It's the beer.'

'No! 'Tisn't the beer,' said Mulvaney. 'I know fwhat's comin'. He's tuk this way now an' agin, an' ut's—ut's bad—for I'm fond av the bhoy.'

Indeed, Mulvaney seemed needlessly anxious; but I knew that he looked after Ortheris in a fatherly way.

'Let me talk, let me talk,' said Ortheris dreamily. 'D'you stop your parrit screamin' of a 'ot day, when the cage is a-cookin' 'is pore little pink toes orf, Mulvaney?'

'Pink toes! D'ye mane to say you've pink toes undher your bullswools*, ye blandandherin','—Mulvaney gathered himself together for a terrific denunciation—'school-misthress? Pink toes! How much Bass wid the label did that ravin' choild dhrink?'

''Tain't Bass,' said Ortheris. 'It's a bitterer beer nor that. It's 'ome-sickness!'

'Hark to him! An' he goin' Home in the *Sherapis** in the inside av four months!'

'I don't care. It's all one to me. 'Ow d'you know I ain't 'fraid o' dyin' 'fore I gets my discharge paipers?' He recommenced, in a sing-song voice, the Orders.

I had never seen this side of Ortheris' character before, but evidently Mulvaney had, and attached serious importance to it. While Ortheris babbled, with his head on his arms, Mulvaney whispered to me—

'He's always tuk this way whin he's been checked overmuch by the childher they make Sargints nowadays. That an' havin' nothin' to do. I can't make ut out anyways.'

'Well, what does it matter? Let him talk himself through.'

Ortheris began singing a parody of 'The Ramrod Corps,'* full of cheerful allusions to battle, murder, and sudden death. He looked out across the river as he sang; and his face was quite strange to me. Mulvaney caught me by the elbow to ensure attention.

'Matther? It matthers everything! 'Tis some sort av fit that's on him. I've seen ut. 'Twill hould him all this night, an' in the middle av ut he'll get out av his cot an' go rakin' in the rack for his 'coutremints. Thin he'll come over to me an' say, "I'm goin' to Bombay. Answer for me in the mornin'." Thin me an' him will fight as we've done before—him to go an' me to hould him—an' so we'll both come on the books for disturbin' in barricks. I've belted him, an' I've bruk his hid, an' I've talked to him, but 'tis no manner av use whin the fit's on him. He's as good a bhoy as ever stepped whin his mind's clear. I know fwhat's comin', though, this night in barricks.

Lord send he doesn't loose on me* whin I rise to knock him
down. 'Tis that that's in my mind day an' night.'

This put the case in a much less pleasant light, and fully
accounted for Mulvaney's anxiety. He seemed to be trying to
coax Ortheris out of the fit; for he shouted down the bank
where the boy was lying—

'Listen now, you wid the "pore pink toes" an' the glass
eyes! Did you shwim the Irriwaddy at night, behin' me, as a
bhoy shud; or were you hidin' undher a bed, as you was at
Ahmid Kheyl?'*

That was at once a gross insult and a direct lie, and
Mulvaney meant it to bring on a fight. But Ortheris seemed
shut up in some sort of trance. He answered slowly, without
a sign of irritation, in the same cadenced voice as he had used
for his firing-party orders—

'*Hi* swum the Irriwaddy in the night, as you know, for to
take the town of Lungtungpen, nakid an' without fear. *Hand*
where I was at Ahmed Kheyl you know, and four bloomin'
Paythans know too. But that was summat to do, an' I didn't
think o' dyin'. Now I'm sick to go 'Ome—go 'Ome—go 'Ome!
No, I ain't mammysick, because my uncle brung me up, but
I'm sick for London again; sick for the sounds of 'er, an' the
sights of 'er, and the stinks of 'er; orange-peel and hasphalte
an' gas comin' in over Vaux'all Bridge. Sick for the rail goin'
down to Box 'Ill, with your gal on your knee an' a new clay
pipe in your face. That, an' the Stran' lights where you knows
ev'ry one, an' the Copper that takes you up is a old friend that
tuk you up before, when you was a little, smitchy boy lying
loose 'tween the Temple an' the Dark Harches. No bloomin'
guard-mountin', no bloomin' rotten-stone,* nor khaki, an'
yourself your own master with a gal to take an' see the
Humaners* practisin' a-hookin' dead corpses out of the
Serpentine o' Sundays. An' I lef' all that for to serve the
Widder beyond the seas, where there ain't no women and
there ain't no liquor worth 'avin', and there ain't nothin' to
see, nor do, nor say, nor feel, nor think. Lord love you,
Stanley Orth'ris, but you're a bigger bloomin' fool than the
rest o' the reg'ment and Mulvaney wired together! There's the
Widder sittin' at 'Ome with a gold crownd on 'er 'ead; and 'ere

am Hi, Stanley Orth'ris, the Widder's property, a rottin' FOOL!'

His voice rose at the end of the sentence, and he wound up with a six-shot Anglo-Vernacular oath. Mulvaney said nothing, but looked at me as if he expected that I could bring peace to poor Ortheris' troubled brain.

I remembered once at Rawal Pindi* having seen a man, nearly mad with drink, sobered by being made a fool of. Some regiments may know what I mean. I hoped that we might slake off* Ortheris in the same way, though he was perfectly sober. So I said—

'What's the use of grousing there, and speaking against The Widow?'

'I didn't!' said Ortheris. 'S'elp me Gawd, I never said a word agin 'er, an' I wouldn't—not if I was to desert this minute!'

Here was my opening. 'Well, you meant to, anyhow. What's the use of cracking-on* for nothing? Would you slip it now if you got the chance?'

'On'y try me!' said Ortheris, jumping to his feet as if he had been stung.

Mulvaney jumped too. 'Fwhat are you going to do?' said he.

'Help Ortheris down to Bombay or Karachi, whichever he likes. You can report that he separated from you before tiffin, and left his gun on the bank here!'

'I'm to report that—am I?' said Mulvaney slowly. 'Very well. If Orth'ris manes to desert now, and will desert now, an' you, Sorr, who have been a frind to me an' to him, will help him to ut, I, Terence Mulvaney, on my oath which I've niver bruk yet, will report as you say. But——' here he stepped up to Ortheris, and shook the stock of the fowling-piece in his face—'your fistes help you, Stanley Orth'ris, if iver I come across you agin!'

'I don't care!' said Ortheris. 'I'm sick o' this dorg's life. Give me a chanst. Don't play with me. Le' me go!'

'Strip,' said I, 'and change with me, and then I'll tell you you what to do.'

I hoped that the absurdity of this would check Ortheris; but he had kicked off his ammunition-boots and got rid of his tunic almost before I had loosed my shirt-collar. Mulvaney gripped me by the arm—

'The fit's on him: the fit's workin' on him still! By my Honour and Sowl, we shall be accessiry to a desartion yet. Only twenty-eight days,* as you say, Sorr, or fifty-six, but think o' the shame—the black shame to him an' me!' I had never seen Mulvaney so excited.

But Ortheris was quite calm, and, as soon as he had exchanged clothes with me, and I stood up a Private of the Line, he said shortly, 'Now! Come on. What nex'? D'ye mean fair? What must I do to get out o' this 'ere a-Hell?'

I told him that, if he would wait for two or three hours near the river, I would ride into the Station and come back with one hundred rupees. He would, with that money in his pocket, walk to the nearest side-station on the line, about five miles away, and would there take a first-class ticket for Karachi. Knowing that he had no money on him when he went out shooting, his regiment would not immediately wire to the seaports, but would hunt for him in the native villages near the river. Further, no one would think of seeking a deserter in a first-class carriage. At Karachi he was to buy white clothes and ship, if he could, on a cargo-steamer.

Here he broke in. If I helped him to Karachi he would arrange all the rest. Then I ordered him to wait where he was until it was dark enough for me to ride into the Station without my dress being noticed. Now God in His wisdom has made the heart of the British Soldier, who is very often an unlicked ruffian, as soft as the heart of a little child, in order that he may believe in and follow his officers into tight and nasty places. He does not so readily come to believe in a 'civilian,' but, when he does, he believes implicitly and like a dog. I had had the honour of the friendship of Private Ortheris, at intervals, for more than three years, and we had dealt with each other as man by man. Consequently, he considered that all my words were true, and not spoken lightly.

Mulvaney and I left him in the high grass near the river-bank, and went away, still keeping to the high grass, towards my horse. The shirt scratched me horribly.

We waited nearly two hours for the dusk to fall and allow me to ride off. We spoke of Ortheris in whispers, and strained our ears to catch any sound from the spot where we had left him. But we heard nothing except the wind in the plume-grass.

'I've bruk his hid,' said Mulvaney earnestly, 'time an' agin.
I've nearly kilt him wid the belt, an' *yet* I can't knock thim
fits out av his soft hid. No! An' he's not soft, for he's
reasonable an' likely by natur'. Fwhat is ut? Is ut his breedin'
which is nothin', or his edukashin which he niver got? You
that think ye know things, answer me thot.'

But I found no answer. I was wondering how long Ortheris,
on the bank of the river, would hold out, and whether I should
be forced to help him to desert, as I had given my word.

Just as the dusk shut down and, with a very heavy heart, I
was beginning to saddle up my horse, we heard wild shouts
from the river.

The devils had departed from Private Stanley Ortheris, No.
22639, B Company. The loneliness, the dusk, and the waiting
had driven them out as I had hoped. We set off at the double
and found him plunging about wildly through the grass, with
his coat off—my coat off, I mean. He was calling for us like
a madman.

When we reached him he was dripping with perspiration,
and trembling like a startled horse. We had great difficulty in
soothing him. He complained that he was in civilian kit, and
wanted to tear my clothes off his body. I ordered him to strip,
and we made a second exchange as quickly as possible.

The rasp of his own 'grayback' shirt and the squeak of his
boots seemed to bring him to himself. He put his hands before
his eyes and said—

'Wot was it? I ain't mad, I ain't sunstrook, an' I've bin an'
gone an' said, an' bin an' gone an' done . . . *Wot* 'ave I bin
an' done?'

'Fwhat have you done?' said Mulvaney. 'You've dishgraced
yoursilf—though that's no matther. You've dishgraced B
Comp'ny, an' worst av all, you've dishgraced *Me!* Me that
taught you how for to walk abroad like a man—whin you was
a dhirty little, fish-backed little, whimperin' little recruity. As
you are now, Stanley Orth'ris!'

Ortheris said nothing for a while. Then he unslung his belt,
heavy with the badges of half-a-dozen regiments that his own
had lain with,* and handed it over to Mulvaney.

'I'm too little for to mill with you, Mulvaney,' said he, 'an' you've strook me before; but you can take an' cut me in two with this 'ere if you like.'

Mulvaney turned to me.

'Lave me to talk to him, Sorr,' said Mulvaney.

I left, and on my way home thought a good deal over Ortheris in particular, and my friend Private Thomas Atkins whom I love, in general.

But I could not come to any conclusion of any kind whatever.

The Story of Muhammad Din*

Who is the happy man? He that sees, in his own house at
home, little children crowned with dust, leaping and falling
and crying.

Munichandra, translated by Professor Peterson.*

THE polo-ball was an old one, scarred, chipped, and dinted. It
stood on the mantelpiece among the pipe-stems which Imam
Din, *khitmutgar*,* was cleaning for me.

'Does the Heaven-born want this ball?' said Imam Din
deferentially.

The Heaven-born set no particular store by it; but of what use
was a polo-ball to a *khitmutgar*?

'By Your Honour's favour, I have a little son. He has seen this
ball, and desires it to play with. I do not want it for myself.'

No one would for an instant accuse portly old Imam Din of
wanting to play with polo-balls. He carried out the battered
thing into the verandah; and there followed a hurricane of joyful
squeaks, a patter of small feet, and the *thud-thud-thud* of the ball
rolling along the ground. Evidently the little son had been
waiting outside the door to secure his treasure. But how had he
managed to see that polo-ball?

Next day, coming back from office half an hour earlier than
usual, I was aware of a small figure in the dining-room—a tiny,
plump figure in a ridiculously inadequate shirt which came,
perhaps, half-way down the tubby stomach. It wandered round
the room, thumb in mouth, crooning to itself as it took stock of
the pictures. Undoubtedly this was the 'little son.'

He had no business in my room, of course; but was so deeply
absorbed in his discoveries that he never noticed me in the
doorway. I stepped into the room and startled him nearly into a
fit. He sat down on the ground with a gasp. His eyes opened,
and his mouth followed suit. I knew what was coming, and fled,
followed by a long, dry howl which reached the servants'
quarters far more quickly than any command of mine had ever
done. In ten seconds Imam Din was in the dining-room. Then

despairing sobs arose, and I returned to find Imam Din admonishing the small sinner who was using most of his shirt as a handkerchief.

'This boy,' said Imam Din judicially, 'is a *budmash**—a big *budmash*. He will, without doubt, go to the *jail-khana** for his behaviour.' Renewed yells from the penitent, and an elaborate apology to myself from Imam Din.

'Tell the baby,' said I, 'that the *Sahib* is not angry, and take him away.' Imam Din conveyed my forgiveness to the offender, who had now gathered all his shirt round his neck, stringwise, and the yell subsided into a sob. The two set off for the door. 'His name,' said Imam Din, as though the name were part of the crime, 'is Muhammad Din, and he is a *budmash*.' Freed from present danger, Muhammad Din turned round in his father's arms, and said gravely, 'It is true that my name is Muhammad Din, *Tahib*, but I am not a *budmash*. I am a *man*!'

From that day dated my acquaintance with Muhammad Din. Never again did he come into my dining-room, but on the neutral ground of the garden we greeted each other with much state, though our conversation was confined to '*Talaam, Tahib*' from his side, and '*Salaam, Muhammad Din*' from mine. Daily on my return from office, the little white shirt and the fat little body used to rise from the shade of the creeper-covered trellis where they had been hid; and daily I checked my horse here, that my salutation might not be slurred over or given unseemly.

Muhammad Din never had any companions. He used to trot about the compound, in and out of the castor-oil bushes, on mysterious errands of his own. One day I stumbled upon some of his handiwork far down the grounds. He had half buried the polo-ball in dust, and stuck six shrivelled old marigold flowers in a circle round it. Outside that circle again was a rude square, traced out in bits of red brick alternating with fragments of broken china; the whole bounded by a little bank of dust. The water-man from the well-curb put in a plea for the small architect, saying that it was only the play of a baby and did not much disfigure my garden.

Heaven knows that I had no intention of touching the child's work then or later; but, that evening, a stroll through the garden brought me unawares full on it; so that I trampled, before I knew, marigold-heads, dust-bank, and fragments of broken soap-dish into confusion past all hope of mending. Next morning, I came upon Muhammed Din crying softly to himself over the ruin I had wrought. Some one had cruelly told him that the *Sahib* was very angry with him for spoiling the garden, and had scattered his rubbish, using bad language all the while. Muhammed Din laboured for an hour at effacing every trace of the dust-bank and pottery fragments, and it was with a tearful and apologetic face that he said, '*Talaam Tahib*,' when I came home from office. A hasty inquiry resulted in Imam Din informing Muhammad Din that, by my singular favour, he was permitted to disport himself as he pleased. Whereat the child took heart and fell to tracing the ground-plan of an edifice which was to eclipse the marigold-polo-ball creation.

For some months the chubby little eccentricity revolved in his humble orbit among the castor-oil bushes and in the dust; always fashioning magnificent palaces from stale flowers thrown away by the bearer, smooth water-worn pebbles, bits of broken glass, and feathers pulled, I fancy, from my fowls—always alone, and always crooning to himself.

A gaily-spotted sea-shell was dropped one day close to the last of his little buildings; and I looked that Muhammad Din should build something more than ordinarily splendid on the strength of it. Nor was I disappointed. He meditated for the better part of an hour, and his crooning rose to a jubilant song. Then he began tracing in the dust. It would certainly be a wondrous palace, this one, for it was two yards long and a yard broad in ground-plan. But the palace was never completed.

Next day there was no Muhammad Din at the head of the carriage-drive, and no '*Talaam, Tahib*' to welcome my return. I had grown accustomed to the greeting, and its omission troubled me. Next day Imam Din told me that the child was suffering slightly from fever and needed quinine. He got the medicine, and an English Doctor.

'They have no stamina, these brats,' said the Doctor, as he left Imam Din's quarters.

A week later, though I would have given much to have avoided it, I met on the road to the Mussulman burying-ground Imam Din, accompanied by one other friend, carrying in his arms, wrapped in a white cloth, all that was left of little Muhammad Din.

On the Strength of a Likeness*

If your mirror be broken, look into still water; but have a care that you do not fall in.   *Hindu Proverb.*

NEXT to a requited attachment, one of the most convenient things that a young man can carry about with him at the beginning of his career is an unrequited attachment. It makes him feel important and business-like, and *blasé*, and cynical; and whenever he has a touch of liver, or suffers from want of exercise, he can mourn over his lost love, and be very happy in a tender, twilight fashion.

Hannasyde's affair of the heart had been a godsend to him. It was four years old, and the girl had long since given up thinking of it. She had married and had many cares of her own. In the beginning, she had told Hannasyde that, 'while she could never be anything more than a sister to him, she would always take the deepest interest in his welfare.' This startlingly new and original remark gave Hannasyde something to think over for two years; and his own vanity filled in the other twenty-four months. Hannasyde was quite different from Phil Garron,* but, none the less, had several points in common with that far too lucky man.

He kept his unrequited attachment by him as men keep a well-smoked pipe—for comfort's sake, and because it had grown dear in the using. It brought him happily through one Simla season. Hannasyde was not lovely. There was a crudity in his manners, and a roughness in the way in which he helped a lady on to her horse, that did not attract the other sex to him; even if he had cast about for their favour, which he did not. He kept his wounded heart all to himself for a while.

Then trouble came to him. All who go to Simla know the slope from the Telegraph to the Public Works Office. Hannasyde was loafing up the hill, one September morning between calling hours, when a 'rickshaw came down in a hu , and in the 'rickshaw sat the living, breathing image of the girl who had made him so happily unhappy. Hannasyde leaned against the railings and gasped. He wanted to run downhill after the 'rickshaw, but that was impossible; so he went forward with most of his blood in his temples. It was impossible, for many reasons, that the woman in the 'rickshaw could be the girl he had known. She was, he discovered later, the wife of a man from Dindigul, or Coimbatore,* or some out-of-the-way place, and she had come up to Simla early in the season for the good of her health. She was going back to Dindigul, or wherever it was, at the end of the season; and in all likelihood would never return to Simla again, her proper Hill-station being Ootacamund*. That night Hannasyde, raw and savage from the raking up of all old feelings, took counsel with himself for one measured hour. What he decided upon was this; and you must decide for yourself how much genuine affection for the old Love, and how much a very natural inclination to go abroad and enjoy himself, affected the decision. Mrs. Landys-Haggert would never in all human likelihood cross his path again. So whatever he did didn't much matter. She was marvellously like the girl who 'took a deep interest' and the rest of the formula. All things considered, it would be pleasant to make the acquaintance of Mrs. Landys-Haggert, and for a little time—only a very little time—to make believe that he was with Alice Chisane again. Every one is more or less mad on one point. Hannasyde's particular monomania was his old love, Alice Chisane.

He made it his business to get introduced to Mrs. Haggert, and the introduction prospered. He also made it his business to see as much as he could of that lady. When a man is in earnest as to interviews, the facilities which Simla offers are startling. There are garden-parties, and tennis-parties, and picnics, and luncheons at Annandale,* and rifle-matches, and dinners and balls; besides rides and walks, which are matters of private arrangement. Hannasyde had started with the intention of seeing a likeness, and he ended by doing much more. He wanted to be deceived, he meant to be deceived, and he deceived himself very thoroughly. Not only were the face and figure the face and figure of Alice Chisane, but the voice and lower tones were exactly the same, and so were the turns of speech; and the little mannerisms, that every woman has, of gait and gesticulation, were absolutely and identically the same. The turn of the head was the same; the tired look in the eyes at the end of a long walk was the same; the stoop-and-wrench over the saddle to hold in a pulling horse was the same; and once, most marvellous of all, Mrs. Landys-Haggert singing to herself in the next room, while Hannasyde was waiting to take her for a ride, hummed, note for note, with a throaty quiver of the voice in the second line, 'Poor Wandering One!'* exactly as Alice Chisane had hummed it for Hannasyde in the dusk of an English drawing-room. In the actual woman herself—in the soul of her—there was not the least likeness, she and Alice Chisane being cast in different moulds. But all that Hannasyde wanted to know and see and think about, was this maddening and perplexing likeness of face and voice and manner. He was bent on making a fool of himself that way; and he was in no sort disappointed.

Open and obvious devotion from any sort of man is always pleasant to any sort of woman; but Mrs. Landys-Haggert, being a woman of the world, could make nothing of Hannasyde's admiration.

He would take any amount of trouble—he was a selfish man habitually—to meet and forestall, if possible, her wishes. Anything she told him to do was law; and he was, there could be no doubting it, fond of her company so long as she talked to him, and kept on talking about trivialities. But when she launched into expression of her personal views and her wrongs, those small social differences that make the spice of Simla life, Hannasyde was neither pleased nor interested. He didn't want to know anything about Mrs. Landys-Haggert, or her experiences in the past—she had travelled nearly all over the world, and could talk cleverly—he wanted the likeness of Alice Chisane before his eyes and her voice in his ears. Anything outside that, reminding him of another personality, jarred, and he showed that it did.

Under the new Post office, one evening, Mrs. Landys-Haggert turned on him, and spoke her mind shortly and without warning. 'Mr. Hannasyde,' said she, 'will you be good enough to explain why you have appointed yourself my special *cavalier servente**? I don't understand it. But I am perfectly certain, somehow or other, that you don't care the least little bit in the world for *me*.' This seems to support, by the way, the theory that no man can act or tell lies to a woman without being found out. Hannasyde was taken off his guard. His defence never was a strong one, because he was always ⸀hinking of himself, and he blurted out, before he knew what ⸀e was saying, this inexpedient answer, 'No more I do.'

The queerness of the situation and the reply made Mrs. Landys-Haggert laugh. Then it all came out; and at the end of Hannasyde's lucid explanation Mrs. Haggert said, with the least little touch of scorn in her voice, 'So I'm to act as the lay-figure for you to hang the rags of your tattered affections on, am I?'

Hannasyde didn't see what answer was required, and he devoted himself generally and vaguely to the praise of Alice Chisane, which was unsatisfactory. Now it is to be thoroughly made clear that Mrs. Haggert had not the shadow of a ghost of an interest in Hannasyde. Only . . . only no woman likes being made love through instead of to—specially on behalf of a musty divinity of four years' standing.

Hannasyde did not see that he had made any very particular exhibition of himself. He was glad to find a sympathetic soul in the arid wastes of Simla.

When the season ended, Hannasyde went down to his own place and Mrs. Haggert to hers. 'It was like making love to a ghost,' said Hannasyde to himself, 'and it doesn't matter; and now I'll get to my work.' But he found himself thinking steadily of the Haggert-Chisane ghost; and he could not be certain whether it was Haggert or Chisane that made up the greater part of the pretty phantom.

* * *

He got understanding a month later.

A peculiar point of this peculiar country is the way in which a heartless Government transfers men from one end of the Empire to the other. You can never be sure of getting rid of a friend or an enemy till he or she dies. There was a case once—but that's another story.

Haggert's Department ordered him up from Dindigul to the Frontier at two days' notice, and he went through, losing money at every step, from Dindigul to his station. He dropped Mrs. Haggert at Lucknow, to stay with some friends there, to take part in a big ball at the Chutter Munzil,* and to come on when he had made the new home a little comfortable. Lucknow was Hannasyde's station, and Mrs. Haggert stayed a week there. Hannasyde went to meet her. As the train came in, he discovered what he had been thinking of for the past month. The unwisdom of his conduct also struck him. The Lucknow week, with two dances, and an unlimited quantity of rides together, clinched matters; and Hannasyde found himself pacing this circle of thought:—He adored Alice Chisane, at least he *had* adored her. *And* he admired Mrs. Landys-Haggert because she was like Alice Chisane. *But* Mrs. Landys-Haggert was not in the least like Alice Chisane, being a thousand times more adorable. *Now* Alice Chisane was 'the bride of another,' and so was Mrs. Landys-Haggert, and a good and honest wife too. *Therefore* he, Hannasyde, was . . . here he called himself several hard names, and wished that he had been wise in the beginning.

Whether Mrs. Landys-Haggert saw what was going on in his mind she alone knows. He seemed to take an unqualified interest in everything connected with herself, as distinguished from the Alice-Chisane likeness, and he said one or two things which, if Alice Chisane had been still betrothed to him, could scarcely have been excused, even on the grounds of the likeness. But Mrs. Haggert turned the remarks aside, and spent a long time in making Hannasyde see what a comfort and a pleasure she had been to him because of her strange resemblance to his old love. Hannasyde groaned in his saddle and said, 'Yes, indeed,' and busied himself with preparations for her departure to the Frontier, feeling very small and miserable.

The last day of her stay at Lucknow came, and Hannasyde saw her off at the Railway Station. She was very grateful for his kindness and the trouble he had taken, and smiled pleasantly and sympathetically as one who knew the Alice-Chisane reason of that kindness. And Hannasyde abused the coolies with the luggage, and hustled the people on the platform, and prayed that the roof might fall in and slay him.

As the train went out slowly, Mrs. Landys-Haggert leaned out of the window to say good-bye—'On second thoughts, *au revoir*, Mr. Hannasyde. I go Home in the Spring, and perhaps I may meet you in Town.'

Hannasyde shook hands, and said very earnestly and adoringly—'I hope to Heaven I shall never see your face again!'

And Mrs. Haggert understood.

Wressley of the Foreign Office*

I closed and drew for my Love's sake,
  That now is false to me,
And I slew the Riever of Tarrant Moss,
  And set Dumeny free.

And ever they give me praise and gold,
  And ever I moan my loss;
For I struck the blow for my false Love's sake,
  And not for the men of the Moss!

Tarrant Moss.

ONE of the many curses of our life in India is the want of
atmosphere in the painter's sense. There are no half-tints
worth noticing. Men stand out all crude and raw, with
nothing to tone them down, and nothing to scale them against.
They do their work, and grow to think that there is nothing
but their work, and nothing like their work, and that they are
the real pivots on which the Administration turns. Here is an
instance of this feeling. A half-caste clerk was ruling forms in
a Pay Office. He said to me, 'Do you know what would
happen if I added or took away one single line on this sheet?'
Then, with the air of a conspirator, 'It would disorganise the
whole of the Treasury payments throughout the whole of the
Presidency Circle! Think of that!'

If men had not this delusion as to the ultra-importance of
their own particular employments, I suppose that they would
sit down and kill themselves. But their weakness is wearisome,
particularly when the listener knows that he himself commits
exactly the same sin.

Even the Secretariat believes that it does good when it asks
an over-driven Executive Officer to take a census of wheat-
weevils through a District of five thousand square miles.

There was a man once in the Foreign Office—a man who
had grown middle-aged in the Department, and was com-
monly said, by irreverent juniors, to be able to repeat

Aitchison's* *Treaties and Sunnuds* backwards in his sleep. What he did with his stored knowledge only the Secretary knew; and he, naturally, would not publish the news abroad. This man's name was Wressley, and it was the Shibboleth, in those days, to say—'Wressley knows more about the Central Indian States than any living man.' If you did not say this, you were considered one of mean understanding.

Nowadays, the man who says that he knows the ravel of the inter-tribal complications across the Border is of more use; but, in Wressley's time, much attention was paid to the Central Indian States. They were called 'foci' and 'factors,' and all manner of imposing names.

And here the curse of Anglo-Indian life fell heavily. When Wressley lifted up his voice, and spoke about such-and-such a succession to such-and-such a throne, the Foreign Office were silent, and Heads of Departments repeated the last two or three words of Wressley's sentences, and tacked 'yes, yes,' on to them, and knew that they were assisting the Empire to grapple with serious political contingencies. In most big undertakings one or two men do the work, while the rest sit near and talk till the ripe decorations begin to fall.

Wressley was the working-member of the Foreign Office firm, and, to keep him up to his duties when he showed signs of flagging, he was made much of by his superiors and told what a fine fellow he was. He did not require coaxing because he was of tough build, but what he received confirmed him in the belief that there was no one quite so absolutely and imperatively necessary to the stability of India as Wressley of the Foreign Office. There might be other good men, but the known, honoured, and trusted man among men was Wressley of the Foreign Office. We had a Viceroy in those days who knew exactly when to 'gentle' a fractious big man, and to hearten-up a collar-galled little one, and so keep all his team level. He conveyed to Wressley the impression which I have just set down; and even tough men are apt to be disorganised by a Viceroy's praise. There was a case once . . . but that is another story.

All India knew Wressley's name and office—it was in Thacker and Spink's Directory*—but who he was personally, or what he did, or what his special merits were, not fifty men knew or cared. His work filled all his time, and he found no leisure to cultivate acquaintances beyond those of dead Rajput chiefs with *Ahir** blots in their scutcheons. Wressley would have made a very good Clerk in the Heralds' College had he not been a Bengal Civilian.

Upon a day, between office and office, great trouble came to Wressley—overwhelmed him, knocked him down, and left him gasping as though he had been a little schoolboy. Without reason, against prudence, and at a moment's notice, he fell in love with a frivolous, golden-haired girl who used to tear about Simla Mall on a high, rough waler, with a blue velvet jockey-cap crammed over her eyes. Her name was Venner— Tillie Venner—and she was delightful. She took Wressley's heart at a hand-gallop, and Wressley found that it was not good for man to live alone; even with half the Foreign Office Records in his presses.

Then Simla laughed, for Wressley in love was slightly ridiculous. He did his best to interest the girl in himself—that is to say, his work—and she, after the manner of women, did her best to appear interested in what, behind his back, she called 'Mr. W'essley's Wajahs'; for she lisped very prettily. She did not understand one little thing about them, but she acted as if she did. Men have married on that sort of error before now.

Providence, however, had care of Wressley. He was immensely struck with Miss Venner's intelligence. He would have been more impressed had he heard her private and confidential accounts of his calls. He held peculiar notions as to the wooing of girls. He said that the best work of a man's career should be laid reverently at their feet. Ruskin* writes something like this somewhere, I think; but in ordinary life a few kisses are better and save time.

About a month after he had lost his heart to Miss Venner, and had been doing his work vilely in consequence, the first idea of his *Native Rule in Central India* struck Wressley and filled him with joy. It was, as he sketched it, a great thing—the work of his life—a really comprehensive survey of a most fascinating subject—to be written with all the special and laboriously acquired knowledge of Wressley of the Foreign Office—a gift fit for an Empress.

He told Miss Venner that he was going to take leave, and hoped, on his return, to bring her a present worthy of her acceptance. Would she wait? Certainly she would. Wressley drew seventeen hundred rupees a month. She would wait a year for that. Her Mamma would help her to wait.

So Wressley took one year's leave and all the available documents, about a truck-load, that he could lay hands on, and went down to Central India with his notion hot in his head. He began his book in the land he was writing of. Too much official correspondence had made him a frigid workman, and he must have guessed that he needed the white light of local colour on his palette. This is a dangerous paint for amateurs to play with.

Heavens, how that man worked! He caught his Rajahs, analysed his Rajahs, and traced them up into the mists of Time and beyond, with their queens and their concubines. He dated and cross-dated, pedigreed and triple-pedigreed, compared, noted, connoted, wove, strung, sorted, selected, inferred, calendared and counter-calendared for ten hours a day. And, because this sudden and new light of Love was upon him, he turned those dry bones of history and dirty records of misdeeds into things to weep or to laugh over as he pleased. His heart and soul were at the end of his pen, and they got into the ink. He was dowered with sympathy, insight, humour, and style for two hundred and thirty days and nights; and his book was a Book. He had his vast special knowledge with him, so to speak; but the spirit, the woven-in human Touch, the poetry and the power of the output, were beyond all special knowledge. But I doubt whether he knew the gift that was in him then, and thus he may have lost some happiness. He was toiling for Tillie Venner, not for himself. Men often do their best work blind, for some one else's sake.

Also, though this has nothing to do with the story, in India, where every one knows every one else, you can watch men being driven, by the women who govern them, out of the rank-and-file and sent to take up points alone. A good man, once started, goes forward; but an average man, so soon as the woman loses interest in his success as a tribute to her power, comes back to the battalion and is no more heard of.

Wressley bore the first copy of his book to Simla, and, blushing and stammering, presented it to Miss Venner. She read a little of it. I give her review *verbatim*—'Oh, your book? It's all about those howwid Wajahs. I didn't understand it.'

*   *   *

Wressley of the Foreign Office was broken, smashed,—I am not exaggerating—by this one frivolous little girl. All that he could say feebly was—'But—but it's my *magnum opus**! The work of my life.' Miss Venner did not know what *magnum opus* meant; but she knew that Captain Kerrington had won three races at the last Gymkhana. Wressley didn't press her to wait for him any longer. He had sense enough for that.

Then came the reaction after the year's strain, and Wressley went back to the Foreign Office and his 'Wajahs,' a compiling, gazetteering, report-writing hack, who would have been dear at three hundred rupees a month. He abided by Miss Venner's review; which proves that the inspiration in the book was purely temporary and unconnected with himself. Nevertheless, he had no right to sink, in a hill-tarn, five packing-cases, brought up at enormous expense from Bombay, of the best book of Indian history ever written.

When he sold off before retiring, some years later, I was turning over his shelves, and came across the only existing copy of *Native Rule in Central India*—the copy that Miss Venner could not understand. I read it, sitting on his mule-trunks, as long as the light lasted, and offered him his own price for it. He looked over my shoulder for a few pages and said to himself drearily—

'Now, how in the world did I come to write such damned good stuff as that?'

Then to me—

'Take it and keep it. Write one of your penny-farthing yarns about its birth. Perhaps—perhaps—the whole business may have been ordained to that end.'

Which, knowing what Wressley of the Foreign Office was once, struck me as about the bitterest thing that I had ever heard a man say of his own work.

By Word of Mouth*

Not though you die to-night, O Sweet, and wail,
    A spectre at my door,
Shall mortal Fear make Love immortal fail—
    I shall but love you more,
Who, from Death's house returning, give me still
One moment's comfort in my matchless ill.

Shadow Houses.

THIS tale may be explained by those who know how souls are made, and where the bounds of the Possible are put down. I have lived long enough in this India to know that it is best to know nothing, and can only write the story as it happened.

Dumoise was our Civil Surgeon at Meridki,* and we called him 'Dormouse,' because he was a round little, sleepy little man. He was a good Doctor and never quarrelled with any one, not even with our Deputy Commissioner who had the manners of a bargee and the tact of a horse. He married a girl as round and as sleepy-looking as himself. She was a Miss Hillardyce, daughter of 'Squash' Hillardyce of the Berars,* who married his Chief's daughter by mistake. . . . But that is another story.

A honeymoon in India is seldom more than a week long; but there is nothing to hinder a couple from extending it over two or three years. India is a delightful country for married folk who are wrapped up in one another. They can live absolutely alone and without interruption—just as the Dormice did. Those two little people retired from the world after their marriage, and were very happy. They were forced, of course, to give occasional dinners, but they made no friends thereby, and the Station went its own way and forgot them; only saying, occasionally, that Dormouse was the best of good fellows though dull. A Civil Surgeon who never quarrels is a rarity, appreciated as such.

Few people can afford to play Robinson Crusoe anywhere—least of all in India, where we are few in the land

and very much dependent on each other's kind offices. Dumoise was wrong in shutting himself from the world for a year, and he discovered his mistake when an epidemic of typhoid broke out in the Station in the heart of the cold weather, and his wife went down. He was a shy little man, and five days were wasted before he realised that Mrs. Dumoise was burning with something worse than simple fever, and three days more passed before he ventured to call on Mrs. Shute, the Engineer's wife, and timidly speak about his trouble. Nearly every household in India knows that Doctors are very helpless in typhoid. The battle must be fought out between Death and the Nurses minute by minute and degree by degree. Mrs. Shute almost boxed Dumoise's ears for what she called his 'criminal delay,' and went off at once to look after the poor girl. We had seven cases of typhoid in the Station that winter and, as the average of death is about one in every five cases, we felt certain that we should have to lose somebody. But all did their best. The women sat up nursing the women, and the men turned to and tended the bachelors who were down, and we wrestled with those typhoid cases for fifty-six days, and brought them through the Valley of the Shadow in triumph. But, just when we thought all was over, and were going to give a dance to celebrate the victory, little Mrs. Dumoise got a relapse and died in a week, and the Station went to the funeral. Dumoise broke down utterly at the brink of the grave, and had to be taken away.

After the death Dumoise crept into his own house and refused to be comforted. He did his duties perfectly, but we all felt that he should go on leave, and the other men of his own Service told him so. Dumoise was very thankful for the suggestion—he was thankful for anything in those days—and went to Chini on a walking-tour. Chini is some twenty marches from Simla, in the heart of the Hills, and the scenery is good if you are in trouble. You pass through big, still deodar* forests, and under big, still cliffs, and over big, still grass-downs swelling like a woman's breasts; and the wind across the grass, and the rain among the deodars say— 'Hush—hush—hush.' So little Dumoise was packed off to Chini, to wear down his grief with a full-plate camera and a rifle. He took also a useless bearer, because the man had been his wife's favourite servant. He was idle and a thief, but Dumoise trusted everything to him.

On his way back from Chini, Dumoise turned aside to Bagi, through the Forest Reserve which is on the spur of Mount Huttoo. Some men who have travelled more than a little say that the march from Kotgarh to Bagi is one of the finest in creation. It runs through dark wet forest, and ends suddenly in bleak, nipped hillside and black rocks. Bagi *dâk*-bungalow* is open to all the winds and is bitterly cold. Few people go to Bagi. Perhaps that was the reason why Dumoise went there. He halted at seven in the evening, and his bearer went down the hillside to the village to engage coolies for the next day's march. The sun had set, and the night-winds were beginning to croon among the rocks. Dumoise leaned on the railing of the verandah, waiting for his bearer to return. The man came back almost immediately after he had disappeared, and at such a rate that Dumoise fancied he must have crossed a bear. He was running as hard as he could up the face of the hill.

But there was no bear to account for his terror. He raced to the verandah and fell down, the blood spurting from his nose and his face iron-gray. Then he gurgled—'I have seen the *Memsahib*! I have seen the *Memsahib*!'

'Where?' said Dumoise.

'Down there, walking on the road to the village. She was in a blue dress, and she lifted the veil of her bonnet and said—"Ram Dass, give my *salaams* to the *Sahib*, and tell him that I shall meet him next month at Nuddea." Then I ran away, because I was afraid.'

What Dumoise said or did I do not know. Ram Dass declares that he said nothing but walked up and down the verandah all the cold night, waiting for the *Memsahib* to come up the hill, and stretching out his arms into the dark like a madman. But no *Memsahib* came, and, next day, he went on to Simla cross-questioning the bearer every hour.

Ram Dass could only say that he had met Mrs. Dumoise, and that she had lifted up her veil and given him the message which he had faithfully repeated to Dumoise. To this statement Ram Dass adhered. He did not know where Nuddea was, had no friends at Nuddea, and would most certainly never go to Nuddea, even though his pay were doubled.

Nuddea is in Bengal, and has nothing whatever to do with a Doctor serving in the Punjab. It must be more than twelve hundred miles south of Meridki.

Dumoise went through Simla without halting, and returned to Meridki, there to take over charge from the man who had been officiating for him during his tour. There were some Dispensary accounts to be explained, and some recent orders of the Surgeon-General to be noted, and, altogether, the taking-over was a full day's work. In the evening Dumoise told his *locum tenens*, who was an old friend of his bachelor days, what had happened at Bagi; and the man said that Ram Dass might as well have chosen Tuticorin* while he was about it.

At that moment a telegraph-peon came in with a telegram from Simla, ordering Dumoise not to take over charge at Meridki, but to go at once to Nuddea on special duty. There was a nasty outbreak of cholera at Nuddea, and the Bengal Government being short-handed, as usual, had borrowed a Surgeon from the Punjab.

Dumoise threw the telegram across the table and said— 'Well?'

The other Doctor said nothing. It was all that he could say.

Then he remembered that Dumoise had passed through Simla on his way from Bagi; and thus might, possibly, have heard first news of the impending transfer.

He tried to put the question and the implied suspicion into words, but Dumoise stopped him with—'If I had desired *that*, I should never have come back from Chini. I was shooting there. I wish to live, for I have things to do . . . but I shall not be sorry.'

The other man bowed his head, and helped, in the twilight, to pack up Dumoise's just-opened trunks. Ram Dass entered with the lamps.

'Where is the *Sahib* going?' he asked.

'To Nuddea,' said Dumoise softly.

Ram Dass clawed Dumoise's knees and boots and begged him not to go. Ram Dass wept and howled till he was turned out of the room. Then he wrapped up all his belongings and

came back to ask for a character. He was not going to Nuddea
to see his *Sahib* die and, perhaps, to die himself.

So Dumoise gave the man his wages and went down to
Nuddea alone, the other Doctor bidding him good-bye as one
under sentence of death.

Eleven days later he had joined his *Memsahib*; and the
Bengal Government had to borrow a fresh Doctor to cope
with that epidemic at Nuddea. The first importation lay dead
in Chooadanga *Dâk*-Bungalow.

To be Filed for Reference*

By the hoof of the Wild Goat up-tossed
From the Cliff where she lay in the Sun,
    Fell the Stone
To the Tarn where the daylight is lost;
So she fell from the light of the Sun,
    And alone.

Now the fall was ordained from the first,
With the Goat and the Cliff and the Tarn,
    But the Stone
Knows only her life is accursed,
As she sinks from the light of the Sun,
    And alone.

Oh, Thou who hast builded the World!
Oh, Thou who hast lighted the Sun!
Oh, Thou who hast darkened the Tarn!
    Judge Thou
The sin of the Stone that was hurled
By the Goat from the light of the Sun,
As she sinks in the mire of the Tarn,
      Even now—even now—even now!
    From the Unpublished Papers of McIntosh Jellaludin.

'SAY is it dawn, is it dusk in thy Bower,
Thou whom I long for, who longest for me?
Oh, be it night—be it——'*

Here he fell over a little camel-colt that was sleeping in the Serai* where the horse-traders and the best of the blackguards from Central Asia live; and, because he was very drunk indeed and the night was dark, he could not rise again till I helped him. That was the beginning of my acquaintance with McIntosh Jellaludin. When a loafer, and drunk, sings 'The Song of the Bower,' he must be worth cultivating. He got off the camel's back and said, rather thickly, 'I—I—I'm a bit screwed,* but a dip in Loggerhead* will put me right again;

and, I say, have you spoken to Symonds* about the mare's knees?'

Now Loggerhead was six thousand weary miles away from us, close to Mesopotamia,* where you mustn't fish and poaching is impossible, and Charley Symonds' stable a half mile farther across the paddocks. It was strange to hear all the old names, on a May night, among the horses and camels of the Sultan Caravanserai. Then the man seemed to remember himself and sober down at the same time. He leaned against the camel and pointed to a corner of the Serai where a lamp was burning.

'I live there,' said he, 'and I should be extremely obliged if you would be good enough to help my mutinous feet thither; for I am more than usually drunk—most—most phenomenally tight. But not in respect to my head. "My brain cries out against"*—how does it go? But my head rides on the—rolls on the dunghill I should have said, and controls the qualm.'

I helped him through the gangs of tethered horses, and he collapsed on the edge of the verandah in front of the line of native quarters.

'Thanks—a thousand thanks! O Moon and little, little Stars! To think that a man should so shamelessly . . . Infamous liquor too. Ovid in exile* drank no worse. Better. It was frozen. Alas! I had no ice. Good-night. I would introduce you to my wife were I sober—or she civilised.'

A native woman came out of the darkness of the room and began calling the man names, so I went away. He was the most interesting loafer that I had had the pleasure of knowing for a long time; and later on, he became a friend of mine. He was a tall, well-built, fair man, fearfully shaken with drink, and he looked nearer fifty than the thirty-five which, he said, was his real age. When a man begins to sink in India, and is not sent Home by his friends as soon as may be, he falls very low from a respectable point of view. By the time that he changes his creed, as did McIntosh, he is past redemption.

In most big cities natives will tell you of two or three *Sahibs*, generally low-caste, who have turned Hindu or Mussulman, and who live more or less as such. But it is not often that you can get to know them. As McIntosh himself used to say, 'If

I change my religion for my stomach's sake, I do not seek to become a martyr to missionaries, nor am I anxious for notoriety.'

At the outset of acquaintance McIntosh warned me. 'Remember this. I am not an object for charity. I require neither your money, your food, nor your cast-off raiment. I am that rare animal, a self-supporting drunkard. If you choose, I will smoke with you, for the tobacco of the bazars does not, I admit, suit my palate; and I will borrow any books which you may not specially value. It is more than likely that I shall sell them for bottles of excessively filthy country-liquors. In return, you shall share such hospitality as my house affords. Here is a charpoy* on which two can sit, and it is possible that there may, from time to time, be food in that platter. Drink, unfortunately, you will find on the premises at any hour; and thus I make you welcome to all my poor establishment.'

I was admitted to the McIntosh household—I and my good tobacco. But nothing else. Unluckily, one cannot visit a loafer in the Serai by day. Friends buying horses would not understand it. Consequently, I was obliged to see McIntosh after dark. He laughed at this, and said simply, 'You are perfectly right. When I enjoyed a position in society, rather higher than yours, I should have done exactly the same thing. Good Heavens! I was once'—he spoke as though he had fallen from the Command of a Regiment—'an Oxford Man!' This accounted for the reference to Charley Symonds' stable.

'You,' said McIntosh slowly, 'have not had that advantage; but, to outward appearance, you do not seem possessed of a craving for strong drinks. On the whole, I fancy that you are the luckier of the two. Yet I am not certain. You are—forgive my saying so even while I am smoking your excellent tobacco—painfully ignorant of many things.'

We were sitting together on the edge of his bedstead, for he owned no chairs, watching the horses being watered for the night, while the native woman was preparing dinner. I did not like being patronised by a loafer, but I was his guest for the time being, though he owned only one very torn alpaca coat and a pair of trousers made out of gunny-bags.* He took the pipe out of his mouth, and went on judicially, 'All things

considered, I doubt whether you are the luckier. I do not refer
to your extremely limited classical attainments, or your
excruciating quantities,* but to your gross ignorance of
matters more immediately under your notice. That, for
instance.' He pointed to a woman cleaning a samovar near the
well in the centre of the Serai. She was flicking the water out
of the spout in regular cadenced jerks.

'There are ways and ways of cleaning samovars. If you knew
why she was doing her work in that particular fashion, you
would know what the Spanish Monk meant when he said—

> I the Trinity illustrate,
>   Drinking watered orange-pulp—
> In three sips the Arian frustrate,
>   While he drains his at one gulp—*

and many other things which now are hidden from your eyes.
However, Mrs. McIntosh has prepared dinner. Let us come
and eat after the fashion of the people of the country—of
whom, by the way, you know nothing.'

The native woman dipped her hand in the dish with us.
This was wrong. The wife should always wait until the
husband has eaten. McIntosh Jellaludin apologised, saying—

'It is an English prejudice which I have not been able to
overcome; and she loves me. Why, I have never been able to
understand. I forgathered with her at Jullundur, three years
ago, and she has remained with me ever since. I believe her
to be moral, and know her to be skilled in cookery.'

He patted the woman's head as he spoke, and she cooed
softly. She was not pretty to look at.

McIntosh never told me what position he had held before
his fall. He was, when sober, a scholar and a gentleman. When
drunk, he was rather more of the first than the second. He
used to get drunk about once a week for two days. On those
occasions the native woman tended him while he raved in all
tongues except his own. One day, indeed, he began reciting
*Atalanta in Calydon,** and went through it to the end, beating
time to the swing of the verse with a bedstead-leg. But he did
most of his ravings in Greek or German. The man's mind was
a perfect rag-bag of useless things. Once, when he was

beginning to get sober, he told me that I was the only rational being in the Inferno into which he had descended—a Virgil in the Shades,* he said— and that, in return for my tobacco, he would, before he died, give me the materials of a new *Inferno* that should make me greater than Dante. Then he fell asleep on a horse-blanket and woke up quite calm.

'Man,' said he, 'when you have reached the uttermost depths of degradation, little incidents which would vex a higher life are to you of no consequence. Last night my soul was among the Gods; but I make no doubt that my bestial body was writhing down here in the garbage.'

'You were abominably drunk, if that's what you mean,' I said.

'I *was* drunk—filthily drunk. I who am the son of a man with whom you have no concern—I who was once Fellow of a College whose buttery-hatch you have not seen—I was loathsomely drunk. But consider how lightly I am touched. It is nothing to me—less than nothing; for I do not even feel the headache which should be my portion. Now, in a higher life, how ghastly would have been my punishment, how bitter my repentance! Believe me, my friend with the neglected education, the highest is as the lowest—always supposing each degree extreme.'

He turned round on the blanket, put his head between his fists and continued—

'On the Soul which I have lost and on the Conscience which I have killed, I tell you that I cannot feel! I am as the Gods, knowing good and evil, but untouched by either. Is this enviable or is it not?'

When a man has lost the warning of 'next morning's head' he must be in a bad state. I answered, looking at McIntosh on the blanket, with his hair over his eyes and his lips blue-white, that I did not think the insensibility good enough.

'For pity's sake, don't say that! I tell you it *is* good and most enviable. Think of my consolations!'

'Have you so many, then, McIntosh?'

'Certainly. Your attempts at sarcasm, which is essentially the weapon of a cultured man, are crude. First, my attainments, my classical and literary knowledge, blurred, perhaps, by immoderate drinking—which reminds me that before my soul went to the Gods last night I sold the Pickering Horace* you so kindly lent me. Ditta Mull the clothesman has it. It fetched ten annas, and may be redeemed for a rupee—but still infinitely superior to yours. Secondly, the abiding affection of Mrs. McIntosh, best of wives. Thirdly, a monument, more enduring than brass, which I have built up in the seven years of my degradation.'

He stopped here, and crawled across the room for a drink of water. He was very shaky and sick.

He referred several times to his 'treasure'—some great possession that he owned—but I held this to be the raving of drink. He was as poor and as proud as he could be. His manner was not pleasant, but he knew enough about the natives, among whom seven years of his life had been spent, to make his acquaintance worth having. He used actually to laugh at Strickland as an ignorant man—'ignorant West and East'—he said. His boast was, first, that he was an Oxford Man of rare shining parts, which may or may not have been true—I did not know enough to check his statements; and, secondly, that he 'had his hand on the pulse of native life'— which was a fact. As an Oxford man, he struck me as a prig: he was always throwing his education about. As a Mahommedan *faquir*—as McIntosh Jellaludin—he was all that I wanted for my own ends. He smoked several pounds of my tobacco, and taught me several ounces of things worth knowing; but he would never accept any gifts, not even when the cold weather came, and gripped the poor thin chest under the poor thin alpaca coat. He grew very angry, and said that I had insulted him, and that he was not going into hospital. He had lived like a beast and he would die rationally, like a man.

As a matter of fact, he died of pneumonia; and on the night of his death sent over a grubby note asking me to come and help him to die.

The native woman was weeping by the side of the bed. McIntosh, wrapped in a cotton cloth, was too weak to resent a fur coat being thrown over him. He was very active as far as his mind was concerned, and his eyes were blazing. When he had abused the Doctor who came with me so foully that the indignant old fellow left, he cursed me for a few minutes and calmed down.

Then he told his wife to fetch out 'The Book' from a hole in the wall. She brought out a big bundle, wrapped in the tail of a petticoat, of old sheets of miscellaneous notepaper, all numbered and covered with fine cramped writing. McIntosh ploughed his hand through the rubbish and stirred it up lovingly.

'This,' he said, 'is my work—the Book of McIntosh Jellaludin, showing what he saw and how he lived, and what befell him and others; being also an account of the life and sins and death of Mother Maturin.* What Mirza Murad Ali Beg's book* is to all other books on native life, will my work be to Mirza Murad Ali Beg's!'

This, as will be conceded by any one who knows Mirza Murad Ali Beg's book, was a sweeping statement. The papers did not look specially valuable; but McIntosh handled them as if they were currency-notes. Then said he slowly—

'In despite the many weaknesses of your education, you have been good to me. I will speak of your tobacco when I reach the Gods. I owe you much thanks for many kindnesses. But I abominate indebtedness. For this reason I bequeath to you now the monument more enduring than brass—my one book—rude and imperfect in parts, but oh, how rare in others! I wonder if you will understand it. It is a gift more honourable than . . . Bah! where is my brain rambling to? You will mutilate it horribly. You will knock out the gems you call Latin quotations, you Philistine, and you will butcher the style to carve into your own jerky jargon; but you cannot destroy the whole of it. I bequeath it to you. Ethel . . . My brain again! . . . Mrs. McIntosh, bear witness that I give the *Sahib* all these papers. They would be of no use to you, Heart of my Heart; and I lay it upon you,' he turned to me here, 'that you do not let my book die in its present form. It is yours unconditionally—the story of McIntosh Jellaludin, which is *not* the story of McIntosh Jellaludin, but of a greater man than he, and of a far greater woman. Listen now! I am neither mad nor drunk! That book will make you famous.'

I said, 'Thank you,' as the native woman put the bundle into my arms.

'My only baby!' said McIntosh, with a smile. He was sinking fast, but he continued to talk as long as breath remained. I waited for the end; knowing that, in six cases out of ten, a dying man calls for his mother. He turned on his side and said—

'Say how it came into your possession. No one will believe you, but my name, at least, will live. You will treat it brutally, I know you will. Some of it must go; the public are fools and prudish fools. I was their servant once. But do your mangling gently—very gently. It is a great work, and I have paid for it in seven years' damnation.

His voice stopped for ten or twelve breaths, and then he began mumbling a prayer of some kind in Greek. The native woman cried very bitterly. Lastly, he rose in bed and said, as loudly as slowly—'Not guilty, my Lord!'

Then he fell back, and the stupor held him till he died. The native woman ran into the Serai among the horses, and screamed and beat her breasts; for she had loved him.

Perhaps his last sentence in life told what McIntosh had once gone through; but, saving the big bundle of old sheets in the cloth, there was nothing in his room to say who or what he had been.

The papers were in a hopeless muddle.

Strickland helped me to sort them, and he said that the writer was either an extreme liar or a most wonderful person. He thought the former. One of these days you may be able to judge for yourselves. The bundle needed much expurgation, and was full of Greek nonsense at the head of the chapters, which has all been cut out.

If the thing is ever published, some one may perhaps remember this story, now printed as a safeguard to prove that McIntosh Jellaludin and not I myself wrote the Book of Mother Maturin.

I don't want *The Giant's Robe** to come true in my case!

THE END

APPENDIX A

BITTERS NEAT*

THE oldest trouble in the world comes from want of understanding. And it is entirely the fault of the Woman. Somehow, she is built incapable of speaking the truth, even to herself. She only finds it out about four months later, when the man is dead, or has been transferred. Then she says she never was so happy in her life, and marries someone else, who again touched some woman's heart elsewhere, and did not know it, but was mixed up with another man's wife, who only used him to pique a third man. And so round again—all criss-cross.

In India, where life goes quicker than at Home, things are more obviously tangled, and therefore more pitiful to look at. Men speak the truth as they understand it, and women as they think men would like to understand it; and then they all act lies which would deceive Solomon, and the result is a heart-rending muddle that half-a-dozen open words would put straight.

This particular muddle did not differ from any other muddle you may see, if you are not busy playing cross-purposes yourself, going on in a big Station any cold season. Its only merit was that it did not come all right in the end; as muddles are made to do in the third volume.*

I've forgotten what the man was—he was an ordinary sort of man—'man you meet any day at the A.D.C.s'* end of the table, and go away and forget about. His name was Surrey; but whether he was in the Army, or the P.W.D.,* or the Commissariat, or the Police, or a factory, I don't remember. He wasn't a Civilian.* He was just an ordinary man, of the light-coloured variety, with a fair moustache and with the average amount of pay that comes between twenty-seven and thirty-two—from six to nine hundred* a month.

He didn't dance, and he did what little riding he wanted to do by himself, and was busy in his office all day, and never bothered his head about women. No man ever dreamed he would. He was of the type that doesn't marry, just because it doesn't think about marriage. He was one of the plain cards, whose only use is to make up the pack, and furnish background to put the Court cards against.

Then there was a girl—ordinary girl—the dark-coloured variety—daughter of a man in the Army, who played a little, sang a little, talked a little, and furnished the background, exactly as Surrey did. She had been sent out here to get married if she could, because there were many sisters at home, and Colonels' allowances aren't elastic. She lived with an aunt. She was a Miss Tallaght, and men spelt her name 'Tart' on the programmes when they couldn't catch what the introducer said.

Surrey and she were thrown together in the same Station one cold weather; and the particular Devil who looks after muddles prompted Miss Tallaght to fall in love with Surrey. He had spoken to her perhaps twenty times—certainly not more—but she fell unreasoningly in love with him as if she had been Elaine and he Lancelot.*

She, of course kept her own counsel; and, equally of course, her manner to Surrey, who never noticed manner or style or dress any more than he noticed a sunset, was icy, not to say repellent. The deadly dullness of Surrey struck her as reserve of force, and she grew to believe he was wonderfully clever in some secret and mysterious sort of line. She did not know in what line; but she believed, and that was enough. No one suspected anything of any kind, for the simple reason that no one took any deep interest in Miss Tallaght except her Aunt; who wanted to get the girl off her hands.

This went on for some months, till a man suddenly woke up to the fact that Miss Tallaght was the one woman in the world for him, and told her so. She *jawabed** him—without rhyme or reason; and that night there followed one of those awful bedroom conferences that men know nothing about. Miss Tallaght's Aunt, querulous, indignant, and merciless, with her mouth full of hair-pins, and her hands full of false hair-plaits, set herself to find out by cross-examination what in the name of everything wise, prudent, religious, and dutiful, Miss Tallaght meant by *jawabing* her suitor. The conference lasted for an hour and a half, with question on question, insult and reminders of poverty—appeals to Providence, then a fresh mouthful of hair-pins—then all the questions over again, beginning with: 'But *what* do you see to dislike in Mr.—?' then a vicious tug at what was left of the mane; then impressive warnings, and more appeals to Heaven; and then the collapse of poor Miss Tallaght, a rumpled, crumpled, tear-stained arrangement in white on the couch at the foot of the bed, and, between sobs and gasps, the whole absurd little story of her love for Surrey.

Now, in all the forty-five years' experience of Miss Tallaght's Aunt, she had never heard of a girl throwing over a real genuine lover with an appointment, for a problematical, hypothetical lover to whom she had spoken merely in the course of the ordinary social visiting rounds. So Miss Tallaght's Aunt was struck dumb, and, merely praying that Heaven might direct Miss Tallaght into a better frame of mind, dismissed the *ayah*,* and went to bed; leaving Miss Tallaght to sob and moan herself to sleep.

Understand clearly, I don't for a moment defend Miss Tallaght. She was wrong—absurdly wrong—but attachments like hers *must* sprout by the law of averages, just to remind people that Love is as nakedly unreasoning as when Venus first gave him his kit and told him to run away and play.

Surrey must be held innocent—innocent as his own pony. Could he guess that, when Miss Tallaght was as curt and as unpleasing as she knew how, she would have risen up and followed him from Colombo to Dadar* at a word? He didn't know anything, or care anything, about Miss Tallaght. He had his work to do.

Miss Tallaght's Aunt might have respected her niece's secret. But she didn't. What we call 'talking rank scandal,' she called 'seeking advice;' and she sought advice, on the case of Miss Tallaght, from the Judge's wife, 'in strict confidence, my dear,' who told the Commissioner's wife, 'of course you won't repeat it, my dear,' who told the Deputy Commissioner's wife, 'you understand it is to go no further, my dear,' who told the newest bride, who was so delighted at being in possession of a secret concerning real grown-up men and women, that she told any one and every one who called on her. So the tale went all over the Station, and from being no one in particular, Miss Tallaght came to take precedence of the last interesting squabble between the Judge's wife and the Civil Engineer's wife. Then began a really interesting system of persecution worked by women—soft and sympathetic and intangible, but calculated to drive a girl off her head. They were all *so* sorry for Miss Tallaght, and they cooed together and were exaggeratedly kind and sweet in their manner to her, as those who said: 'You may confide in *us*, my stricken deer!'

Miss Tallaght was a woman and sensitive. It took her less than one evening at the Bandstand to find that her poor little, precious little secret, that had been wrenched from her on the rack, was known as widely as if it had been written on her hat. I don't know what she went through. Women don't speak of these things, and men ought not to guess; but it must have been some specially refined torture, for she told her Aunt she would go Home and die as a governess sooner than stay in this hateful—hateful—place. Her Aunt said she was a rebellious girl, and sent her Home to her people after a couple of months; and said no one knew what the pains of a chaperon's life were.

Poor Miss Tallaght had one pleasure just at the last. Half-way
down the line, she caught a glimpse of Surrey, who had gone down
on duty, and was then in the up-train. And he took off his hat to her.
She went Home, and if she is not dead by this time must be living
still.

* * * * *

Months afterwards, there was a lively dinner at the Club for the
Races. Surrey was mooning about as usual, and there was a good deal
of idle talk flying every way. Finally, one man, who had taken more
than was good for him, said, apropos of something about Surrey's
reserved ways: 'Ah, you old fraud. It's all very well for you to
pretend. I know a girl who was awf''ly mashed on you—once. Dead
nuts she was on Old Surrey. What had you been doing, eh?'

Surrey expected some sort of sell, and said with a laugh:—

'Who was she?'

Before any one could kick the man, he plumped out with the name;
and the Honorary Secretary tactfully upset the half of a big brew of
shandy-gaff all over the table. After the mopping up, the men went
out to the Lotteries.

But Surrey sat on, and, after ten minutes, said very humbly to the
only other man in the deserted dining-room: 'On your honour, was
there a word of truth in what the drunken fool said?'

Then the man who is writing this story, who had known of the
thing from the beginning, and now felt all the hopelessness and
tangle of it—the waste and the muddle—said, a good deal more
energetically than he meant:—

'Truth! Oh, man, man, couldn't you *see* it!'

Surrey said nothing, but sat still, smoking and smoking and thinking, while the Lottery tent babbled outside, and the *khitmutgars**
turned down the lamps.

To the best of my knowledge and belief that was the first thing
Surrey ever knew about love. But his awakening did not seem to
delight him. It must have been rather unpleasant, to judge by the
look on his face. He looked like a man who had missed a train and
had been half stunned at the same time.

When the men came in from the Lotteries, Surrey went out. he
wasn't in the mood for bones* and 'horse' talk. He went to his tent,
and the last thing he said, quite aloud to himself, was:— 'I didn't see.
I didn't see. If I had *only* known!'

Even if he had known I don't believe . . . .

But these things are *Kismet*, and we only find out all about them
just when any knowledge is too late.

APPENDIX B

HAUNTED SUBALTERNS*

So long as the 'Inextinguishables' confined themselves to running picnics, gymkhanas, flirtations, and innocences of that kind, no one said anything. But when they ran ghosts, people put up their eyebrows. 'Man can't feel comfy with a Regiment that entertains ghosts on its establishment. It is against General Orders. The 'Inextinguishables' said that the ghosts were private and not Regimental property. They referred you to Tesser for particulars; and Tesser told you to go to—the hottest Cantonment of all. He said that it was bad enough to have men making hay of his bedding and breaking his banjo-strings when he was out, without being chaffed afterwards; and he would thank you to keep your remarks on ghosts to yourself. This was before the 'Inextinguishables' had sworn by their several lady-loves that they were innocent of any intrusion into Tesser's quarters. Then Horrocks mentioned casually at Mess that a couple of white figures had been bounding about his room the night before, and he didn't approve of it. The 'Inextinguishables' denied, energetically, that they had had any hand in the manifestations, and advised Horrocks to consult Tesser.

I don't suppose that a subaltern believes in anything except his chances of a Company; but Horrocks and Tesser were exceptions. They came to believe in their ghosts. They had reason.

Horrocks used to find himself, at about three o'clock in the morning, staring wide-awake, watching two white Things hopping about his room and jumping up to the ceiling. Horrocks was of a placid turn of mind. After a week or so spent in watching his servants, and lying in wait for strangers, and trying to keep awake all night, he came to the conclusion that he was haunted, and that, consequently, he need not bother. He wasn't going to encourage these ghosts by being frightened of them. Therefore when he woke— as usual—with a start and saw these Things jumping like kangaroos, he only murmured: 'Go on! Don't mind me!' and went to sleep again.

Tesser said, 'It's all very well for you to make fun of *your* show. You can *see* your ghosts. Now I can't see mine, and I don't half like it.'

Tesser used to come into his room of nights, and find the whole of his bedding neatly stripped, as if it had been done with one sweep of the hand, from the top right-hand corner of his cot to the bottom left-hand corner. Also his lamp used to lie weltering on the floor, and generally his pet screw-head, inlaid, nickel-plated banjo was lying on the cot, with all its strings broken. Tesser took away the strings, on the occasion of the third manifestation, and the next night a man complimented him on his playing the best music ever got out of a banjo, for half an hour.

'Which half hour?' said Tesser.

'Between nine and ten,' said the man. Tesser had gone out to dinner at 7.30 and had returned at midnight.

He talked to his bearer and threatened him with unspeakable things. The bearer was grey with fear. 'I'm a poor man,' said he, 'If the Sahib is haunted by a Devil, what can I do?'

'Who says I'm haunted by a Devil?' howled Tesser, for he was angry.

'I have seen It,' said the bearer, 'at night, walking round and round your bed; and that is why everything is *ulta-pulta** in your room. I am a poor man, but I never go into your room alone. The *bhisti** comes with me.'

Tesser was thoroughly savage at this, and he spoke to Horrocks, and the two laid traps to catch that Devil, and threatened their servants with dog-whips if any more '*Shaitan-ke*-hanky-panky'* took place. But the servants were soaked with fear, and it was no use adding to their tortures. When Tesser went out at night, four of his men, as a rule, slept in the verandah of his quarters, until the banjo without the strings struck up, and then they fled.

One day, Tesser had to put in a month at a Fort with a detachment of 'Inextinguishables'. The Fort might have been Govindghar,* Jumrood,* or Phillour;* but it wasn't. He left cantonments rejoicing, for his Devil was preying on his mind; and with him went another Subaltern, a junior. But the Devil came too. After Tesser had been in the Fort about ten days he went out to dinner. When he came back he found his Subaltern doing sentry on a banquette across the Fort Ditch, as far removed as might be from the Officers' Quarters.

'What's wrong?' said Tesser.

The Subaltern said 'Listen!' and the two, standing under the stars, heard from the Officers' Quarters, high up in the wall of the Fort, the '*strumty tumty tumty*' of the banjo, which seemed to have an oratorio on hand.

'That performance,' said the Subaltern, 'has been going on for three mortal hours. I never wished to desert before, but I do now. I say, Tesser, old man, you are the best of good fellows, I'm sure, but . . . I say . . . look here, now, you are quite unfit to live with. 'Tisn't in my Commission, you know, that I'm to serve under a . . . a . . . man with Devils.'

'Isn't it?' said Tesser. 'If you make an ass of yourself I'll put you under arrest . . . and *in my room!*'

'You can put me where you please but I'm not going to assist at these infernal concerts. 'Tisn't right. 'Tisn't natural. Look here, I don't want to hurt your feelings but—try to think now—haven't you done something—committed some—murder that has slipped your memory—or forged something . . . ?'

'Well! For an all-round, double-shotted, half-baked fool you are the . . .'

'I dare say I am,' said the Subaltern. 'But you don't expect me to keep my wits with that row going on, do you?'

The banjo was rattling away as if it had twenty strings. Tesser sent up a stone, and a shower of broken window-pane fell into the Fort Ditch; but the banjo kept on. Tesser hauled the other Subaltern up to the quarters, and found his room in frightful confusion—lamp upset, bedding all over the floor, chairs overturned and table tilted sideways. He took stock of the wreck and said despairing, 'Oh, this *is* lovely!'

The Subaltern was peeping in at the door.

'I'm glad you think so,' he said. "Tisn't lovely enough for me. I *locked up* your room directly after you had gone out. See here, I think you'd better apply for Horrocks to come out in my place. He's troubled with your complaint, and this business will make me a jabbering idiot if it goes on.'

Tesser went to bed amid the wreckage, very angry, and next morning he rode into cantonments and asked Horrocks to arrange to relieve 'that fool with me now.'

'You've got 'em again, have you?' said Horrocks. 'So've I. *Three* white figures this time. We'll worry through the entertainment together.'

So Horrocks and Tesser settled down in the Fort together, and the 'Inextinguishables' said pleasant things about 'seven other Devils.' Tesser didn't see where the joke came in. His room was thrown upside-down three nights out of the seven. Horrocks was not troubled in any way, so his ghosts must have been purely local ones. Tesser, on the other hand, was personally haunted; for his Devil had moved with him from cantonments to the Fort. Those two boys spent three parts of their time trying to find out *who* was responsible for the riot in Tesser's rooms. At the end of a fortnight they tried to find out *what* was responsible; and seven days later they gave it up as a bad job. Whatever It was, It refused to be caught; even when Tesser went out of the Fort ostentatiously, and Horrocks lay under Tesser's charpoy with a revolver. The servants were afraid—more afraid than ever—and all the evidence showed that they had been playing no tricks. As Tesser said to Horrocks: 'A haunted Subaltern is a joke, but s'pose this keeps on. Just think what a haunted Colonel would be! And, look here—s'pose I marry! D'you s'pose a girl would live a week with me *and* this Devil?'

'I don't know,' said Horrocks. 'I haven't married often, but I knew a woman once who lived with her husband when he had D.T.* He's dead now and I daresay *she* would marry you if you asked her. She isn't exactly a girl, though, but she has a large experience of the *other* devils—the blue variety. She's a Government pensioner now, and you might write, y'know. Personally, if I hadn't suffered from ghosts of my own, I should rather avoid you.'

'That's just the point,' said Tesser. 'This Devil thing will end in getting me *budnamed*,* and you know I've lived on lemon-squashes and gone to bed at ten for weeks past.'

"Tisn't that sort of Devil,' said Horrocks. 'It's either a first-class fraud for which some one ought to be killed or else you've offended one of those Indian Devils. It stands to reason that such a beastly country should be full of fiends of all sorts.'

'But why should the creature fix on *me*?' said Tesser, 'and why won't he show himself and have it out like a—like a Devil?'

They were talking outside the Mess, after dark, and, even as they spoke, they heard the banjo begin to play in Tesser's room, about twenty yards off.

Horrocks ran to his own quarters for a shot-gun and a revolver, and Tesser and he crept up quietly, the banjo still playing, to Tesser's door.

'Now we've got It!' said Horrocks as he threw the door open and let fly with the twelve-bore; Tesser squibbing off all six barrels into the dark, as hard as he could pull trigger.

The furniture was ruined, and the whole Fort was awake; but that was all. No one had been killed, and the banjo was lying on the dishevelled bed-clothes as usual.

Then Tesser sat down in the verandah, and used language that would have qualified him for the companionship of unlimited Devils. Horrocks said things too: but Tesser said the worst.

When the month in the Fort came to an end, both Horrocks and Tesser were glad. They held a final council of war, but came to no conclusion.

'Seems to me, your best plan would be to make your Devil stretch himself. Go down to Bombay with the time-expired men,' said

Horrocks. 'If he really *is* a Devil, he'll come in the train with you.'

"Tisn't good enough,' said Tesser. 'Bombay's no fit place to live in at this time of the year. But I'll put in for Depôt duty at the Hills.' And he did.

Now here the tale rests. The Devil stayed below, and Tesser went up and was free. If I had invented this story, I should have put in a satisfactory ending—explained the manifestations as somebody's practical joke. My business being to keep to facts, I can only say what I have said. The Devil may have been a hoax. If so, it was one of the best ever arranged. If it was not a hoax . . . But you must settle that for yourselves.

EXPLANATORY NOTES

3 *The Wittiest Woman in India*: it has often been asserted, notably by Kipling's sister Trix, that this dedication was addressed to their mother, who was indeed well known for her ready wit and gift of repartee. Trix was, however, an unreliable witness in her old age, and it is now established beyond doubt that the dedication was addressed to the wife of Major F. C. Burton of the 1st Bengal Cavalry, then stationed at Peshawar on the North-West Frontier. Kipling had met Mrs Burton at Simla—there is good reason to suppose from references in his letters that she was the original of Mrs Hauksbee—and on 26 October 1887 he wrote asking permission to dedicate the book to her: 'If I put on the title-page, *sans* initials or anything, just this much, "To the wittiest woman in India I dedicate this book," will you, as they say in the offices, "initial and pass as correct"?' And the copy he presented to her in January 1888 bears the inscription 'To the Lady of the Dedication, in sign of service the writer sends this little book, praying that she will forgive a hundred faults.'

5 *Eight-and-twenty of these tales*: for a more accurate account see above, p. xvi–xviii.

7 LISPETH: first published in the *Civil and Military Gazette* (henceforth referred to as *CMG*), 29 Nov. 1886, as No. VIII of the 'Plain Tales' series.

   the Sutlej Valley: the Sutlej is one of the great rivers of the Punjab: it flows westward through the Himalayas from its source in Tibet.

   Kotgarh: some 55 miles by road N.E. of Simla, Kotgarh is described in Murray's *Handbook of the Panjáb* (1883) as 'a pretty little place with a Post-office, a pretty church, and a Missionary Station' (p. 214).

   Moravian missionaries: the Moravian Church was a Protestant sect which originated in Moravia in central Czechoslovakia in the eighteenth century.

   Diana: the virgin goddess of hunting in Roman mythology.

8 *Narkunda*: the first stage on the road to Simla, some ten miles from Kotgarh.

9 *P. & O.*: the Peninsular and Oriental Steamship Company, which provided regular services between England and India.

Dehra Dun: a garrison town far to the S.E. of Kotgarh. As Simla lay to the S.W. a traveller from Dehra Dun would not have come through there, which is why 'no one at Simla . . . knew anything about him'.

10 *Muttiani*: the next stage after Narkunda on the way to Simla, some twelve miles further on.

11 *pahari*: hillman.

Tarka Devi: Hindu goddess, transformed from a demon by the sage Agastya.

her beauty faded soon . . .: an alternative version of Lispeth's future is given in *Kim*, where she reappears as the formidable Woman of Shamlegh, 'fair-haired . . . with turquoise-studded head-gear', and polyandrous in the manner of some of the Hill tribes. ' "Once, long ago, if thou canst believe [she tells Kim], a Sahib looked on me with favour. Once, long ago, I wore European clothes at the Mission-house yonder." She pointed towards Kotgarh. "Once, long ago, I was *Ker-lis-ti-an* and spoke English as the Sahibs speak it. Yes. My Sahib said he would return and wed me—yes, wed me. He went away—I had nursed him when he was sick—but he never returned. Then I saw that the Gods of the Kerlistians lied, and I went back to my own people. . . ." ' Far from being beaten by a woodcutter she imperiously commands her two husbands to help carry Kim's lama in a litter to the Plains, and she does not conceal the attraction she feels towards Kim himself.

12 THREE AND—AN EXTRA: first published in the *CMG*, 17 Nov. 1886, as No. IV of the 'Plain Tales' series.

gram: pulse crop used in India to feed horses.

went off at score: broke away at full speed.

13 *tiffined*: lunched.

Peliti's: Peliti's Grand Hotel, a famous Simla rendezvous for cakes, ices, gossip and flirtation.

A.-D.-C.: Aide-de-Camp; in this context a young officer responsible for arrangements for the Viceroy's social programme.

Lord and Lady Lytton: Lord Lytton was the Viceroy from 1876 to 1880.

Peterhoff: the viceregal residence at Simla. Too small for an official residence—Lytton described it as 'a sort of pigsty'—it was replaced during Lord Dufferin's viceroyalty (1884–8) by a more magnificent Viceregal Lodge on Observatory Hill.

13 *Phelps's*: Phelps and Company, Military Tailors, Court Milliners and Costumiers, had establishments in Calcutta, Simla, and Lahore.

14 *slight mourning*: not funereal black, but a muted colour such as grey.

15 *'The Roast Beef of Old England'*: traditional tune played to indicate that the meal was now being served. From Fielding's *Grub Street Opera* (1731).

dandy (this was before rickshaw days): the roads of Simla were too narrow for carriage traffic. Men were expected to ride, and ladies were usually transported by dandy, jampan or rickshaw. A dandy was 'a kind of vehicle . . . consisting of a strong cloth slung like a hammock to a bamboo staff, and carried by two (or more) men' (H. Yule and A. C. Burnell, *Hobson-Jobson*, new edn., London, 1985, p. 296). The 'rickshaw or ginrickshaw was a light two-wheeled vehicle with padded seat and waterproof hood, pulled by one or more men. Once imported from Japan it quickly replaced the dandy and the jampan, which was a kind of sedan chair mounted on poles and carried by several bearers.

'cloud': light wrap for head and neck.

16 THROWN AWAY: first published in *Plain Tales from the Hills*, 1888.

lunge: horse-breaker's term for making a horse canter in a circle while controlling it from the centre by a long rope.

Old Brown Windsor: brand name of a well-known soap.

Sandhurst: the Royal Military College where officers were trained for the Infantry and Cavalry. Officers for the technical arms—the Artillery and Engineers—were trained at the Royal Military Academy at Woolwich. By the 1880s entry was by competitive examination.

17 *depôt battalion*: the depôt was the regiment's permanent base, where recruits received their initial training. The main function of the depôt battalion would be to provide drafts for the service battalion overseas.

acting allowances: additional pay for work on a higher grade undertaken on a temporary basis.

old as the Hills: the capitalization converts the cliché to a pun.

18 *two-goldmohur*: the goldmohur was the chief gold coin of British India, worth 15 rupees (approximately £1 sterling at this time). Two goldmohurs was a very modest sum, indicating the unimportance of the race.

maiden ekka-ponies: an *ekka* was a one-horse carriage often used by natives, and an *ekka* pony was not likely to have high potential for racing. 'Maiden' is a term for a horse which has never won a race.

19 *Canal Engineer's Rest House*: a rest house or dâk-bungalow was accommodation provided for the use of Government officials travelling on business. It could be used by other travellers on payment of a fee.

tetur: partridge.

shikar-kit: shooting clothes.

20 *A country-bred*: as opposed to imported horses.

22 *seals*: worn on watch-chain.

big hoes: mattocks used for digging in India.

23 *Valley of the Shadow*: see Psalms 23:4.

24 MISS YOUGHAL'S SAIS: first published in the *CMG*, 25 April 1887, as No. XXX of the 'Plain Tales' series.

Sais: groom.

Kazi: judge (in Moslem law).

passed by on the other side: cf. Luke 10:31.

hide-dresser: very low caste in contrast with the priest.

the Ghor Kathri: Hindu temple, formerly a Buddhist monastery, in Peshawar, near the entrance to the Khyber Pass.

the Jamma Musjid: the Great Mosque at Delhi.

'going Fantee': going native.

Sat Bhai: lit. the Seven Brothers, a popular name for birds of a certain kind; here presumably a secret society.

Sansis: gypsy tribe of Northern India.

Hálli-Hukk dance, etc.: deliberate mystification on Kipling's part?

Jagadhri: village to S.E. of Umballa in the Punjab.

25 *chángars*: gangs of female labourers.

Eusufzai: member of Pathan tribe on North-West Frontier, within whose territory Attock lies.

Sunni Mollah: Moslem religious teacher in orthodox tradition.

Baba Atal: 'Baba' is a term applied to Sikh ascetics. Atal Raí, youngest son of Har Govind (a great seventeenth-century military leader and religious teacher), was said to have given up his own life after raising a child from the dead.

25 *shikar*: hunting, pursuit of game.

26 *Tarn Taran*: town 12 miles south of Amritsar.

Arab: i.e. her Arab horse.

the blanket: the horse blanket.

Naik: corporal.

Isser Jang: village south of Lahore.

27 *knuckle-bones*: game played with small bones from sheep's legs.

jhampánies: carriers of *jampans* or *jhampans* (sedan chairs), or pullers of 'rickshaws. Cf. note to p. 15.

Gaiety Theatre: the focus of amateur theatricals in Simla till it was replaced in June 1887 by a new theatre, also named the Gaiety, in the recently completed Town Hall.

Jemadar: native officer in Indian Army; here a leader or overseer.

Benmore: a Simla residence purchased in 1869 by Herr Felix von Goldstein, Bandmaster to the Viceroy, who added a ballroom and skating rink to the house and established it as a central feature of social life in Simla.

as Jacob served for Rachel: see Genesis 29:18–20.

28 *in purple and fine linen*: see Luke 16:19.

29 *leads to Simla*: i.e. to a permanent appointment in the Secretariat.

30 'YOKED WITH AN UNBELIEVER': first published in the *CMG*, 7 Dec. 1886, as No. XI of the 'Plain Tales' series. For the title see 2 Corinthians 6:14: 'Be ye not unequally yoked together with unbelievers: for what fellowship hath righteousness with unrighteousness? and what communion hath light with darkness?'

the Gravesend tender: in the 1880s P. & O. liners moored in the Thames off Gravesend, and a tender ferried passengers and their friends out from shore, taking the friends back when the ship was ready to sail.

'tea': tea-growing on plantations in India was developed from the mid-nineteenth century.

Darjiling: hill station some 300 miles N. of Calcutta, the summer HQ of the Bengal Government. Tea-growing was begun in the Darjeeling district in 1850 and rapidly became its chief industry.

31 *the Morning Sun*: old saying 'The morning sun never lasts a day'.

the Bengal Ocean: no such ocean is known to geography, and Darjeeling is some 300 miles from the Bay of Bengal.

Kangra: the capital of Kangra District, another tea-growing area hundreds of miles N.W. of Darjeeling.

32 *Rajput*: member of Hindu warrior caste.

ex-Subadar-Major: Subadar-Major was the highest commissioned rank to which a native officer could then rise in an Infantry regiment of the Indian Army.

33 *Watson's Hotel*: a very well-known hotel in Bombay.

35 FALSE DAWN: first published in *Plain Tales from the Hills*, 1888.

fain: thus in *Songs from Books*, collected editions of verse, and Sussex Edition; 'faint' in earlier editions.

a Civilian: a member of the Indian Civil Service.

36 *Behar*: province to N.W. of Calcutta.

37 *an old tomb*: many tombs are listed as objects of architectural interest in Murray's *Handbook of the Panjáb* (1883).

'Noah's Ark' picnic: in which the animals would come in two-by-two—i.e. the guests would ride in couples.

the ruined tank: a tank was an artificial pond or cistern.

38 *picketed*: tethered to pegs driven into the ground.

puggree: turban cloth; here in the sense of a scarf wound round her helmet.

40 *brown holland habit*: unbleached linen riding clothes.

'dust devils': whirling columns of sand.

bad even to ride pig over: pig-sticking, or hunting wild boar on horseback with a spear, was a favourite Anglo-Indian sport which called for daring and good horsemanship. This stretch of ground would have daunted even pig-stickers.

41 *Umballa*: city about 170 miles S.E. of Lahore; the railway station nearest Simla.

43 THE RESCUE OF PLUFFLES: first published in the *CMG*, 19 Nov. 1886, as No. V of the 'Plain Tales' series.

the 'Unmentionables': Kipling was always inclined to the facetious when inventing regimental nicknames.

seat or hands: i.e. skill in horsemanship.

44 *Captain Hayes*: Captain M. Horace Hayes, author of *A Guide to Training and Horse Management in India*, and famous in Anglo-India for his demonstrations of horse-breaking and horse-training.

44 *tonga driver*: a tonga was a light, two-wheeled vehicle, drawn by two horses, which was much used on the roads leading to Simla and other Hill Stations.

Elysium: as generally used, a place or state of ideal happiness, but here the reference is to Elysium Hill, to the N. of Simla (so called in compliment to Emily and Fanny Eden, who had lived there in the 1840s when their brother Lord Auckland was Governor-General), and possibly also to the Elysium Hotel.

a married subaltern: marriage for subalterns was frowned on, partly because of their low pay, but more because they were expected to devote themselves wholeheartedly to regimental life.

45 *Mrs. Cusack-Bremmil*: see 'Three and—an Extra', pp. 12–15 above.

the Seven Weeks' War: by analogy with the Seven Years War of 1756–63, and the seven weeks' war between Austria and Prussia in 1866.

Jakko Hill: mountain at Simla, with a shrine to Hanuman, the Monkey God, at the summit. The road round the mountain was a favourite ride for Simla residents.

46 *held him on the snaffle*: managed him gently.

fifteen: a clue to Mrs Hauksbee's age. Pluffles was twenty-four; Mrs Hauksbee must therefore have been thirty-nine at the time of this episode, which took place 'some years ago' (p. 43).

47 *the curse of Reuben*: a reference to Jacob's dying words to his son Reuben, 'Unstable as water, thou shalt not excel' (Genesis 49:4).

48 CUPID'S ARROWS: first published in *Plain Tales from the Hills*, 1888.

Bund: dam or embankment.

a Commissioner: for a Commissioner's place in the administrative hierarchy, see p. 82.

open-work jam-tart jewels in gold and enamel: insignia of the Orders of the Indian Empire and the Star of India.

Member of Council: the Viceroy's Council was the supreme governing body in India.

a Lieutenant-Governor: the head of the Government of a Province (e.g. the Punjab) or a Presidency (e.g. Madras).

six letters: presumably C.I.E., C.S.I. (Companion of the Order of the Indian Empire, Companion of the Order of the Star of India).

49 *steles*: shafts of arrows.

   Tara-Devi: mountain peak near Simla.

50 *deodars*: Himalayan cedars.

   Annandale: wooded glen near Simla; site of race-course.

   the Judgment of Paris: a competition between the goddesses Hera, Aphrodite, and Athena, judged by Paris, in which the prize for the most beautiful was given to the Goddess of Love.

53 THE THREE MUSKETEERS: first published in the *CMG*, 11 March 1887, as No. XXI of the 'Plain Tales' series. The title derives, of course, from that of Dumas the elder's famous novel *Les Trois mousquetaires* (1844), with an ironical contrast between the aristocratic background of the original trio and the proletarian quality of Kipling's.

   An' when the war began . . .: this ballad, which seems to be an authentic soldiers' song, refers to events of the Second Afghan War (1878–80), including the British occupation of Kabul and its citadel the Balar Hissar. Cf. the verse headings to 'The Taking of Lungtungpen' (p. 86), 'The Daughter of the Regiment' (p. 150), and 'The Madness of Private Ortheris' (p. 207).

   Ghazi: fanatical Moslem warrior.

   a Line Regiment: a regiment of regular Infantry other than the Guards. Kipling was drawing on his contacts with several different battalions he had known in Lahore.

   Umballa: see note to p. 41.

   Impedimenta: in Latin this means heavy baggage—used here in the sense of encumbrances.

   a Cossack: the suggestion is that Cossacks (Ukrainian light cavalry in the Russian Army) lived off the country, and so did Lord Benira Trig.

   a Radical: antagonistic, therefore, to the Empire and armed forces.

   on a Thursday: Thursday had become a customary though unofficial holiday, perhaps because it was the day on which letters had to be posted to catch the English mail.

54 *fower rupees, eight annas*: the rupee was worth about one shilling and six pence. There were sixteen annas to a rupee.

   decoity: sc. dacoity, armed robbery.

   mallum his bat: understand his language.

54 *b'roosh*: barouche.

   ekka: see note to p. 18.

55 *jildi*: fast.

   Jhil: marsh or lake.

   Jehannum ke marfik, mallum: like Hell, understand.

   bukkin': talking.

   samjao: understand.

   bolos: says.

   choop and chel: shut up and go on.

   Dekker: Do you see?

   arsty: slowly.

   arder: half.

   Shaitan ke marfik: like the Devil.

   kooshy: pleased.

   Bote achee: very good.

   a tat an' a lookri: a pony and a stick.

56 *Victoria*: the Victoria Theatre in London.

   budmash: evil-doer.

57 *tattoo*: pony.

   Ahmid Kheyl wid Maiwand: Ahmed Khel and Maiwand were
   battles in the Second Afghan War.

   Bobs Bahadur: Sir Frederick Roberts, the Commander-in-Chief,
   India, nicknamed 'Bobs'. Bahadur is a term of respect.

   Clink: prison, or cells for soldiers undergoing punishment.

58 *Sherapis*: the *Serapis* was one of the troopships which plied
   between England and India.

59 HIS CHANCE IN LIFE: first published in the *CMG*, 2 April
   1887, as No. XXIV of the 'Plain Tales' series.

   Kafir: inhabitant of Kafiristan in the N.W. of Afghanistan.

   Derozio: Henry Louis Vivian Derozio, author of *Poems* (Calcutta, 1827), *The Fakeer of Jungheera. A Metrical Tale; and Other
   Poems* (Calcutta, 1828), etc.

60 *tussur*: inferior kind of silk.

   immortelles: brightly coloured dried flowers.

   huqa: sc. hookah or hubble-bubble pipe, despised by D'Cruze
   since it was smoked by natives.

   Dom: honorific title in Portuguese.

Poonani: Ponnanni, a town on the Malabar Coast of S.W. India.

Cochin: small state in S.W. India, where a settlement was established by the Portuguese early in the sixteenth century. There was also a Jewish settlement, divided between the Black Jews, who claimed to have settled there in the third and fourth centuries AD, and the White Jews who were said to have arrived at a much later date.

61 *In nomine Sanctissimae*: in the name of the most holy.

Intermediate: compartments on Indian trains were First, Second or Third Class, or Intermediate, and conditions in the last of these are well described by Kipling in 'The Man who would be King'.

a Bengali Babu: originally a term of respect, 'Babu' had come to be used among Anglo-Indians 'with a slight savour of disparagement, as characterizing a superficially cultivated, but too often effeminate, Bengali. And from the extensive employment of the class, to whom the term was applied as a title, in the capacity of clerks in English offices, the word [had] come often to signify "a native clerk who writes English" ' (*Hobson-Jobson*, p. 44).

Orissa: a state on the east coast of India between Calcutta and Madras.

the Collector-Sahib: the Collector was the chief administrative officer for a District. The term derives from his responsibility for the collection of revenue, but he had many other functions, including magisterial authority.

62 *Mohurrum*: Moslem festival, not infrequently the occasion of clashes between Moslems and Hindus.

Donnybrook: Donnybrook Fair, held in a village near Dublin, had become a byword for unruly, riotous behaviour.

63 *ancientry*: old-fashioned style.

65 WATCHES OF THE NIGHT: first published in the *CMG*, 25 March 1887, as No. XXIII of the 'Plain Tales' series.

Brahmin: member of the Hindu priestly caste.

Waterbury: a kind of pocket watch, mass-produced and therefore moderate in cost.

a plain leather guard: in place of a watch-chain which was usually gold or silver.

Kismet: fate or destiny.

66 *ayah*: lady's maid or children's nurse.

66 *the butts of the territs*: the thicker ends of rings screwed into the saddle for the attachment of harness.

feu-de-joie: rolling volley fired as a salute.

vessel of wrath: see Romans 9:22.

67 *somebody in Revelation*: presumably 'the great whore . . . with whom the kings of the earth have committed fornication, and the inhabitants of the earth have been made drunk with the wine of her fornication' (Revelation 17:1–2).

other Scripture people. . .: presumably including Jezebel.

68 *tail-twisting*: from the practice of Indian bullock-drivers who twisted the animals' tails to make them go faster.

69 *compounds*: enclosed areas round Anglo-Indian houses.

an Engineer. . .: see *Hamlet*, III. iv: 'For 'tis the sport to have the enginer/Hoist with his own petard' (i.e. the maker of engines of war blown up by his own bomb). Kipling seems to suppose that a petard was a gun or mortar.

71 THE OTHER MAN: first published in the *CMG*, 13 Nov. 1886, as No. III of the 'Plain Tales' series—the first of those by Kipling himself (see above, p. xvii–xviii).

Public-Offices: it was during Lord Ripon's period as Viceroy (1880–4) that a number of government offices were built at Simla, instead of the work being carried on in existing buildings.

the broad road round Jakko: this road had been widened on the instigation of Lord William Beresford, Military Secretary to Lords Lytton, Ripon, and Dufferin in succession.

P.W.D.: Public Works Department.

two hundred rupees a month: about £180 per year—a rather miserly sum for someone of his seniority.

Commissariat or Transport: branches of the service which were not highly esteemed.

72 *Simla Mall*: the main thoroughfare.

Terai hat: felt hat with wide brim.

73 *tonga*: see note to p. 44.

sixty-mile uphill jolt: from Kalka to Simla.

two stages out of Solon: Solon was about half-way between Kalka and Simla.

buckshish: tip or gratuity.

Babu: see note to p. 61.

74 *'Peterhoff' it was then*: i.e. before the Dufferins had built the new Viceregal Lodge on Observatory Hill. See note to p. 13.

75 CONSEQUENCES: first published in the *CMG*, 9 Dec. 1886, as No. XII of the 'Plain Tales' series.

Rosicrucian: connected with a secret society or order whose members sought secret or magic knowledge. It was much indebted to the teachings of Paracelsus (Theophrast Bombast Von Hohenheim), a sixteenth-century Swiss philosopher, doctor, alchemist and astrologer.

Jacatâlâ's Hill: Jakko? See note to p. 45.

Flood the Seeker: Robert Fludd (1574–1637), who defended Rosicrucian doctrines.

Luna at her apogee: the moon at her furthest distance from the earth.

they call Pachmari a Sanitarium: 'Sanitarium' is another term for a Hill Station, and Pachmari *was* a Hill Station in the Central Provinces. The patronizing note indicates the sense of superiority felt by North India men.

behind trotting-bullocks: instead of horses; indicating the uncouth, benighted nature of Central India.

A.-D.-C.: see note to p. 13.

76 *interest*: influence.

The particular Viceroy: probably Lord Lytton, Viceroy from 1876 to 1880.

Lord Dufferin: Governor-General of Canada before becoming Viceroy in 1884.

Lord Ripon: Viceroy from 1880 to 1884. He had resigned from office in 1873 because of his spiritual struggles which led to his joining the Roman Catholic Church the following year. He had been active in its affairs before re-entering public life on his appointment as Viceroy.

77 *Vakils and Motamids*: authorized representatives.

Native States: in addition to the Provinces which came under British rule, there were Native States governed by their traditional Princes, Maharajahs, etc., with only indirect supervision by the Indian Government.

soft crinkly paper: i.e. flimsies—thin paper used for copies.

Annandale: see note to p. 50.

no book to sign: i.e. to acknowledge receipt of the package.

79 *chlorodyne*: a patent medicine.

What the Viceroy said . . .: an allusion to the game of Consequences with its formulae '*He* said', '*She* said', 'And the consequence was', etc.

81 THE CONVERSION OF AURELIAN McGOGGIN: first published in the *CMG*, 28 April 1887, as No. XXI of the 'Plain Tales' series.

Life's Handicap: used as the title of another volume of stories. It implies the comparison of life to a race in which each competitor rides carrying appropriate weights, to even the odds.

Comte: Auguste Comte (1798–1857), French philosopher who rejected metaphysics and revealed religion in favour of a religion of humanity.

Spencer: Herbert Spencer (1820–93), English philosopher who promulgated theories of evolution in the ethical as well as physical sphere.

Town: i.e. London.

82 *Deputy*: Deputy Commissioner.

Secretary of State: the Secretary of State for India, who was a member of the British Government.

'*beany*': too full of energy.

Wesleyan preachers: both of Kipling's grandfathers were Methodist ministers, and a preaching strain was to manifest itself in him too.

Blastoderm: layer of cells in early stages of segmentation in the life of an embryo.

83 *eighteen annas in the rupee*: there are only 16 annas to a rupee; hence 'overdoing it'.

84 *Pioneer*: the *CMG*'s sister paper at Allahabad, to which Kipling was transferred late in 1887.

aphasia: loss of speech.

'*Punjab Head*': slang for forgetfulness.

86 THE TAKING OF LUNGTUNGPEN: first published in the *CMG*, 11 April 1887, as No. XXVI of the 'Plain Tales' series. The story is based on an actual incident in the Burmese War, which Kipling himself had summarized in the *CMG* for 1 January that year: 'Private Thomas Atkins of today may be five foot four in his ammunition boots, less than thirty-three inches round the chest, and hard to keep in hand; but he still has a good

deal of the spirit that sent his predecessors of the Light Division up the shot-torn vineyards of the Alma [in the Crimean War]. Twenty soldiers in the Ninghyan district are ordered to cross a river and burn a village. The boat in which they are to cross is pointed out to them. Unfortunately the boat has its bottom knocked out of it by dacoits. Obviously it is the duty of the party to return and point out this distressing fact to the authorities. But the party continues to go on; and a detachment of five men and a bugler, a small boy, take off their garments and proceed to swim the river; losing one man as they cross. Then, clad as was Lady Godiva on a certain memorable occasion, they walk up the bank, advance upon the village, wherein, for anything they know, there may be a hundred dacoits, and set it alight. Luckily the village is deserted, and the dacoits are flying further into the jungle; so no one is hurt, and the little band returns naked, but not ashamed, having done what they were told to do. The idea of Thomas, whom a paternal Government has supplied with a rifle and a uniform, discarding these trifles, and running about the country with nothing on in pursuit of dacoits, is very ludicrous; but the little affair has its more solemn side, and it is impossible not to admire the reckless bravery of the four men and the bugler of the 2nd Queen's on the Sittang river.' A full report of the episode was printed on 5 January 1887.

Barrack-Room Ballad: see note to p. 53, and cf. pp. 150 and 207.

Dagshai: site of cantonment on the road from Kalka to Simla. The parapet was a low wall to reduce the risk of travellers falling down the precipitous mountainside below the road.

scutt: term of contempt—a low dirty fellow.

pipeclay: whitening material used on soldiers' belts, etc.

Bobs Bahadur: see note to p. 57.

Wolseley: Lord Wolseley, previously Sir Garnet Wolseley (1833–1913), had had a distinguished military career, and was a leading exponent of Army reform. Mulvaney's loyalty is to Sir Frederick Roberts, later Lord Roberts, the Commander-in-Chief (India), who was sometimes seen as Wolseley's main rival.

Saysar and Alexandrier: Caesar and Alexander.

three-year-olds: short-service troops.

87 *dacoits*: armed bandits; guerillas.

dah: Burmese sword.

Snider: an obsolescent type of rifle.

87 *puckarowed*: caught, laid hold of.

bohs: Burmese leaders.

jingles: sc. *jingals*: long tapering swivel guns.

88 *nullah*: river-bed, usually a dry one.

89 *blindin' and stiffin'*: cursing.

melly: mêlée.

Diarmid: a hero of Irish legend.

90 *the 'Ard*: Portsmouth Hard, an area by the harbour used as a Sunday promenade.

flat: covered barge towed by paddle-steamer.

91 *honey-dew*: a kind of tobacco sweetened with molasses.

92 A GERM-DESTROYER: first published in the *CMG*, 17 May 1887, as No. XXXV of the 'Plain Tales' series.

94 *Peterhoff*: see note to p. 13.

Red Lancers: of the Viceroy's Bodyguard.

Chaprassi: Office Messenger.

96 *a Seepee Picnic*: the Fair held annually at Sipi, some six miles from Simla, was one of the social events of the year, at which the Viceregal Staff gave famous lunch parties.

97 KIDNAPPED: first published in the *CMG*, 21 March 1887, as No. XXII of the 'Plain Tales' series.

98 *K.C.I.E.*: Knight Commander of the Order of the Indian Empire.

Gazette Extraordinary: i.e. a special edition of the official Government publication, the *Gazette of India*.

Honorary Lieutenant: a promoted ranker. Cf. p. 86.

99 *the Solon dip*: on the way from Simla to Kalka.

Summer Hill: one of the two main spurs jutting out from the ridge at Simla, the other being Elysium Hill (see note to p. 44).

100 *Bikaneer*: state in Rajputana consisting largely of desert.

'peg': drink with soda added.

102 THE ARREST OF LIEUTENANT GOLIGHTLY: first published in the *CMG*, 23 Nov. 1886, as No. VI of the 'Plain Tales' series.

Choop: shut up.

cantle: rear part of saddle.

solah: pith.

riding post: changes horses at each stage.

103 *Pathankote*: the railhead for Dalhousie, 40 to 50 miles away.

solah-topee: pith helmet.

104 *khitmutgar*: table-servant.

Khasa: near Amritsar (Umritsar).

105 *an 'intermediate' compartment*: see note to p. 61.

Rogue's March: tune played when an unsuitable soldier is drummed out of his regiment.

106 *clink*: see note to p. 57.

blind, stiff and crack on: curse.

Martini: the standard rifle in the British Army at this time.

108 IN THE HOUSE OF SUDDHOO: first published in the *CMG*, 30 April 1886, under the title 'Section 420 I.P.C. [Indian Penal Code]'.

Churel: ghost of a woman who has died in childbirth.

Djinn: spirit with magical powers in Moslem mythology.

Taksali Gate: one of the gates of the walled city of Lahore, on the west side.

Edwardes' Gate: named after Sir Herbert Edwardes, one of the great soldier-administrators of the Punjab in the middle of the nineteenth century.

109 *ekka*: see note to p. 18.

Ranjit Singh: the last independent Maharajah of the Punjab.

Huzuri Bagh: gardens in Lahore.

Sirkar: Government.

110 *the Financial Statement*: the basis of the Indian Budget, presented annually by the Financial Member of Council.

jadoo: magic.

112 *thermantidote*: a device for blowing air through moistened screens over doors or windows, to cool the interior.

113 *Poe's account*: see Edgar Allan Poe's short story, 'The Facts in the Case of M. Valdemar'.

teraphim: small household gods or images.

Lazarus: see John 11:1–44.

Asli nahin! Fareib!: glossed in Sussex Edn. as 'Not real. A trick'.

114 *bunnia*: merchant.

mantras: sacred words, spells.

114 *purdahnashin*: woman who lives in purdah or seclusion. Cf. p. 32.

cow-devourer: beef was forbidden food for Hindus, since the cow was held sacred by them.

116 HIS WEDDED WIFE: first published in the *CMG*, 25 Feb. 1887, as No. XIX of the 'Plain Tales' series.

giants or beetles: cf. *Measure for Measure*, III. i; 'And the poor beetle that we tread upon / In corporal sufferance finds a pang as great / As when a giant dies.'

Shikarris: lit. Hunters.

117 *broke*: cashiered.

121 *a case something like this. . .*: see 'In the Pride of his Youth', p. 156–61.

122 THE BROKEN-LINK HANDICAP: first published in the *CMG*, 6 April 1887, as No. XXV of the 'Plain Tales' series.

long-neck: type of spur?

big beam tilts: at the weighing-in prior to a race.

'ten-three': 'official weight (10 stone 3 lbs) to be carried by a four-year-old for a three-mile Steeplechase' (*The Readers' Guide to Rudyard Kipling's Work*, p. 66).

G.R.: Gentleman Rider.

running a horse . . .: cheating.

larrikin: hooligan (Australian slang).

brumby: wild horse (Australian slang).

chumars: low-caste leather-workers.

ekka ponies: see note to p. 18.

demirep: female of doubtful character.

flag: tail.

shroff: money-lender.

b.w.g. 15 1⅜: bay, waler [horse imported from Australia], gelding, 15 hands 1⅜ inches height. (Abbreviations used at race meetings.)

123 *Harpoon, The Gin*: presumably horses famous in the racing world.

Ajmir: city in Rajputana, some 350 miles south of Lahore.

Chedputter: unidentified. A fictional course?

124 *Stewards*: officials responsible for the proper conduct of races.

country-bred: cf. note to p. 20.

jarrah: Australian eucalyptus tree.

1-53: one minute, 53 seconds.

125 *plunging in the lotteries*: spending heavily to secure tickets with the name of the horse(s) most likely to win.

126 *Currency Commission*: a body investigating the problem of the declining value of Indian currency (which was based on the value of silver) against sterling (which was based on the value of gold).

127 BEYOND THE PALE: first published in *Plain Tales from the Hills*, 1888.

bustee: quarter.

Gully: alley.

128 *dhak*: a bushy tree sometimes called 'Flame of the Forest'.

bhusa: straw and chaff.

129 *boorka*: long enveloping garment, usually worn by Moslem women in public.

133 IN ERROR: first published in the *CMG*, 24 Jan. 1887, as No. XVII of the 'Plain Tales' series.

Salsette: island linked to the Island of Bombay.

L.L.L. and Christopher: whisky and cherry brandy (from brand names).

135 *P.W.D.*: see note to p. 71.

136 *peg*: see note to p. 100.

137 A BANK FRAUD: first published in the *CMG*, 14 April 1887, as No. XXVII of the 'Plain Tales' series.

between four and ten: i.e. 4 p.m. to 10 p.m.

between ten and four: i.e. 10 a.m. to 4 p.m.

when a man crossed: i.e. committed a foul by riding across the path of an opponent.

a two-thousand rupee loan: about £150 , which could never be loaned on the security proposed.

138 *hoondi*: bill of exchange.

140 *accommodation*: credit.

burked: smothered.

a Gilbarte or a Hardie: authors of standard nineteenth-century works on banking.

144 TOD'S AMENDMENT: first published in the *CMG*, 16 April 1887, as No. XXVIII of the 'Plain Tales' series.

ayah: nurse.

Boileaugunge: western area of Simla.

Peterhoff: see note to p. 13.

Red Lancer: see note to p. 95.

salaam: greeting.

Moti: Pearl.

145 *jhampanis . . . saises*: see notes to pp. 27 and 24.

dhobi: washerman.

khit: i.e. khitmutgar: table-servant.

Chota Simla: suburb of Simla (*chota*: small).

chotee bolee: baby talk?

146 *Durbaris*: persons attending Durbars or levées given by the Viceroy.

red Chaprassis: office messengers in Government service.

Burra: great, large.

bunnia: see note to p. 114.

Lat Sahib: Lord Sahib.

147 *Ryotwary*: a *ryot* was a peasant or tenant farmer; *ryotwary* was a technical term for the system of landholding by such cultivators.

murramutted: repaired.

theek: correct.

lakhs: hundreds of thousands.

148 *Sirkar*: see note to p. 109.

bundobust: arrangement, regulation.

Jehannum: Hell.

vakils: pleaders, attorneys.

burnt: cremated.

dikh: trouble.

150 THE DAUGHTER OF THE REGIMENT: first published in the *CMG*, 11 May 1887, as No. XXXIV of the 'Plain Tales' series.

Old Barrack-Room Ballad: see note to p. 53, and cf. pp. 86 and 207.

Circassian Circle: a country dance.

vis-à-vis: person opposite.

cant—: the word 'canteen' broken off.

Jhansi: town S.W. of Cawnpore.

151 *Pummeloe*: large orange-like fruit.

strapagin': strapping?

Presidincy: Bombay, Calcutta, and Madras (with their subordinate territories) were known as Presidencies, since in the days of the East India Company they had each been governed by a Council headed by a President.

152 *Saint Lawrence*: invoked because he had suffered martyrdom by being broiled on a gridiron.

Ludianny: Ludhiana, a town in the Punjab.

153 *tope*: grove.

lotah: small brass pot.

grand-roun's: formal inspection of guards and sentries at night.

155 *a three-year-ould*: a short-service soldier.

his—savin's: the implication is that in the Commissariat there would be rich pickings, not all honestly acquired.

I will tell you about that: see 'In the Matter of a Private', *Soldiers Three*.

156 IN THE PRIDE OF HIS YOUTH: first published in the *CMG*, 5 May 1887, as No. XXXIII of the 'Plain Tales' series.

weight-cloths: used in handicapping horses for races.

Life's Handicap: cf. note to p. 81.

The Worm: see 'His Wedded Wife', pp. 116–21.

The Voice that breathed o'er Eden: hymn often sung at formal wedding ceremonies.

157 *Addison Road Station*: now Kensington Olympia station.

Gravesend: cf. note to p. 30.

at 1-6⅞: the rate of exchange being one rupee for one shilling, 6⅞ pence (old currency, at 12 pennies to the shilling and 20 shillings to the pound).

chummery: house shared by a number of bachelors.

158 *filter*: for purifying water for drinking.

screw: salary; in billiards, an element of spin on the ball.

159 *the crushing Exchange*: the deteriorating value of the rupee against the pound was a matter of great concern to Anglo-Indians in the 1880s.

159 *Parsee*: descendant of Persians who practised Zoroastrian religion and settled in India to avoid Moslem persecution.

160 *'If a youth would be distinguished...'*: attributed by Kipling to 'old song' in his marginal notes to an 'Index of First Lines' of verses in Kipling's works, compiled by Admiral Lloyd H. Chandler.

162 PIG: first published in the *CMG*, 3 June 1887, as No. XXXVIII of the 'Plain Tales' series.

Shikarri: see note to p. 116.

the Strid: a deep, narrow fissure in the channel of the River Wharfe in Yorkshire.

Assistant Commissioner: a humble level of administrator.

countrybreds: see note to p. 20.

Bannu and Kohat: towns and districts on the frontier between the Punjab and Afghanistan.

Ghaznevid: from the reign of Mahmud of Ghazni (in Afghanistan), the founder of the Moslem Empire in India.

163 *Sutlej*: see note to p. 7.

164 *Dravidian*: from area of Southern India.

the Rechna Doab: area of the Punjab west of Lahore, between the Chenab and Ravi rivers.

the Derajat: area of the Punjab west of the Indus.

165 *the gentlemen in Keats's poem*: see *Isabella*, ll. 119–20 ('Half-ignorant, they turn'd an easy wheel, / That set sharp racks at work, to pinch and peel').

166 *give offence to the Mahommedan population*: pig was an unclean animal to Moslems, and pork unclean meat.

167 *Sus*: pig.

Competition-wallah: entry to the Indian Civil Service was now by competitive examination—a competition-wallah was one who had succeeded by this means.

169 THE ROUT OF THE WHITE HUSSARS: first published in *Plain Tales from the Hills*, 1888.

The White Hussars: it has been suggested that this fictional regiment is based on the 9th Lancers.

170 *cast*: sold as unfit for further service.

Waler: horse imported from Australia (New South Wales).

ewe-neck, rat-tail, and cow-hocks: all defective features in a horse.

Keel Row: a traditional Northumbrian tune, played as cavalry moved past at the trot.

171 *Parsee*: see note to p. 159.

Black Jew: see note to p. 60.

'*The Place where the old Horse died*': song by C. J. Whyte-Melville (1821–78), soldier, fox-hunter, novelist and poet, who wrote especially about sporting life.

172 *the regimental number burnt in . . .*: every cavalry horse had its number branded on a hoof.

Fontenoy: battle fought in Belgium in 1745 between the French on the one hand and the British and their allies on the other.

173 *en échelon*: like rungs on a ladder.

175 *cantle*: rear part of saddle.

176 *troop*: at that time a division of a Cavalry squadron, commanded by a captain.

178 *Charity and Zeal, 3709, E.C.*: the title of a Masonic Lodge.

179 THE BRONCKHORST DIVORCE-CASE: first published in *Plain Tales from the Hills*, 1888.

three-cornered: awkwardly shaped.

country-blood: i.e. an Indian element in his ancestry.

Hutt: Get up, or Get out.

180 *on the criminal count*: on the grounds of adultery, which under the Indian Penal Code could be punished by imprisonment as well as the award of damages.

181 *Oorya . . . khit . . . ayah*: from Orissa (see note to p. 61); and see notes to pp. 145 and 66.

182 *khitmutgar*: see note to p. 104.

184 *Waler*: see note to p. 170.

185 VENUS ANNODOMINI: first published in the *CMG*, 4 Dec. 1886, as No. X of the 'Plain Tales' series.

And the years went on . . .: these lines are from a poem *Diana of Ephesus*, first published in the *Englishman*, a Calcutta daily, on 18 March 1887, collected in the 3rd edn. of *Departmental Ditties*, 1888, but not subsequently reprinted until it appeared in the posthumous Sussex Edn. It may be that 'Diana' was too recognizable as a figure on the Simla social scene. (There was a famous temple of Diana at Ephesus in Asia Minor.)

Number Eighteen in the Braccio Nuovo: presumably a statue of Venus Anadyomene (rising from the sea) in the gallery indicated. Kipling is punning on 'Anadyomene' and 'Annodomini' (in the year of our Lord) used as slang for old age.

186 *a Bengal Civilian*: member of the Bengal Civil Service.

187 *Ninon de L'Enclos*: Anne Lenclos (1620–1705), a Frenchwoman famous for her wit and beauty, who maintained a salon in Paris till an advanced age.

Babus: see note to p. 61.

Nero . . . Scylla . . . Charybdis: garbled classical allusions.

Darjiling: the Hill Station for the Government of Bengal.

190 THE BISARA OF POOREE: first published in the *CMG*, 4 March 1887, as No. XX of the 'Plain Tales' series.

Pooree: a town on the coast some 300 miles south of Calcutta.

Kulu: a mountain valley north of Simla in the lower Himalayas.

a Kafir: i.e. an inhabitant of Kafiristan (cf. note to p. 59).

a Lahouli: i.e. an inhabitant of Lahoul or Lahaul, north of Kulu.

khitmutgar: see note to p. 104.

Hanlé: town in Kashmir.

balas-rubies: red spinels used as gemstones.

Nizam: the ruler of Hyderabad, the greatest of the Native States.

191 *Theog*: village 22 miles from Simla.

192 *Ashtaroth*: pagan goddess of fertility. For Solomon's action see I Kings 11:1–8.

193 *zenana*: women's quarters.

Benmore . . . office: see note to p. 15. In 1885 Herr Felix von Goldstein, seeing the challenge the new Town Hall would pose to his establishment, sold Benmore to the Punjab Government for use as offices. See Kipling's poem 'The Plea of the Simla Dancers' in *Departmental Ditties*.

194 *Gubernatis or Max Müller*: authorities on Indian religions, myths, etc. Count Angelo de Gubernatis (1840–1913) was an Italian Professor of Sanscrit who produced an Indian encyclopaedia and translated works of Indian literature and mythology; and the Right Hon. Friedrich Max Müller (1823–1900), as Professor of Comparative Philology at Oxford, edited *The Sacred Books of the East* and was famous as a translator of and commentator on works of Hindu religion, etc.

195 A FRIEND'S FRIEND: first published in the *CMG*, 2 May 1887, as No. XXXII of the 'Plain Tales' series.

Hadramauti: inhabitant of the Hadramaut in S.E. Arabia.

side: i.e. side of India.

T.G.s: travelling gentlemen, or globe-trotters; amended to Globe-Trotters in Sussex Edn.

197 *'The Roast Beef of Old England'*: see note to p. 15.

198 *Hakodate*: Japanese port.

199 *luted*: cemented, sealed.

goldbeaters' skin: membrane used to separate sheets of gold that are being hammered into gold leaf.

isinglass: kind of gelatine used for glue.

201 THE GATE OF THE HUNDRED SORROWS: first published in the *CMG*, 26 Sept. 1884.

pice: copper coin of small value.

Gully: alley.

Mosque of Wazir Khan: one of the sights of Lahore.

Black Smoke: opium.

pukka: proper.

chandoo-khanas: opium houses.

203 *Babus*: see note to p. 61.

Anarkulli: area of Lahore.

Macsomebody: see 'To be Filed for Reference', pp. 234–41 above.

206 *'first-chop'*: top quality (from the word for an official seal).

207 THE MADNESS OF PRIVATE ORTHERIS: first published in *Plain Tales from the Hills*, 1888.

Barrack Room Ballad: see note to p. 53, and cf. p. 86 and 150.

a file o' Dooks: a pair of Dukes.

burning-ghaut: platform for the cremation of the dead.

209 *bullswools*: leather boots (Army slang).

Sherapis: the troopship *Serapis*.

'The Ramrod Corps': not identified, but cited by Kipling as the source for two lines which form the heading of 'In the Matter of a Private' (*Soldiers Three*): 'Hurrah! hurrah! a soldier's life for me! / Shout, boys, shout! for it makes you jolly and free.' Kipling denies his authorship of the lines in his marginalia to Admiral Chandler's bibliography.

210 *loose on me*: fire at me.

Ahmid Kheyl: battle in Second Afghan War.

210 *rotten-stone*: kind of limestone used for polishing.

Humaners: Royal Humane Society.

211 *Rawal Pindi*: military station near the North-West Frontier. Kipling had visited it in 1885, when he was reporting as a Special Correspondent on the state visit by the Amir of Afghanistan.

slake off: make less intense.

cracking-on: cursing.

212 *twenty-eight days*: period of detention as penalty.

213 *had lain with*: had been quartered alongside.

215 THE STORY OF MUHAMMAD DIN: first published in the *CMG*, 8 Sept. 1886.

Professor Peterson: Peter Petersen (1847–99), Professor of Sanscrit at Elphinstone College in Bombay, and compiler of catalogues of Sanscrit MSS, which he discovered and edited.

khitmutgar: see note to p. 104.

216 *budmash*: rogue, evil-doer.

jail-khana: prison.

218 ON THE STRENGTH OF A LIKENESS: first published in the *CMG*, 10 Jan. 1887, as No. XVI in the 'Plain Tales' series.

Phil Garron: in 'Yoked with an Unbeliever' (pp. 30–4 above).

219 *Dindigul, Coimbatore*: Stations in south India.

Ootacamund: Hill Station in south India.

Annandale: see note to p. 50.

220 *'Poor Wandering One'*: from *The Pirates of Penzance*. (Gilbert and Sullivan's operas were very popular in Anglo-India.)

221 *cavalier servente* (cavaliere servente): gentleman in attendance on a married woman.

222 *Chutter Munzil*: 'Umbrella Mansion' built by a Nawab of Lucknow in the early nineteenth century (the umbrella having been an emblem of royalty).

224 WRESSLEY OF THE FOREIGN OFFICE: first published in the *CMG*, 20 May 1887, as No. XXXVI in the 'Plain Tales' series.

225 *Aitchison*: Sir Charles Umpherston Aitchison, Lieutenant-Governor of the Punjab 1882–7, and author of an authoritative work entitled *A Collection of Treaties and Sunnuds [Deeds] Relating to India and Neighbouring Countries*.

Thacker and Spink's Directory: *Thacker's Bengal Directory*, expanded from 1885 to *Thacker's Indian Directory*, was published by Thacker and Spink, a Calcutta firm which also published *Plain Tales from the Hills*. It listed holders of official positions, etc.

226 *Ahir*: cowherd (low caste).

Ruskin . . .: see John Ruskin's *Sesame and Lilies* (1865), especially the lecture 'Of Queens' Gardens' on women's role in love, marriage, and human life in general.

228 *magnum opus*: great work.

229 BY WORD OF MOUTH: first published in the *CMG*, 10 June 1887, as No. XXXIX of the 'Plain Tales' series. In this original publication the story ended 'Now this is the last of the Plain Tales, because there are no more to follow.'

Meridki: some 20 miles north of Lahore.

Berars: an imaginary regiment, named after the Berar region in Central India.

230 *deodar*: see note to p. 50.

231 *dâk-bungalow*: see note to p. 19.

232 *Tuticorin*: near the southernmost tip of India.

234 TO BE FILED FOR REFERENCE: first published in *Plain Tales from the Hills*, 1888.

Jellaludin: a Moslem name, assumed by McIntosh, presumably, when he changed his creed to that of Islam. (See pp. 235–6.)

'Say is it dawn . . .': from D. G. Rossetti's 'The Song of the Bower'.

Serai: caravanserai or resting place for travellers.

screwed: tipsy.

Loggerhead: bathing place on the Cherwell at Oxford.

235 *Symonds*: proprietor of well-known stables in Oxford.

Mesopotamia: walk beside the Cherwell near Magdalen College.

'My brain cries out against . . .': reference unidentified.

Ovid in exile: the Roman poet Ovid was banished in AD 8 to Tomis on the shores of the Black Sea, where he died ten years later. His poem *Tristia* describes the tedium and hardships of his exile.

236 *charpoy*: bedstead.

gunny-bags: coarse sacking.

237 *excruciating quantities*: false quantities of vowels in pronouncing Latin.

'*I the Trinity illustrate . . .*': from Browning's 'Soliloquy of the Spanish Cloister'.

Atalanta in Calydon: verse drama by Swinburne.

238 *a Virgil in the Shades*: the spirit of Virgil acts as Dante's guide through the Inferno (Hell) and Purgatorio (Purgatory) in his *Divina Commedia*.

239 *the Pickering Horace*: William Pickering (1796–1854) was a publisher responsible for the 'Diamond Classics', including the works of Horace, in the early nineteenth century.

240 *Mother Maturin*: Kipling's letters reveal that he worked for several years in India on an ambitious project for a novel, to be called *Mother Maturin*, revelatory of the horrors of lower class and Eurasian life in India as they existed outside official reports.

Mirza Murad Ali Beg's book: a work of fiction, *Lalun, the Beragun or The Battle of Paniput: A Legend of Hindoostan*, published in 1884. The identity of the author is not known.

241 *The Giant's Robe*: title of a novel by F. Anstey (i.e. Thomas Anstey Guthrie), published in 1883, on the fate of a man who passes off a friend's novel as his own.

243 BITTERS NEAT (Appendix A): first published in the *CMG*, 19 April 1887, as No. XXIX of the 'Plain Tales' series. Collected in Vol. I of the Outward Bound Edition and the Edition De Luxe in 1897, and in Vol. I of the Sussex Edition in 1937, in all of which it follows 'Miss Youghal's Sais'. It was included also in Vol. I of the Burwash Edition (1941), which follows the Sussex Edition text.

the third volume: i.e. in the conclusion of a three-volume novel.

A.D.C.s: Aides-de-Camp.

Civilian: member of the Indian Civil Service.

P.W.D.: Public Works Department.

six to nine hundred: i.e. rupees.

244 *Elaine and . . . Lancelot*: Elaine, the Fair Maid of Astolat, in Malory's *Morte D'Arthur* and Tennyson's *Idylls of the King*, dies for love of Sir Lancelot.

jawabed: refused.

245 *ayah*: lady's maid.

from Colombo to Dadar: Colombo is in Sri Lanka (formerly Ceylon); Dadar is a district of Bombay.

246 *khitmutgars*: see note to p. 104.

bones: dice (slang).

247 HAUNTED SUBALTERNS (Appendix B): first published in the *CMG*, 27 May 1887, as No. XXXVII of the 'Plain Tales' series. Collected in Vol. I of the Outward Bound Edition and the Edition De Luxe in 1897, and in Vol. I of the Sussex Edition in 1937, in all of which it follows 'The Other Man'. It was included also in Vol. I of the Burwash Edition (1941), which follows the Sussex Edition text.

248 *ulta-pulta*: topsy-turvy.

bhisti: water-carrier.

Shaitan-ke: devilish.

Govindghar: fort at Amritsar.

Jumrood: fort near Peshawur on the North-West Frontier.

Phillour: near Ludiana in the Punjab.

250 *D.T.*: *delirium tremens*.

budnamed: in bad reputation.

*The
Oxford
World's
Classics
Website*

www.worldsclassics.co.uk

- Browse the full range of Oxford World's Classics online

- Sign up for our monthly e-alert to receive information on new titles

- Read extracts from the Introductions

- Listen to our editors and translators talk about the world's greatest literature with our Oxford World's Classics audio guides

- Join the conversation, follow us on Twitter at OWC_Oxford

- Teachers and lecturers can order inspection copies quickly and simply via our website

www.worldsclassics.co.uk

American Literature

British and Irish Literature

Children's Literature

Classics and Ancient Literature

Colonial Literature

Eastern Literature

European Literature

Gothic Literature

History

Medieval Literature

Oxford English Drama

Poetry

Philosophy

Politics

Religion

The Oxford Shakespeare

A complete list of Oxford World's Classics, including Authors in Context, Oxford English Drama, and the Oxford Shakespeare, is available in the UK from the Marketing Services Department, Oxford University Press, Great Clarendon Street, Oxford OX2 6DP, or visit the website at www.oup.com/uk/worldsclassics.

In the USA, visit www.oup.com/us/owc for a complete title list.

Oxford World's Classics are available from all good bookshops. In case of difficulty, customers in the UK should contact Oxford University Press Bookshop, 116 High Street, Oxford OX1 4BR.

JANE AUSTEN	**Catharine and Other Writings**
	Emma
	Mansfield Park
	Northanger Abbey, Lady Susan, The Watsons, and Sanditon
	Persuasion
	Pride and Prejudice
	Sense and Sensibility
ANNE BRONTË	**Agnes Grey**
	The Tenant of Wildfell Hall
CHARLOTTE BRONTË	**Jane Eyre**
	The Professor
	Shirley
	Villette
EMILY BRONTË	**Wuthering Heights**
WILKIE COLLINS	**The Moonstone**
	No Name
	The Woman in White
CHARLES DARWIN	**The Origin of Species**
CHARLES DICKENS	**The Adventures of Oliver Twist**
	Bleak House
	David Copperfield
	Great Expectations
	Hard Times
	Little Dorrit
	Martin Chuzzlewit
	Nicholas Nickleby
	The Old Curiosity Shop
	Our Mutual Friend
	The Pickwick Papers
	A Tale of Two Cities